THE HOME FRONT

THE
HOME FRONT

COLLECTED STORIES BY
MARGARET CRAVEN

G.P. Putnam's Sons
New York

Library of Congress Cataloging in Publication Data

Craven, Margaret.
  The home front.

  I. Title.
PS3553.R277H65   1981   813'.54   80-25717
ISBN 0-399-12568-X

PRINTED IN THE UNITED STATES OF AMERICA

For my dearest friend and agent
Jo Stewart . . .

CONTENTS

THE HOME FRONT

THE HOME FRONT

When the town learned that Julie Devon was coming home at last, it went into as fine a collection of front-stoop and back-fence huddles as had ever been seen in that part of the country.

Julie and Martha Devon were twins, and partly because a pair of almost anything is so much more interesting than a mere one, the town had always considered them a civic pride and concern, along with the oaks in the square and the tannery on the south side.

Mrs. Peabody declared that from their birth each of the Devon twins had set her own pace in this world.

"Martha arrived in bed like a lady," Mrs. Peabody reminded the town. "But not that Julie. She had to get here fifty minutes early in the back of Sam Westmore's hack and upset everybody. Just like her!"

There was truth in this. When the twins were small, almost the whole town marched up the hill in relays to have a look at them, and usually it was to find Martha quietly playing with her toes, and Julie whooping it up for attention. She got it too.

Mr. Devon was one to turn all matters of infant correction over to his wife, and Mrs. Devon was one to think that in the production of twins she had achieved the ultimate and was provided thereby with a permanent alibi. "Oh, I couldn't possibly; I have twins. . . . No, I'm afraid not; the twins, you know."

When Julie and Martha were six years old, it was Julie who got the skates with the ball bearings. When they were eight, it was she who got the Peter Thompson suit with the larger anchor on the dickey. When they were ten, it was she who got the pretty blue bicycle instead of the brown. When they were sixteen, it was she who got Ned Burkes, the only boy in town with a car of his own.

Julie had brains, charm and looks. Martha had everything Julie had except what Mrs. Peabody called "the brass." Oh, the town saw it coming all right!

13

The twins were in their last year at the state university when Mrs. Devon was killed in an automobile accident and Mr. Devon crippled and invalided for life. They came home. Martha cried bitterly, took a look at the bank balance, dismissed the cook and the nurse, and put on an apron. Julie held Ned Burkes' hand and cried twice as hard. Mrs. Peabody said that Julie cried so hard the reservoir went up two inches, and the town said that this was outrageous of Amanda Peabody and for once she'd gone too far.

She was right, though. Six months later Julie had a job on a city newspaper and was sending Martha a check each month. The next year she sent home three checks and Ned's ring. The third year she went to Paris and sent no checks at all.

No one knew how she got over there, but everyone knew how neatly she left Martha trapped on the home front. The town's snoopy big heart ached for Martha. Every time Julie's name came up, someone said, "Poor Martha! Poor dear Martha!" as if it were an epitaph.

Martha said nothing. Just at first she went around looking as if she'd been smacked between the eyes. The look went away, and Martha settled down to holding the home front alone and unaided. Her father lived twelve years, and no sooner had he gone than she inherited Aunt Em, a sweet dear old lady with a genteel income of $2.16 a month. Martha wrote books for children, and every fall she borrowed a little money from the bank, and every spring she paid it back when her royalties dribbled in. Her garden was really lovely. She had the finest begonias in town. She made the best spongecake—with only four eggs too.

The town soon took Martha for granted. She was part of the scene, so everyday, so commonplace as to be almost invisible. But not that Julie!

Julie was spoiled and selfish. Julie was a sinner. Julie was on the wrong side, and the wrong side simply must lose. For years the town kept its ears hopefully cocked for the crash. Like an apple defying gravity, Julie refused to tumble. She went right on climbing to success. Europe began to send off sparks around her pretty ears. . . . Julie had a byline. . . . Julie had a column. . . . Julie was well known. . . . Julie was famous. . . . Good heavens! Julie was coming home.

The town was excited, curious and mad, all at once. It took Mrs. Peabody, of course, to put the civic sentiment into words. "For years, Samuel, I've planned to take that young woman by the ear and tell her a few things for her own good," said Mrs. Peabody to her husband. "And now, just because a lunatic has upset the universe, and Julie's famous, and I'm head of the British Aid, I'll have to be nice to her instead. Samuel, it hurts. I tell you it hurts. Oh, poor Martha! This is going to be so hard on her."

Mrs. Peabody was wrong.

The morning Julie came home Amos Westcott was down on his hands and knees, planting flowers in the big circle plot of the town square. Amos was nobody at all except the town gardener. He was almost as much a part of the square as the oaks, always around and about, pottering among his flowers, muttering of sow bugs, slugs and leaf molds, saying little and missing nothing.

The town was mighty jittery, Amos was thinking. Blamed if it didn't take a man back to '18; only then people had been more excited than scared. Why, the town was like one of those round tables on the radio—everybody courteous and taking his turn at first, and suddenly everybody talking louder and louder, and getting madder and madder, until you couldn't hear one clear word. It had got so bad lately a man couldn't get away from it anywhere. Blamed if he wasn't afraid to open his mouth for fear of starting somebody up again. Blamed if he could walk one side of this square without being stopped three or four times. Did you hear Kaltenborn? . . . Terrible, isn't it? . . . Did you hear Raymond Gram Swing? . . . Awful, isn't it? . . . What's the use of saving money? Inflation's coming. . . . No, it isn't. . . . Yes, it is. . . . We all ought to stand by Roosevelt. . . . No, we should hang him. . . . Yes, we should. . . . No, we shouldn't. . . . Now, to add to the general squeamishness, Julie Devon was coming home. Even so early in the morning Amos could feel the town's bump of curiosity growing and swelling.

Julie was due on the 9:38, and Amos figured that Martha would walk through the square on her way to the station to meet her. She wouldn't drive that ancient car of hers. Not this day. The whole town knew that Sam Westmore had called her up and begged the honor of transporting her and Julie home from the station in his new taxi. Free too!

Amos watched and waited, and, sure enough, at 9:10 he saw Martha coming through the trees, arms swinging, head up.

It struck Amos that Martha was looking mighty pert. She was thirty-six. No-o-o-o, she was thirty-eight coming up; old enough to wither a little on the bough. No doubt about it. Martha was holding her bloom. When she came close it struck Amos with a sudden shock that, except for the children, Martha Devon had the only pair of eyes in town with no jitters in them. Probably the worst had already happened to her.

She said, in that slow gentle way of hers, "Hello there, Amos. How's the planting?"

Amos said, "It's coming along, Miss Marthy. I took your advice. Nothing but blue and pink this year. Borders of ageratum and lobelia, and masses of petunias. Kind of thought it might soothe the town. God knows it needs it!"

Martha laughed. "Afraid it'll take more than petunias, Amos, but it's a good idea. You remember the winter stock you gave me last fall? They were beautiful."

"I got some slips started in pots for you, Miss Marthy," Amos said. "I snipped 'em off Mrs. Peabody's prize fuchsias, only she don't know it. She's fightin' the war so hard with her tongue, she won't even miss 'em."

"How nice of you, Amos." Martha looked at her watch. "Well, I must go now. You know, Julie's due home this morning. Isn't it exciting?"

Amos searched her face for any trace of sarcasm, and found none. "Be mighty interesting to see Miss Julie," he admitted dryly. "She's a—she's a right smart girl."

"Good-by, Amos." Martha smiled and strode on toward the station. Amos went back to his planting.

He saw Cy Matthews, the photographer, and Clem Stewart, the editor, pop out of the Mercury office and dogtrot for the station. He saw a shiny black automobile pass by, a white card reading PRESS CAR on its windshield, a city license on its tail.

Thirty minutes after the train had come and gone, Amos saw Sam Westmore driving Martha and Julie past the square on their way home. That is to say, he had a brief glimpse of Julie, smiling and talking a mile a minute to Clem and one of the men who had been in the press car. Amos couldn't see Martha. She was probably in the corner under a hatbox.

Amos felt uneasy in his mind. Afterward it seemed to him he saw a grass fire start that day. He saw the sparks blow in and catch, and begin to smolder. At 10:30 he saw Sam Westmore park his taxi under an oak and strut into the cigar store. Amos put down his trowel and strolled over for some tobacco for his pipe.

"And she remembered me," Sam was telling the boys. "She called me by name right off, and she said, 'Hello, Sam. Have you the hack waiting for me? You know I won't let anybody else drive me home.' She ain't spoiled a bit. You should have seen those city fellows popping questions at her, and her answering them as nice as you please. She gave me a two-dollar tip, and she said—"

Amos went out quickly. Not one word about Martha. But Amos knew. Amos knew as well as if he had seen it all. Julie fluttering across the platform to Martha, kissing her and making over her, and after that Martha standing there forgotten in the background.

And even if she showed nothing in her eyes, she must have felt it in her heart, mustn't she? She must have felt all those long years pressing there, and thought of her father breaking up, disintegrating slowly until there was nothing left of him but a querulous, whining, demanding voice.

Amos felt so upset he stepped on three petunias. Drat that Julie! Drat her, anyway! The station wasn't cold yet where she'd stood, and already she'd begun to set the men back on their heels. Wait until the women got started! That would be something for Martha to swallow.

It seemed to Amos that the whole town was stirring that day. In the afternoon the mayor's emergency-defense committee met at the city hall, and when it was over the members began to straggle down the white steps into the square. Amos had a fine opportunity to watch some of the town's super citizens.

Ned Burkes and Ed Twitchell came out first, walking slowly, talking earnestly, both heads nodding.

"H'm'm'm," said Amos to himself, "Ned's got on his best blue serge. On a weekday too. He's got his hair combed to hide the bald spot. Might as well try to save a lawn once the devil grass gets in it. Now what do you suppose he's up to?"

Ed Twitchell seemed to be arguing with Ned, and Ned seemed to be holding back. Amos had a strong hunch as to what was going on. Both men were leaders in the Town Hall group, and Amos would bet anybody a dollar that Ed was saying, "Now look here, Burkes; you can do it. Don't you see what a drawing card she'll be? If we wait, old lady Peabody'll get to her first. You know how these women are."

Ned and Ed Twitchell went on, still talking earnestly. Almost immediately Mrs. Peabody and Ella Hobart, her shadow, came down the steps with Mrs. Pritchart.

Mrs. Peabody headed the town's Aid-to-Britain group and Mrs. Pritchart headed the Red Cross group. They were being very, very polite to each other. When they reached the bottom of the steps they smiled and bowed. Mrs. Pritchart hurried one way. Ella and Mrs. Peabody came into the square.

Amos made himself as inconspicuous as possible. Glory, glory, they were coming his way!

Mrs. Peabody was saying, "Ella, there's no use. I'll just have to bury my pride and go out there. If Jane Pritchart gets her first, we'll be left with this big benefit tea and no outstanding attraction. We've got that yarn shipment coming, and heaven knows we need money. She'd be a drawing card, Ella. We could hold the benefit on a Sunday afternoon. Why, even the men would come to hear her, the spoiled, selfish thing! I hope I know my duty, Ella."

This was too much for Amos. His emotions got the better of him. "Gabble-gabble-gabble!" he muttered.

Mrs. Peabody heard him and halted. "I beg your pardon, Amos," she said. "Were you speaking to me?"

"No, ma'am," said Amos. "I was talking to myself."

Mrs. Peabody and Ella Hobart went on.

"That Amos Westcott gets stupider every year," said Mrs. Peabody. "I'll just get my car, Ella, and go right—"

Amos put down his trowel, dug a nickel out of his jeans, walked over to the drugstore, sequestered himself in the telephone booth and dialed a number.

"Miss Marthy?" he said. "This is Amos Westcott. Just thought I'd better tell you they're a-comin'. They're on their way, Miss Marthy, and they all want something."

Martha said, in that quiet way of hers, "How thoughtful of you to call me, Amos. I'll put the teakettle right on, and the coffeepot too. Thank you, Amos."

Amos wiped his brow. It was out of his hands. He'd done all a man could.

Mrs. Pritchart drove to Martha's house by the Middlefield road. Mrs. Peabody drove by Holly Street. Neither lady saw the other, and each was absorbed in her own thoughts.

Mrs. Pritchart thought, *Well, there's one thing. This war may be hard on the grocery bill, but it's good for the hips. I've lost two pounds this week, and that reminds me, I forgot to get the meat, and Norah's probably ordered a two-dollar roast. I just won't let Herbert know, that's all. I'll pay the difference in the butcher's bill out of miscellaneous. What he doesn't know isn't going to hurt him. I do hope I get there before Amanda Peabody. You can't tell me she doesn't want Julie for that British Aid tea of hers. But there's one thing. I was a better friend of Julie's mother than Amanda ever was, and if I just remind Julie of it nicely, maybe—Oh, dear, I must hurry.*

Mrs. Peabody thought, *I'm so tired I could scream. I don't know why it is, but every time there's a war, all the women in this town come down with telephonitis. They start in at seven and they keep it up. And that reminds me, I must call up Sue Smith and ask her to be on the benefit committee. I left her off last time and she was furious. Well, Amanda, you never know anything about women until you work in clubs and committees with them, but don't tell that to Samuel. You know what he'll say. I must hurry. If that Jane Pritchart thinks for one minute—And another thing. I must be especially nice to Martha. Poor dear Martha. You can't tell me this won't be hard for her. But I mustn't overdo it, because if I do, Julie'll notice, and then I won't get—Heavens! I've missed Kaltenborn. Maybe I can still catch the tail end.*

Mrs. Pritchart arrived first. Mrs. Pritchart was a slow parker, and when she'd finally maneuvered her car close enough to the curb and climbed out, it was to see Amanda Peabody pulling up briskly. Mrs. Peabody recovered first.

She said, "Well, Jane, I see you have the same idea I have. Shall we go in? H'm'm'm—isn't that Ned Burkes' car coming around the corner? Do you suppose he's still in love with Julie after all these years, or does he want her for the Town Hall? You ring, Jane, while I put on my gloves."

Martha came to the door. She looked happy and at ease. She said, "Why, how nice! Come in. Julie'll be so pleased. . . . Julie, here are some old friends to welcome you. . . . And Ned? Come in. Come in."

They went in. Julie came forward. It was like the moment at the theater when the curtain goes up. Julie came forward, smiling and eager, her eyes bright and intense. Before they knew it, they were in Martha's cheerful living room, seated by the fire. Julie was gay. Julie was charming. Of course she'd speak at the Town Hall. Of course she'd speak at the British benefit and help the Red Cross. How awfully nice of them to ask her, and besides, there was so much to tell, and so little time.

Julie sat by the fire, the light on her face, and she told them of her days in France, Poland and England. How brilliantly she spoke! They all sat on the edge of their chairs, excited and thrilled and—yes, terribly frightened deep down inside.

For two hours not one of them knew Martha was there. Martha was the dumb waiter. She brought a log for the fire. Ned Burkes didn't even see her, much less help put it on the coals. She carried in the coffee and the tea. She brought hot water for Mrs. Pritchart's cup. She refilled the cake dish, took a shawl to her Aunt Em, who was in bed with a cold, and answered the telephone four times.

Twice Martha spoke. The first time she was sitting a little to the rear. She spoke softly, as if she knew no one was listening to her, as if she spoke only for herself.

"Now I know why an old soldier never tells you how he lost his arm," Martha said. "It's because while he was off there dying a little bit at a time, he knew that at home there were still so many, many people fighting the war with words."

At last the afternoon was over. It was time to go.

"Oh, Julie," said Mrs. Peabody, "your coming is going to be a great thing for this town. It's going to wake up at last."

"But, Mrs. Peabody," said Martha, louder this time, "I think this town's already awake. What it needs is to stop talking and disagreeing with itself, to settle down and go to work on all the little jobs at hand."

Mrs. Peabody heard that, and she suddenly remembered Martha and felt a slight twinge of conscience.

"Martha, you're a dear," she said warmly. . . . "Doesn't Martha look well, Julie? We're so proud of her."

Julie said, "Indeed she does, Mrs. Peabody. I'm just amazed how much Martha's grown. She's so competent, so efficient and capable."

She could have said the same of a washing machine, ten dollars down and five a month. Nobody noticed it. There was one last chorus of good-bys. Julie went with them to their cars. Martha picked up the tea dishes to carry to the kitchen.

Twenty minutes later telephones were buzzing all over town. The smoldering grass fire had burst into flame.

For the next two weeks Julie made speeches. Julie appeared on a national hookup. Julie signed a contract for a book. Julie charmed the town. Strange people descended from the city and sat on Martha's chairs, and spilled ashes on Martha's rugs, and stayed to lunch. The telephone rang all day long, and Aunt Em's cold settled in her bronchial tubes.

Martha moved quietly in the background. She swept up the ashes, replenished the larder, answered the telephone, and put mustard plasters on Aunt Em, front and back, twice a day. Martha made ten dozen cookies and two spongecakes for the British benefit. Martha knit and handed in two sweaters for the Red Cross.

"I don't see how Martha does it," declared Mrs. Peabody. "Here I've been working on my sweater for weeks, and I still have both sleeves to go. She must knit very fast."

The town had never been in such a dither. Ed Twitchell met Sam Westmore in the square one noon and all but pushed his face in. Ed said the underpass was the only possible shelter in town. Sam said only a fool would suggest such a thing, since everybody knew the railroad would be bombed first.

Ella Hobart announced that if it came to the worst, she was going to pack up and go to her sister's in Iowa. Mrs. Pritchart said, well, she wasn't. She was going to sit tight in her own home and not budge for anything.

* * *

The group of women who met twice a week to make infant clothes for the French and the Dutch got into a large squabble one day as to whether they should put featherstitching on the necks. Some said yes, they didn't want those foreign women to think Americans can't sew nicely, did they? Others said fiddlesticks, the foreign women would be so glad to get the wrappers they wouldn't notice the featherstitching. This discussion lasted forty-five minutes, and while it raged, not one woman sewed as much as an inch.

Ned Burkes turned himself into a chauffeur for Julie, and the town said he must be in love with her still, and the town said that this was hard on poor dear Martha, to whom he had paid desultory court for some ten years, but what could you expect?

Martha said nothing—except to Amos. One afternoon she walked down to the farmers' market to pick out a young hen to stew for Aunt Em, and she stopped to chat a moment with Amos in the square.

"Amos," she said very seriously, "am I imagining things or is this town's steam pressure getting very high?"

"You ain't imagining, Miss Marthy," said Amos. "I've been noticing it too."

"Amos, when the steam pressure gets too high, something has to give where it's weakest, doesn't it?"

"That's right, Miss Marthy. Something lets go with a pop. I been kind of listening for it."

"So have I." Martha laughed. "Maybe we're a couple of old fossils, Amos. Maybe it's you and I who are out of step. Well, I must hurry home. I have to get this chicken on for Aunt Em. Good-by, Amos."

Four days later the manganese plant ten miles out of town blew up. It was an accident. Everybody said so. But the next day there was a bad fire in the lumberyard. It was scarcely out before the freight depot began to blaze.

SABOTAGE . . . SPY . . . MANIAC . . . ARSONIST—the words leaped at the town from every newsstand. Business almost stopped. Mothers plucked their small children off the streets and stayed at home, glued to the telephone. Fathers talked on every street corner.

Old Doctor Schultze, who had taught German in the high school for twenty years, locked himself in his room. So did Mrs. Korthauer, whose grandparents had escaped from Germany in a load of hay. A little Italian boy was stoned at recess and went home in tears.

Martha said nothing. Every afternoon she walked down to see Amos. Nobody noticed her.

Everybody noticed Julie. Julie was at her best now. Julie stood out like a blackberry in a pan of milk. Julie was everywhere. She was with the sheriff, running down rumors. She was in a city press car. Julie was whetted, avid, intense—with a voice too high with fatigue and excitement.

A pile of lint and shavings, soaked in kerosene, was found in the basement of the farmers' market. A rail was found dislodged on the main tracks. Something must be done. Everybody said so. Something must be done at once. The mayor called a special meeting of the emergency defense committee.

Mrs. Peabody was there. Mrs. Pritchart was there, and Ella Hobart, and Ned Burkes, and Ed Twitchell. The sheriff was there, and the police chief. Of course, Julie was there. Julie was asked to sit in by popular request.

All such good people! So serious and so worried! Each one hurried up the city-hall steps. Mrs. Peabody remembered that, when he came home from a trip abroad ten years ago, Ed Twitchell had said that Hitler had done a lot for Germany, and she felt a frost in her heart. Ed Twitchell thought of old Doctor Schultze and doubted him, and hated himself for it. Each one hurried up the steps with his own private fears and suspicions, and not one of them noticed that Amos Westcott was not pottering among his flowers in the square that day.

The meeting was hectic. They all talked at once. Mrs. Peabody said it must be the Japanese. Tricky little people, those Japanese. Ed said it must be a German. Mrs. Pritchart said it must be a Communist. Julie took the bit in her teeth and told them why France fell—because of the dry rot inside of her. The mayor pounded on the table for attention. He was still pounding when the telephone rang. It was for the sheriff.

The sheriff said, "Hello. . . . Who? . . . What? . . . Well, who is it? . . . Oh. . . . Yes-s-s-s. . . . Yes-s-s-s-s. . . . Yes, right away. . . . Yes, I'll bring them. . . . All right. All right."

He put down the receiver. "It was Amos Westcott," he told them. "Says he and Martha Devon have the man who has been setting the fires. Says he's at Martha's house. Wouldn't tell me who it is. Says we're to come out right away, all of us, and come quiet."

Mrs. Peabody said, "Oh, poor Martha!"

Julie said, "What are we waiting for?"

The committee dived for the door, down the steps and onto the square. The sheriff and the police chief gave orders, and in a few minutes a cordon of cars moved quickly up the street.

It drew up quietly at Martha's house. Everybody got out and stood there, excited and scared and thrilled.

Amos was waiting for them. Amos looked stern, almost angry. Amos said. "Marthy thinks only the sheriff and the police chief are comin'. But there's something I want you all to hear. You follow me, and don't talk."

They filed around to the kitchen door. They crowded into the kitchen, and Amos opened the swinging door into the front part of the house and motioned them to be still and listen.

They heard a man's voice, a troubled, whimpering voice, saying, "And, Miss Martha, I had to do it. I had to burn it to keep them from getting it. I had to do it before they got here. They're coming. Can't you hear 'em, Miss Martha? They're almost here."

Why, that voice didn't belong to a spy, a maniac, an arsonist. It was Jeb Bown's voice. Jeb wouldn't hurt a fly. Of course, he wasn't smart. He was the town moron, but Jeb wouldn't——

"And, Miss Martha, tonight I've got to burn the hospital. I've got to keep them from getting it. Everybody knows they're coming to kill us next and——"

They heard Martha speak then. "Why, Jeb, of course you must burn the hospital. I'll help you. I'll help you every way I can. You've told me all about it, Jeb, and now you must rest. You lie down here, and I'll cover you up. I'll wake you when it's time."

They heard Martha moving around, talking to him in that same gentle, quiet, soothing way.

Then, after what seemed a very long time, Martha came to the door and into the kitchen.

She spoke to the sheriff. She had her chin up, and tears in her eyes. She said, "You're not to hurt him, sheriff. It isn't his fault. He's terribly sick. He's always been on the border line, and all this fear has just pushed him over. It isn't his fault, and don't you hurt him. Do you understand?"

"I won't hurt him, Martha," the sheriff said gently. "I promise you. I won't let anybody hurt him. You and I'll wake him, and I'll tell him I've come to help him. I'll have a doctor waiting."

It happened that way, easily and quietly. The sheriff, the mayor and the police went away with Jeb. The rest stayed.

No one spoke. Only Martha. Martha babbled along like a brook, trying to make them feel better:

"You must all be just worn out. . . . Amos, get another log for the fire. I'll put on a big pot of coffee right away. It'll make you all

refreshed. . . . Ned, you help Mrs. Peabody with her coat.
. . . Julie, you get the cookies. They're in the big brown crock.
. . . Come in by the fire, everybody, and sit down. . . .
Sit down, Ella. . . . Here, Mrs. Pritchart; you take this chair."

They did as they were told. No one spoke, not until after Martha
had brought the coffee. Then Mrs. Peabody rediscovered her
tongue.

"Martha," she asked, "how did you know it was Jeb?"

"Oh, I didn't, dear. Amos and I just suspicioned it. We watched
him, and finally Amos brought him out here. Jeb used to rake
leaves for me each fall. I know him, and I just sympathized with
him, and pretty soon he was telling me all about it. It was that
simple."

Julie spoke then, resentment in her voice, "But how did you
know how to handle him? How did you know how to talk to him
like that? Weren't you—weren't you afraid?"

"Why, Julie dear, I guess you've forgotten I took care of pa all
those years. Right at the end, when he was delirious, I had to learn
how to soothe him. You learn a lot of things on the home
front."

It was as if everybody in the room was seeing Martha for the
first time, and, through Martha, themselves. Ned got up and went
over to her and took her hands.

"Oh, Martha," he said, "I'm so ashamed."

"Nonsense, Ned," said Martha brusquely. "Here, pass the cookies to Mrs. Pritchart. Her plate is empty."

Presently Mrs. Peabody thought she must go. They all got up.
This time it was Martha who went with them to the door, and told
them good-by, and thanked them for coming.

On the way to the cars, Mrs. Peabody walked by Amos, and she
said to him, "Go on, Amos, say it."

"Say what, Mrs. Peabody?"

"Say gabble-gabble-gabble. I deserve it."

The men climbed into one car. It was a time when men wanted
to be alone, without any women cluttering up their thoughts. The
women climbed into Ella's car. It was a time when women wanted
to straighten out their minds before they bumped into their husbands. They all thought the same thoughts.

Mrs. Peabody sat stiff as a board between Ella and Mrs. Pritchart.
And she kept thinking of Jeb, and she knew that the town was
responsible for what had happened to Jeb, and she knew she was
part of the town—a very loud part. And she kept thinking of Julie
and Martha. Martha knew things Julie had never learned, never
could learn on this earth because it wasn't in her. She kept seeing

Martha holding down her home front all those long years, holding it quietly, without fuss, without talk, as the whole town had to learn to hold its home front now.

They reached Mrs. Peabody's house first. She eased her width through the door. She looked around to be sure no man was looking, grasped her girdle firmly on each side, and give it a quick downward tug, the better to fortify herself for what she was about to say.

"Well, girls," said Mrs. Peabody, "I guess it's apparent to all of us that all these years this town has been sorry for the wrong twin. As for me, I'm not very pleased with my part in this. I'm going to make a few changes. Martha's knit more sweaters and done more war work than anyone else in town, and she didn't do it by chattering. God knows I'm sixty-eight, but they say even an old dog can learn a new trick if she wants to enough. . . . Ella, don't call me in the morning. I'm working mornings, and hereafter I'm answering no telephone until noon. Good-by, girls."

She started up the walk, stopped, turned back.

"Poor Julie," she said. "Poor dear Julie! This is going to be hard on her."

—*January 31, 1942*

FOR WOMEN ONLY

When the women announced
that they were going to raise twice as much money for war relief as
had ever been raised in the town for anything except taxes, the
men said flatly they couldn't do it. The men smiled tolerantly and
said it was impossible, any man would know better, but bless the
little women for trying.

The women smiled, too, and said nothing. Then they went
ahead and raised the money anyway, and $105.16 besides.

All over town, in some of the best families and some of the
worst families, husbands prepared to admit they had been wrong.
The mayor did it. The banker did it, and the courthouse janitor
who lived across the tracks, he did it too.

Now, the janitor's wife ran to steaming washtubs and faded
aprons. The banker's wife ran to dull black crepe and sables. The
mayor's wife had babies, and ran to flannelette and hair done for
the night in pigtails. Yet when their husbands told them they had
done well, there was no difference among them. They did not say,
"I told you so." They did not crow, or boast, or rub it in. Each said,
modestly and entirely too casually, "Thank you, dear, but it was
nothing, really," and then all three shut up tighter than an aba-
lone clinging to a rock.

The janitor said it was strange. The mayor said it was unnatural.
Why, here the women had a chance to make every man in town
wriggle and squirm, and they hadn't taken it. That was unnatural,
all right.

The banker said it was abnormal. Apples might as well start
jumping back on the trees. Why, everybody knows women have
no sex loyalty and can't keep a secret. "Yet they have a secret, and
they're keeping it too," said the banker. "You can't tell me, boys.
The women of this town have been up to something, but
what?"

Now, the Reverend Appleby, seventy years wise, borrowed one
from the women. He said nothing. It seemed to him that the
women were getting along together better than they used to. Why,

26

even Mrs. Terwilliger, who sang in the choir and whose disposi-
tion had certainly not been handed down from heaven, exchanged
none but sweet words with anyone. Yes, the women had been up
to something, and the Reverend Appleby sensed somehow that it
was important.

He simmered in the soup of curiosity and then he began to
snoop. Not a murmur came to his ears. The Reverend Appleby
couldn't stand it another day. He waylaid Madge Westcott in the
vestry after Guild meeting.

"Now, Mrs. Westcott," said the Reverend, "remember that the
Lord hates a liar and tell me the truth. What happened during that
drive you women put on? How did the women of this town learn
suddenly to work together so well? Who taught the lioness and
the ewe lamb to lie down in the same field? I've been here
forty-three years and I've never been able to do it."

Madge Westcott was cornered. The Reverend Appleby had married her, buried her first child and christened the others. There
was only one thing to do, and she did it. She gathered together all
the oomph that was left her at fifty-two, and she picked up the
truth and gave it to him. She gave it to him so glibly and so fast
that the poor dear ducked by involuntary action and missed it.

"Why, Reverend Appleby," said Madge Westcott, "of course I'll
tell you. It was perfectly simple. We just dug up Melinda Brown.
She's been buried for twenty years. We helped bury her, so we just
dug her up and dusted her off. And though I'm the first to admit
Melinda did a lot for all of us"—and here Madge Westcott stopped
to catch her breath and beam at the Reverend—"I do think we did
a little something for Melinda. Good-by."

The Reverend stood perfectly still to let his head clear. He was
sure of only one thing. Whatever the truth, it was for women only.
He sighed and walked to his study, finding solace in the reflection
that there were some things in this world that the Lord just never
intended a man to know anyway.

It began down at volunteer headquarters. All day long the big
office had been in one of its finest dithers. A steady stream of
people poured in the door. The telephone rang every minute, and
pretty girls—some in uniform—darted back and forth like shiny
minnows.

In the small rear room a private conference was going on. Here
were gathered the women who held the town's most important
volunteer war jobs. All ages and shapes, they were, with certain
common denominators. Each had the poised air that goes with
having at least some degree of local and social prominence. Each
had a nice face, bright with sincerity.

"Well, girls," said Madge Westcott—she was the leading doctor's wife—"it looks as if we'll have to dig up another man."

Everybody moaned.

"I know," said Madge cheerfully, "they're not worth a whoop. Their names are fine on committees and letterheads. That's all. If men are any good, they're too busy to take on another thing. If they have time, they're worthless. But what else can we do?"

"How about Helen Westmore?" somebody asked.

"She's in the hospital with a bad appendix," somebody answered. "Wouldn't you know it?"

The women moaned again, as if Helen Westmore had done it on purpose.

"Wait a minute," Madge said, "I've just thought of something." She rummaged around in a bottom drawer and came up with a shoe box. "I just happened to remember that right after Pearl Harbor, when every woman in town volunteered for emergency service, Mary Patton checked their cards. She's lived here forty years, and knows every woman clear to Eve. She picked out several dozen women she thought would be especially good in case of some big need."

She lifted a bunch of cards and began to examine them.

"H'm'm'm—'Mary Higgins.' No, she won't do. She's efficient, all right, but she's officious too. 'Alice Tremaine'—no, she's moved away. . . . Here's one—"

She lifted out a card, inserting her finger to hold its place.

" 'Melinda Brown. Aged thirty-eight. Single. Five feet nine.' " She looked around to be sure nobody present was more than five feet five. "Well, girls, that sounds hopeful. You have to admit one thing about the tall brigade. They're blunt, maybe, but they're capable."

Madge's head bent over the card as she read silently. When she looked up again, she was smiling and a little excited.

"I think we have something here," she declared. "Mary's made a notation. This Melinda Brown was with one of the big advertising firms in the city for twenty-some years. Mary says she's a woman of outstanding ability, especially as an executive and organizer. Her aunt died and left her an income. She's retired and living here again."

"But who is she?" somebody asked. "Does anybody know her?"

The bright, sincere faces looked at one another blankly.

"I do," said little Sue Collins from a corner. "She used to live in the same block. We went to school together as children. I remember, when the rest of us went on to college. her father died and she went to work. I always thought I'd keep track of her, but somehow I never did."

Lili Hopkins spoke then. She was the banker's wife. "I think I've met her," she said. "I'm almost sure I met her at some Sunday supper a few years back. There was a tall girl there anyway who worked with an advertising firm in the city. My husband said she was one of the most attractive women he'd ever met. He wanted me to have her over." Lili raised both hands in a gesture of futility. "You know how it is," she finished.

Yes, indeed! The women understood perfectly. If you asked a girl like that to luncheon or tea, she couldn't come because she was working. If you asked her to a dinner party, she was that most unwanted of guests, the extra woman.

"But, good heavens!" said Madge Westcott. "We can't just call up and ask her, please, to take charge of the hardest job this organization has ever tackled."

"Of course we can't, darling," agreed Lili Hopkins. "We shorter women can be subtle, can't we? Now, let me see. . . . First, Sue, you must go call on her."

The women put their nice heads together and set to work to unearth Melinda Brown. It never occurred to any one of them that maybe she wasn't going to enjoy being dug up just to be handed the largest, sourest gooseberry job on the home front.

Meanwhile Melinda was home by her fireside, feeling just a little sorry for herself. All the years that she had struggled for a living she'd anticipated this day.

A little white house with a garden. Rain on the roof and a wind at the eaves. A Crown Derby teapot on a slim mahogany table, and her great-grandmother's spoons on an old silver tray. A fire on the hearth. Chairs drawn close. And above all else, friends, people—women, and maybe a man or two—filling the room with the warmth of their talk and the glow of their laughter.

Well, here she was! Here was the white house and the Crown Derby teapot. Here was the fire on the hearth, and even the rain on the roof. But where were the people? Where were the friends? Melinda Brown had come back home where she'd been born and raised. She had come home to the woman's world where she belonged—where every woman belongs—only to find, as most working girls find sometime in their lives, that there was no place for her here. She was a stranger.

Not even a neighbor had called. The woman who lived on the left had sent over her gardener to inquire as to the clipping of the hedge which separated the two places. The woman who lived on the right had actually smiled and spoken. "Oh, Miss Brown," she'd called out, "we're so glad you're going to live next door! We were afraid it would be somebody with children or dogs!"

It had been amusing at first, this negative welcome. Now, suddenly, it was a little frightening.

All week it rained, and all week Melinda wrestled with her problem, pacing the room on her long legs. In the kitchen big black Dulcy—Melinda had inherited Dulcy along with the spoons—banged the pots and pans. Dulcy was frightened too.

But Madge Westcott was right. Tall girls are blunt—blunt enough to want the truth, and capable enough to wrestle until they find it. By the end of the week Melinda had reached a curious conclusion.

She was lonely. Not for the business world. In her heart she'd always been an alien there. Not for men. Melinda had always had more than her share of attention from men. It was women that she missed. It was women that she wanted.

There comes a time, thought Melinda, *when every woman longs to reach out her hand in good fellowship to her own sex, and if she tries it, what happens? She gets her knuckles rapped. She finds out that women are seldom drawn together by their sameness. They are separated by their differences. "I'm married; you're not. I have children; you haven't. I work; you don't." She finds that women, who are so amazingly clever at many things, know little of each other, and that though individually they may like each other, collectively they look upon each other with suspicion, if not downright distrust.*

It is barbaric. It is stupid. Why, good gracious, thought Melinda Brown, *a fourth of the women in this country are already working. By the end of the war perhaps one half will be working. When at last they earn the right to return to the woman's world, will they, too, feel like strangers? Will they be conscious of what they have missed? Will they, too, feel lonely and set apart?*

"Miss Melinda?" This was Dulcy speaking. "You got to stop this traipsin' back and fo'th. You is weah'in' yo'self to a frazzle."

"Now, Dulcy, go away. I'm thinking."

"Dat's one of yo' troubles, Miss Melinda. Jest thinkin' and a-thinkin'. You is a retired lady and you is supposed to act lak one. I tell you, Miss Melinda—" Dulcy left her words in mid-air.

"What is it, Dulcy?"

"Bless my soul," said Dulcy, "we's got callahs."

"H'm'm—probably an insurance salesman."

"No, 'tain't. He's a-helpin' a lady out of a cah; he's got on one of dem brown suits with shiny shoes and a big brown belt. He's got a little cap with gold—"

Melinda looked too. "Why, so he has. Why, Dulcy, it's Sue

Collins, I do believe. She used to be Sue Wells. And that must be her brother."

"Ain't he pretty, Miss Melinda? My! My! Ain't he the prettiest thing?"

"Put on the teakettle, Dulcy. Make coffee too. And don't cut the cake into little sissy pieces. You know how men are. Hurry now."

Melinda went to the door herself. "Why, Sue," she said, her voice warm with friendliness. "How lovely this is."

"It's been too long, Melinda," said Sue Collins. "You remember my brother, Jim?"

"He turned the hose on me when I was six. Of course I remember him. . . . How do you do, major?"

Jim Wells smiled down at her. "I only turned the hose on you because you ignored me," he told her. "I learned to wiggle my ears just to impress you, and you walked the other way with your nose up."

How nice he was! Not pretty, of course. A bit on the owlish side. A fine twinkle to the eye, gray at the temples, and just barely middle-aged enough so that he had to stand very straight and remember to hold his stomach in, lest somebody guess he had one.

Melinda was suddenly so grateful that she felt the tears pressing behind her eyes. Rain on the roof. Chairs drawn close. A fire on the hearth. Big black Dulcy carrying in the tea tray. All of them talking at once. Major Jim eating four pieces of cake and laughing louder than anybody. And finally Sue saying very casually, "Melinda, I'm giving a little dinner next Tuesday. I do hope you can come. Oh, it isn't big. Just Madge and Bill Westcott are coming, and Lili and Sam Hopkins. Jim will call for you. Do say yes."

Melinda said yes.

The next few days passed in a flurry of preparation. Melinda brought a new dress. It wasn't practical. It wouldn't wear well. It cost too much. It was exactly the kind of dress a working girl plans to buy someday, if and when.

Melinda had her hair done a new way also. It would never stay in such fine swirls. Dulcy would have to fuss with it. A hat would ruin it. How lovely it was!

Tuesday arrived. The major came and carried off Melinda and brought her home again.

The next morning she told Dulcy all about it—well, almost all about it. She didn't tell her that she and the major had sat in the car in front of the house when he brought her home and exchanged pertinent comments—namely: "Miss Brown, do you know that

you are a most unusual person? You have all the feminine attri-
butes. . . . Oh, yes, you have. You're one of the most feminine
women I ever met. At the same time, you have some strong
masculine traits mentally. Oh, only mentally. That's the most
attractive combination of them all."

"Can you believe it, Dulcy?" asked Melinda. "I am thirty-eight
years old and I have met a man who isn't married. There's nothing
wrong with him either. It's a miracle."

"Dose married women went to all de trouble to find an extra
man jest for you,," asked Dulcy, "and you not eben a related?"

"Yes, Dulcy, they did. And you know something? I've always
felt that married women weren't really interested in a working
girl. But Madge Westcott and Lili Hopkins were just as nice as they
could be. They even wanted to know all about my work."

"It don't sound right to me," said Dulcy slowly. "I been married
three times, Miss Melinda."

"Dulcy, get my coat, please. Lili Hopkins asked me to drive
down to the volunteer headquarters with her this morning. I
thought maybe I'd pick up some knitting."

"You bettah stay home," said Dulcy. "It don't sound right to me.
Dem women are up to somethin' sure nuff."

Melinda laughed. "Why, Dulcy, I wouldn't have your suspicious
mind for anything. There's Lili honking now. Where are my
gloves? Here they are. Good-by, Dulcy."

Poor Melinda! She walked into it like a lamb trotting into a
corral wagging its sweet little tail behind it.

Two weeks later Major Jim Wells had weekend leave. He rushed
into town from the nearby air base, and he hurried to a telephone
to call up that tall, attractive Miss Brown.

Give him a tall girl every time, thought the major. None of those
petty female wiles about Melinda. A man knew where he stood
with her. She wasn't the kind to go off half-cocked about something. Feminine, too, and just old enough to have some sense.

Dulcy answered the phone and reported that Melinda was
down at volunteer headquarters. She sounded ominous, but the
major was too pleased with himself to notice. He bounced up the
headquarters steps, feeling like a boy.

It was early Saturday afternoon. Madge Westcott and Lili Hopkins were just leaving.

Both ladies were in uniform, looking like lady generals and
knowing it. They greeted him effusively.

"Oh, Jim," said Lili, "we're so grateful for Melinda. My dear,
she's a treasure!"

"A perfect treasure!" Madge agreed. "I don't know what in the world we'd do without her."

The major smiled and escorted the two ladies to their station wagon. They walked down a side corridor and passed a large room. In it were several pieces of massive and ancient furniture in various states of repair.

On the floor sat a woman engaged in removing the filthy stuffing of a decrepit sofa. She was pinching her nose with one dusty hand, trying to keep from sneezing.

Lili Hopkins stopped in the door. "This is where we're doing over the furniture for the new lounge at the air base, Jim," she said.

The major made approving sounds in his throat.

"Oh, Mrs. Martin," said Lili Hopkins to the woman on the floor, "you're doing a beautiful job. It's going to be just lovely. Can we do anything to help you?"

Now, if the major had known one-tenth as much about women as he thought he did, he would have recognized the look that passed over Mrs. Martin's face.

It said, without words, "Yes, Mrs. Hopkins, there's something you can do to help me. You can get down here on the floor on that soft rear end of yours, and get your hands filthy, and get dust up your nose and in your ears—"

The major missed the look. So did Lili Hopkins.

"Nothing, thank you," said Mrs. Martin with great restraint.

The major helped the ladies into their car. When he returned, Mrs. Martin was waiting for him in the hall. She was the kind of inconspicuous little woman you see a hundred thousand times and never remember.

"If you're looking for Melinda Brown," she said dryly, "she's in there. Just go in. Nobody ever bothers to knock around here."

He thanked her and went in.

The room was nothing more than a huge closet shelved on three sides. Piled on the shelves was the accumulated junk of years. On top of a stepladder, left center, perched Melinda Brown, or what was left of her. She was looking for something on the top shelf, and she was dirty. She had her head tied up in a towel, and rubber gloves on her hands. She would fish into a mess of junk, come out with something, mutter, put it back and try again. She had reached the state where she was talking to herself.

"Madge said it was here somewhere," she said, "if I only live long enough to find it."

The major cleared his throat. She turned her head and saw him. For a moment she just sat and stared, and then the light of battle gleamed in her eye. "Well, well," said Melinda Brown slowly and too politely, "if it isn't the decoy duck. I'm surprised you recognize me."

"I beg your pardon?" said the major.

"You know perfectly well what I mean," said Melinda, beginning to steam up to the job at hand. "One of those wooden things that sit on the water and look innocent, and the poor little duckling sees it and flies down to get shot."

"Miss Brown," said the major, "I assure you I haven't the slightest—"

"Oh, you haven't, have you?" said Melinda. "Do you mean to stand there and deny that you and Susan planned every bit of it? I suppose you figured I just couldn't resist a uniform at my age. Trust a little woman to think of that."

"Melinda, I swear I never—"

"Well, you were right. I couldn't. And to think of how easily they hooked me. I didn't know I was caught until it was too late to back out." Melinda began to descend the ladder, backing the major, step by step, into the jam shelf.

"Oh, Miss Brown," she said in an excellent imitation of Madge Westcott, "don't you think you could help us out just a little? Oh, Miss Brown," she said in an excellent imitation of Lili Hopkins, "we really don't need very much help. Just somebody to take the responsibility. That's all."

"Melinda," said the major frantically, "I swear Susan never told me a word! Are you—are you well?"

"Well? After what I've been through? I'm practically dead. That's what I am. Why, do you know what I'm supposed to do? I'm responsible for raising a dollar and a half for every man, woman and child in this town. There isn't a man who thinks it can be done."

All the steam was gone now. Melinda sat on the lowest step of the ladder and, without any fuss at all, began to cry.

"Oh, Jim-m-m," she said, "I hoped, at a time like this, women would come to understand one another. I hoped maybe they'd all take hold of the business end of the mop and go to it."

"And they will," he said gently. "It's always this way at the beginning of a war, Melinda. But you want to remember something. The women with the orchids on their shoulders who smile and take the bows, while women like you do the work, they aren't important. They either turn into Melinda Browns or they get brushed aside into the discard."

"Do they?" she asked him.

"Yes, they do. War's hell on the middle-aged, Melinda. Take me.

I'm just a bay-window major. Do you know what the boys at the base call me? Pop. Good ole Pop. Pot-bellied Pop."

"How outrageous!" said Melinda fiercely, trying not to look at the region under discussion.

"I flew all through the other war. I even got some medals. And now look at me. I'm an earthbound goose with my wings clipped. Why, I can't even get one foot off the earth unless I lift it myself."

"Not really," said Melinda.

"It's true. I do the dirty work, the pesky, unromantic, tiresome detail. Men like me, we're just buffers between the generals and the kids. Don't you see, Melinda? In my way I'm nothing but a male Melinda Brown."

They sat there looking at each other, and then they began to laugh. They were still laughing when there was a knock at the door and little quiet Dora Martin came in.

"I know it isn't polite to knock," she said, "but I thought I'd better tell you I heard every word. I just had to come in and tell you that I've been a Melinda Brown all my life. All this week I've been down on the floor, getting dirtier and madder and madder. I just want you to know that whatever you do, Miss Brown, I'll help you." She stood there nervously. "You are going to do something, aren't you?" she asked. "I mean, it's quite an opportunity, isn't it?"

"Why, yes-s-s," said Melinda. "It is, isn't it? Of course I'm going to do something. Why, yes, of course I want your help."

They sat down, the three of them. They put their nice heads together and went to work.

Melinda learned something about women those next weeks. They can put down their differences. They can work together and understand each other, if the cause is great.

The drive was on. Women came to help from everywhere. They gathered like harvesters when the wheat is ready. They came seeking no personal recognition. Rich and poor, they came because they believed in the same things.

Melinda put them to work and worked herself harder than any of them. They sent out hundreds of letters, stating the cause and the facts in short simple words. They formed teams and solicited the town, door to door, the hard shoe-leather way. They erected booths at banks and street corners. They took collections in movies. They asked every store in town to give a line in their ads. They sent out little please-give slogans with bills and milk deliveries.

The money trickled in, then poured, then died again to a trickle. Melinda called in her committees and dug up new wrinkles.

Melinda permitted no persistent dunning. Several of the richest people in town were so surprised and pleased at this that they sent in large donations—one check in four figures.

The men were solicited just once. After that they were permitted to go back to sleep again, only half conscious of the rumpus going on right under their noses. Well, the women were certainly steamed up this time. They'd never make it, of course. Good for them, though. Kept them out of trouble.

Now, this was strange. Melinda noticed that these dozens of women who worked so tirelessly and so hard minimized their own efforts. They forgot one another. They remembered, as did she, only the women who didn't do their part, and in their names they indicted their whole sex.

She and Mrs. Martin kept strict account of the women who were drips. The officious know-it-all. The one who thinks that an executive's job consists of picking up the telephone and asking somebody else to do the hard work. The sweet thing who says, "Oh, I couldn't possibly do it. I'm not clever enough."

"And, Jim, out of all the dozens who've worked in this drive," Melinda told the major one night, "we've collected just six flops."

"That's all it takes," said the major. "Six women in the wrong place can make a noise like six hundred."

Now, the final event, scheduled for the last day of the drive, was a huge community luncheon. At nine that morning Madge, Lili and Susan appeared at the town center where the luncheon was to be held. Each was dressed in her best, and each wore flowers. Presently, other women joined them. In all, there were six.

They all talked at once. They explained to one another that they didn't care one bit about having their pictures in the paper, but Melinda Brown had absolutely insisted.

"Do you think we'll make our quota?" one woman would ask another, and the other woman would respond, "Well, really, my dear, I don't know. I hope so. We've all worked so-o-o hard."

"I do wish Melinda would come," Madge Westcott said presently. "She said she'd be here exactly at nine with the photographer."

No Melinda at nine-fifteen. No Melinda at nine-thirty.

The six women were beginning to get provoked at Melinda Brown and showing it, when the door to the kitchen opened and in scurried inconspicuous little Mrs. Martin, wearing gingham and no flowers.

"Oh, Mrs. Westcott," said Mrs. Martin, "I'm so glad you're here. Melinda just called to say she'll be very late. The last minute she couldn't find any women to do this room. She said she was sure you women wouldn't mind—"

"Well, of course," said Madge, "but, you see, we—"

"Oh, there isn't very much to do," said Mrs. Martin quickly. "The tables to set and the flowers to arrange. And potatoes to peel and dishes to unpack. And then, of course, Mrs. Parks' little boy dropped three glasses of jelly and somebody walked in it, so I'm afraid one of you will have to mop the floor. A shame, isn't it?"

"We'll have to get on the telephone right away," said Lili Hopkins. "We'll have to find somebody."

"I'm afraid it's a little late for that," said Mrs. Martin. "Saturday morning's not a very good time. And most of the women in town are cooking for us already."

"But we're not dressed to work. We're not—"

"Melinda said you could take off your dresses and work in your slips. She left the key in the front door, so you could lock it and no men could burst in on you. I'll be getting back to the kitchen, ladies. I think you'll find everything you need right here."

Mrs. Martin scurried back to the kitchen.

Madge giggled nervously.

"Hoist by our own petard," she said; "I think that's Shakespeare."

"Madge, for heaven's sakes," said Lili, "don't be erudite at a time like this."

"I can't help it. We were proud of digging up Melinda Brown. Now Melinda has turned the tables on us. She didn't even bother to be subtle. That's one thing about those tall girls. They may be blunt, but, my, they're effective!"

"Madge, stop babbling. What are we going to do?"

"Well, I don't know what you're going to do, Lili. I'm going to pick up this potato peeler and go to work. Then I'm going to get down on my hands and knees to Melinda Brown and ask her, please, not to tell my husband about this, because if she does I'll be hearing about it at dinner parties for the rest of my life."

"Madge," said Lili, "I never thought of that. Just hand me that mop."

The luncheon was an immense success. No one noticed that six of the women who were helping looked more wilted than the others.

Late that afternoon Major Jim Wells dropped in at volunteer headquarters to see how the drive had come out. The place was a madhouse. The women were counting the money. They looked as worried and distracted as presidential candidates waiting for the final returns to come in. Lili was counting dimes. Madge was counting quarters. As for Melinda, she scarcely spoke to the major. She just nabbed him and put him to running an adding machine.

Presently the confusion died down.

"All right, Jim," said Melinda wearily. "How much do we lack?"

"Six hundred fifty-two," he told her. "And we still have a few more checks to count."

The big room hushed as she read him the figures and he added them.

"Now what is it?" she asked, and the women held their breaths.

"Three hundred and thirty-three short."

Everybody moaned again. Madge looked at Lili. Lili looked at Susan. Susan looked at three other women. They all nodded, and Madge stepped forward.

"I'm sorry, Madge," said Melinda.

"Oh, no," Madge said quickly. "It isn't your fault. If you'd had the cooperation you needed, we'd have made it."

"But we're going to make it," said little Mrs. Martin loudly. . . . "Major, lend me your pencil."

She scribbled for a moment.

"Now, let me see," she said. "Five from ten is—Nine from thirteen is four—We're not only going to make it. We're going over by one hundred five dollars and sixteen cents."

"But, Mrs. Martin, I'm sure you must be mis—"

"No, I'm not, Melinda. I've just tossed in my fur-coat money. Been saving for years to buy one. What does a plain little mouse of a woman like me want with a fur coat, anyway? Now don't thank me. You see, I've never liked my own sex. I think I've always been afraid of women and—well, I'm—I'm not any more. That's all. It's worth the money to find it out." She chuckled quietly. "There's just one thing," she added. "I don't think we should tell the men a word about this. You know how men are."

They all nodded and looked at the major.

"If I have any luck, I can't talk," he said, looking at Melinda. "A man can't testify against his own wife."

Now, Sam Hopkins was not a man to give up easily. He still wanted to know the inside truth.

"Lili," said Sam one night, "whatever happened to that uniform you bought with sixty-three dollars of my money?"

"I sold it to Cousin Lucy in the city for sixty-five dollars and fifty cents, Sam, dear," said Lili. "I'm not a banker's wife for nothing."

"But I thought you volunteer executives needed uniforms."

"We do and we don't," said Lili. "We women have learned, Sam, that you can't judge a war worker by her clothes. All you have to do is look at her hands."

"Lili, who taught you that? I didn't."

"It's not a thing a man teaches a woman," Lili said slowly. "It's a thing a woman learns from another woman."

"What other woman?" he asked.

Lili walked over to his chair and perched on the arm. "Oh, Sam," she said, "you're a sweet thing. What in the world would I do without you?"

She leaned down and put a kiss where she thought it would upset him the most and take his mind from a subject which was none—absolutely none—of Sam's business.

—*January 16, 1943*

WHITE-COLLAR TOWN

Mrs. Goodhue was ready to turn the heel. She put down her knitting to rest a moment, and she removed the glasses which Maud, her daughter, had given her because they made her look like a dowager duchess. Mrs. Goodhue wasn't the least interested in looking like anyone at all, thank you, except herself, eighty years old and reconciled to it.

She sat there on the porch in the sun, looking out at the town which was her slice of America, fighting now for its freedom. A small worry swam up from the depths of her mind and paddled lazily on the surface. Bethie, her granddaughter, had come home from the bookshop for lunch today. She hadn't seemed quite like herself for some time now. This noon Mrs. Goodhue had tried to tempt her appetite with a cheese soufflé. Such a lovely one too! Fluffy on the inside and crusty on the outside, with a fine pinkish tinge from the tomato juice. But Bethie had not been tempted. She'd scarcely taken a bite. She'd scarcely said a word throughout the meal. Her grandmother had noticed, also, that Bethie was letting her nails and hair go a little. Such bad signs in a girl.

Mrs. Goodhue saw Helen Proctor's big black car pulling in at the curb. It was Helen's turn to drive the women to the Red Cross board meeting. She was early, which was unusual. Today she didn't honk frantically for Maud to hurry-up, please. She climbed out. Two other women emerged from the back seat. They stood on the curb, nice heads bent to the huddle, voices high and sibilant.

Across the grass came that peculiar buzz-buzz which, even after eighty years, still filled Mrs. Goodhue with misgiving. Oh, dear, what now? It couldn't be good news. Not in this town. Not in times like these.

The huddle broke. The women sauntered up the walk. One voice disentangled itself from the others and soared alone. "Well, my dear, there's one thing," it said dramatically. "If it had to happen to anybody, thank heaven it happened to them."

The other ladies agreed.

40

"Not that I'd wish it on anyone," added the voice hastily. Oh, no, no! The ladies understood perfectly.

"Just the same, it's their turn. You can't deny that. That family's never met a thing. It's just sailed along while the rest of us have had to get out and push. It just proves that everybody gets his sometime or other."

It did indeed. They had reached the steps. The front door opened and Maud hurried out to greet them.

"So glad you're a little early!" she cried brightly. "I'm almost ready. Blanche, darling, what a cute dress. Where in the world did you get it? I looked all over town and they didn't show me anything like that. Come up on the porch while I get my hat."

The women came up onto the porch. For the first time they saw Mrs. Goodhue, sitting quietly at the far end.

"Mother dear," Maud said, "you remember Helen Proctor and Catharine Ober and Blanche Seymour."

Remember them? How could Mrs. Goodhue forget them? She had bounced and burped all three. And how could she possibly live long enough to forget that time—let's see, it was in 1894, wasn't it?—when Helen Proctor's mother had gone away on a trip and left Helen with her for ten dreadful, interminable days? Why, actually on the sixth day Mrs. Goodhue had removed the young lady to the bathroom, laid her across her knees, pulled up her little skirts, pulled down her little—

"How nice to see you all," she said calmly. "Lovely weather, isn't it? Sit down, my dears."

They sat down. Helen Proctor ignored a chair, ran a tentative finger over the white porch railing and entrusted her well-girdled end to its support.

How well Mrs. Goodhue looked, they said. Did you ever in your life see anything lovelier than her white hair? Perfect with that blue dress. Just absolutely perfect!

Good heavens, thought Mrs. Goodhue. *I must be getting very old. They're using the same pussy-pussy tone that I've always reserved for infants, small animals and Jed Davis.* Jed Davis was the town half-wit.

Maud came out then, hat on, gloves in hand. Helen Proctor slid quickly off the railing. The other women stood up. They couldn't wait another minute. Not an instant. Mrs. Goodhue saw it in their eager faces and their bright eyes. Like gulls, they looked. Like gulls ready to swoop down upon some poor hapless little fish stupid enough to flip a fin out of the water.

"Maud, you'll never guess," said Helen Proctor. "On our way

here we passed the old Labadie house, and what do you think? The awnings are up, and so are the curtains."

"They must be going to rent it," Maud said. "After all these years."

"No, they're not, Maud," said Blanche Seymour. "The utility man was there connecting up the gas. He came out just as we drove along, and who do you think was with him? Old Ben, the Labadies' butler."

Maud said, "You don't suppose—"

"Yes, Maud. We asked him. The Labadies are coming back here to live. They're due any day now."

"No." Maud sank against the railing. "Well, girls, we won't be bored to death through this war, will we? We'll have something to talk about, anyway."

"But that's not all, Maud," said Catharine Ober. "Wait until you hear the rest. We stopped at the drugstore, and Helen called up Norah Cummings. She always knows everything. She says they've lost their money."

"But how dreadful!"

"Isn't it? All those lovely millions; it seems they were invested in the oil fields of Sumatra or some such place. The wells were blown to smithereens to keep the Japs from getting them."

Maud said, "Well, if it had to happen to somebody, thank goodness—"

"That's what I said," Helen put in quickly. "Isn't it, girls? It's the Labadies' turn." Her voice slowed. "Of course it's harder for you, Maud, because of Bethie. I mean she was so terribly in love with Tim Labadie, wasn't she?"

Maud drew on her gloves slowly. "Oh, I don't know, Helen," she said. "She thought she was in love with him, but that was years ago. You know how it is with puppy love. Terribly hard, but soon over. Bethie will be sorry, of course, but she's happy in her little bookshop. She's quite a careerist these days." She looked at her watch. "Heavens! We're going to be late. Mother dear, do be careful if you make a cup of tea. I'm always so afraid you'll leave the gas on."

"Yes, Maud."

The women prepared to leave. There was a final flurry of farewells. A general exodus.

"And, Mother," Maud called back, "do watch the steps, dear. I don't want you to fall and break a hip."

"Yes-s-s, Maud."

Mrs. Goodhue watched the women walk to the car and climb in.

Hands waved. Doors slammed. They were gone. She was staring into an empty street.

They wouldn't admit it, she told herself, *but they were pleased as Punch. Why didn't I smack Helen Proctor harder that time I had her laid over my knees? I'd like to shake them all. Yes, I would. Sometimes human nature is so irritating that honestly—*

She stood up quickly and walked down the steps into the garden. She pinched the blooms from the new plants to make them spread. Such a fine emotional outlet usually, and good for the flowers too. Today it didn't work.

Maud had been as bad as the others. Maud had been cold and brittle. But Maud was a good woman, even if she was a bit bossy and exasperating at times. They were all good women. They liked a little gossip now and then—what woman doesn't?—but never before had Mrs. Goodhue seen them pleased because misfortune had singled out another victim. Furthermore, they were common denominators for their sex in the town. If they felt this way about the Labadies, so did the majority of the town's women. My goodness! Probably there were gabbling huddles all over town by this time.

Mrs. Goodhue returned to the porch. Her mind kept slipping back into the past. It didn't seem yesterday since the Labadies had come first to the town. Let's see, it was in 1922, wasn't it? Yes-s-s-s. It was after the First World War. It was the year Bethie had the measles. My, the town had been excited when the Labadies came. They were the town's first millionaires, and they had turned out to be a surprise all right. As homey as an old shoe and just about as pretentious. Why, they weren't settled in the big old house a week before every child in the neighborhood was howling to go there right after breakfast and stay until bedtime.

Mrs. Goodhue chuckled to herself. Do you suppose Matilda was still alive? No, of course not. Matilda was a huge white English bulldog, perfectly beautiful in an ugly sort of way. Sometimes when you were calling in the Labadies' charming big room with its comfortable chairs and faded chintz, and you heard a sudden shriek from the children outside, and you thought, *Oh, glory! Bethie's fallen in the fish pond,* Mrs. Labadie would look up over the tea tray and smile, and she'd say, "Don't worry, my dear. Matilda will look out for them," and Matilda always did.

Once Bethie had hurt Maud terribly. She'd announced, aged six, that she thought she'd just go back up to heaven and come down a baby in the Labadie house. Maude had cried for an hour, until Mrs. Goodhue had explained that it wasn't because Bethie preferred Mrs. Labadie to her. It was Matilda's new puppies. The children got into some fine pickles that year. Poor Matilda had more than she could handle.

Mrs. Goodhue felt very uneasy. One memory topped the rest—that of Bethie's face the time Tim had come to tell her good-by when the Labadies moved away East, eight years ago. Bethie was eighteen then and she'd been wearing Tim's ring two years. No, not a diamond. Nothing but an agate in a silver setting that Tim had made himself.

You're wrong, Maud, said Mrs. Goodhue to herself. *It wasn't puppy love. Not at that moment.*

She went into the house to her room. When she returned, she was dressed to go out. It was too nice a day to stay in, anyway. She needed some bias tape. She needed a spool of white cotton No. 50 to hem the new dishcloths. She'd drop in to see Bethie, of course. Just casually in passing.

"Oh, stop fooling yourself, Nancy Goodhue," she said aloud. "You're too old for that. You're going downtown because you're worried about Bethie. There's something afoot in this place, and you want to know what it is. You're just as bad as any other woman."

She shut the front door with a slam and marched up the street to the bus corner.

Usually, Mrs. Goodhue rode in state in the back of Maud's car. It was quite an adventure to take the bus by herself. The very first person she saw was Mr. Lucca, the butcher, who had sold her meat when Paul, her husband, was alive and they lived in the little house on Elm Street.

Mr. Lucca was looking old and tired. When he saw Mrs. Goodhue he smiled and came over, and said, "It's nice to see you, ma'am," and Mrs. Goodhue said, "How are you, Mr. Lucca?" Mr. Lucca was poorly, thank you. The meat situation, you know. Might have to close his shop after forty years in business. He sat down across the aisle and told her about it, and Mrs. Goodhue listened and said, "Oh dear, dear" at the proper intervals.

Later it seemed to her that the whole afternoon she was making elderly, sympathetic, clucking sounds to somebody about something.

She made them to the bus driver when he said he was working himself half to death. Not enough drivers and too long a run. She made them to John Higgins, the lawyer, whom she met as she climbed off the bus. Yes, he was getting by, he told her, but that was about all. She made them to the girl who sold her the bias tape and the thread. Her husband was out on the Pacific, she said. Hadn't heard from him now for three months. Not so much as a postal.

Surely she had heard these same words before and made the same answers. They were strangely familiar, buried somewhere deep in her past, like a melody that haunts the memory while its exact tune evades the mind.

As Mrs. Goodhue walked toward Bethie's bookshop, she saw Doctor Biggs coming toward her. Doctor Biggs was eighty-one, and jaywalking.

"Why, Nancy Goodhue!" he declared. "You look younger every year. Always were a good-looker. How in the world did you get away from that daughter of yours?"

Mrs. Goodhue blessed him silently and thanked heaven Maud wasn't along to hear his flattery. Maud would just think he was an old fool.

"I'm A. W. O. L., John. I think that's the term," she told him. "How did you get away from yours?"

"I sneaked out the back door," said Doctor Biggs. "She'll give me the devil if she catches me. Well, Nancy, I suppose you're excited about the new ruins."

"What new ruins?" asked Mrs. Goodhue.

"Why, the Labadies, of course. They're coming home broke."

"Well, it'll be like old times, John. Do you remember how Mr. Labadie used to take rooms at the Elks Club when his family got too much for him? Shocked everybody."

"Yes, yes. I'm glad I'm retired, Nancy. There'll be a flock of grandchildren by this time. Bound to be. When they start getting the croup in the middle of the night, Mrs. Labadie can't call me."

"You know perfectly well you'd go if she did," said Mrs. Goodhue. "You'd love it. Oh, John, I was thinking this afternoon about the time Mrs. Proctor and your wife and I paid our first call on Mrs. Labadie. She was out working in the flower bed. Mud to the ankles and not one bit embarrassed. I remember she was just as cordial as could be. She led us into the house. Had to leave her shoes on the porch. Mrs. Proctor never did get over it."

They both chuckled.

"Mr. Labadie is gone, isn't he?" said Mrs. Goodhue. "Tell me. Is Tim coming?"

She knew at once something was wrong.

"Yes, Tim's coming," he said heavily. "Nobody else knows it yet, Nancy. Tim was hurt down there in the Solomons. I don't know yet how bad it is. I'm not going to mention it to anyone else until I know the facts."

Mrs. Goodhue was all sympathy. The town was going to be mighty sorry to hear that. If there was anything she could do, the doctor must let her know. She wouldn't tell a soul Tim was hurt. She'd tell Bethie he was coming. It was going to be a shock to Bethie. She'd have to sort of get her ready for it. Oh, dear, dear! So many fine boys going these days. So many changes. Well, probably they'd all have to get used to them. The doctor was to remember. If there was anything she could do—anything at all—

Mrs. Goodhue walked on down the street to Bethie's bookshop. Bethie was sitting at the circulating-library desk in the rear, a droop to her shoulders, a hopeless look on her face. She looked up and saw her grandmother.

"Darling, how nice!" she said. "I'm so glad you dropped in." She pulled up a chair close to the desk.

Mrs. Goodhue sat down and chattered a few moments about nothing at all. Then she said casually, "I suppose you've heard the news, Bethie, about the Labadies coming back here to live."

For a moment she thought Bethie hadn't heard her. When Bethie spoke, it was almost in a whisper. "Oh, Grandmother," she said. "When are they coming?"

"Right away, I believe. Any day now."

"Is—is Tim coming too?"

"Yes, dear. Tim's coming too."

"Then he's on furlough. He must be. Oh, grandmother, I know it's silly. I haven't heard from him for six months. I haven't seen him for seven years. There isn't anybody else like Tim. Grandmother, do you think he will like me the way he used to? Do you?"

"Of course, child. Of course he will."

"It's been so lonely. It's hard to be young and the men gone to war. It'll be wonderful to have Tim back just for a little while. I could always talk to Tim about anything. He's such fun. I'll buy a new dress. I'll do my hair a new way. I'll make an appointment right now and have my nails done tonight. You tell mother I won't be home for dinner."

"Yes, Bethie. I must go now. Good-by, dear."

Mrs. Goodhue walked slowly up the street to the bus corner. She hadn't even told Bethie that the Labadies had lost their money. It didn't seem important, somehow. Her small worry had grown large now. She stood on the corner and she took a long honest look at her town. The strange familiar feeling was back again stronger than ever. And suddenly she had it, the tune and the melody. She knew why Maud and the women were callous and brittle. It fell into place. All of it.

Of course, it was familiar. It had been like this in '17 and in '98; even after Bull Run, if anybody could remember that far back. It was always like this in any war, because the town fought all wars from the same old spot, the hardest one of them all.

Other towns were defense towns and fought with a hullabaloo and a holler. Other towns were Washington, D.C., and turned into a madhouse. Other towns were that sassy little burg on the Coast whose citizens talked about how terrible war was and earned three times what they'd ever made before in their lives. But this town, like hundreds of others, was the white-collar town that had never made a nickel out of war and never would.

My goodness, thought Mrs. Goodhue. The town couldn't even listen to itself go to pot with a bang. It just plugged along, struggling with priorities, taxes and its own white-collar misery.

Mrs. Goodhue understood Maud and her friends now. She thought of Blanche Seymour. Her husband's income was reduced to a fourth of what it had been. Her daughter was home for the duration with a brand-new baby. Had Blanche complained? No, she hadn't. She'd oiled up the old washing machine and announced she was going to dye her nice light rugs dark.

And take Helen Proctor. She'd worked for years to help her husband get established. Now they were fighting to keep their new home. And Catharine Ober was helping her husband in his office half time now.

Oh, yes, Mrs. Goodhue saw it all. War's long prying fingers had reached into the small corners of lives all over town. It wasn't that the women were pleased at the Labadies' misfortune. It wasn't that they were really cold and brittle. It was just that when you were having a hard time yourself, it helped somehow to know that everybody else was also. That's what it was.

At dinner that night, Maud and Sam, her husband, discussed little else but the Labadies. The Labadies were always exciting and fun. You had to say that for them. Couldn't have got away with it, of course, if they hadn't had money.

Mrs. Goodhue was silent up to this point. She could be quiet no longer.

"I met Doctor Biggs downtown this afternoon," she said. "He says Tim's coming too. Bethie was quite excited about it. I didn't have a chance to tell her the Labadies had lost their money. Not that it would matter to her anyway."

"Well," said Maud decisively, "it matters to me, I can tell you. I've never wanted Bethie to marry into wealth especially. But I certainly don't want her to marry into a family that's lost out and is discouraged and heartsick. I don't want her to marry into unhappiness."

"The Labadies were always a joyful sort of family," said Mrs. Goodhue.

"Of course they were. Why not? They hadn't a care in the world. That's all changed now."

"Their circumstances have changed, Maud."

"That's what I mean, Mother. The Labadies are bound to be changed too."

Mrs. Goodhue chose her words carefully. "I don't think human nature is as frail as all that, Maud," she said slowly. "Money never spoiled the Labadies. It never made them smug or selfish. I don't think the loss of it is going to ruin them. You have to believe in people, Maud. You have to believe that no matter what happens to any of us these days, we can keep our—our essential decency."

"That sounds fine," Maud said sharply. "I prefer to be practical about it. I want something better for Bethie than we've had. Look at this town. Look at people like us. We're wellborn and well-educated. We're honest and hard-working. We're the people in the middle, the forgotten millions."

"I know, Maud. It isn't an easy place."

"Easy?" Maud's voice was shrill. "The top people can pay their way always. The people on the bottom are helped. Who helps us? Nobody. We have to crawl out of trouble on our hands and knees. We're always the hardest hit. I want something better for Bethie."

She put down her napkin and left the table.

"Oh, dear, dear!" said Mrs. Goodhue. "Now what have I done, Samuel?"

"Maud's upset," Sam said. "Don't you worry, Mother. She'll be all right."

Mrs. Goodhue didn't sleep well that night. The old bones couldn't rest because the mind was too active. Her heart winged back to the house on Elm when Paul was living, to the sitting room and rainy days, and Maud leaving Bethie with her while she went to a party. Bethie was never in the house two minutes before Timmy was over from the big place across the street.

The past was safe. Did Bethie think so too? Was she looking back to a day that was no longer real? Was Maud right?

Mrs. Goodhue told Bethie at breakfast the next morning that the Labadies had lost their money. Bethie was sorry, but not concerned. She could hardly wait until they arrived. It was going to be wonderful.

Mrs. Goodhue waited until Maud had gone to do the marketing, and then she telephoned Doctor Biggs and asked him to let her know, please, the minute he knew the extent of Tim's injury.

He didn't call for two days. They were among the worst days Mrs. Goodhue had ever spent. Waiting days were always the hardest, she reminded herself.

Finally, on a Sunday night, Doctor Biggs called. His voice was flat. The Labadies had arrived. Tim had a badly shattered right leg. Always have to hobble around with a cane.

Mrs. Goodhue marched straight up to Bethie's room and told her as gently as she could.

Bethie took it well. She said, "We'll send flowers tomorrow morning. Mrs. Labadie loves flowers, Grandmother. We'll send a big box of Talisman roses. I'll include a book for Tim and a welcome-home note. Something perky and cheerful. I'll work on it right now."

Bethie left the house early the next morning before either Maud or Mrs. Goodhue was up. Her grandmother knew she had gone to the bookstore, so that she'd have her desk cleared and could take plenty of time to choose the flowers.

Mrs. Goodhue didn't mention Tim's injury to Maud. She was busy about her room all morning. Maud went out to luncheon. It was just after she'd left that Mrs. Goodhue saw Ben, the Labadies' old butler, come up the street.

Ben brought a note from Mrs. Labadie asking Mrs. Goodhue and Bethie to come to tea that same afternoon, and thanking them for the flowers. "We're not settled," she wrote. "Everything's just stuck in, but do come. Tim and I are so eager to see you."

Mrs. Goodhue telephoned Bethie. She wrote a note to leave for Maud. She told of Tim's injury. She explained why she hadn't mentioned it before. She smiled a little while she wrote. She knew so well how Maud would feel and what she would do. She'd get right on the telephone and call up Helen Proctor. How the words would fly.

Mrs. Goodhue left the note on the hall table for Maud. Then she went downtown and met Bethie at the bookshop.

They spoke little on their way to the Labadies'. They had to walk two blocks from the streetcar, and they passed the little house on Elm. The new owners hadn't cut back the honeysuckle, Mrs. Goodhue noticed. The heliotrope was almost dead. Paul had carried it home to her from the nursery. It had been placed in the morning sun and grown so tall that it had covered the whole end of the porch.

Mrs. Goodhue and Bethie walked right by. When they reached

the driveway to the Labadie house, Mrs. Goodhue dreaded to go in. She was frightened suddenly. Bethie had no fear. She looked radiant and eager. She put her hand on her grandmother's arm.

"Here we are," she said. "This is it."

Together they walked up the drive to the house. In the flower bed to the left of the porch stood Mrs. Labadie. She was lifting a little plant from a flat, careful to lose none of the earth around it. She stopped and tucked it in place, tamping down the earth gently. Then she looked up and saw them.

"Oh, how nice," she said. "How good of you to come. Bethie, darling, give me a kiss, if you can find a clean spot."

Everybody laughed and talked at once. Mrs. Labadie said, yes, she knew she shouldn't be out in the garden with the whole house to settle, but the day was so fine, and if she had any flowers at all, she simply had to get them in.

Mrs Goodhue had the queerest feeling—as if she'd stepped back into the past. Only, the first time she'd caught Mrs. Labadie in the damp earth, it had been amusing because of the millions. Now it seemed merely normal.

The big old living room was the same too. Ben had had the movers place the furniture as it had stood before. Mrs. Goodhue looked around her and remembered that when the town went in for a flurry of pastel living rooms, Mrs. Labadie had clung to her old Orientals. The room was as homey and comfortable and as charming as ever.

"We can't afford Ben," Mrs. Labadie was saying, "but he won't leave us. I've fired him three times this week, and four times last week. He simply won't leave. He says if he can't stay any other way, he'll rent a room and board here."

Bethie laughed, and so did Mrs. Goodhue. Wait until Maud and the town heard that the Labadies were boarding their ex-butler.

"Tim's downtown getting a haircut, Bethie. He said he couldn't have you catch him looking seedy. He ought to be home in a few minutes now. Come into the kitchen while I put on the kettle. I have a surprise for you."

"I know," Bethie said. "Lace cookies."

"That's right. Ever since Tim came home from the hospital he's been asking for lace cookies. I've been saving sugar for a month, and this morning I baked up a whole batch, if the grandchildren haven't found where I hid them."

They all helped get the tea. Bethie carried the tray back into the living room. She had scarcely set it down before there was a clatter from below, accompanied by howls of childish laughter and a furious barking.

"Eva's children," said Mrs. Labadie. "Hubert's too. I think they're sliding down the coal chute. We've been home one day and those children have acquired a dachshund, a cocker and a cat. I don't know where in the world they come from. Cream or lemon, Mrs. Goodhue?"

They were sampling the lace cookies and sipping the tea when they heard Tim's step on the porch. For the first time Bethie's joy left her for a moment. She became tense. The tap-tap of Tim's cane came louder and louder, and he opened the door and entered.

He walked in. First he went over to Mrs. Goodhue and he said, "Hello there," exactly as if he'd never been away, and he kissed her. Then he went to Bethie, who stood up to meet him. He grinned and he said, "Got a hug for the old man?" and Bethie laughed and took his face in both hands and kissed him hard on each cheek.

"How's that, Timothy?" she asked, and he said, "Bum. We'll go into it later." Then he sobered and looked down at her as if he couldn't get enough. "I used to sit in a foxhole at a place called Matanikau," he said slowly, "and I used to think that more than anything on all this earth I'd like to see one certain funny face—"

"Me?" Bethie asked. "My face, Tim?"

"If that isn't the conceit of a girl—if that isn't like a woman—"

They both laughed, and she slipped her arm through his, and they went out, both talking at once, unconscious of anyone or anything except themselves and the fact that they were together again.

Mrs. Labadie found her handkerchief and blew her nose hard. She said, "I think we better have some hot tea."

After the third cup of tea, Mrs. Goodhue said she must go. She wouldn't bother Bethie. She'd just run along. No, Ben needn't take her home. She'd take the streetcar. It was only a block or two to walk. Mrs. Labadie walked with her down the steps, and thanked her for coming, and said good-by.

Mrs. Goodhue went down the drive by herself. She looked back once. Mrs. Labadie had returned to her flowers. She was pulling on her gloves. She was standing again in the damp earth, humming a little tune to herself. Through the trees Mrs. Goodhue could see Bethie and Tim holding hands like children. She walked on to the street.

Maud and Helen Proctor were getting out of Helen's big black car. Maud held an armful of flowers. When she saw her mother, she looked a bit abashed.

"I—I got your note, dear," she said quickly. "Helen and I thought it would be nice if we came right over. We won't go in, of course. We'll just leave the flowers at the door."

"I think it's a lovely idea, Maud," said Mrs. Goodhue. "Mrs. Labadie will be so pleased. She's right there in the garden. Bethie's there with Tim. I'll just go along home. No, no, dear, I won't wait for you. Mrs. Labadie will want to chat. It's a nice day for a streetcar ride."

Maud and Helen Proctor walked up the drive, Mrs. Goodhue following them with her eyes. She saw them stop and stare. She heard Mrs. Labadie's greeting and Bethie's eager cry. She saw Maud smile and start forward.

Mrs. Goodhue walked down the street. She had to wait awhile for her streetcar. She sat on the bench in the shadow of the elms, thinking of the Labadies. It didn't matter whether they were the rich or the poor Labadies, she thought. They were bigger than what they had or what they lost. They were bigger than what happened to them. They had overcome adversity, and so would the other people of the town when it was their turn.

Mrs. Goodhue sat there on the bench in the lazy summer sun, looking out over her town. She could see the tall church steeple, grimy now and in need of paint. The town would need more than paint before the war was over, but it didn't matter now. It didn't matter, because the town held safety within itself. *Why, my goodness*, thought Mrs. Goodhue, *one couldn't ask a better place to live.*

—*June 26, 1943*

THE WALL BETWEEN

The new class of women welders from the defense school had passed through the gate and was crossing the yard to report for work. From doors and windows, men watched, some openly, some surreptitiously, each from that small pigeonhole through which every man observes the woman who steps from her world into his own.

From a second-story window in the executive office, Mr. Sheldon, grandson of the founder, looked down with the relief of a distracted mother whose children are sick and whose sink is piled high with dishes. Mr. Sheldon welcomed any help the Lord might see fit to send him. Any help at all.

From an adjoining room, Ned Landis, the assistant manager, saw the entry and moaned softly. Just another ton of trouble arriving on the hoof.

A small wake of patter followed the women across the yard. "Here comes the sisterhood," the men said. This was a Ned Landis coinage, short for Sisterhood of Boilermakers, his favorite phrase. Some of the men preferred diminutives. "The dollies," they called them, or "the fillies."

One man used no pet word or phrase. To Ben Morrow, the new workers were simply "the women." Nobody noticed Ben sitting there in the sun outside his little gatekeeper's house. He was a leftover. He was a relic, like the gate he tended in the old wall.

The wall was staunch brick and mortar. It surrounded the executive buildings, and had been built originally to shut out the noise of the foundry and to keep stray livestock from trampling the stiff garden that fronted its offices. A high steel fence surrounded the whole plant now. Stray horses and cows no longer roamed here. The foundry had grown so huge its noise could be heard in the town. But the old wall still stood, and Ben Morrow still tended its main gate.

Ben could see both ways. To him, the grass plots in front of the executive buildings and the hard-packed earth of the foundry yard were the shores of Africa, the Aleutian Islands—any place and

53

every place where a man like himself, who took a stroll once at Belleau Wood, could no longer go as an active participant.

Ben watched the women cross the yard. Queer thing, he was thinking. Sometimes war puts big men in little jobs, and little men in big jobs. Then, when it's over, they both go back where they belong. With women it's different. Women never go back. Yes, individually they may, but their sex stays forward. War picks up some women and drops them rudely into new kinds of life, and because of them all women live a little differently and a little more freely thereafter.

The telephone rang in Ben's gatehouse. Without leaving his chair, he turned and plucked the receiver with his good hand. It was Miss Patton, secretary to Ned Landis, her voice tart and dry. When a young woman by the name of Ann Burkett presented herself at the gate, she said, Ben was to send her up.

"She's taking Mr. Phillips' place, Ben," she explained. "The Army's grabbed him. And if you see Mr. Landis, tell him Mr. Sheldon wants him to show her the plant. Poor man, he's already had about as much as he can stand."

Ben said he would, and hung up. He felt a little excited now, as if he were waiting for the overture to finish and the curtain to go up. Ann Burkett coming here to work. Wasn't that like life? Wasn't that the way life could change and deal it out? She was a town girl. She was Doctor Tremaine's daughter. The old doc was gone now, but Ben could remember way back when Ann had been a mere sprout, a curly-headed little tyke skating up and down in front of her dad's clinic with her pigtails flying.

Let's see—that was in 1920, wasn't it? Yes-s-s, that was after Ben had come home from France and Doc Tremaine was trying so hard to save his bad arm. He'd had to go to the clinic almost every day for a while then. He remembered that once little Ann had set up housekeeping on the clinic porch with her dolls. Ben had thought then that she was as cute a trick as they come.

No man ever had a better friend than the old doc. Maybe that was why Ben had been interested in watching his kid grow up. Ben knew a lot about the town's youngsters. He knew the ones who grew up too soon, and the ones who grew up too late. It had seemed to him that Ann Tremaine did it just about right. She had had it neither too hard nor too easy. She had had just enough necessity to give her impetus.

Why, even when she came home from college—with all the honors, too—she hadn't been one bit uppity or smart. She hadn't forgotten Ben, the gatekeeper. She'd found a job and gone to work.

Ben remembered teasing her once about being a career girl. He remembered her answer: "Oh, no, Ben. I know my place. I know where I belong. I'm just marking time until that tall dark stranger comes along. You know, Ben, I'm beginning to think he's bogged down somewhere."

Ben had said nonsense, he'd be chugging round the bend any minute now, and he probably wouldn't be tall and dark, and he probably wouldn't be a stranger either. It had always tickled him, because not six months later he'd read of Ann's marriage to a towheaded lad from across state who'd gone to school with her. She'd gone away to live, and every time Ben met the old doc he'd reached in his pocket and come up with a new snapshot of his grandbaby. And this, Ben had thought, was the happy ending. This was the place where the reel ended and you found your hat and went out.

Then life played the joker and took her ace. Her husband went to China to help build dikes to keep the Yellow River from flooding. He stayed to blow up the same dikes he'd helped build, to flood the river and hold back the Japanese. He stayed too long.

Ben sat there in the sun, mulling it over. War had stretched out its cold fingers and derailed this girl's life exactly as war had derailed his own life so long ago. It gave them a kind of kinship. He sat there watching for her. If she was to take Mr. Phillips' place, she was coming here as an executive, not in one of those subordinate positions where a woman makes it easier for some man. She'd handle the whole insurance department. The women welders were here because women in England and Russia had proved themselves at the work. But Ann Burkett would be a trail breaker, and trail breakers had it hard. It took war to do it. It meant that Mr. Sheldon had scoured the Coast and couldn't find a man.

Ben waited eagerly. Finally he saw her coming. She was walking toward him across the yard from the bus stop. She was still young and attractive, and she walked with her head up, like her dad. He stood up to welcome her. Even then, Ben knew she was not going to be merely important to the plant and to her sex. No, this girl was going to be the significant one.

When the bus had stopped at the outside fence of the foundry, she was a few minutes early. She walked aside and sat down on a bench and looked at this huge sprawling plant where she had come to build herself a fine new life.

She wanted to enter, and she was frightened too. She had that waiting-room feeling, when a woman stands on the threshold of any big new experience, and knows the seams of her stockings are crooked and her lipstick is smeared, and knows she's going to tumble and fall on her face any minute now.

Nonsense. She was well prepared for this job. Seven years' experience in all, four before her marriage and three since John's death. It was just that—that a woman doesn't really know what working means until she has others dependent upon her, somebody like her own little Nanny, and John's mother too. It was just that a girl doesn't realize how heavily she's leaned on her father's and her husband's names until she enters some place like this foundry, where even the shadow of their protection cannot follow her.

Ann Burkett stood up and pulled down the jacket of her suit and straightened her blouse. She walked to the big outside gate and handed in her letter of admittance. For one brief instant she looked back. She said good-by to the girl she'd been and the woman she'd expected to be. Then she stepped quickly inside.

She walked across the yard toward the small gate in the old inner wall. She didn't recognize Ben until she was almost up to him. When she saw him standing there, smiling and waiting for her, she was frightened no longer. "Oh, Ben," she cried, "I'd forgotten you worked here! Ben, I never was so glad to see anybody in my whole life!"

Ben said, "How are you, Mrs. Burkett? How are you?" He took both her hands in his one hand, and he said, "Blamed if you haven't grown into a nice-looking woman. Never thought you'd make it."

"Why, Ben Morrow! You know perfectly well I was a beautiful angel child. Oh, Ben," she said, "it's good to know you're here." She told him about her little Nanny and the new job. No, Nanny wasn't with her. Not yet. She was with John's mother. But they'd all be together again when she was sure she'd make good at her work and had found a house.

Then it was time to go in. Ben walked with her to the door of the executive building.

"It's the second floor first door on the right," he said, "and don't you be scared of Ned Landis. He roars loud, but he's never bit anybody yet."

She said she wouldn't. She thanked him and went up the steps. She took the elevator to the second floor and stopped at the first door to the right. She went in. Miss Patton was typing at a desk. She looked up with curiosity and without friendliness. A flicker of something—was it amusement?—played across her nice middle-aged face. Her tone was polite.

"The shop's just called to say that Mr. Landis was on his way over, Mrs. Burkett," she said. "Won't you be seated, please?"

Ann chose a chair by the door, so that she could see Mr. Landis before he saw her. Miss Patton went back to her typing. Ann studied her. A blotter to sop up the surplus emotions of her employer. A mirror in which to see his reflection. A little black boy from a fairy tale who fans flies from a royal brow. That was Miss Patton.

Footsteps sounded in the hall. The door burst open. All the confusion and the tension of the war was reflected in the man who entered.

"Well, what is it now, Miss Patton?" he demanded. "Hurry, please. I'm due back at the shops."

"Here's a new ruling from the government, Mr. Landis," she said. "I can't figure out what it means. I thought you ought to see it."

"Good heavens! Another one?" He took it. Silence lay thick in the room. Then the explosion. "Who in the devil thought this up?" he roared. "Madame Perkins? Here, take it. I haven't seen it. It'll hold up our whole shipment. Tear it up. Throw it away. Show it to me Monday."

"Yes, Mr. Landis. Mrs. Burkett is here. The woman to take Mr. Phillips' place. Mr. Sheldon asked if you'd mind showing her—"

"Oh, he did, did he? Of course I mind. Does he think I have nothing better to do than show some fool woman around—Stick Dewey with her. You couldn't find me, Miss Patton. You looked everywhere and you couldn't find me."

He turned. Ann Burkett had stood up to meet him. She spoke first. "I know just how you feel," she said slowly. "You feel the way a woman does when she gets up in the morning with a million things to do and finds ants all over her nice clean kitchen. I'm an intrusion." She laughed a bit shakily. "I'm not a man," she said, "but maybe I'll be better than nothing. Mr. Sheldon did hire me, so I guess you'll have to give me a chance to prove I can do the work. And now, Miss Patton, if you'll tell me where I can find this Dewey person who is to be stuck with me, I'll go, and gladly."

Mr. Landis grinned suddenly. "Mrs. Burkett," he said, "I've averaged three hours' sleep a night for the last week. I hope you'll give me another chance. I'm not always so ill-tempered. Really I'm not. I hope you'll permit me to show you the plant."

It was a strange tour for Ann Burkett. In the first place, Mr.

Landis, who was a possible forty and in no way decrepit, showed no awareness of her sex. What impressed her about him above all else was his attitude toward the foundry.

Why, he loves the place, she thought with surprise. *His whole life is here.*

It showed in the eagerness and pride with which he spoke of the work. It showed in the way he greeted the men. He wasn't surly now or tired. He told her that he had started in the shops himself. There was scarcely a job he hadn't held sometime or other. No, he'd never married. Never had time for it.

After the tour of the shops, he introduced her to the office personnel. The women were all like Miss Patton—curious and polite, and a little amused. The men were alike too. Their faces wore a courteous withdrawn look, as if they were deferring judgment and hoping for the best. Last, Mr. Landis took her to the office of Winthrop Tolman.

"You're not under him in any sense," he explained. "However, your work does cross his desk. I'll let him explain the details, since he knows more about your department than I do. He is Mr. Sheldon's son-in-law."

There was a final flurry of amenities. If there was anything she didn't understand, if she met any problem which she would like to talk over, she was to remember that he was at her service. She thanked him. He was so kind. Then he turned her over to Mr. Tolman and left her—no doubt with relief.

There was nothing withdrawn in Mr. Tolman's manner. He had made up his mind. He had passed judgment without even giving her a trial. Mr. Tolman showed her her new office. He did hope she would like it, he said too politely. He had chosen it himself with the greatest of care. They sat down at her desk. She listened carefully while he went over the work in detail.

Once he looked up and said, "I assume, Mrs. Burkett, that you understand what I'm saying."

The implication was obvious—that she was quite incapable of understanding anything so complicated—but Ann ignored this and said easily, "Thank you, Mr. Tolman, I believe I do."

In everything Mr. Tolman said and the way he said it, he showed antagonism. She tried frankness, which had worked so nicely on Mr. Landis.

She said, "I know it's difficult to accept a woman in a position that no woman has ever held here, Mr. Tolman. But I do think I can prove to you that I can do the work."

Mr. Tolman said coldly, "The war means a good many changes

for all of us, Mrs. Burkett—at least temporarily. I admit I don't feel this position is suitable for a woman. Frankly, I told Mr. Sheldon so. He didn't agree with me."

When at last he had gone, Ann told herself it couldn't be real. She must be imagining things. She must be exaggerating. That's what it was. It was the strain that comes from a new job in strange new surroundings. And all the time she knew this wasn't true. She knew that Mr. Tolman was her call to battle stations, and she sensed also that no matter how hard and how well she fought, he wouldn't change.

Ann knew that when working women got together and talked shop, they spoke frequently of the prejudice which men held against their sex in those top jobs where women compete with men. She had never met it before. She had never even admitted its existence. When some woman complained bitterly that she was expected to do better work for less pay than a man, Ann had always felt that, whether she knew it or not, this woman wanted favors because of her sex. Now she wasn't so sure.

Footsteps sounded in the hall. A voice said, "Oh, hello, Win. Your lady executive arrived yet?"

Mr. Tolman's voice answered, "Yes, she's here. She won't last two months."

He spoke loudly. He meant her to overhear. He meant his tone to be contemptuous.

The Venetian blinds were drawn tight at the windows. Ann walked over and pulled them open. She stood there staring out. Her room, which Mr. Tolman had said he chose with such great care, looked straight into the inner wall.

She stared at the wall. In that instant it became a sort of symbol to her. It wasn't brick and mortar. It wasn't the old wall whose gate Ben, her friend, tended. It had become a wall of prejudice, and she knew that whatever else she had to do here, first she must find a way to tear it down.

When winter came, Ben pulled his chair outside the shadow of the wall, so that the morning sun could reach him.

No one bothered to watch the women cross the yard these days. The shoddy, careless workers had been weeded out long ago, and those women who remained were accepted without curiosity and without comment.

Ann Burkett had been here five months now. Every morning she came through the gate, chin up and courage high. But sometimes when she left at night she looked too tired, and at other times she showed anger and resentment in her eyes. No doubt about it. The girl had a war on—a private war, one of those inner conflicts about which a man could not ask, about which he could do nothing except wait.

She never complained. Whatever was wrong, she held it tight within her. Frequently she stopped to chat with Ben. She was always bright and smiling and full of news about her little girl, who had come with Ann's mother-in-law to live in a trim little house near the foundry.

It couldn't be her job. Ben asked Mr. Sheldon one day how the young woman was doing who had taken Mr. Phillips' place. Mr. Sheldon had lost his distracted-mother look and smiled.

"Splendid, Ben. I have to admit I've been pleasantly surprised. She's a good worker, and no nuisance to anybody."

No, it couldn't be that Ann Burkett was worrying over holding her job. It must be a man. Ben hoped it wasn't Ned Landis. He liked him. Of course, Ned didn't know much about women. If Ned Landis wanted to lift a woman to heaven with the compliment supreme, he told her she could do something or other as well as a man. If he wished to reduce her to the lowest possible pulp, he said, "Well, what can you expect from a woman?" Nevertheless, Ned was a fair man. Ben was sure of that.

Once Ben saw Ned and Ann Burkett together. They left work at the same time. She was taking him home to dinner. They were laughing and talking, and she was teasing him a little about something. No, it couldn't be Ned.

After that, Ben looked for the little man put by war in the big job. It didn't take him long to single out Winthrop Tolman, who had been at the plant scarcely a year. Ben watched him carefully.

Meanwhile Ann Burkett asked no favors and worked as hard as anyone. Gradually the men lost their look of withheld judgment. They accepted her as one of them—all except Mr. Tolman. At first she thought perhaps he was just a difficult person with whom to work—difficult for men as well as women. But no, the men seemed to like him. He was fair to them.

She tried to make Mr. Tolman bring his prejudice into the open. She said to him, "I know you don't like me. But can't we discuss the reason frankly? I'm willing to make any concessions that are right."

Mr. Tolman said, "I'm too busy today, Mrs. Burkett, for emotionalism. Some other time—"

She tried to ignore him. In her mind she declared an armed truce. But Mr. Tolman's desk was the clearinghouse for her work. He couldn't fire her. Neither could she avoid or go around him.

Once when Mr. Sheldon sent down an important new government ruling, Mr. Tolman neglected to refer it to her. She made a mistake which might have involved the foundry in serious difficulty and cost her her job. She caught it in time quite by accident.

When she asked Mr. Tolman why he had failed to give her the ruling, he said, "Mrs. Burkett, I am sure that you are mistaken. I distinctly remember asking my secretary to take it in to you."

After that he was careful to send in anything which she needed to see. If it involved any work on her part, he had his secretary take it to her at a quarter of five or just before noon on a Saturday. She worked late many a night because of Mr. Tolman, and many a weekend too. She found herself living in a world of pettiness with a growing resentment which she could not ignore or shake off. She didn't go over his head to Mr. Landis. She sensed somehow that this was what he hoped she'd do.

There was one bright chapter in those months of work. She wasn't satisfied with one form of contract used in her office. She devised another. She worked out a new system to deal with one phase of her work. Then she took it to Mr. Landis.

She remembered the first time he'd shown her the plant. There was the same pride in his voice now, and the same eagerness. Only this time she understood them and was part of them.

"You've done a swell job on this," Ned Landis said. "Talk it over with Tolman. It will help his department too. The board must approve the change, of course."

Ann took her plan to Mr. Tolman. It was the first time she had entered his office without resentment. She was so interested in what she was saying, she forgot her dislike. When she was finished, she saw that he had been listening with a smile on his lips. His words told her nothing.

"You may leave your plan, Mrs. Burkett," he said. "I'll go over it when I have time."

Days passed. Weeks.

When she asked him if he had considered her plan yet, Mr. Tolman said no; later perhaps. She knew then that he'd shelved it.

Mr. Sheldon was giving his annual party for the executives and their wives that night. Ann told herself she was too discouraged to go. She stayed late at her desk, and for the first time she felt defeated. You couldn't beat prejudice. It was the problem of the man who held it.

When she left the office, it was dark. Old Ben was still at the gate. He looked at her carefully. He spoke slowly, almost sadly.

"So you're licked," he said. "He's won, has he? Well, I'm disappointed in you, girl. Didn't know I'd care so much."

"What do you mean, Ben?" she said. "How—how did you know?"

"You've always come out this gate with your spunk up," he told her. "Sometimes you were tired and mad, but you always came out fighting, your chin up."

"But, Ben, what can I do? Oh, I know not all men are that way. He's not fair. He's not just."

Ben took out a packet of matches and lighted his pipe. "I've been watching him," he told her. "I've been watching Mr. Tolman quite a spell now. I'm kind of sorry for him myself. Doesn't seem natural for a man to be mean to a nice girl like you. Must be a mighty strong reason for it. Yes, I'm right sorry for the man."

She was too amazed to answer, and she was angry. She turned to go. His next words stopped her.

"Your dad said something to me once, Ann. I was griping about losing my arm. He said I'd either lick the way I felt about it or it would lick me."

"I can't lick it, Ben," she said quickly. "I've tried everything."

"You mean you can't solve it maybe," Ben said. "A man can only solve his little problems, Ann. He has to outgrow his big ones. This is a good time to grow up. Lots of women are growing up these days. Why don't you try it?"

She was furious. She turned and hurried on home. When she reached home she was more perplexed than angry. All through dinner she kept thinking of what Ben had said. When little Nanny was in bed and she was alone by the fire, she still tried to puzzle out his meaning.

The doorbell rang. There stood Ned Landis, hat in hand, smile on face.

"I came by to see if I might take you to the party," he explained. "Old Ben waylaid me at the gate tonight. He says we're working you too hard. He says the foundry doesn't deserve a pretty lady executive unless it learns how to treat her."

"Ben said that?"

"He certainly did. I promised to rush right over and make amends. Ben insists the Sheldon party will do you good. Come on, Ann."

"All right, Ned. I'll go."

At the Sheldon home, the men were gathered into huddles, talking war and business. The women were in small groups, too, talking children and rationing. Inside of five minutes Ned Landis was talking shop with the men and Ann was talking women's talk with the wives, which is the same the world over.

After a time she excused herself and went to the powder room by herself. She was marooned there for a few moments because when she was ready to go, some couple held a domestic argument outside the door.

The woman's voice was high and angry. "I'm not going to waste the whole evening on the hired help. We'll leave at eleven. I told Helen we'd be at her—"

It was Mr. Tolman's voice that answered. "Maud, I've told you twenty times if I've told you once that I won't—"

"Oh, Win, for heaven's sakes, do we have to go over all this again? You seem to forget that if it weren't for me, you wouldn't be—"

The voices drifted off. Ann returned to the party. It was Mr. Sheldon himself who introduced his daughter, Maud Tolman, all smiles now, and graciousness. Her talk was entirely of herself. It was a running stream of my children, my house, my husband, until the only word Ann heard was the possessive pronoun. A selfish woman. A spoiled and arrogant woman. A cold woman at whose heart no man could ever warm his hands.

For the first time Ann knew why Mr. Tolman disliked her. It was because he disliked his own wife. It was because he was afraid of any woman in a position of authority. And she knew now, too, why Ben was sorry for Mr. Tolman and why Ben had wanted Ned to bring her here. If some men built a wall of prejudice against women, she thought, it was because women themselves—the ones who wouldn't grow up—had given them the bricks with which to build it.

It was a disturbing thought. It meant that some of the responsibility for that prejudice—all of which she had placed on Mr. Tolman and men like him—belonged back on her own sex, and, therefore, in part upon herself.

All that evening she thought of this. When she reached home she mulled it over. She had contributed to the misunderstanding. She knew that now. It seemed to her that without appreciating it, she had spent her life absorbing the old idea that a woman deserves love and care and protection because of her sex.

It wasn't true. It never had been true. Jane Addams knew it when she first saw the Chicago slums. Florence Nightingale knew it at Scutari. Maybe the great women were born knowing what Ann had just learned—that a woman can do whatever she must do, and go wherever she is needed.

She did not feel alone in a man's world any longer. She was in the vanguard of her sex with thousands of other women who had left behind their safe and possessive lives to follow their country's heart and encompass a new world. It was dangerous here in front, and frightening, too, and yet it had a kind of glory.

The next morning Ann Burkett was late to work for the first time. There at the gate waited old Ben and Ned Landis.

Ned spoke first. He said, "Ann, this morning we had an early executive-board meeting. Mr. Tolman got up and presented your plan as his own. He didn't say it was his plan in so many words. He let us assume it."

"It doesn't matter," she told him. "Yesterday it would have mattered a lot to me. Today it doesn't seem so important."

"It matters to me," he protested. "I got up at once and said I considered the plan excellent, and that I had told you so when you first talked it over with me. Ann, you've been having trouble with Tolman for months. Why—why didn't you tell me?"

"I couldn't until I'd licked it. You wouldn't have believed me, and anyway it was partly my fault. I've always been the center of my little world. I had to learn that I was a mere cog in something bigger than myself. You and Ben taught me that. . . . Oh, yes, you did, and I'm grateful to both of you."

No one spoke. Then Ben put his hand on the gate. "You two heard the news?" he asked loudly. "Mr. Sheldon's going to tear down this old wall. Says it's outlived its usefulness. And that's not all either." He opened the gate wide. "The new personnel director is to be a woman. I understand the new head accountant's to be a woman too. I expect you had a hand in bringing them here, Mrs. Burkett."

She was shocked. "Oh, no, Ben. I didn't even know it. No, Ben. I'm afraid you're wrong there. I'm just an everyday woman with a job."

Ben said, "Sure. I know. Just another woman with a job."

—September 25, 1943

THE GENERAL
AND THE LADYBIRD

Who tells the children of the running wind? When the long twilight comes to the pebbled beaches of the Northwest, who sits on the white drift log and tells them of the days before the stumps and the slashings? Who keeps clear the life line that binds the children to their heritage? The mothers don't bother, the fathers haven't time, and where are the oldsters grown wise with failure, like Uncle Rod?

Long before they met him, the children knew Uncle Rod was a failure. The grownups said so. They spread their apology like a carpet before his name.

"He was born too late," they said. "He should have been a pioneer. Poor Roderick!"

Tim asked Papa what was a pioneer, please, and Papa said a pioneer was a person who went to a new land and got there first. And Johnny asked if they had any in their family, please, and Papa said they did indeed, son; why, the Pomsbys had marked their path across this continent with their own bones.

First had come Samuel, who gave a note thus: "I promis to pay enough beare skins well dressed to make any common man a pare of ample briches." Samuel paid up and lost his life to a Red Coat. Then there was big Jim, scalped by the Pawnees, and after him William, who stood in a Montana wagon bed and cried out, "Boys, you can't hang him until he's had a trial." And that, said Papa, picking up his paper, was enough pioneers for the time being.

Little Cathy asked if there were any lady pioneers, please, and Papa sighed behind the financial page and admitted to Sarepta. Quite a girl—Sarepta. She'd helped her husband cut his own bolts on the Nooksack. She'd chased a cougar from her cabin roof with a broom, and she'd had twelve children.

Cathy said, "Why don't we have twelve children?" and Papa stuck his head out from behind the paper and said, "Oh, Cathy, do we have to go into this?"

Cathy said, "But Papa, why don't we—" And Mamma said quickly, "Cathy, dear, would you mind running upstairs and

65

getting me a handkerchief from the top drawer of my chest?" And
Cathy was so delighted at permission to snoop a little in Mamma's
dresser drawers that she forgot the pioneers.

But not for long. You couldn't forget the family's past when you
lived in the Old House. The Pomsbys had halted their long trek
when they reached Puget Sound. Here among the firs on the very
brim of the bay Papa's father had built the Old House from trees
cut from his own timber claims and planed in his own mills. From
the Old House you could hear the whine of the saws. You could
see the tugboats pulling cribs of logs up the sound. You could
watch the Alaskan fleet set out for the salmon run, and you could
count the snow-capped peaks standing watch in the distant sky.

It was an easy house, mellowed by much rain. It had plenty of
places to hide, even with the neighbor children playing, and of
course it had the attic. The attic had trunks full of the most
wonderful cast-off treasures. On a drizzly day the children could
go up there and dress up and parade around. Sometimes Mamma
played with them as if she were no older than they. Then it was
almost as if they were in that magic place, the grown-up world,
which every child is so eager to enter.

Each house has its own sounds. The sounds that belonged with
the Old House were the patter of rain on the roof, the racing of
small feet on the stairs, quick bursts of laughter, and Norah's voice
from the kitchen telling Tim to get right out of that refrigerator,
young man, and no please about it.

Every night Mamma asked Papa how his day had gone, and
every night Papa said business was bad, business was terrible, and
what were they going to have for dinner? Mamma always said that
if business was that bad there wasn't a bit of use worrying about it,
was there, and Norah had baked two beautiful wild-blackberry
pies.

"Bless Norah!" said Papa. "Tell her I think I'll have her pay by
Monday." And Mamma said Papa needn't bother, because Norah
had agreed to take her old muskrat coat for two months' wages.

"There's still a lot of wear in it," said Mamma, "and Norah says
it's exactly what she needs when she goes to visit her sister at
Friday Harbor."

Then one night the routine changed. Business was picking
up . . . business was pretty good . . . business was excellent . . . business was booming.

Norah got a raise. Mamma got a new fur coat. The children got
skates with real ball bearings. The Old House got a coat of paint.
And Agatha Weston, Mamma's mother, came out from the East to
live with the family, and this was the beginning of the change.

Nobody told the children that Nana Agatha was one of those disappointed, determined little gentle-women who see in their daughters' marriages a chance to fulfill their own ambitions. Nobody needed to tell them. In their own way they knew it.

They knew that the sweet silly little things parents do in an easy house stopped when Nana came. Mamma never took Papa by the ear anymore to push down his head and kiss him. He never pretended to spank her or tickled her—with the children squealing, Mamma begging him to stop, the dog barking, and Norah rushing in from the kitchen to see what in the world was causing all this hullabaloo.

Once Mamma brought Nana up to see the attic. The children heard Papa's voice from the landing.

"You won't find any old Chippendale up there, Mother Weston," he said. "All our ancestral antiques were dumped on the plains to lighten the load."

Nana looked at the boxes of cast-off treasures, and she said, "Really, Susan, you must have Norah clean out this place. It isn't healthful," and Mamma answered, "Yes, Mother. I'll tell her. I meant to do it long ago," exactly as if she were a child herself, as if she were Cathy promising amends for a mistake.

Nana told the children of their Great-great-grandfather Weston's house back East—of its flying staircase, its carved-oak-leaf cornices, and of the dining-room chairs that were now in the Metropolitan.

The children knew that Nana didn't like the Old House, and that she didn't like the pungent smell of the tide flats which lay below it.

"Well, good Lord!" said Papa when he heard that. "The tide goes out in the East, too, doesn't it?"

Mamma said, "Please don't raise your voice, Hubert," and Papa said, "Oh, all right, all right."

"All I want you to do," said Mamma, "is just look at the lots on the hill."

"Now look here, Susan. I was born in this house and I'm going to die in it. Your mother needn't think she can come out here and—"

Mamma cried, "Hubert, I won't have you speak of my mother that way! She's a good woman!"

Papa said, "She's the kind of a good woman who drives a man absolutely—" and the door banged shut, and the children heard no more and felt their small safe world tremble beneath them.

After that, Mamma wore the harassed look of one who is yanked two ways. She spent more and more time in her room and she began to have sick headaches. Papa made more and more money and worried about losing it, and when he came home at night he was too tired to play with the children.

One morning neither Papa nor Mamma came down to breakfast. Nana Agatha ate with the children.

"Finish your cereal," she said. "When you're all done, I have a surprise for you."

The children ate their cereal to the last spoonful. Then Agatha said gently, "My dears, your father is going to build us a lovely new home on the hill. It will be quite like your Great-great-grandfather Weston's house."

And so the New House was built and the family moved in. It was fine and altogether beautiful, but it was not an easy house. It had no attic and no cast-off treasures. It had no place where the children could play at being big, which was strange, since it had a fine room in the basement where the bigs could play at being little. Its roof was so well insulated that the children couldn't hear the patter of the rain. It was set so high on the hill they couldn't see the boats clearly or hear the whine of the saws.

The children were homesick. Tim took Cathy down and sat on her. Johnny kicked Tim in the shins, and Tim hauled off and whacked him in the stomach.

Mamma came running and cried out, "What in the world has got into you children? Why, I've never known you to behave so badly."

And this is the way things were on the day Uncle Rod came home.

Tim and Johnny were outdoors that afternoon, looking for trouble. Cathy was inside, perched on the top of the stairs, trying to avoid it. Mamma and Nana Agatha were having tea by the living-room fire, their voices low and tantalizing. Cathy slipped down the steps to the door.

Mamma was speaking, "And did I tell you that when Marcella Collins was in Nome last summer, she saw him?"

Nana said, "No-o-o-o. Of all people, it would have to be Marcella, wouldn't it? What did she say, Susan?"

Mamma looked up, saw Cathy, and began to spell, "She said he looked o-l-d and s-h-a-b-b-y. It seems he has some mining interests up there somewhere. She said wasn't it a shame that no matter how hard they tried, some such nice people simply couldn't make a d-e-c-e-n-t l-i-v-i-n-g?"

"It's a pity, of course," said Nana, "but I can't see, my dear, that it's your responsibility. Mind you, I'm not criticizing H-u-b-e-r-t for asking him here. I just feel there must be a better s-o-l-u-t-i-o-n."

Mamma said, "Cathy, we're very busy. Here dear, you may have one of Mamma's wafers. Now run along, run outside and play."

Cathy accepted the wafer and inched for the door.

Nana said, "Susan, didn't you tell me that as a b-o-y he g-r-e-w up on the old f-a-r-m on the i-s-l-a-n-d?"

"Yes, Mother."

"But, my dear, don't you see? That's it. That's your answer."

Mamma said doubtfully, "But it's so lonely t-h-e-r-e in the w-i-n-t-e-r. I'm afraid H-u-b-e-r-t wouldn't like the idea."

"Nonsense," Nana said firmly. "It's all in the way you present it."

Mamma said, "Cathy, are you still here? Did you hear Mother?"

Cathy heard. She scooted for the door and out. She sat on the porch step, lonelier than ever now. Presently Tim and Johnny spied her and asker her to play war. She was the girl. She could be the settler's wife, inevitably caught and scalped. She could be General Lee, who always had to stand up and hand over his sword.

Cathy said no. Johnny said, yes, she would, too, and he stung her bare legs with pebbles, and she ran, and the boys chased her. She ran through the trees, her legs pounding, tears on her cheeks. She ran through the new rose garden, around the house, up the path and smack into the knees of the tall, straight, gray-haired man who looked and spoke like a general.

He dropped his suitcase and caught her. He saw the tears on her cheeks. He said, "Gentlemen! Gentlemen! What is the meaning of this?"

He straightened up and pointed his cane at Tim, and he said, "Sir, you've left your left flank exposed." And then he pointed his cane at Johnny and said, "Captain, dispatch a platoon to encircle the hill. Move up the artillery."

The boys stood goggle-eyed, then ran to do his bidding. He offered Cathy his arm exactly as if she were grown up—nothing so wonderful had ever happened to her before—and they walked to the front door.

He said slowly, "So this is the New House," and she knew he didn't like it either.

"Chin up, Ladybird," he said. "We're going in," and they did.

It was a memorable night for the children. When Norah saw Uncle Rod, she had to wipe her eyes on her apron. He tweaked her

plump cheek and teased her until she grew pink with pleasure.
When Papa came home, he laughed as he used to laugh in the
Old House. After dinner, he and Uncle Rod started right in to talk
about the days when Papa was a boy on the old farm on the island.
Now Mamma had always told the children that Papa was a good
little boy, but that's not the way Uncle Rod remembered it.

Presently Mamma said, "As a matter of fact, Uncle Rod, we're
going over to the island next week to spend the summer. We do
hope you'll come along."

Uncle Rod said, "Thank you, Susan."

Mamma said, "It's such a shame the old place has been so
neglected. The orchard hasn't been pruned properly for years."

"Now, Susan," said Papa, "it's not so bad as all that."

"Oh, yes, it is, Hubert. And the roof leaks, and the boathouse
needs painting. . . . I was hoping, Uncle Rod, that perhaps you
might take an interest in the old farm. It needs a good
man—"

Papa said quickly, "Now wait a minute, Susan. Maybe that's not
what Uncle Rod wants—"

"Oh, I don't know, son," said Uncle Rod. "It sounds good to
me. . . . It was thoughtful of you to think of it, Susan."

The children were permitted to stay up an hour later that night.
Just before bedtime, Mamma and Nana Agatha went to the kitchen
to make some hot cocoa.

When they had left the living room, Papa stood up quickly.
"Things have changed, Uncle Rod," he said.

Uncle Rod looked around the fine new living room, and he said,
"Yes, son, I see that. I guess you're the first Pomsby to find the pot
and pick it up."

"It isn't easy," Papa said. "I—I find I have four children."

Uncle Rod got up and put his hand on Papa's shoulder. "I
know," he said. "Now don't you worry."

Then he picked up little Cathy, and he said, "I've been looking
for a frontier all my life. Maybe I had to come home to find
one. . . . That right, Ladybird?"

No one told the children the truth that night. Theirs were the
small words, the spelled words, the half-hidden gestures. Yet, in
the wonderful way children have of taking the gleanings and
arriving at the whole, they knew. They knew that Uncle Rod was
the finest cast-off that had ever come to them from the grown-up
world. Why, he was better than any treasure from the attic of the
Old House. The grownups didn't want him, and he was wonderful—and he was theirs.

Summers on the island took the place of the Old House. They, too, were easy and much the same. The day after school was out, the family took the early-morning boat from the mainland. It was June and often raining. When the boat whistled for the village dock, the children strained at the rail for the first glimpse of Uncle Rod.

They would see his great black cotton umbrella bobbing in the distance, and sure enough, there he'd be, smiling and pipe in hand, the dog at his heels. Sometimes he caught the headline and slipped its loop over the pile, and always when the gangplank was down the children were first off the boat. The grownups followed—Norah's face pink above the bundles, Mamma fearful that the children might fall in, and Nana Agatha already complaining of her hay fever and positive she was going to begin to sneeze any minute now.

There were only a few miles of roads on the island, and almost no cars. Mr. Higgins, who ran the general store, had one to deliver groceries, and it fell to him to transport the bundles and the grownups to the farm. Uncle Rod took the children in the spring wagon with old Nell between the shafts.

When at last they pulled in at the gate, the children piled out over the wheel to race ahead. They ran past the house and down the path through the orchard to the little private beach which was their own, their special domain. It was always there, waiting for them and unchanged, and when they broke through the trees that grew to the pebbles' edge, the first thing they saw was not the sun on the sound or the green islands across the strait. They saw the *Blue Peter* pulled up on the beach out of the reach of the tide, bottom side up on two sawhorses, scraped and caulked and ready for the new summer's paint.

Sometimes the *Blue Peter* was green, other times she was red, and once—the year Cathy chose the color—she was a virulent pink. But her name never changed, and the night Mamma and Norah struggled to remove the paint from the children's hair they knew that vacation was here, summer had really begun.

During the second summer the family acquired a new member by mutual adoption. Cathy came racing up from the beach to say that a little boy was sweeping fish out of their bay with a broom and he'd just fallen in.

Uncle Rod said, "Bless my soul! He's trying to use a herring rake," and rushed to the rescue. He fished out a bright-eyed object, Thad Brooks by name, who had returned with his widowed mother to live on the old Brooks farm next door. After that, Thad was one of them.

Nana Agatha said Mamma must put a stop to it at once. "You

shouldn't permit the children to grow too friendly with these islanders, Susan. They're such common people."

When Uncle Rod heard that, he made the chips fly in the woodpile, but, fortunately, Nana never stayed long enough to press her point. The hay fever got her. She sneezed and put drops up her nose. She gave up at the end of a week and returned to the mainland.

Papa was too busy to come often, and sometimes Mamma grew bored and left the children with Uncle Rod and Norah. They liked these times best. Every night they had a picnic and a bonfire on the beach. When the twilight fell, Uncle Rod told them of the old days—about the chinook, which the Indians called "the running wind." He would lift his cane and say, "Once the Indians paddled through that strait on their way to the fishing grounds. They scraped their canoes on the pebbles of this beach. They were angry and they wanted water." On these times his voice was keen and whetted, as is true of the Westerner when he speaks of the long past deep within him.

Uncle Rod never intruded upon the children. He was just there when they needed or wanted him. He wasn't quaint or given to whimsical remarks that belonged in a play. He was one of the big people you find sometimes in the little places who have acquired the wisdom of the unobtrusive corners where more successful men never have time to go.

Once a year Uncle Rod went to the mainland—at Christmas. Otherwise he spent the long winters alone on the farm. At first the family felt called upon to explain his exile, but soon it was unnecessary. Nobody in town asked about him anymore. His status was accepted. He was just one of those people you find in almost every family who are like an old sofa, too worn to be redecorated and therefore tucked away where it won't show too much and nobody will trip over it.

These were the summers on the island. At the time, nobody considered them important. Nobody thought they mattered very much. They were the recesses in the school year when the children ran wild and acquired freckles on their noses and bumps on their knees. Then one year the children slid into their teens. A fine new road was built around the island. Papa bought the boys a car. The family began to outgrow the little farm as it had outgrown the Old House. The summers began to change.

At first it was a change of small things. Old Nell was sent to pasture. A specialist found out that Agatha's hay fever was due to cat fur. The cat and her kittens were banished to the Brooks farm, and Agatha stayed over all summer long. Norah retired to live with her sister at Friday Harbor, and in her place came a Japanese boy who bowed and smiled all the time and said yes to everything. Thad Brooks went to the mainland to work and save money for college, and Cathy forgot she was going to marry him when she grew up, and developed puppy love for an adolescent sprout who owned a pair of white pants and came over weekends on his father's yacht.

Then the changes began to grow larger and more important. The children went away to school. When they returned, they wanted house parties at the island all the time, and they wanted something doing every minute. The *Blue Peter* wasn't fast enough. The farmhouse wasn't big enough. Business was splendid. Papa bought a speedboat with a solid-mahogany trim. Papa bought adjoining land and built a huge rambling lodge. And Mamma and Agatha plundered Victoria and Vancouver, and furnished the lodge with beautiful old English pieces and silver, relinquished by families that had not been so fortunate as to find the gold pot and pick it up.

One day on the mainland Cathy met Thad Brooks. Each was conscious of the difference between them. She thought how dear he was, but so callow, so unsure of himself. He thought what a pity that so nice a girl should be growing into another frozen young beauty from the rich family of the middle-sized town, destined no doubt to marry some incipient youth from the richer family of the bigger town.

Only Uncle Rod did not change. He stayed alone in the old farmhouse, and what he thought he kept to himself until one afternoon when Cathy found him sitting motionless on the drift log staring out at the strait.

For the first time Cathy saw that he was old and somehow saddened. She sat down beside him and tucked her arm through his.

She said lightly, "What are you thinking about, darling?"

Uncle Rod patted her hand. "I was looking out at the sound," he said. "I was remembering the great families who have lived here in the West."

He flicked a pebble into the water with his cane, watched the rings form.

"I tell you, Ladybird, there's nothing finer than an American family on the climb up the hill. It has everything—the character, and the humor, and the fight. All our tradition as a country, all our pattern is behind it."

He flicked another pebble into the water, and another, silent for some moments.

"And then too often a family comes out on the peak and stands there alone, and the pattern stops. It's a hard thing for a man to have to sit and watch that happen." He sighed heavily. "I suppose it's inevitable, Ladybird. A family gets rich and starts dressing itself up. I suppose that's natural. But pretty soon nothing's good enough for it. It grows smug and humorless. It doesn't even know it's in mortal danger of losing its guts. . . . I beg your pardon, Ladybird."

"Darling," she said, "you're so serious today."

"Yes, Cathy, it's a serious subject. You know, I'm beginning to think the time comes when a man has to let go for a while of the things he loves. Maybe it's like the mother whose son marries. She knows she's lost him. The bride's family has gobbled him up. But she knows, too, that if she's done her work well, he'll come back someday in his heart."

Cathy did not realize at all that he was speaking of the Pomsbys and of himself. She held his arm close and said, "Now look here, Uncle Rod. That's enough of this sort of talk. You come over to the new beach with me. I'll give you a ride in the speedboat. That'll blow these cobwebs away."

"It'll blow what little hair's left me right off my head," he said, laughing, and he began to speak of happy and trivial things.

Uncle Rod went to California the next winter. Nana Agatha and Mamma said it was just right for him. It was just what he needed. All that nice sunshine would be so good for his rheumatism. And of course he'd be back by June.

But Uncle Rod wasn't back by June. The old farmhouse remained shuttered and blind. The *Blue Peter* looked shabby and forlorn, pulled up on the little beach. Uncle Rod had stood it as long as he could and pulled out. And with him had gone the last of the warmth and the glow.

The family rode high. It was the most prominent family on the bay now. All doors were open and all hinges greased. All its labels were the best of brands. The children's colleges were the finest in the land, and their manner was that nice assurance of those well-bred young people to whom the pleasant things of this world are available with no ugly strain and no waiting.

The Pomsbys loved Uncle Rod and missed him. They always remembered him at Christmas. It can't be said that they thought of him often. It can't be said that they thought of anything very much except themselves, but this was natural. The world was full of exciting things to do, and they were the people who were doing them.

When Europe began to rumble, the family was irritated. It had little sympathy for anybody in trouble. You would suppose those people over there would learn to manage their own affairs. But when the Japanese attacked Pearl Harbor, the Pomsbys were shocked and angry.

Tim and Johnny came home for the Christmas holidays. They asked Thad Brooks over one night, and the three of them shut themselves in the library of the New House and talked until dawn.

Mamma said she wasn't going to stand for it; she knew what they were up to.

Papa was firm. "Susan, you're not going in there. Do you hear me?" he said. "This is the boys' problem. They're going to decide it."

Once Johnny's voice rose above the others. "You know what Uncle Rod would say, Tim," he said. The next day the rest of the family knew also. Right after breakfast the boys went downtown and enlisted. The marines took Johnny and Thad and sent them to training camp together and later to the South Pacific. The Navy took Tim and sent him East for specialized work. You could pick up the paper almost any Sunday now and see a picture of Susan looking very trim in her volunteer uniform, or one of Cathy modeling what the well-dressed welder will wear, in some charity fashion show. Cathy, of course, did no welding.

Then one day a telegram came from the War Department saying that Johnny had been wounded. Thad's mother received an identical message, and Susan Pomsby sat with her, and they talked quietly with no difference between them.

Susan took off her uniform and went to the Red Cross surgical-dressing room to work. She counted the bandages as she rolled and folded . . . "one . . . twenty-four . . . thirty-six . . . seventy-two. . . ." Every day she rolled at least a hundred.

Nana Agatha said that Susan must stop this, she was working too hard, and Susan answered shortly, "Oh, nonsense, Mother. I've been a child long enough."

Cathy took nurses' aid, and worked four hours every day at the county hospital. When the supervisor saw her the first day, she sighed and said, "This bud won't last a week. I'll give her the bedpans." The second week she gave Cathy the basins to hold for patients who were coming out of ether. The second month she put her in the delivery room.

The Pomsbys didn't go to the island that summer. The Navy had taken over the speedboat and the fine new beach. The Army had set up an antiaircraft gun on the new terrace and moved into the

new lodge. Only the old farm remained, neglected and deserted.
The Pomsbys learned to wait, groping their way back to their
own roots, and finally a wire came from Thad in San Francisco that
he and Johnny had arrived safely, and that he was bringing
Johnny home, time of arrival indefinite. The Pomsbys waited
three more days. They prowled the house. They called Tim twice,
long distance.

It was a summer evening and twilight when Cathy heard the
taxi stop at the curb. The family gathered and rushed to the
door—and stopped. They saw it all at the first glance. Johnny and
Thad had gone away boys and were coming home men. They saw
the Purple Heart and service ribbons. They saw that it was Thad
who prompted Johnny to speak, and that, although Johnny knew
them, he was still dazed from shock. Part of him still lingered on
some distant battlefield. Part of him was a stranger.

The evening was chilly. Cathy made a hot drink, and Susan sat
on a stool by Johnny's feet and held his hands.

He said gently, "You mustn't worry about me, Mother. I'll be
fine. I'm tired. That's all. If I can just get home, I'll be all right—if I
can just get home—" And the Pomsbys cried out in their hearts,
But, Johnny, you are home, and nobody said it.

Susan said, "You shall go home, Johnny. I promise you."

When Johnny had been put to bed, Thad told the family everything. All about how brave Johnny had been, and what the doctor
said. That he'd been through more than any man should be asked
to take. That he had an excellent chance for complete recovery.
That the thing to do was let him slip back into the old familiar
ways.

"We were in the same ward in the hospital," Thad said. "At
night when we couldn't sleep, we talked about the summers on
the island. Even when he was sickest, Johnny wasn't confused
about them. We talked of the farm and of Uncle Rod. Johnny
always called him 'the General.' He said a man had to go halfway
around the earth and pretty near get himself killed before he
knew the warp and the woof of his life. Then the trimmings fell
away and he knew. When we reached San Francisco, the first
thing I did was try to get hold of Uncle Rod. I finally got the house
where he'd boarded. The woman said he was gone. She said he
packed up and went away weeks ago, without a word to anybody."

Cathy went to him and put her hand on his arm. "But, Thad,"
she said, "don't you see? He's gone back to the farm. It's what he
would do. He never failed us. Don't you see? Before he went away,
he told me that sometimes you have to let loose of the things you

love, but if you'd done your work well they'd come back to you. He's over there waiting for us, Thad. He must have started as soon as he heard that Johnny had been injured."

Hubert said heavily, "Maybe you're right, Cathy. We'll go to the island. We'll take Johnny home."

The family took the early-morning boat for the island. When the boat whistled for the village dock, the Pomsbys saw that a barge was unloading Army supplies, a young officer was giving orders, a jeep was tearing up the dusty road. Everything was changed. Even Mr. Higgins was gone and his store was run by strangers who knew none of the old-timers. Thad found a man to drive them to the farm. He'd never heard of Uncle Rod and had to be directed to the Pomsby place. The family was silent on the way. Only Cathy spoke, trying hard to be gay and amusing.

They left the car at the gate. Johnny walked ahead as he always had. The family saw him reach the bend in the road, stop, raise his hand in greeting.

It heard him cry out, "Hello there, Norah," and saw Norah coming out the back door of the farmhouse and heard her say, "Bless my soul! It's Mr. Johnny, and me making ginger drops and both hands all over flour!"

Then the Pomsbys saw Johnny lean down and put a kiss on Norah's old cheek and reach around and untie her apron strings, and they heard Norah let out a bellow and say, "Oh, you young scalawag, you haven't changed a bit. Not a bit! Off with you now!" and she saw them and came forward.

For a moment the air was filled with chatter. Thad and Hubert piled the luggage on the porch. Nobody went into the house.

Johnny said, "I wonder where Uncle Rod is. Probably down at the beach. Let's find him."

He started down the path through the orchard, the rest of the family accompanying him. When they broke through the trees onto the beach they saw the *Blue Peter*, bottom side up, scraped and caulked and ready for the summer's paint. On the old drift log were set the brushes and the paint pots, and hovering over them, stirring some concoction with a stick, stood Uncle Rod.

Johnny laughed and said, "What color are we going to paint her this year, General?" and Uncle Rod looked up with no surprise at all, as if Johnny had never been away, and he said, "Well, son, I'll tell you. I thought we'd do something radical. I thought we'd paint her a nice bright blue," and then he chuckled, dropped the stick and put his hands on Johnny's shoulders and held him off to see him. They both talked at once and laughed, and for the first time Johnny was completely like himself, relaxed and natural.

When the greetings were over, Hubert took Susan's hand and they strolled to the water's edge. Hubert scooped up a handful of pebbles and began to skip them, and Susan said slowly, "You know something, dear? One doesn't marry into a family. One isn't even born into a family. One grows into a family."

Uncle Rod said loudly, "It's going to blow up a rain by tomorrow. I'll have to go trolling today and catch us some fish for supper. Do you want to come, Johnny, boy? . . . How about you and Thad, Cathy?"

Johnny said yes, but Cathy said no.

"I can't leave Thad, darling," she said. "I've just found him again. He hasn't seen his mother yet, and I'm going with him."

"Bring Thad back to dinner," Susan called, "and his mother, too, of course. And don't hurry back, dear. I'll help Norah."

Something had happened to the beach and to the Pomsbys. The beach was an easy beach as the Old House had been an easy house, and the family was tight unto itself, compact and whole. No one said so, but the Pomsbys all knew it. They knew they had been waiting and hoping for this for a long, long time, until at last the time had come. The time was now.

—*January 29, 1944*

The Gentle Heart

This is the train that cuts the night gently. When the rails thunder with the urgency of war, and great freights screech their need to reach the ships that await them, this is the train that moves gently through the dark. Sometimes, by day, it stands in the port station, its berths made up, a sentry guarding it, and a little boy asks shrilly, "What's that?" and his mother says, "Sh-h-h! Nothing, dear," and pulls him along by one arm.

This night few people heard it come. No one saw it arrive. It came in the lost hours when the sleepless face little worries suddenly grown big. The engine that brought it had been dug from the boneyard. The man at the throttle had been called from retirement. But when at last they came to the new siding where no train had yet stood, they slipped the cars thereon without a jolt, and the engineer said, "Thank God, that's that!" and the old engine, free of her burden, kicked her heels in the air and bounced down the track with a huff and a flourish. The cars were lost there in the dark until day found them. First it picked out the big white squares on their sides, then the Red Crosses that told what they were.

At the new hospital beyond the trees, everything was abustle and astir. In the kitchens the cooks moved swiftly, ladling out cereal, filling pots with steaming coffee. From their barracks, the wardmen hurried to mess. They stumbled sleepily through the mist, an occasional voice calling, "Has it come yet?"; the answer floating back eerily, "I don't know!"

In the nurses' mess, the chatter was shrill and high, broken by sudden bursts of laughter, like a college dorm on the morning of finals. Quick hands reached for a last sip of coffee.

Over in a corner by herself sat Captain Pilkins, serene amid the confusion. She showed no tension, no strain of the long waiting, of the weary weeks of preparation. Captain Pilkins had been on Corregidor, and never spoke of it. She had a medal which she never wore: She was impassive now as a pelican sitting on a rock,

79

and rather looked like one, which she would be the first to admit. Nurse Pilkins never shied from the truth. She was the old campaigner. She was the tough one.

"Look at Pilkie!" cried the sweet young thing in the new cap. "Look at old Pilkie! Nothing excites her! She's ice and salt and steel shavings!"

"She's quinine and iodine," said another, with respect in her voice. "She's everything that's bitter and burns."

"She's pickled in the vinegar of her own disillusion," said the erudite one loftily. "And that's what we're all going to be if we don't watch out. Oh, I'm sick of waiting! Why doesn't it come? Why doesn't it begin?"

In the distance a bell rang. The nurses began to drift out quickly, their chatter quieting, their laughter gone.

Captain Pilkins finished her coffee. She walked slowly to the door and out into the new day, then briskly up the path to Ward D.

One of her young nurses was waiting at the door. "Has it come yet?" she asked eagerly.

"I think so," said Pilkie. "The ambulances are warming up. I rather think it came in the night. . . . And—and who is this?"

The second girl was small and fair in crisp whites and cap. "I'm Lieutenant Merrill," she said. "Colonel Davies said you were short over here. I volunteered to come and help out. I'm the new P.T."

"You the new P.T.?" said Pilkie incredulously. "We need three physiotherapists and they send us one? They send us you, looking like a daffodil escaped from a flower bed? Ridiculous!"

The little P.T. looked at her carefully. "I weigh a hundred and seven," she said gently. "That's two pounds over regulations. And I'm a whole quarter inch taller than I need be." The shadow of a smile flickered across her face. "And anyway," she added modestly, "there's one thing you have to admit. I may not be very big, but I'll be better than nothing."

"Bless you, child," said Pilkie. "That remains to be seen. But I'm glad you've come. You can unpack the box the Red Cross sent over yesterday. There are some flowers to be arranged also. Perhaps you can make this place seem a little more homelike."

The little P.T. made it seem considerably more homelike. She put magazines on the tables by the beds. She laid out the crossword-puzzle books, each with its pencil. She gave the last bed—the one that was in the cubicle at the end of the ward—its own small radio.

"Why?" asked Pilkie, who had come silently on her big white shoes.

"Because it has a corner view," said the little P.T. "Because it's almost a private room back here by itself. And because you're saving it for the boy who needs it most."

"You're smart," Pilkie told her. "Guess you pretty little things have to be."

"We P.T.'s have to be. All it takes is two good hands and a head. At least that's what the director of training used to tell us," said the little P.T.

Presently, everything was ready. And this was the hardest time, this last brief moment of waiting. Captain Pilkins stood in the open door, and beside her waited the P.T. The sun was up now, slanting through the trees. From the siding came the rumble of the first ambulance as it moved slowly up the road.

The little P.T. said breathlessly, "It's beginning, isn't it? We're not just a big, dead, inert place any more, are we? We're alive. Now our fight's begun—the wonderful one—the battle of the build-up after the tear-down."

"Most people wouldn't agree with you," said Pilkie dryly. "When they pass a place like this, they shudder and turn away."

"Not all of them," said the little P.T. "How about the youngsters who went from door to door collecting coat hangers for us, and pencils and ashtrays? How about the mountain people up at Markleeville who held town suppers all winter long and worked like mad on the puzzle books?"

"You're a sentimentalist," said Pilkie severely. "You'll have to watch that, P.T. But you're right about one thing. It's begun, all right. Here comes the first ambulance through the gates."

And now there was an end to waiting. The tension was done. Everything began to click. Everything began to fall into place. The doctors, the nurses, the wardmen, even to the least of them, knew their jobs, were deft with long training. They gave orders and took them. They cleared the ambulances, checked the records, segregated, arranged and directed. Slowly the great place began to take on life and purpose. And presently the first boys came to Ward D.

They walked in, grinning. When one of them was helped down from the truck and found himself standing there on the good old U.S.A. in his own home state, he reached down and picked up a handful of dirt and he let it trickle through his fingers. Then he laughed all over his big freckled face and he said, "Oh, blessed land!" and nobody thought him silly and everyone echoed it.

The next boys were wheeled in. The dark-haired lad who came first grabbed Pilkie's skirt in passing and said, "Hey, nurse, my mom's only sixty miles away and I got to phone her right away. I got to, I tell you. She'll come. I know she'll—and I got to—" and Pilkie said, "Of course she'll come. I'll phone her myself, right after I pop you boys in bed."

They carried the last boy carefully. A doctor came with him and talked to Pilkie for a moment. She nodded her head and called out, "Take him down to the last bed, please! The one at the very end! . . . P.T., come help me."

They put the last one in the bed in the cubicle. The little P.T. helped Pilkie place a cradle to lift the weight of the blankets from his left leg. It was then that she saw that there was no bump—no bump at all—where the boy's right leg ought to be. He didn't smile. He made no jokes, as had the others. He lay quietly, a good-looking lad, withdrawn, white and very polite.

He said to the P.T., "Nurse, would you pull down the shade, please? The light hurts my eyes."

The little P.T. drew the shades, so he could not see the sun shining on his own lovely country, and she went away and left him.

The boys were all in bed now. From the diet kitchen came the rattle of the breakfast trays. They had had coffee on the train, and were hungry now and tired. The little P.T. helped carry in the trays, and she fed one boy who couldn't use his hands yet. When the letdown had begun and the ward was quiet and relaxed, she still lingered.

"Well-l-l-l," said Pilkie. "Out with it. What is it? What's bothering you?"

"It's the last one," said the little P.T. "The others were all so glad to get here. He wasn't. He didn't care. He's not like the others."

"He's been sicker. The Japs threw the book at him, and hit him too. His left leg is fractured badly in two places, one of them the heel. Do you know what that means?"

"Yes," said the little P.T. "It means a job for me."

"In this case, it means the cast has been on three months. It means it'll come off in a few days, probably, and when it does, his leg will be ugly and sore and blue."

"I'll rub the life back in it. That's why I'm here. The doctors make the boys feel worse, and then the P.T.'s come along and make them feel better."

"You're cocky," said Pilkie severely.

"Have to be. Nobody ever thinks a little girl like me knows anything. It's very tiresome."

"Indeed? Then, of course, there's his other leg—what's left of it. You'll have to help get him ready for the new one. You won't like it, P.T."

"I won't, but I'll do it. He'll walk again. He'll go fishing. He'll dance too."

"You have a gentle heart," said Pilkie. "You like this lad. Well, he's too sick to be taken to you, so I expect you'll be over here almost every day. I suppose you'll be falling over that soft little heart of yours and I'll be picking you up. Probably you'll be a nuisance, but thanks for coming."

The little P.T. said it was nothing, nothing at all, and walked away, a small straight white arrow with a gold tip. Pilkie watched her go. The battle had begun.

The boy lay in his small white cubicle, trying to put together the broken pieces of his life. Snatches came back to him. Being picked up by the litter bearers. A little of the ride on the ambo-jeep through the green jungle. A calm voice saying, "More plasma, please." The whir of a plane's engines, and then nothing clearly until that day on the boat when he had looked down at the foot of the berth and understood.

For the first few days his eyes followed the big middle-aged nurse everywhere. They clung to her, depended on her, asked without words, "Can I?" and always her presence, unhurried and confident, gave him her unspoken answer, "Of course you can, son."

Sometimes when he woke at night and couldn't sleep, Pilkie came and rubbed his back and tucked a pillow in exactly the right spot. Once she brought him a cup of warm milk and sat beside him in the hushed ward, and told him softly of the time she'd gone fishing in the Rogue River Valley and of the spring she'd helped with the lambing in Colorado.

Two beds up lay the boy whose mother lived only sixty miles away. Pilkie telephoned her and she came at once. She was a little Italian woman from the artichoke farms. She had stood up on the bus all the way. She had arrived too late to come to the hospital and trudged from hotel to boardinghouse, vainly seeking lodging. Yet when she came into the ward and saw her son, she did not look tired. She laughed and cried. She called him her little *bambino* and she rocked with joy, as the Italian women do. And that night in the white cubicle the boy's temperature shot up three degrees.

Pilkie gave him a pill and asked casually, "Do you have a family, John?" and he said, very quietly, no, he didn't. His mother and father had been killed in an automobile accident just after he'd gone overseas. All he had was a trust fund and some furniture in storage somewhere.

Pilkie asked no more questions, but she knew. She knew that in that long weary stretch from two A.M. until dawn, the boy took the furniture out of storage and unpacked it, piece by piece, in his mind, because it was all he had left of home. And she knew now why it looked so big to him, the mountain waiting there on the white ceiling, the peak which somehow he had to learn to climb. All the boys faced the same thing. Trained in the courage of attack, now they had to discard it and learn the other, the harder kind— the courage of acceptance.

The boy in the private room could do it. His head and neck were packed in sandbags because he must not move his eyes. He could lie there absolutely still, hour after hour. He had to. His wife was coming in a month, bringing their new son, and the doctor said if he did just what he was told, he'd be able to see them.

The boy at the other end of the ward, who had lost an arm, could do it too. He had a mother and a dad, and two kid brothers and a sweetheart. They all thought he was the most wonderful, courageous, marvelous man in the whole Army. They didn't know he was just an ordinary boy, homesick and scared. He could do it. He couldn't let them down.

All the other boys had homes and families whose love reached out to them, by whose faith they could take hold and hoist themselves over the peak. But Johnny Reid had gone to war before he'd found the right girl. He had no one, no one special, no one close.

Every day the doctor came in to see him. The doctor was a plump-stomached major with a persistently genial all-is-well-with-the-world air. He'd say, "Good morning, lieutenant. You're better today, I see. We're going to have you up and walking in no time now," and the boy would lie there longing for a good leg with which to kick him.

Then one day the doctor and Pilkie removed the cast from his left leg. The following day, the doctor brought the little P.T. with him. He told her what to do, and went off and left her. The boy didn't want the little P.T. to look at his leg. It was too ugly and she was too sweet and small. He didn't want her fussing over him. He opened his mouth to say something cross, but she spoke first.

She said. "I know, soldier. Go ahead. Swear at me. I don't care." Then she smiled at him a little shyly, and she said, "But don't you dare say I look like a kitten. And don't you say I belong home with my mother. That's fight talk in this camp, soldier."

He grinned. He didn't mean to. He said, "Spunky, hm'm'm'm? I always did like spunky girls."

Every day the little P.T. worked on his left leg. She put on the heat and began the long rubbing. She worked on the other leg also. Her hands were strong, but gentle. Sometimes the boy questioned her, and she told him about her work and how she had happened to go into it. She told him how desperately the Army needed P.T.'s, and spoke so convincingly he said, "Now stop worrying, P.T. The minute I'm better, I'll join up," and she laughed and said he'd look sweet in the cap.

Oh, it was a fine thing to see, and then one day it went cold. The boy retired into a steelbound cell in his own mind and shut her out. She couldn't reach him and she couldn't extricate him. It made Pilkie bite her lip to see the girl try. She was game, this little one, and she was bright, too, and doomed to fail. One afternoon she sought out Pilkie.

The elder nurse was getting ready to sterilize the hypodermics. She put them down as she listened.

"And I don't understand it," concluded the little P.T. "Just when he's getting better too. His left leg isn't even going to be stiff. He's due to begin the exercises to get him ready for his new leg. He's beginning to look well again. But I can't reach him. He's lost in a sort of vacuum. I can't get through to him. Why? Do you know?"

"Yes," said Pilkie. "Yes, child. I know." She sat down rather heavily, the little P.T. standing patiently beside her.

"Look, P.T.," she said slowly. "Some boys don't know it, but in their minds they carry around a picture of their mothers. Unconsciously they choose a girl who resembles it. Johnny's like that. His mother was small like you. She used to go around humming at her work. You do that. Johnny doesn't like the hard, brittle girls who go through life, palms up, selfish and taking. He likes the palms-down girls, the giving ones—like you."

"Then why can't I help him?"

"Because you're the kind he wants. You're the kind he thinks is lost to him forever because—because he's crippled."

"But it isn't true," said the little P.T. "He's not shut away from anyone."

"Oh, yes, he is," said Pilkie, "as long as he thinks so. That's the hardest problem we have to meet with the boys who have lost arms and legs, P.T.—their belief that they're due to miss all the warmth and the loving in this world."

"And you think I can't help him? You think he'll keep on

steeling himself against me until he's built a wall that grows larger and larger? That's it, isn't it?"

"That's it," said Pilkie.

"Then I'll tunnel under the wall. I'll climb over it. And don't tell me I like this boy, because it's true. And don't tell me I have a gentle, soft little heart, because I know it." The little P.T. walked out, very stiff and straight. Pilkie went back to her hypos.

The little P.T. seldom came to the ward after that. The boy went to her department. A wardman took him in a wheelchair, and it was a fine thing to be up and moving about again, even in so halting a fashion.

There were other boys in the physiotherapy department, taking their exercises and their treatments. The P.T. was nice to all of them, and too busy to single him out for her pity. He was sure, of course, that's what it was. She was a fine girl—no doubt of it—but he couldn't stand people being nice to him because they were sorry for him. He didn't intend to give her a chance.

He grew much stronger. Every day he sat outdoors in the sun in his wheelchair. When he learned to walk again on his left leg with the help of crutches, he made his way to the open court, pleased because he could get there now by himself.

One day the little P.T. came by and stopped to chat a moment. "Hello, Johnny," she said, and he clenched his fingers to keep from reaching up and pulling down her little capped head, so strong was his impulse. He didn't do it, of course. He was very polite and impersonal to her, and relieved when she went away and left him to fight his loneliness and his bitterness.

Then came the day he tried his new right leg for the first time. Despite the warnings, he had expected to walk right off on it. He couldn't. It was just another thing to be learned in his long adjustment to his new world. The first time he tried it alone, he had a bad fall. After that, he took it slowly and carefully, sure that anybody could spot him for a hopeless cripple as far as the eye could see.

Pilkie was wonderful to him. When he was in the ward, she kept him too busy to brood. She brought him an airplane model some civilian had sent in. It required two months to build and the help and advice of every man in the big room.

He had told Pilkie once that he had been taking engineering at Stanford when the war caught him. One night she plopped some pamphlets on his bed. They were from the engineering department, and he knew then that she expected him to go back to school. The thought appalled him. He saw himself as an old, old man of twenty-three, back with a bunch of infants, but when his eyes asked "Can I?" he found his answer in Pilkie's steady gaze.

One afternoon the hospital held a small dance for the boys who were learning to use their new arms and legs or who were loosening up limbs stiff from injuries. No outsiders were permitted, just patients and a few nurses, doctors' wives and daughters to make enough girls.

Johnny went because he had to. He wasn't going to dance, of course. Nobody was going to catch him making a spectacle of himself. Nobody tried to. He sat on the sideline in the big Red Cross recreation room, relaxed and easy, enjoying the music. He began to wish he had nerve enough to try dancing, too, but he didn't know quite how to go about it. Then he saw Captain Burke come in with a girl. Captain Burke had had a badly broken ankle, which was almost well. He looked exactly as an officer should, and he knew it. The girl with him was the most beautiful Johnny had ever seen. She was the palms-up type. She was the dazzler, the girl who takes what she wants, who knows nothing of pain and suffering. She was out of the old world where Johnny had lived long ago, and she fascinated him. He watched her covertly.

The captain pretended to be lamer than he was, so he could lean on the girl. He teased her and she flirted back outrageously. Pretty soon she pretended to grow tired of him and left him flat—the captain following her across the room, and every man following her with his eyes—and she saw Johnny sitting there a little apart, and she came straight to him and she said, "Leap year, lieutenant. My dance."

He knew she only did it to tease the captain. He knew she didn't give a whoop for him. She wasn't trying to help him. She wasn't sorry for him. And somehow this released him, this opened the door on his cold cell. Before he knew quite how it happened, Johnny was up and had her in his arms.

Then the miracle happened. He was part of life again. He was off the bench and the sideline, and in it again. He knew he must be clumsy, but it didn't matter. The girl danced so well she gave him the illusion that he was dancing well too. She chattered every minute. Her name was Marcia West, she said, and she was visiting the colonel's wife for a whole month, and she was having a marvelous time—just too divine—and weren't the boys simply darling?

That night when Pilkie made her rounds, she scowled down at him.

"I saw you," she said. "I saw you dancing with that silly twirp.

You men are all alike. We nurses break our necks trying to help you, and then you turn us down for some beauty all wrapped up in orchids and mink. I think I'll scratch her eyes out. I'm the jealous type."

That night the peak on the ceiling did not seem so high. For the first time, Johnny felt that he was going to be able to climb it. In his heart there burned a small new flame at which to warm his life. Its name was hope.

The next day he went eagerly to the exercise room. He practiced so hard that the little P.T. congratulated him, and finally told him that was enough for today—my goodness, he'd just wear himself out! For a moment he forgot to feel shut in and surly, and grinned at her, and felt a sudden qualm of conscience that this girl, who had tried so hard and to whom he owed so much, had not been the one to open the door of his cell.

Three times a week he went to the recreation center, where the boys practiced their dancing. Every time Marcia West managed to forget her captain long enough to dance with him, each time giving him that wonderful sense of freedom. The third week the captain was sent out again. After that, she was Johnny's girl.

Each time she released him further, drew him back into life, made him feel part of it again. Once he obtained permission to leave the hospital for a few hours. Marcia borrowed the colonel's little car and they went for a ride in the big outside world on two whole gallons of gas. They stopped at a village store and he bought ice-cream sodas. They sat at the counter and laughed and talked, and one old lady said to another, "Nice-looking young couple, aren't they?" and through Johnny's heart sang the words, *She doesn't know; she doesn't even guess,* and the flame within him grew strong and bright.

He scarcely knew that Pilkie and the P.T. lived those days. He thought of Marcia all the time. The world glowed because of her. He even thought he was in love with her. Then one Sunday afternoon at the end of visiting hours, she told him she was leaving the next day.

He was appalled. She walked with him down the path toward Ward D. When they came to a leafy secluded spot and were alone for a moment, he kissed her hungrily and long, and in that instant he knew that something was wrong about it—it wasn't any good.

They walked on without speaking, her hand in his. When they reached the ward, they stopped and looked at each other searchingly. There was no gayness about her now.

She said slowly and a little sadly, "You see, Johnny, I'm not your girl. It's time for me to go. My job's done here."

He said, "Marcia, I don't understand it. I was so sure. I'm so grateful."

"Nonsense. I don't want that. We have to stand by each other, Johnny, we who are alike, people with legs like ours."

He didn't know what she meant for a moment, and when he did, he couldn't say a word.

"Didn't you know?" she asked. "Didn't you guess? Oh, it's such a trite ending. It's a movie finish. Yet it's happening all over the country now. You boys are all from Missouri, Johnny. You can't be told. You have to be shown, and the only ones who can show you are the ones like me who have gone ahead." She put her hand on his arm. "Look at me and tell me the truth," she said. "Does it shock and appall you?"

"No," he said slowly. "It surprises me. I'm deeply sorry."

"You're sorry for me, Johnny?"

"No one could be sorry for you."

"If you loved me—and you don't—would it make any difference?"

"Yes," he said quickly and truthfully, "I'd love you more."

"You see," she said softly. "You see. Oh, Johnny, I almost wish that kiss had been right. I envy you. I envy you because the one who asked me to come here loves you so much," and she kissed him very lightly on the cheek and went quickly down the path through the trees.

And this night the mountain was gone from the ceiling. When Pilkie made her rounds, she found the boy lying there smiling to himself. "Pilkie," he said, "do you love me very much?"

She set down the tray of thermometers so hard it rattled.

"For goodness' sakes!" she said. "Should I love a man who won't swallow his medicine? Should I love a man who has nightmares and wakes up the whole ward? Certainly not—and anyway I love all my patients. At my age and with a face like mine, it doesn't mean a thing."

"Pilkie, did you know why Marcia was here? Did you send for her?"

"I didn't know and I didn't send for her. The P.T. sent for her. She nursed her when Marcia had her accident. I didn't even guess. I thought she was a selfish, spoiled butterfly. I've always considered myself one of those big plain bright women. Let me tell you, young man, it's a shock to find out I'm merely big and plain." Pilkie went on about her rounds.

Presently the boy saw the little P.T. enter the ward at the far end. She had come to rub the hands of a young pilot who had bailed out of a burning plane. Twice a day, morning and evening, she rubbed his hands with castor oil. The boy could see her fair head leaning over the bed, and he knew the pilot's eyes followed her every move, and that she was talking to him softly and fanning the hope within him.

Finally she had finished. She came down the ward and she stopped—oh, so casually—to speak to him. "Hello, Johnny," she said.

She was going to walk right by, but he stopped her. He said, "That was a big thing you did for me, P.T., asking Marcia West to come here."

She halted then. She said, "It wasn't anything, Johnny. I knew you'd like her. She's a wonderful girl."

"Yes, she is," he agreed. "She taught me a lot. I guess I was mighty dumb there for a while. I guess I was very difficult."

"You weren't dumb," she said quickly, "and you weren't difficult. It was new. That's all. It takes a while to learn to walk in a new country."

"P.T." he said, "the hospital's giving its first dance tomorrow night. The Red Cross is sending in a hundred junior hostesses. There's going to be a real orchestra and professional entertainment. Thought maybe I'd go."

"That's fine, Johnny. I was hoping you would."

"Yes, I thought I'd try it—that is, if you'll go with me."

For the first time she seemed unsure of herself, a little frightened.

"I don't dance very well," she told him. "I guess I've never had time to practice enough."

Pilkins was opening the next bed for a new patient to be moved in from another ward. She put down the pillow. "Let him say it now," she prayed. "Let him make a joke about it. Then I'll know he's over the hump. Then I'll be sure."

"I'm not much of a dancer, Johnny," said the little P.T., "but if you don't mind, why, I guess—"

He said quickly. "I don't mind, P.T. I don't care. Why, you can step on half my toes and I won't mind one bit."

And suddenly they both burst into laughter, and he reached up and drew her head down, so that her fair cheek rested a moment against his tanned one, neither ashamed to show his need for the other.

Pilkie, the old campaigner, the tough one, saw it. She barged out of the ward so fast she fell over a wheelchair which some hapless wardman had left where it did not belong. She found him and told him so. En route, she scolded two enlisted men and three young nurses for minor infractions, and leaving a line of chastened souls behind her, and feeling a little better, but not much, she walked hastily out into the evening and blew her nose hard.

—July 22, 1944

THE CRUMPLED LEAF

He came in the early twilight. He brought his sloop skillfully through the strait, heading for the thick green firs that edged the island bay. He did not know how long he had been sailing. On and on, endlessly. Anywhere to keep going. Anything to still the restless urge within him. Now he could put it off no longer. He had to stop. He had to take a stand somewhere and stick it out. This was as good a place as any—or as bad.

He let her drift in slowly before the wind, past hidden coves and little pebbled beaches, the water so clear he could see the orange and purple starfish on the rocks below. In the middle of the small bay was another island, big enough only for three junipers, hoary with age, in whose branches the Indians had once buried their dead. High in the sky above it, an eagle soared. For an instant he forgot himself. *This is it*, he thought, and felt the old eagerness flicker and die out.

The pier was small. No large boats stopped here. From the float a lone cat fished for minnows, her head hung close to the surface, her paw darting in and out. When she saw him, she put her tail in the air and stalked off, angered at the intrusion, and he made his boat fast and followed her up the runway to the pier and down the pier to the road.

The fragrance of burning pine lay in the air. Then a woman's voice called out in that rising tone mothers use to summon their offspring home to bed, and up the dusty road came a small boy clutching a cardboard box. He leaned down and opened it, and out scrambled several dozen little crabs, scurrying back to the beach to be caught again tomorrow.

He met no one else. He walked slowly, as if he were walking in a dream, past a brown church, past a sign that pointed the way to the inn, until he came to the one store, its front door still open. He went in.

It was an ancient and easy store with that unmistakable musty

smell that is made up of a thousand different little smells all shut
up together and never aired out.

A nondescript white dog with battle-scarred ears came over and
held up his head to be rubbed, and an old man who was doing
accounts at a rear counter looked up and called out cheerfully,
"Well, young feller, what can I do for you?"

He was glad that the moth-ball smell was gone from his clothes.
He explained what he wanted—a cabin not too near the village,
something with a little beach of its own, where he could moor his
boat. Then he felt the old defensive edge whet his words.

"I don't know how long I'll be here," he said. "Two or three
months maybe; perhaps only a few days."

Now it would come—the polite questions of the stay-at-homes
or the elaborate avoidance of them. But the old man asked nothing, avoided nothing.

He gave him a long look, and he said casually, "Guess all our
plans are kind of uncertain these days, mister," and he walked to
the wall telephone and rang three longs and a short, holding the
receiver four inches from his ear as if he didn't quite trust it.

"That you, Bert?" he bawled loudly. "This is Sam Fry. . . .
Yes-s-s, that's right. How's things going out your way, Bert?"

He put his hand over the mouthpiece and grinned.

"I'll just let him gabble a while," he explained softly. "This is a
party line, mister. Nine people on it. Hear that click? That's Lottie
Trumbull takin' her receiver off the hook. A mighty fine woman,
but awful nosy. Knew she'd be listenin' if she was home."

He looked very pleased with himself and spoke loudly again
into the mouthpiece, "My, Bert! You don't say? That's bad, ain't it?
Well, I guess it'll come out all right. Usually does, if you give it
time. . . . Say, Bert, I got a young feller down here needs a
cabin, something kind of off by itself the other side of the
Point. . . . No, that won't do. Hasn't got a beach, and anyway,
the roof leaks. . . . No, that won't do either. Lucy Simon'd spend
her whole time hangin' over the fence gogglin' her eyes at him.
He wants rest, not diversion. . . . Don't know exactly, Bert.
Just puttin' in time, I reckon. Have a hunch he's writin' a
book. . . . Well, if you hear of anything, let me know."

He hung up the receiver and chuckled.

"That'll get her," he said. "Nobody's ever written anything
worth readin' 'bout this place, but Lottie's mighty liter'ry and
hopeful. She's got a nice little cabin to rent. Best on the island. You
have any grub with you mister? . . . Then you'll be needin'
enough to keep you going until you can stock up proper." He took

a carton from under the counter. How about bacon and eggs," he said, "and coffee and bread and milk? That sound okay?"

The young man said it sounded fine. Anything sounded fine as long as it wasn't dehydrated and out of a can. That was a bad slip, but Sam Fry didn't seem to notice it. He was busy filling the carton.

"Criminy! Almost forgot the matches and the salt," he said. "I'll put in some newspapers, so you can start a fire. The cabin'll be a mite damp maybe. . . . Guess that's everything." He took a pencil from behind his ear and wrote down the items. "No, you don't have to pay for them now. You can pay by the week or the month, same as other folks."

The telephone rang shrilly.

"That'll be Lottie Trumbull. I'll let her get good an' anxious. Can't handle some women direct, son. They don't know what you're talkin' about. Took me thirty years to learn that."

On the third ring, he answered.

"Sam Fry's store," he bawled. "Who's talkin'? . . . Why, hello, Mrs. Trumbull. How've you been? . . . Yes, that's right. Kind of a friend of mine. . . . No, he's not a mainlander. Not a regular one anyway. . . . No, Mrs. Trumbull, I can't promise he'll dust every day, but he won't break up the furniture either. He's got a fine mother. Had a proper bringin' up."

He put his hand over the mouthpiece. "Got to kind of pacify her some, son," he said. "'Taint lyin' exactly. Just dentin' the truth a trifle."

"All right, Mrs. Trumbull. . . . Yes-s-s-s. Yes-s-s-s, I'll tell him. Awful nice of you. . . . Yes-s-s-s. Good-by, Mrs. Trumbull."

He hung up the receiver and mopped his brow.

"Talkingest woman this side of Anacortes," he said. She'll rent you the cabin for twenty a week, fifty a month. Can't do better than that. You want it?"

The young man wanted it.

"You got your boat tied up to the float? Well, leave her there till tomorrow. Nobody'll trouble her. You go down and get your dunnage. I'll come by in my pick-up in about two shakes and take you to the cabin. It's right on my way."

It wasn't real. None of it was real—the ride in the truck through the firs or the glimpse of a snow-capped mountain standing guard in the distant sky. He schooled himself for the questions he was sure the old man would ask. But Sam Fry, occupied by the road, asked nothing.

"Worse darn road west of the Rockies," he muttered savagely. "Jake Morrow's got the contract and he's doin' his courtin' other side of the island. Widow over there's been after him all year. Be a relief when she stops runnin' and lets him catch her."

The road left the shore line and turned past a clearing. Sam slowed carefully.

"Got to watch this stretch," he said, "'specially in the mornings and evenings. The deer cross here. . . . Yep, there's one now."

A little brown, unspotted fawn not much larger than a dog gamboled into the road. The mother doe darted out after it, keeping herself between it and the truck, trying to nudge it off the road.

The boy stared. When he spoke, he had a kind of wonder in his voice. "I didn't know there was a peaceful spot left upon this earth," he said slowly. "I had forgotten."

"That's what the Russians said," Sam told him. "Bunch of 'em came over from Seattle last summer while they was waitin' for planes to take back to the fight. Nice boys too. Kind of stocky and disciplined. Always said they'd be back."

"Did they come back?"

"Nope. But the island's never been quite the same somehow. They made us feel the smallness of the world at war. We've been part of the great waiting room ever since. Guess we've been kind of watchin' for you, mister. Maybe you're the first one to come home."

The boy said nothing. The doe and the fawn had disappeared among the trees. Old Sam speeded up. Beyond the clearing, the road led back to the shore. Presently, Sam drew up to one side and stopped.

"Here we are. No road in. Got to lug the stuff."

The boy took his dunnage and Sam Fry carried the carton of groceries and led the way up the path. The cabin was unlocked. It had one large room with a fireplace, a small kitchen and bath. Sam set down the carton. The boy walked over and felt the studio couch.

"It's not too soft," Sam said dryly. "Lottie Trumbull's a Scotch Presbyterian. She's got a good stiff soul. Probably sleeps on a board out of the dining-room table. . . . Don't leave a fire without the screen up. Driftwood snaps something fierce. And drop in at the store anytime. I'm there till eight every night. Short of help. Got to do my own cleaning up."

"I'll be in," the boy promised. "I'll sweep out the store for you, Sam."

He did not try to thank him. He couldn't. He was too touched by the kindness of the stranger, more effective sometimes than the kindness of family or friends because it is so unexpected. He waited in the door until he heard the truck rattle off down the road. Then he went into the cabin and unpacked his gear. And by the magic of small possessions—the tobacco pouch on the table, the old pipe on the mantel—it was as if no one had ever lived here before. It was his.

He made a fire and put the bedding to warm. He prepared supper. There was still a little light, and he went outdoors for a quick look. The little shell beach was just right. Tomorrow, he'd dig himself a fine mess of clams for chowder. Maybe he'd troll for salmon. He'd gather drift for the woodpile, and he'd rig up a buoy for his sloop. He went back into the cabin, banked the fire and lighted his pipe, holding his mind firmly to the comfort of the moment. He did not know how long he sat there. He knew only that suddenly he was alert, his hand reaching for the knife he no longer wore, the old foxhole reflexes keen and ready. Then he heard it—something big moving stealthily outside, and he was on his feet and slipping out the door into the night.

The moon was up now. Not a bird stirred or a leaf fell. He became part of the shadows next to the cabin, watchful and waiting, and he knew that in some other shadow someone, something, watched him also. Then he saw him—a brown buck beneath a fir some forty feet away. The buck stepped directly into the moonlight and stood there, head up and listening, pawing the duff. Then, quite unafraid, he moved off slowly through the trees. The boy followed.

Once the buck stopped to rub his horns against the bark of a pine, and again he stopped to graze in a small clearing where the rains and the mists from the Sound had made the young green things grow. Then he came to a white cottage, a light in the window, and he walked directly to its door and began to whiffle.

The boy watched. He saw the door open and a girl stand there, framed in light.

She said, "You're late tonight," and she held out something which the buck ate from her hand. She patted him and talked to him. Then a man's voice, querulous and demanding, called from the house.

"I'm coming, dear!" she called back. "Just a minute!" and she said to the buck, "Now that's all you get tonight, you big spoiled nuisance. That's all you get." When she went to the door the buck followed her, and she laughed and said, "Why, I think you'd come right in and sit on the sofa. I think you would."

The boy felt that he had watched something not meant for his eyes, and he turned and went quickly to his cabin.

That night taut nerves did not snap him awake with every sudden sound. He did not prowl the house or dream. He slept as a child sleeps, confident that tomorrow will be a fine, a splendid day. So much to do. He must go for his boat. He must build the buoy. And above all else he must ask old Sam about the brown buck and the girl.

It was late the next morning when he awoke. After breakfast he walked directly to the store. He bought materials for his buoy, and so many supplies that old Sam had to help carry them to the sloop. On the way the boy told him about the buck and the girl, and asked who she was. Sam was silent. Then he held the box he was carrying with one hand and with the other he plucked two leaves from a silver maple by the road, one perfect, the other quite as lovely, but curled at the edge.

"Well, son," he said slowly, "I guess you'd say she's the crumpled leaf. . . . See that little fir over there? Mighty pretty, isn't it? Not a branch out of line. Be nice on a calendar. Well, she's not it. But see that red madroña down close to the beach? A storm twisted it maybe when it was a sapling. Had to kind of fight its way up. Says something, doesn't it? Reckon it would make a great etching. Well, son, she's that one."

They walked down the pier to the sloop. Sam helped him stow his supplies.

"Oh-h-h, you don't have to bother about Laird Hunt," he said cheerfully. "She won't bother you none. Probably be scared to say howdy. She's too young to know it's the thing that makes a person different that makes 'm valuable."

The boy could contain his curiosity no longer. "What happened to her?"

"Just trouble," Sam said. "Her parents died early. Their boat was swamped one night while the young doc was trying to reach a patient on another island. No money left and no relatives. Ed Peters raised her. He didn't have to. He wasn't obligated in any way. Mighty brilliant man in his day, but always did drink too much. He laid off the bottle and brought her up and educated her, and loved her like his own. And then he slipped. Some people think she ought to commit him and be done with it. . . . You all set?"

The boy was set. He pushed off. All the way back to the cabin, he kept thinking of what Sam had told him. The crumpled leaf. It was a strange way to have expressed it, and an apt way. He had never known a girl of whom it could be used. He had known the girl whose life follows the nicer pattern—the one you meet under the clock at the Biltmore, soft hair on her shoulders, and on her face that smooth assurance that hides the fear that in her quick and easy flowering she may fail to find what she wants and grab it.

The crumpled leaf. It tolled through his mind, and suddenly he knew why. It was because it was true of him also, and of those like him whose lives had been wrenched from the pattern and tossed into the confusion and bewilderment of war.

All afternoon he worked on the buoy, restless and waiting. At last the day slipped into dusk, but the buck did not come that night or the next. On the third night the boy heard him moving through the trees. It was exactly as it had been before. He was on his feet with the first sound and out the door into the shadows. Again he was stalking the buck through the moonlight, scarcely aware of what he did, and again the buck led the way to the cottage, pawing the duff and whiffling for the girl to come out and feed him. Only this time the boy did not hide in the shadows. He stepped directly into the light from the open door as she came out.

She was slender and fair, and when she saw him she looked so startled he thought she was going to run.

He spoke quickly. "I followed him here," he said. "I have the cabin next to yours. I heard him three nights ago and I stalked him then. You see, I've been bushing Japs off little islands in the Pacific, and I guess I don't know how to stop."

She stared at him and sat down slowly on the step. The buck came up to her and put down his head to be patted.

"You want to talk about it, soldier?" she said gently, and he went over and sat down beside her without even being asked.

It was the first time he had wanted to talk to anyone. At home, he had been able to say no more than a casual word. Now the unreality of this moment, of sitting here beside the girl in the quiet night released him, and he heard the pent-up words flowing freely.

He told her about his job out there—about going in at night in a rubber boat with three other men to pick up Japanese stragglers. Sometimes he heard certain of his words stand out stark with dramas.

"We hid the boat in the jungle. We couldn't see the Japs, but we could hear them. They carried sticks and rapped them in a kind of code. The natives hated them because they'd taken their pigs and chickens. They used to bring us the Japs' feet."

Toward the end he heard himself say a strange thing:

"I suppose before the Japs came there, those little islands were much like these, as peaceful and as still, the natives minding their own business and wanting only to be let alone. I suppose so."

Then he was silent, and the girl also. She made no trite remark. When she spoke at last, it was as if she had picked up his narrative.

"And then you came home," she said slowly, "and nothing had changed. It was as you had wished it. Nothing had changed."

"Except myself," the boy said.

"Except yourself. You couldn't sit still. You were restless. You couldn't relax. You wanted to go right back into it."

"Yes," the boy said quickly, and so loudly that the buck drew away. "Yes, that's right. Everything irritated and annoyed me. At first I thought it was the specific things—the strikes, the smugness, the graft. But it wasn't. It isn't anything I can put my hand on. It's just the remoteness of the people here at home from the realities of war."

"It's because you've been through an experience that has set you apart," the girl said. "Nothing lonelier can happen to one. You thought you'd come back into the old world with a bang, and instead you found you don't belong."

"That's right. So I came away for a while. I came across the continent and bought a little sloop and put in here to find myself. How did you know?"

"Because I've been to the wars too," she said. "I've been the only young person on this island whose youth was different. Now there are two of us." She laughed and she said, "Do you like to fish, soldier? I know a place where the salmon run."

In the next weeks, theirs was the world of discovery frequented only by lovers. They fished off the point and sailed in the strait. They knew the place where the maidenhair fern grew thick against the bank, and the slope where the little wild strawberries grew. They watched the sunset from the mountain and the early mist rise from the Sound.

They saw no possible danger, felt no threat. They did not hear the chinook in the treetops blowing up rain.

Sam Fry heard it. Every Saturday night he hung the CLOSED UNTIL MONDAY sign on the front door of his store and opened the back door, so the islanders could come in and discuss the mainlanders in decent privacy and catch up on the week's goings-on.

Eisenhower didn't know it, Sam always said, but Fry's General Merchandise was one of the better battlefields of the war. Here

Guadalcanal, Saipan and Tarawa had been fought all over again, and twice as fiercely. Here Lottie Trumbull had taken her stance by the cracker barrel to announce that Germany must be cut up and passed out like a pie, and Sadie Peabody had tipped over a crate of strawberries in her vigorous insistence that Japan be squashed flat.

But when the young stranger came to live in Lottie's spare cabin, the islanders called a truce in their war talk. They had a returned soldier in their midst, and everybody knows that the returned soldier is a civilian problem—so much more fun than shooting off the same old adverbs and adjectives. Lottie Trumbull had a lot to say about the gulf that separates the soldier from his old civilian life, and about how they must all help him to cross it.

"And we mustn't ask him where he's been or what he's been through," said Lottie, and Sadie Peabody agreed loudly—she had just read an article on that very point.

And so the islanders accepted him and gave him that most precious of gifts, the gift of privacy. Then gradually they began to take him for granted, and their attitude began to change.

Sam felt it first. Lottie Trumbull came into the store one afternoon to buy some potatoes.

"Well, Sam," said Lottie, out of breath with annoyance, "I just passed Laird Hunt and the returned soldier on the road. They were so busy holding hands they didn't even see me. Spend their whole time together, those two. Why, even that brown buck she brought up on a bottle sleeps under the firs by my cabin he's renting. That girl needs a mother. Why, she doesn't know one thing about the boy! You know me, Sam. I'm no gossip, but really, he's the closest-mouthed young man I ever saw."

"Guess he doesn't like to talk about the war," Sam said slowly. "They don't make 'm any finer than Laird Hunt. It's a mighty nice thing to see her blooming for a change."

Lottie agreed that it was, and picked up her potatoes. "Seems to agree with that adopted uncle of hers too," she said. "They say he's been sober for three months," and Lottie walked out, annoyance still set on her nice face.

It wasn't, Sam thought, that she resented the girl's happiness. She knew Laird deserved it. No, it wasn't that. It was just that Lottie Trumbull, along with all the other island women, had always been sorry for poor little Laird Hunt—such an easy emotion to feel for another, and so satisfactory to the one who holds it. Now they could be sorry no longer. Now Laird had flowered into unexpected radiance. Naturally, they resented this just a little, and the glow on her face made them feel suddenly dowdy, middle-aged and plump in the wrong spots—a thing hard to forgive.

Two weeks later, another small waft of air added itself to the growing breeze. Sadie Peabody came into the store dying to talk to someone. "Sam Fry," said Sadie, "I never was so insulted in my life."

"That so?" asked Sam because it was expected of him. "What happened, Sadie?"

It seemed that Sadie had met the young stranger down the road a piece and stopped to tell him all about the movie she'd seen in Anacortes last week. Such a wonderful picture it was too! All about a wonderful young flier—a kind of modern Sir Galahad with his head in the clouds—who died so bravely—for democracy, of course, and freedom. Sadie had told it well, but the young stranger had not been impressed. He had looked as if he were about to be sick in the bushes, and he'd said rudely that he was glad to hear that the movie boys knew what they were dying and fighting for, because there had been plenty of times when he and his buddies hadn't been so sure—except, of course, that it was because they had to. With that, he had walked off and left Sadie nursing an angered and deflated ego.

"And do you know what I think, Sam?" asked Sadie. "I think he's one of those combat-fatigue cases you read about. I think he just couldn't take it."

Sam protested loudly, but Sadie was already out the door, hurrying home to call up Lottie Trumbull on the nine-party line, and every one of the nine listening in.

Nothing more would have come of it, probably, if it hadn't been that the next week one of the island women gave a Sunday supper for her nephew, a captain and his wife, who were visiting from the mainland. The captain did considerable talking.

"We'll have to carry it through to the finish this time," he declared loudly, "even if it means machine-gunning the women and children in the streets of Tokyo."

The stranger had said nothing all evening. Now he spoke.

"Did you ever machine-gun anybody, captain?" he asked.

It was a tactless question. The captain had fought the war across a shining desk top. He had run no more danger than is required to cross a city street to buy himself a good lunch. He was a little touchy on the subject.

"No," he said angrily, "but I'd like to."

The stranger didn't think so. The captain might do it, but he wouldn't like it. And having said so, he refused to say more.

The next day the captain's wife told her aunt that she thought

the stranger was a pacifist, and the aunt told Lottie Trumbull that
probably he was a Communist. A week later, someone told Sam at
the store that the FBI was looking for a deserter on the other side
of the island, and Sam knew then that it was only a matter of hours
until some perfectly good, kindly person would feel it his duty to
report that there was a young man over here on the bay who
didn't talk about himself at all, who wasn't quite—didn't fit.
Anyway, it wouldn't do any harm to check on him as a matter of
routine, would it?

Two days later, a courteous, quiet man came to the store and
asked the way to the Trumbull cottage—the one said to be rented
to a returned soldier. And late that afternoon a second man
appeared in a shabby little coupé with a press sticker on its
windshield. He was a cheap, smarty-looking chap who sampled
everything he could reach when he thought Sam was not looking,
bought a package of cigarettes, asked the way to the cottage also,
and drove on up the road.

When the early twilight came and brought no news, the islanders began to gather at the store. Jake Morrow came in presently.
The widow had caught Jake at last, and he was working on the
roads near the Hunt cottage.

"Say, Sam," Jake said, "isn't Laird Hunt keeping that pet buck of
hers fenced in the meadow while the hunting's on? She always
does."

"Yes," Sam said. "Why, Jake?"

"Gate's open and the buck's gone," Jake said shortly. "I just
happened to notice it when I drove by. There was a car sitting
inside the open gate with a press sticker on it."

"Another man went out there early," Sam said. "Quiet fellow in
a blue sedan."

"He came along when Laird Hunt and that fellow of hers were
starting off on a picnic. Talked to them a few minutes and went
right on. It's this other chap I'm worried about. He asked me a lot
of questions and I was fool enough to answer 'em. Said he guessed
he'd chin a little with the girl's uncle."

The islanders began to feel a little nervous now. They stood
around the store, restless and waiting. At last they heard it—the
shabby little coupé come rattling down the road. They saw the
smarty-looking young man climb out and walk up the steps.

He said, "Hiya, Grandpop? Where's your telephone?" and when
Sam motioned toward the wall, he went over and rang the operator. It took him a few moments to get his mainland connection.

"Hi. That you, boss?" he said loudly. . . . "Sure I got
it. . . . Sure he's the man, but he's no deserter. He's an ex-G.I. Joe,

released because of wounds. Got more decorations than a Christmas tree. Say, boss, this guy's story will make Commando Kelly's look like a nursery rhyme. . . . Certainly I got it. . . . No, he's not the talkative type and anyway he was out fishing with his girl friend. But I gave her old uncle a coupla drinks, and after that it was easy. . . . Okay, boss. . . . Yes, I got a picture. Cost me half a bottle of Scotch. You can put it on the expense account. The girl had a picture, and the old man got it for me. . . . Okay, boss. . . . okay."

He hung up, took a coin from his pocket, flipped it to Sam to pay for the call, and sauntered out. For a long time, nobody said a word. Then Sam walked slowly to the door and took his hat from its nail. "I'm going out there," he said. "Somebody's got to be there when the boy and the girl come in from fishing. Somebody's got to tell them."

"I'm going with you, Sam," said Lottie Trumbull; and Sadie Peabody and Jake Morrow said they were going too.

They got into Sam's old truck, the women in front beside Sam, Jake in the back, and all the way up the road through the firs no one spoke. When they were almost there, they saw Jed Brown come into the road from the underbrush, carrying his rifle and his red hunting cap. Sam stopped to give him a lift, and they saw then that Jed's face was haggard.

"I shot the girl's buck," he told Sam. "I didn't recognize him until too late. I'm on my way to tell her."

He stood there in the dusty road, telling them all about it. When he was done at last, Sam told him to get in the back with Jake.

"We're going to the Hunts' too," he said. "It's more our fault than yours. We didn't aim to be mean. Guess we were just thoughtless."

They drove on until they came to the cottage, and they climbed out and walked up the path. Uncle Ed Peters was lying in a deck chair on the porch, sleeping off his drunk. No one else was around.

The men got Ed into the house and put him to bed, then joined the women on the porch. Finally they saw the boy and girl coming through the trees.

They were talking and laughing together, Laird carrying the lunch hamper, the boy carrying the fishing gear. When they came to the clearing and saw the open gate and the buck gone, their laughter ceased. They came on quickly. When they saw the group waiting on the porch—Jed with his red hunting cap—they must have guessed something of what had happened, because they stopped as if a blow had hit them.

It was Sam who stepped forward to meet them and found words to speak. "We failed you," he said to the boy. "Some one of us reported you to the FBI man who was lookin' for a deserter. This morning when he came here, a cheap newspaper kid followed him and got Ed drunk, and found out all 'bout you, and left the gate open. And that's not all either. Laird's buck wandered up on the hill, and Jed shot him. He says it damned near killed him when he knew what he'd done. He says he'll never forget the way the buck looked at him before he fell—just kind of surprised."

The boy and girl said nothing.

"You came here lookin' for peace," Sam said desperately. "And you found it. Even after all you'd been through, you hated no one. If you hate now, I reckon it's because we've taught you." Then Sam said one more thing that went through them all with the cut of a knife. "Guess it doesn't do us much good to know what rights this war's bein' fought for way off there," he said heavily, "if we haven't brains enough to recognize those same rights when they're threatened right here on our own doorstep. Then he stepped back with the others.

The islanders waited for the boy to speak, knowing that what he said now was of tremendous importance to them. He and the girl seemed to know it also. They looked at each other, needing no words.

The boy spoke first to Jed. "I know how you feel, Jed," he said. "I know the way the buck looked at you. I know the look well."

And then he walked over and put his hand on Sam's arm. "It wasn't anybody's fault, Sam. We're not blaming Jed or you or anyone."

In that moment, the islanders had a glimpse of the gulf that separated the boy from the rest of them—him and the girl. They couldn't help him to cross it. They knew that now. It was they who had to learn somehow to cross over to that other side.

—March 31, 1945

UNSEEN LOVER

They are changed, these great places built for youth. By day they bustle with vicarious activity. Squads in blue fatigues tramp the roads, and young men in khaki bend their heads to the green shades and the scarred desk tops. But sometimes of a lovely evening in the latter part of the war, when most of the trainees have gone over, they seem to take on a lonely and a lost enchantment. It is as if they knew and were asleep, guarding all they have to give, waiting for the boys to come back and awaken them to the accustomed life.

It was on such a night that here at Stanford in one of the women's halls a girl had just finished packing her bags ready to leave. The room was stripped now. It was like her life. It was like the lives of most girls who go to a university in wartime, adequate but streamlined, ineffably changed in a hundred big and little ways. Bread-and-butter girls. That's what they were, she thought. Not the kindergarten youngsters to whom college was once a country club at which to prolong their play. Not the culture crowd who had time and money to blot up leisurely some of the beauty and the learning of the world. Bread-and-butter girls, who carry twenty hours instead of fifteen, who go through quickly and slip out quietly into a desperate world that needs their bright young heads. Well, she had been more fortunate than some, one of the lucky ones who liked her own sex. She'd had fun here, made friends, worked hard, been content with an occasional date. It was only now at the time of leaving that she felt a sort of nostalgic yearning for a normal peacetime part of youth that she and her generation had missed—and would never have.

This was thought and feeling from the adult world, and it frightened her. War had brought her early to "the shadow line" which separates youth from maturity. Tonight when she left, she would cross it. She had one more hour. She wished it were longer, that she might linger yet a little while.

She slipped on the cardigan of her suit and walked quickly out the door, down the hall and past the beau parlors. In one, a seventeen-year-old boy waited for a date, trying hard to look twenty-one. In another sat a 4-F, wearing the too-old assurance that hides the fierce hurt pride. She walked out the main door into the evening, and up the road until she came to the beginning of Governor's Lane.

It was shadowy and mysterious here in the gathering dark, the old aromatic eucalyptus grove so tall the trees met overhead, shreds of bark hanging eerily from their smooth sides. "Barby, did I ever tell you about the time your mother took me spooning up Governor's Lane? She kept me out so late that when I finally got her back to the hall, she was locked out. Had to hoist her through a window. You'd never guess it now, but she was a giddy young thing in those days." Yes, her mother had walked here as a girl, and her older sisters also. But they had come with the boys they met here and later married. She came alone.

She turned away and walked on slowly. Then her steps quickened. She had a sudden impulse to go one last time to the spot she had been avoiding on nights like this—an impulse so strong it was almost an urgency. She walked faster, scarcely aware that she was hurrying, past the open fields, up the steps of the Outer Quadrangle and under the deep arcades until she came to the Inner Quad.

This was the place she would remember first, as it was now, muted by moonlight, hushed and deserted, the stars coming out, the arches and the palms defined against the sky. This was the place. It had a kind of magic, an out-of-the-world feeling, so beautiful that when she stepped into the open, she walked softly lest she break its spell. In the center of the Quad she stopped, facing the church.

"Your father and I were married there, Barby, on a lovely moonlight night. And it was something to remember even if Dad did say 'I do' at the wrong time. Someday you'll have a wedding like that."

There were weddings here still. The quick ones of the girls who grew panicky and couldn't wait, who met the boy on Friday and married him a week from Thursday. And the other ones, the weddings of the girls who had met their men before they went over, who waited months for the promised furlough, trying then to crowd into a few days enough living to last a lifetime, if it must be.

High in the sky directly overhead a plane hummed. She was scarcely aware that she heard it. She did not look up. She stood there in the soft moonlight, her mind open and receptive, and it was then that for the first time she thought of him, the man who might have been, the boy she would have met here in normal times, detoured by war to some distant sea or sky.

Strange, but in this moment she knew him well. The kind of boy a girl loves because she sees in him the man he's going to be. The kind with whom she is content, not only in the exciting thrilling moments but in the quiet, wordless times that are not empty because he's there.

The thought of him was so real, it was as if she felt his presence. She almost put her hand out to touch him, and just then a group of girls entered the Quad from a far corner, their laughter strident in the silence. The spell was broken.

She looked at her watch. It was late. She hurried back to the hall, called a taxi, put on her hat and picked up her bags. Some of her friends left their studying to say another good-by to the one of them whose work was in and who was leaving early. The corridor was filled with eager young voices.

As the taxi went down Palm Drive, she looked back and had one brief glimpse of the church in the Inner Quad, and she remembered the depth and the intensity of her moment there. She felt a little apologetic for it now. It had been childish and sentimental, she thought, but it was behind her. Already it belonged to the past. Now she was just another bread-and-butter girl on her way to her first job, her mind focused steadily ahead.

She took the train to the city and the night bus to the town where she was to report for work the next afternoon. Here in the bus station centered the hurly-burly of war. All the seats and the benches were filled. The girl sat on the floor, leaning against her bags. A large fat woman sat down beside her.

"You waitin' for your boyfriend, dearie?" she asked, and the girl said no—no, she wasn't. "He's overseas, dearie?" and the girl said yes—yes, he was. The fat woman looked at her anxiously and said, "He ain't missin', is he?" and, to her own amazement, the girl said yes he was, he was certainly missing, and the woman said, "My, that's bad, dearie," and moved on to talk to someone more cheerful.

At last the bus was called. The trip was like life itself, a jostled rush through the dark, interspersed by moments of light. And when she was sure she would never get there in this world, she arrived. She stepped out into a deserted street and carried her own bags three blocks to a hotel.

Yes, lady, they had her reservation, but the room wouldn't be ready until nine o'clock, and she'd better sit right here in the lobby.

She sat there from three A.M. until nine. When she reached her room, she left a call for noon and sank into bed, utterly exhausted, and finally into a fitful sleep.

And this was the second time she thought of him—the man who might have been. She dreamed that she was walking down a winding country road, dark oaks against dry, tawny hills, misty mountains against a distant sky, pepper and eucalyptus trees along the fence, and across the fields the soft gray-green of olives. And suddenly she saw him, a dim figure far ahead, waiting for her. She felt the depth and the promise, and she ran toward him, happy and expectant. She seemed to run a long, long time, the sky losing its color, the dusk coming, and then, just as she was about to reach him, just as she was about to see his face, she awoke.

The telephone was ringing shrilly. For a moment she could not shake off the dream to answer it.

"It's twelve o'clock, madam," said the girl at the switchboard. "It's twelve o'clock, madam."

It was ridiculous, she told herself, to be so impressed by a dream. It was the sort of thing that happens to anybody.

She took a shower, dressed, snatched a bite to eat in the hotel coffee shop, and walked up the street to report for work. She came to a building with the sign Courier above it in large letters, and went in. The girl at the desk said the editorial rooms were at the back of the building; walk half a block to the right and follow the cobblestoned alley; the door was marked, she couldn't miss it.

She found it and walked up a dark stairway into a small entrance hall. An office boy disentangled his feet from a table, removed his nose from the sports page and looked up.

"Miss Burke," she said, "to see Mr. Kemp. He's expecting me."

He ambled down a hall, knocked at a door and went in. Through the open transom she heard him announce her, and she heard a dry old voice say, "What's that, Henry?. . . . Oh-h-h, yes. Forgot about her. The journalism department's sending her down. . . . Well-l-l-l, it took a war to make me appeal to the professors. Probably won't be worth a whoop, but we'll soon find out. Show her in, Henry."

Ten minutes. later, her hat and jacket were hung on the back of the door in the tiny room which was to be her private office, and she was seated beside the editor's desk, ready to take down tomorrow's editorials in her chicken-track college shorthand.

The editor began to dictate. He was enjoying himself now. He had a fine voice, and he knew it. He let it soar and roar. Then casually he dropped the first bomb, an unknown five-syllable word, followed almost immediately by another, and presently by two small innocuous words familiar only to crossword-puzzle addicts, and lastly by a strange specimen that sounded like "boitrioidal," and probably wasn't. He must have had to stretch for that one!

She asked no questions. She did not hesitate. Her pencil moved on smoothly. Twenty minutes later, the editor stopped.

"Is that all?" she asked politely.

Yes, that was all. When she had typed the editorials, would she give the copy to Henry, please, and ask him to have it set up at once? And while she waited for the proofs, would she answer these letters, please? He had made notations on each.

She went into her cubbyhole and transcribed her notes. When she came to the place where the editor had loosed his fine vocabulary, she stopped, faced by a yawning hole. She had not only missed the rare words. She had lost the context. She filled in the hole with her own words and her own thought, and another, and another. Then she gave the copy to Henry and tackled the letters. They were easy. An hour and a half later, Henry brought in the proofs.

"He fired you yet?" he asked, and she answered, "Any minute now, Henry," and took in the damp proofs and placed them quickly on the editor's desk, lest he see her hand tremble.

His pencil moved slowly down the page. Then a little flicker of surprise crossed his grizzled old face.

"Good heavens!" he said. "Did I say that?"

"Well-l-l-l," she said slowly, "you said something like that."

The pencil moved on. He looked up.

"There is an *a* in 'irrelevant,' " he said, "and two *m*'s in 'accommodate.' Your spelling, Miss Burke, is deplorable."

He sat there looking at her, a challenge in his eyes. And she stood looking back, a challenge in hers.

It was eleven o'clock that night when she reached her hotel. She did not dream. She did not remember the winding road or the moonlit Quad. The man who was had pushed out the man who might have been.

I hate him, she told herself fiercely. *He's a dreadful, cantankerous, smug old man. He thinks he's going to fire me, but he isn't. If I go out of that place, it'll be feet first in a pine box with a lily on top. I loathe him, but I won't give up.*

She did not know that he had given her those most valuable assets—a furnace in which to refine her own metal, a wall against which to prove herself. The battle was on.

Every morning she went to secretarial school, where for an hour a patient little woman fired large words her way, and for another hour she endeavored to fire them back. Every afternoon and evening she worked on the paper. She lost ten pounds and learned a great deal, almost none of it in the college curriculum.

At the end of the third week, Mr. Kemp announced that he was going to the county seat to play golf over the weekend.

"And while I'm gone you are going to write the editorials," he said. "Why not? You're writing most of them, anyway. Now let me see—write me a lead on the Constitution of the United States, and a second on the outlook in the Far East."

Just like that! When he returned the next Monday afternoon, he called her into his office.

"I saw the publishers this morning," he told her. "They are greatly impressed by your editorials. Both are excellent, almost profound." He tamped his pipe slowly. "Your brains, Miss Burke?"

She looked into his wise gray eyes. "No, sir," she said. "The one on the Constitution was Professor Collins' brains. I had him in political science. The other was Professor Train's brains. Both very bright men."

He took a pull on his pipe. "Well-l-l—I'd like to meet these gentlemen sometime," he said. "I expect they'll be writing quite a bit of the paper. Tell me, Miss Burke, what are you going to do when you run out of professors?"

"I'm going to stand revealed in ignorance," she told him. " 'An ill-favored thing, sir, but mine own.' I believe that's from *Hamlet*."

He chuckled. "I think you'll find it's from *As You Like It*," he said. "Act five, scene four."

Two weeks later, she ran out of professors. She couldn't remember a profound thing any one of them had ever said in class or out of class. And this unfortunate day she was on her own. She wrote a small piece in memory of a planked steak. It wasn't learned, but the butcher shop was in it, and the line of women waiting and waiting, and the one who had no intention of taking her turn, and the other who walked out with a huge hunk of meat, having placed sixty red points smugly on the counter, to the envy of all. She relegated the planked steak to the museums along with the dodo bird. And what did it matter, she wrote. We have proved we can be plump and apple-cheeked without it.

The editor passed this gem without comment, but the next afternoon when she came to work, she had to push her way through the hall. It was filled with men, all of them angry. And when she asked the editor who they were, he said sadly that they were butchers.

"Show them in," he ordered, "and go into your little office and shut the door."

She could hear the butchers protesting loudly, and she could hear the editor patting down the irate egos, and promising amends. He did not give her away or let her down. He took the blame, and when the butchers were mollified and gone, he called her in. She stood on the worn spot beside his desk where many an erring neophyte had stood before her.

"Are you impressed with the power of the written word?" he asked calmly.

"Yes, sir," she said humbly. "Especially of the wrong word. Why didn't you stop me?"

"Would you have learned anything if I had?"

"No, sir, I wouldn't."

The editor lighted his pipe. "I suppose now you'll be going back to the professors?"

She knew suddenly she wouldn't. "Not unless you make me," she said stoutly. "There's no fun leaning on other people's fifty-cent brains and trying to pretend they're your own. I'd rather struggle with my own penny thoughts—only—"

"Yes-s-s?"

"Only the next time I ruffle any feathers, I'll do my own smoothing down."

For the first time in all those weeks, she had pleased him. He chuckled, then sobered. "You don't like me, do you?" he said.

"I didn't. Now I'm beginning to, in spite of myself. Heaven knows I fought it."

"Well, I like you. I like you very much indeed."

The war was still on, but the first battle was won.

The next week she left the hotel to rent a room from a Finnish couple, and because their immaculate old house was inconvenient to the bus line, she bought an ancient small car to drive back and forth to work. For her first ride she chose her supper hour, picked up some sandwiches and a carton of coffee, and sought a hillside on the edge of town where she could enjoy the late sun and a respite from tension. After she had eaten, she rambled along any road that seemed attractive until time to return to work.

She was thinking of her job and the editor. She felt a loyalty to him now stronger than any she had known. By some quality of personality, he had put his hand upon her shoulder, and she knew that twenty years from now she would still feel it resting there lightly.

The late sun was gentle on her face, a little breeze blowing in the treetops. She rambled along slowly, enjoying them, and suddenly the road began to seem strangely familiar. Dark oaks against dry, tawny hills. Misty mountains in the distance. Pepper and eucalyptus trees along the way. Where had she seen them recently? When had she been on a road like this? And then she remembered the dream, and for the third time she thought of the man who might have been.

Instantly, her mind swung to her defense. There were countless roads like this, it told her. You came to a place you were sure you recognized, you met a stranger you felt you'd known, and all the time you knew it wasn't true. That was normal. It happened to everybody.

She stopped the car and climbed out. She stood there in the road, a little uncertain. High in the sky overhead, a plane sounded. There had been a plane that first time in the moonlit Quad, hadn't there? She tried to remember. Yes, she was almost sure of it. It meant nothing, her mind told her quickly. There was scarcely a time on the coast these days when the sky did not throb with some life.

It did no good. She was afraid. She bolted. She jumped back into the car and drove away from there. By the time she reached the paper, she was a little ashamed of her retreat and, feeling a need to justify herself, she told the old editor all about it.

Oh, she told it well and gaily. She made a fine bright story of it. She told him of that first time in the Inner Quad, and of the tradition that a Stanford girl is not a Stanford woman until she's been kissed there by a senior on a moonlit night.

"I'm the first woman in my family who didn't make it," she admitted with a laugh. "There just weren't enough seniors. I suppose that's why I got into such a fine sentimental dither and imagined a boy who should have been there and wasn't. Did you ever hear anything so silly?"

She told him of her wait in the bus station and of her dream.

The editor didn't laugh. He knocked out his pipe slowly. Then he began to tell her of Einstein, who had given up his search for truth, admitted he was licked, and that night the formula had popped into his head. He told her of Claude Bernard, the French physiologist, who sought vainly certain knowledge of the body, and found himself suddenly on a side road leading to other and greater knowledge than he had even imagined.

"Scientists admit that often their minds are led to discovery by a process they do not understand and cannot explain," he said thoughtfully. "If it happens to the big people, why can't it happen also to the little ones like you and me?"

He did not discuss it further, but the next afternoon he tackled the work with a flourish, cleaned up the desk in record time. Then he picked up his pipe and took his hat from the back of the door.

"Now, Miss Burke," he said brusquely, "just where is that road?"

She stared at him. "You mean you're actually—"

"I mean I'm going there. I'm a curious old cuss and I don't mind one bit poking my fingers in the pies of others. If you don't want to come along, that's your business, but I, for one, shall never have another peaceful moment until I find out where the road leads."

He started for the door, looked back.

"You coming too?" he asked casually. She said she was.

They drove to the road. In the bright early-afternoon sun it seemed attractive, but in no way unusual. Whatever strange and haunting quality had possessed it was gone now, as a room mysterious by lamplight turns commonplace with day.

The editor stopped his car alongside the first mailbox and looked at the name.

"Giuseppe Pasquale," he said. "Used to be the worst bootlegger in this part of the country. I did him a favor once. We'll call first on Giuseppe."

They emerged fifteen minutes later with a jug of red wine and a box of homemade raviolis, bread upon the water returned after many a year.

The next place was a small ranch. They walked to the house and knocked at the back door. The editor explained to the woman who answered that they were looking hopefully for fresh-laid eggs, and she smiled and said, why, yes, she thought she could let them have a dozen. They emerged ten minutes later with a box of eggs, two fryers and a glass jar of cream.

"No answer for the imponderables yet," said the editor, "but a fine trip for the larder."

The last place on the road was charming—an old white house, with green shutters, set on a knoll surrounded by orchards. The editor read the name on the mailbox.

"William H. Husted," he said. "Hm'm'm—that must be Judge Husted's boy. Yes, I remember he came home from Harvard when the judge died, and reopened the old law office. Married the Bixby girl and lost her in childbirth. Took it hard too. Was determined to go to war, but they turned him down flat because of some leg injury from childhood."

They walked up the winding road to the old house. A curly-headed little girl of about four came to meet them, surveying them gravely with big brown eyes.

The girl said, "Hello there, dear. How are you today?" and the little girl said shyly she was fine, thank you, and took her hand.

"Your daddy around?" the editor asked, and the little girl said yes, he was playing in the water, but he wouldn't let her play too. Sure enough, when they neared the house they heard a pump chugging, and out in the orchard stood a tall man in overalls and rubber boots, directing the flow of water around the fruit trees. He saw them and called out he'd be right over. To the girl, he seemed quite out of her generation—at least twenty-nine or thirty.

He said, "Hello, Mr. Kemp. It's about time you checked up on your farmer readers," and the editor introduced her and explained that they had seen his name on the mailbox and thought they'd stop by for a minute.

"You have a nice place here," he said, and the young man asked if he might show him around.

They saw the orchards and the gardens, and the house. Soon Bill Husted and the editor were off on a fine political discussion as to the farmer's problems, and the little girl had brought out her dolls, which she and the girl dressed and redressed.

An hour later they left. Bill Husted and his little daughter walked with them to the car and waved them good-by. The editor was quiet all the way back. The girl was talkative.

"I'm so glad we went," she said. "You see, there was nothing to it. It was all perfectly natural and normal. I'm just so glad we went. Did you ever see a nicer child?"

The editor never had.

"But I'd certainly like to get my eyes on his housekeeper. I suppose she was in town doing the weekend marketing. The way she skins that baby's hair back! And her little dress was too long. Nothing makes a child more gawky than a dress that's too long. I could hardly keep my hands off her."

The editor said he hadn't noticed.

"I suppose the housekeeper is one of those overly particular women. Did you notice the living room? So prim and proper, and the drapes pulled against the sun. I hope she feeds the child properly. She looked a little thin to me."

That evening the editor suggested that the girl write an editorial on the farmer's problem. When it was done and the proofs on his desk, he pronounced it excellent.

"I expect Bill Husted will read it and come up to thank you," he said casually, and the girl said oh, no, she didn't think so; why, he'd scarcely noticed her.

"He'll be up," the editor predicted sadly. "I'll probably stumble over him every time I come back to work at night. And just when you're beginning to learn to spell."

It was a quiet and a slow growth, her acquaintance with Bill Husted. Sometimes when she had finished her afternoon's work, she would find him in the hall at the top of the stairs, waiting to take her to dinner, a twinkle in his eye, a droll smile on his nice face. She liked him. Gradually she told him about her work, and he told her about his. He was very serious about the law. They dined and danced and went to the city to the theater. They did all the conventional, amusing things. But the times she liked best were the quiet ones—the day they drove into the country to buy a puppy for his little girl, the Saturday afternoons they took her with them and sought a picnic spot beneath the trees.

Even when their love was an acknowledged fact between them, the girl did not associate Bill with the man who might have been. He was like him. But the boy in the Quad, the one who had been waiting at the end of the road, belonged in a small secret place of his own. She did not think of him. She never mentioned him except indirectly to the editor.

"People are all alike," she told him one evening. "Something occurs by happenstance and they build it up into a mystery. Wasn't it Shakespeare who said that we all love to partake of a mystery because it makes us bigger?" and the editor smiled and said, no, it was Robert Louis Stevenson.

All her days were happy and busy. There was the work at the paper and the wedding to plan. New drapes and slipcovers to choose for the house. New clothes for her and the little girl. Hotel rooms to find for her family. Announcements to order and gifts to unwrap.

The day before the wedding, she and Bill moved her belongings to his house, and hung the new drapes, and put on the new slipcovers. She gave the little girl her supper and put her to bed while Bill drove back to town for the new housekeeper who was to stay with the child while they were on their wedding trip.

She sat on the front step by herself. It was where she belonged, she thought—here with the man she loved and the youngster. It was exactly right. It was the life she wanted above all else, loving them and making a home for them, and writing a bit for the paper. And yet she felt now as she had felt the night she left college. She felt a kind of yearning. But that was natural, she told herself quickly. You always feel it when you are about to leave one phase of your life to enter another.

It was quiet there on the step. She saw a squirrel scamper down the trunk of the old oak, and a covey of quail run across the grass to find cover before the coming dusk. She saw the town bus come up the road and pull in at the gate to let off a passenger.

It was a woman, nice-looking, but no longer young, who hesitated a moment and then came forward. The girl walked down the drive to meet her. It was no one she knew.

"Mr. Husted will be back in about an hour," she told her. "Won't you come up on the porch and wait for him?"

The woman smiled. "I don't know Mr. Husted," she said. "You see, we used to rent this house in the summers long ago when my children were small. I just happened to be in town today on business, and I had a sudden impulse to see the place again. Do you think Mr. Husted would mind if I walked around the yard a little?"

"I know he wouldn't," the girl told her. "And I'll show you the house too. You see, I know Mr. Husted rather well. I'm going to marry him tomorrow."

The woman wished her happiness. They walked up the driveway, the woman smiling to herself and looking at everything eagerly and carefully.

"There's the old oak," she exclaimed. "It's larger, of course. We used to eat our suppers under it on warm evenings. And there's the place where the children had their turning bar." She laughed softly. "I used to hang out an upstairs window and watch them skin the cat. The bar was so high I was sure they were going to fall off and break their arms and legs, but they never did."

They walked on.

"The orchards are new," the woman said. "When we were here, there were only brown fields studded with oaks. The children used to ride their ponies across them. They'd gallop off single file, brown as Indians—Johnny in the lead, of course."

"Johnny?" the girl asked slowly.

"Yes, Johnny was my eldest. We all loved the summers here, Johnny most of all. He always said that when he grew up he was going to buy the place and come back every year."

They walked up the steps and into the house. The woman stood in the doorway, her face glowing with memory.

"Johnny gave up finally," she said. "He used to sit over there in the corner working on his plane models. He was a great one to build things. He always knew just what he wanted to do. Even then he wanted to go to the Stanford Engineering School."

"And did he?" the girl asked.

"No-o-o. He took his undergraduate work in the south. I remember my husband and I drove north with him when it was time to put in his credentials at Stanford. He was fascinated with the place. He spent the whole evening rambling around the Quad by himself. But when it was time for him to transfer, the war broke out."

They went on through the house and out again into the garden. The woman asked when the bus would be back, and the girl looked at her watch and said it was due in seven minutes, and she'd walk with her to the road.

They walked down the drive, the woman saying nothing, the girl asking nothing. They sat down on the bench under the pepper tree at the gate, each with her thoughts.

Then the woman said gently. "When he was last seen, he was flying toward the sunset, apparently in no trouble. He was bringing his squadron in from a mission. You see, Johnny was the one who led the boys home."

And me also, the girl thought, *and me also*.

When the bus came around the bend, the woman thanked her. "You don't know what it means to me to have come here," she said. "I feel so much better about it somehow."

"I'm glad you came," the girl told her. "You'll always be welcome here."

She helped her on the bus and said good-by. She watched the bus until it disappeared in the gathering dusk. Then she walked slowly back up the driveway and along the little path that led into the orchard, luminous now with its white bloom. The stars were coming out and the moon had begun to glow. Where the sun had set, the sky was still touched with pink. She stood motionless, waiting, listening.

Then she heard it—a faint hum far away. Was it a pump in some distant orchard across the quiet hills? Perhaps; but this time the sound seemed to be going away from her toward the sunset, and she knew suddenly that he would not come again, or the thought of him, whichever it had been. This was the last time.

And in this moment at the very end she did not deny him or try to explain him. She accepted him. She let him in.

"Johnny", she called softly across the space. "Oh, Johnny, thank you."

And then, as if she had said too much, she walked quickly up the path to the house, up the steps and home, shutting the door gently behind her.

—*June 23, 1945*

EASY STREET

Old Mrs. Courtney always called
it the Street of the Impeccables. She said—but only to herself—
that if she were a bolt of lightning looking for a place to strike, this
would be it. The temptation would be irresistible.

Mrs. Courtney lived on the street, but not of it. Yet, in a way, she
felt responsible for its being. Once it had been a mere strip of land
devoted to cabbages, and part of her inheritance. In the fall, when
the heads were gathered and the outer leaves stripped and left to
rot in the sun, the whole new south section of the nearby city had
been forced to shut its windows and protest loudly. Mrs. Courtney
had been importuned to sell, and the street was born.

It was a beautiful street. She had to admit it. It had grown
slowly, until now it was one of the nicest streets in one of the
nicest suburbs. Not a red geranium dared show its face in a pink
pot. If any vegetable had the temerity to smell, the latest in
ventilators removed the evidence, and should one rude whiff
remain, a maid went around with an atomizer and put upon the air
the spicy fragrance of pine.

A silver service on every buffet. Solid mahogany in every living
room. The best labels in all the clothes. The newest books on all
the tables. Why, there wasn't a tonsil left on the street, and only
one appendix, and two doctors had their eyes on it. Surely this was
Easy Street, the epitome of the American dream successfully ful-
filled. This was the spot of security where most of us want to live
before we die and take the next step into celestial spheres.

And yet, when she retired to her upstairs sitting room every
afternoon and looked down upon the street, old Mrs. Courtney
found herself wishing the same thing. She wished she had left it
in cabbages.

It was the people who bothered her. Such nice people! Such
consciously respectable people—in fact, impeccable—and all come
to the street by a route so typically American and dear to us all.

You marry before you can quite afford it. You set up housekeeping in a small apartment, and every night you move a lamp, a table

118

and two chairs to get the bed down. When the baby's coming, you move out into a house jowl to jowl with other houses almost exactly alike. You work and worry, save and slave, and finally one year, if the luck is with you, you find yourself a leap ahead of the battle. You have begun to acquire what, in Mrs. Courtney's day, was called a competence.

Immediately the house seems too small, the furniture too nicked by little feet. You want more and better advantages for your children. You want to spare them the hard experiences which are responsible for most of the wrinkles in your brow and practically all your character. You buy a nice lot in a good neighborhood. You build a nice house with the help of a good architect. You furnish it with the help of a good decorator. And there you are, all set and ready to enjoy the last and best of life, for which, according to Robert Browning, the first is made.

But is it? Mrs. Courtney had begun to wonder.

One late afternoon just before the war, she sat in her upstairs sitting room, book in lap, watching the women of the street come home from their sundry days. The first was Mrs. Wilcox.

A sweet little woman, Mrs. Wilcox. Her children were in school. Her husband was away on business most of the time. Her house was complete to the last tea towel. Mrs. Wilcox had never had time to think about herself. She was making up for it now.

Mrs. Courtney looked upon her with the wisdom of seventy-eight years—with honesty, with affection and without malice.

Dora's been to the doctor again, she said to herself. *Now let me see; the last time I talked to her she was swallowing twenty pills a day to keep her strength up.*

A sleek dark car turned into a driveway three houses up the street, and out stepped Mrs. Burke, forty-five and childless. Every detail was perfection. Mrs. Burke looked as if she had been plucked in the prime from the advertisements in *Vogue* and kept in a quick freeze.

Helen's been shopping again, said Mrs. Courtney to herself. *Tomorrow the packages will arrive. They won't stay long. She'll return most of them the day after.* And come to think of it, this was typical of attractive Mrs. Burke. Hers was the look you see on the faces of too many smartly dressed shoppers in the best city stores—the dissatisfied look of one who seeks endlessly for something she can never hope to find because she doesn't know what it is.

A large handsome woman walked by in a good suit three years old and the kind of felt hat which is never in style or out.

It's Mrs. Matthews, thought Mrs. Courtney. *She's been to the board meeting of the Children's Hospital auxiliary.*

Mrs. Matthews was the street's do-gooder. She was on numerous committees, and chairman of three, all aligned to that semicharitable activity which carries with it considerable social distinction.

Three nice women of widely divergent types, and yet it seemed to Mrs. Courtney that they and the other women of this street—with some notable exceptions—all had a kind of sameness, and suddenly she knew what it was.

They were ladies emeritae. They were wives and mothers retired from active service, but retained in an honorary position. It wasn't their fault. They had done their main jobs, and well, too. Middle age and the success of their husbands had moved them back from the fierce front lines of living in a country still too new to have any real tradition of leisure. They were putting in time, some wisely, some not so well. They read good books, but they wrote none. They listened to fine music and made little of their own. They were consumers, no longer producers. They were onlookers, too infrequently participants.

Now the men of the street had begun to straggle home from work in the city. The first was John Hinsdale, walking briskly, his fifty years resting easily on broad shoulders. Mrs. Courtney knew him well and liked him. He was typical of the men of the street, she thought. He was a perfectly normal schizophrenic. He was two different persons living in two entirely different worlds. In the city he was a leader in his profession and among men. He liked good food, good friends and good talk. He had the affection and respect of the people under him. He had a fund of salty anecdotes which he told remarkably well, but never in the drawing rooms of the impeccables.

Mrs. Courtney watched him coming up the street. He wore that reminiscent glow that lingers on the face of the man who has tackled a tough nut this day and cracked it. When he reached the corner, the glow faded. His steps slowed, a little of the alertness went away. Mr. Hinsdale didn't know it, but he was shifting gears and approaching his second world in low.

Mrs. Courtney wished she knew what he was thinking. She waited until he had crossed the street. Then she sighed, left the Street of the Impeccables to muddle along as best it could, and went back to her book.

Mr. Hinsdale was thinking about his stomach. He was humming softly to himself, his mind at ease and grazing. "La-de-da," he hummed. "Dum-de-dum. . . . Wish I hadn't taken that second helping of lobster thermidor at the party last night."

Heaven knows he hadn't meant to. He had been about to utter a resolute no when Julia—she was his wife—had spoken for him, and loudly, "Now, darling, you know you shouldn't." Then of course he'd had to take it or admit he was a dead duck and a gone goose. He had regretted it all night long and most of the day.

He went slowly up the walk to his house. The lawn was looking well. Not a dandelion in it. That reminded him that he must ask Julia if she had paid the new gardener. That reminded him that he must call the tree surgeon to come fix the old elm. And that reminded him that he had a cavity in his own tooth and must make an appointment with the dentist. Well, it was always something.

Relax, Mr. Hinsdale cautioned himself. *The day's work is over. Relax.*

The flowers were looking well also, although there were not enough of them. Probably the gardener put them out with a slide rule. He wished Julia would work in the garden. When he walked to the train in the morning, down the lesser streets, he always liked the fresh, eager faces of the women who were out early with the trowel and the watering can. He often wondered what in the world Julia did with her time. He did so now, and today he had his answer.

As he reached the front step he was met by that high unmistakable buzz made only by women in the huddle. Oh-oh, this was the day of Julia's bridge club. He had forgotten it.

He hesitated. *A strange sound,* he thought. *Old ladies don't make it. All the edge has gone out of them, until they purr like teakettles. Men don't make it*— and just then Julia's voice disengaged itself from the parent body and swooped down upon him through the open window.

"He took the lobster," said Julia. "I know perfectly well he didn't sleep one wink all night long. I'll say one thing for John— he didn't—"

Mr. Hinsdale's reaction was reflex. *Relax,* he said to himself quickly. *Relax,* and he prepared to enter his castle silently by the side door.

As he rounded the corner of the house, little Lady, his daughter's cocker, came racing to meet him, her ears flopping in her own wind.

Lady was a friend to man. She knew all about men and how to get along with them. To her, Mr. Hinsdale was no leader-among-men-in-the-city, no mere-husband-at-home. He was God. He could do no wrong.

Lady knew her job. Every day she met Mr. Hinsdale, plumped up his ego and sent him in, feeling rested. He stooped over her now.

"Nice little puppy dog," he said. "Is she glad to see me? Is she glad I'm home? Well-l-l, the nice little doggie—"

Mr. Hinsdale explained that he could not take Lady into the house while the guest beds were afloat with the wraps of the bridge club. He promised to take her for a walk before night. Then, feeling much better, he let himself in the side door and down the hall to the kitchen.

Minnie Mae, big, black and wonderful, picked up the plumping job where Lady had left it. Mrs. Hinsdale said Minnie Mae spoiled Mr. Hinsdale outrageously.

"Good evenin', Mistah Hinsdale," she greeted him. "Ise got your coffee hot on the stove, but don't you let Mrs. Hinsdale catch you drinkin' it this time of day."

She poured a cup of coffee and brought the cream pitcher from the refrigerator. He sat down at the kitchen table. This was more like it. Nobody could make coffee like Minnie Mae. Thank heaven he was home. As he lifted his cup, a prolonged buzz-buzz floated from the living room under the pantry door.

"The ladies are certainly at it today," said Mr. Hinsdale cheerfully, "What are they talking about in there, Minnie Mae?"

"Theyse talkin' 'bout their husbands. Been at it toof and nail."

"Well, do they like them?"

"Oh, yes, suh," said Minnie Mae positively. "And anyway theyse used to them. They all say their husbands is little boys."

"Me too?" asked Mr. Hinsdale.

Minnie Mae giggled. It was one of the nicest sounds ever heard in this nice house.

"Oh, Mistah Hinsdale," she said, "you know you is the littlest boy of the bunch."

It was fair enough, thought Mr. Hinsdale, who was a fair man. He'd often noticed that when men get together, they refer to their wives as "the little woman." It was part of the natural superiority which each sex feels about the other. He pointed this out to Minnie Mae, who nodded vigorously.

"That's the truth," she declared. "That's sutainly the truth, but there's one difference. When men discuss their womenfolks, they admit right off they don't know nothin' 'bout 'em. But when wives discuss their husbands, there ain't nothin' they don't think they know. Theyse filled clear up to heah with an absolute envelopin' comprehension."

Probably it was true. Mr. Hinsdale didn't know. He considered the understanding of women below a man's best rational effort. Thanks to Minnie Mae's coffee, he was feeling very affable now, and relaxed. The cares of the day had begun to fall away.

"Any mail?" he asked.

Reluctantly, Minnie Mae brought forth two letters and handed them over. The first letter was from his son, Bill, not quite sixteen, and incarcerated in one of the very best private schools. The handwriting resembled a picket fence. The spelling was phonetic. The punctuation was sprinkled therein entirely for its artistic effect.

School was okay, Bill wrote. The Latin teacher was rugged. Chemistry was rugged. The food was terrible. Could he come home weekend after next? Maybe Dad had better say it was an emurguncy. One of the boys was going to sell him a 1931 coop for forty dollars. He would pay for it himself at the rate of two bucks a week out of his allowance. To buy it he had to have a purmit from his parents. Would Dad please send him a purmit?

The second letter was from the school and enclosed Bill's report without comment: Latin—C. Chemistry—D. English—C minus. Algebra—B.

"Minnie Mae," said Mr. Hinsdale, "for heaven's sakes pour me some more coffee."

And now the little gremlin of worry which was forever waiting at the door of his mind stepped inside and took over. What was the matter with the boy? He wasn't stupid. Would he never wake up? Why, at his age Mr. Hinsdale would have given his right arm for such an opportunity. And what did Bill do with it? He dreamed of junk. He studied with radio earphones glued to his head and pieces of rusty metal in his hands. He came home with a frank avowal to do better next time, and an engaging grin that never failed to win Julia over to his side immediately. And carefully secreted in his luggage, lovingly wrapped up in one of Julia's better pillowcases, was the inevitable and oily defunct engine part. And his talk! The very thought of it chilled Mr. Hinsdale. Bill's talk abounded in large words from the magic world of science and engineering which he confidently expected to enter someday without benefit of education or higher learning.

There's nothing for it, thought Mr. Hinsdale. *I'll have to drive up to the school next Saturday and have this out.* And he started right in to make up his speech.

"Now, son," he'd say casually, "this is your problem. It's up to you. If you can't see that the work you do now lays the foundation for the work you'll want to do later, you'll have to find it out the hard way."

"Mistah Hinsdale," said Minnie Mae quickly, "don't you think you'd bettah lie down a little 'fore dinner?"

Mr. Hinsdale thought so. He stood up wearily.

"Minnie Mae," he begged, "go easy on the rich sauces tonight, will you? And where's Miss Gerry?"

"Now don't you worry none," she told him soothingly. "Ise got your stomach on my mind. I won't have a lump in anything bigger than a pinhead. Miss Gerry's up in her room, dressin' to go out. She's been doin' her hair since four. Mistah Hinsdale, if that chile don't stop fussin' with her hair, she's goin' to wear it plumb off at the roots."

Bless Minnie Mae! Mr. Hinsdale thanked her and went up the back stairs to his room.

He took the evening paper from his pocket and tossed it into the wastebasket, careful not to glance at the headlines and be reminded all over again that the European situation was growing worse and nearer, day by day. He changed his shoes and his coat, lay down on the bed and lighted his favorite pipe, which smelled horrible and emitted a low, pleasant gurgle. Somewhere in the back of his mind he was still composing speeches to Bill.

Relax, he told himself. *You're home, relax.*

Perhaps he dozed a little. The next thing he knew, his pipe was cold in his hand. He was sitting upright, listening to a sound he had never heard before in his nice house—the sound of someone sobbing bitterly.

One of the bridge club, no doubt—in the guest room with her feelings hurt. Well, she could stay there. He was not going to investigate. Not John Hinsdale. He knew better.

Nevertheless, he arose and approached the door cautiously to be sure it was shut. But the bridge club had gone. The feminine buzz had ceased. Julia was evidently in the living room with the radio going. Minnie Mae was moving about the kitchen rattling the pots and pans. The sobbing did not come from the guest room. It came from the opposite end of the hall, from his daughter's room. Nothing could have surprised Mr. Hinsdale more than this.

Gerry was seventeen. Gerry was long, lithe loveliness, soft hair on her shoulders and absolute surety on her face. Gerry's was that air of youthful arrogance which made Mr. Hinsdale know he must be old, because it amused him, it irritated him and it filled him with a twinge of envy. Lately Mr. Hinsdale had wondered how in the world he and Julia had ever managed to produce so lush, so confident a young creature. Gerry didn't like her father's neckties. She didn't like her mother's hats. And as for Bill's sibilant sipping of the family soup, Gerry said if anybody heard him, and how could they help it—

It had been a long time since Mr. Hinsdale had heard her cry. He could remember her anguished howl when the little neighbor boy used to take her toys away from her, and the high whimper when she had hurt herself. This was different. This held an adult tone of hopelessness

He walked down the hall and listened. The sound of sobbing was stifled now. He knocked softly. There was no answer. He tried the knob and went in. Gerry was collapsed in a slipper chair in her best housecoat. In one hand she clutched a wet washcloth, as if she were trying to repair the damage as fast as she made it, as if she were not quite reconciled to reducing her eyes to a state of red puffiness. On the bed were her party sandals and bag. From a hanger hooked over the top of the closet door was suspended her new evening gown, long, white and gossamer.

She glanced up. The defenseless look on her face changed to one almost of accusation. Mr. Hinsdale knew the signs well from business. Gerry was filled with the fires of indignation, ready to send off sparks. He had caught her with her guard down, her mask off, and was elected to be the target.

She did not wait for him to ask her what was the matter. She did not wait for any invitation to tell Dad all about it.

"It won't make any difference what you say," she told him quickly. "I'm not going. It's stupid. It's silly. It isn't worth it, and I'm not going."

She got up and walked up and down the room, gathering her attack. Then she stopped, the accusation plain on her face.

"Do you know what I'm up against?" she demanded. "I'm one of the luckiest girls in town. Just ask Mother. I'm invited to Mrs. Bradbury's dinner dance for her daughter, Maud. It's the nicest affair of the season. Only the very nicest young people are asked to it."

Why, she's scared, thought Mr. Hinsdale, with a kind of wonder. Here she was, a product of so much expense, so much love and thought. She'd been to the best schools. She'd had her teeth straightened. She'd had dancing, music, riding, tennis and heaven knows how many other lessons. And here she was all bumped out in goose pimples. He could not believe it and he knew it to be true.

"Oh, I do fine at the school dances," Gerry said defiantly, as if she had to prove it. "The boys from Hatcher come over. They can't help themselves, the poor things! They'd do anything to get out of that place. They're loaded into buses and delivered like a bunch of sheep. Oh, I do well then. And I'm all right when a boy asks me to play tennis or go to a show, or when I'm out with a few couples who know each other. This is different."

She stopped pacing back and forth, stood perfectly still, looking at him.

Go on, said the brown eyes so much like his own. *Say I have to go because it will develop my character.*

Mr. Hinsdale didn't say it.

"This is different. Ned Stephens is coming for me. He has to. It's been arranged. He'd rather take the Dupont girl—the one Mrs. Bradbury's snagged for her out-of-town nephew. Oh, I know what I'm in for this time. He'll dance the first dance with me and dish me behind a potted palm, and there I'll be, in a crowd that's older and I don't know very well. There I'll be with nothing to do but hide in the bastille."

"In the what?" asked Mr. Hinsdale faintly.

"That's what they call the women's locker room at the country club, Dad. You don't know what it's like. When the music starts, you wait to see if anybody is going to ask you to dance, and if nobody does, you wish you were dead, but you aren't. You go down to the locker room and you pretend you've broken a strap or something, but you don't fool anybody. That's what I'm in for tonight, and I'm not going."

Go on, said the brown eyes. *Say it. Tell me I have to go because I'm scared.*

Mr. Hinsdale didn't say that either. Now, meeting no resistance, Gerry relaxed a little.

"Do you know what I think, Dad? I don't think it's much fun to be young. It's overrated. One day at the yacht club some of us girls were acting kind of silly, and two old women, at least forty-five, were watching us. One of them said, 'Do you suppose we were ever that young?' and the other said she guessed so, but thank God they were done with it, thank God they didn't have to go through that again. I know what she meant. Yes, I do. Youth's cruel, Dad. You never like yourself. You're too fat in the wrong spots or your bones stick out. You're too short or you think you'll never stop growing until your head comes through the roof. Youth's cruel."

Had she found it out so soon?

"Oh, Dad," Gerry said fiercely, "if you're ever born a woman, be an itty-bitty, wishy-washy blonde with long eyelashes. Don't have brains. You'll trip over them. Do you know something? Mother thinks we're still in the Gentle Julia era Tarkington wrote about. She thinks all a girl has to do is sit out on the front porch, and the boys will break their legs rushing up the steps. It isn't true. It's so horribly competitive. The boys don't take the initiative anymore. They don't have to. It's the girls who do the chasing. They hang on the telephone and plot and plan and scheme. And I'm no good at it. It's predatory. That's what it is. It's against nature. It's disgusting . . . and I wish I could do it."

It was out at last, the gist of it. Gerry rested her case. She sank down on the edge of the bed, her eyes bright, cautious and watchful.

Go on, they said to him. *Say it. Tell me a nice, sensible, intelligent girl inevitably comes into her own. Oh, do say that.*

Mr. Hinsdale didn't say it. *What does a parent say to a child at a time like this?* he asked himself desperately, and found no answer. It was a moment he knew in business, when, hot at the collar and weak at the knee, a man prepares to cut off a little piece of himself to give courage to the fainthearted. He prepared to do it now for Gerry.

He was still holding his pipe. He took a box of matches from his pocket and lighted it slowly.

"Well, Gerry," he said casually, "I think you have something. You're grown-up enough to know your own mind. If you don't wish to go, I haven't the slightest intention of urging you."

Gerry had not expected this. She was surprised, relieved, and for the first time a bit doubtful.

"Now don't worry about it, Gerry," he told her quickly. "I'll call up Mrs. Bradbury myself and make your apologies."

He walked back and forth across the room, puffing on his pipe, concentrating on his speech to Mrs. Bradbury.

"Now let me see," he said, "shall I tell her that you don't feel that you can compete with this older crowd?"

Gerry looked doubtful no longer. She pounced off the bedside. "Oh, no, Dad. Not that."

"Then you'll have to have a headache. It's worn, but it's always good."

He sat down in the slipper chair as if it were settled. When he spoke, his tone was one almost of apology.

"I had forgotten," he said slowly—"I had forgotten that horrible painful time when you don't like yourself."

He struck another match to his pipe and drew on it carefully.

"You're right about it, Gerry. There's no argument. I remember going home from high school and passing the hardware store. It had the best plate-glass windows in town. Every time I went by I tried not to look at my reflection, and failed. There I'd be—a human string bean. I always looked as tall and thin as a telegraph pole, and I could always see the shine on my old blue suit."

He laughed ruefully, as you laugh at something the years have never succeeded in making really funny.

"I suffered agonies over that old blue suit, Gerry," he said. "It was the only suit I owned those days that I didn't outgrow almost at once. It was a good suit and wore like iron. It shone and shone, and I wore it to everything. I remember the first really nice private dance I was asked to attend. All the other boys had new white flannels, but I had to wear that darned blue suit. I didn't want to go, but I didn't have the courage you have, Gerry. I was too proud to admit I was scared, so Mother sponged the suit, and off I went like a martyr going to the lions."

"Why, Dad!"

"I went, and I'm not saying it developed my character. I'm certainly not saying that. I did learn one thing, though, Gerry. I didn't learn it from any fine, sweet, sensible, intelligent girl either. I learned it from what you call a wishy-washy blonde. Her name was Fernie Andrews, and she didn't have a thimbleful of brains. At least I thought so at the time. I think now she must have been a lot smarter than I knew. I've always been grateful to her, in a way. You see, she taught me something that night about getting myself off my hands."

Don't tell me I don't know anything about psychology, he thought. *I'm doing all right. I'm doing fine. Now, if she'll just bite.*

"What did she do?" Gerry asked. "And how did she do it?"

Mr. Hinsdale put down his pipe. *Here I go,* he thought, *about to make a fool of myself. I hope Julia doesn't catch me at this.*

"Stand up, Gerry," he said, "and I'll show you. Now you take the part of the boy. I'll be the girl."

She was delighted and horrified. She reverted to ten years. She giggled. "Oh, Dad, you can't."

"I certainly can," declared Mr. Hinsdale stoutly. "You don't need to think, Gerry, just because I'm a bit ancient, that I know nothing whatsoever about women. At least I can tell you what happened."

He went over to her.

"I went to the dance," he said. "I arrived late. The first person I saw was one of those stuffy dowagers they always had for chaperons in those days. She was ready to pounce on me, ready to nab me as a partner for a perpetual wallflower. To avoid it, I bolted. I walked up to the first girl I saw and asked her to dance."

"Fernie?"

"No, this was an awfully nice girl, as unhappy as I was. She walked to the dance floor with me like this, Gerry. She was too proud and too conscious of herself to bend an inch. We treated each other exactly as if each was in danger of hydrophobia."

"So you dished her behind a potted palm," said Gerry bitterly.

"I got rid of her as fast as I could. I wondered what to do next, and it was then that Fernie Andrews saw me. She sidled up like this, Gerry. She said, 'Aren't you going to ask me to dance, John?' and she looked up as if dancing with me would make her the proudest girl in the room."

"Dad, you didn't fall for that?"

"Oh, yes, I did. The first thing I knew, I was dancing with her. She didn't say, 'Is it cold up there?' the way some of the girls did. She said, 'I'm so glad you're tall. I love to dance with tall men.' She said I danced well too. I didn't, I suppose, but all the time I was dancing with her I thought so. I was a tall, gawky kid, but I had the illusion for a little while that I was the best-looking boy on the floor."

"Well-l-l-l," said Gerry. "That does it. That goes to prove you can put it on with a scoop shovel and a man will swallow it."

"If you mean men like flattery, Gerry, they do. There's more to it than that. Fernie Andrews was as friendly as a puppy. She liked people. She had herself off her hands and she was sufficiently interested to help a boy get himself off his. She was adept at building little conversational bridges across the unknown, and every boy in town felt it, even if he wasn't smart enough to know it." He chuckled. "Oh, she was a smart one, all right. She didn't think of herself every minute. She seemed to know when a boy was scared and nervous and shut up in his own little box. And she knew just how to let him out."

He was through.

"Well," he said, "that's all I know about small talk and breaking the ice. That's every bit. I'll go call Mrs. Bradbury now," and without one look at Gerry, he walked to the door. He was through it before she stopped him.

"Dad. Wait a minute."

"Yes-s-s?"

"I'll go. I'm just the kind of an idiot who'll try anything once," and then she was across the room and in his arms.

"Dad," she whispered, "can I do it? Can I?"

"Of course you can."

"Are my eyes red?"

"No, they're fine. They're perfectly all right."

"Dad, when Ned Stephens comes for me, suppose Mother greets him. Suppose she says, 'Have a good time, children.' Suppose she tells him to take good care of me. I'll die, Dad. I'll just die."

"She won't say it," promised Mr. Hinsdale. "I'll take care of that. Now you get dressed, Gerry."

He went out the door. He'd been put through a mangle and drawn through a knothole.

Relax, said Mr. Hinsdale to himself, and he went quickly down the back stairs to call out the reserves.

Minnie Mae was taking the dinner plates out of the oven.

"There is a young man coming for Miss Gerry," explained Mr. Hinsdale. "She doesn't know him very well and she's nervous.

She's afraid Mrs. Hinsdale and I will—will act like parents. Now, Minnie Mae, do you suppose—"

"Now don't you worry none," said Minnie Mae. "Dinner's ready. After it's over, you take Mrs. Hinsdale upstairs and talk to her nice. I'll let Miss Gerry's young man in and I'll unlax him good."

Very much relieved, Mr. Hinsdale went in to dinner. It was like a hundred others. There sat Julia, attractive and animated, her appetite quite spoiled by the bridge club, her mind bubbling with chitchat. And there sat Mr. Hinsdale in that monosyllabic corner which is the retreat of the nicer men who are interested in their wives' gossip and trying hard not to show it.

But this night Mr. Hinsdale's thought kept flowing upstairs to Gerry. She was so vulnerable, so defenseless. She was exactly as he had been at her age, a little more grown-up in some ways, a little less in others, but still shy beneath her mask, and frightened.

Gerry's words kept coming back to him: "Do you know what I think? . . . Youth's cruel." It was true, though he had hoped she would never know it.

"Julia," he said suddenly, "do you think Gerry will have a good time tonight?"

Julia, who had been interrupted in one of her better bridge bits, looked up with amazement and said, "Why, darling, of course she will. Every girl in town would love to go to this party. Besides, Gerry has a new dress. You paid eighty dollars for it and it's a dream." And after that, Mr. Hinsdale, who was fond of Julia, couldn't say a word.

When Julia went upstairs to her room after dinner, Mr. Hinsdale tagged along. He emerged from his monosyllabic corner and became what he imagined to be quite scintillating. He turned on the radio. Shamelessly and a little sheepishly, because it made him feel like a conspirator in a low comedy, he did his best to keep his wife's mind off their daughter. Poor Julia had not yet learned that the time comes when all a child asks of his parents is that they should be invisible, and mum. Heaven knows, Bill had tried to teach her. Every time Julia came near his school, he acted as if he were ashamed of her, and when she showed a maternal desire to inspect his room, he insisted desperately that the hall was full of boys, all running up and down minus clothes and taking showers. Having noticed Bill's fingernails, Mr. Hinsdale doubted this, but he understood, as he understood Julia now.

Finally he heard a faint swish from the hall. The new dress no doubt, descending the stairs to meet the escort. He turned up the radio.

"Be right back, Julia," he said. "Just want to get my pipe."

He shut the bedroom door behind him and stood at the top of the stairs, listening. Thump, thump, thump! That was Lady's tail doing its diplomatic best. Then he heard Minnie Mae say, "Lan' sakes, Lady, I declare I is goin' to have you stuffed," and he heard a young, boyish voice protest that he liked dogs; why, he had one himself.

Mr. Hinsdale was so nervous he couldn't find his pipe. When he returned to the hall, he knew it was all right. Everything was all right. He could hear laughter, and he could hear Minnie Mae saying, "My goodness, Miss Gerry, you two is goin' to be the best-looking couple at the ball."

He went quickly into Julia's room. When he heard the sound for which he had been waiting, he said casually, "I believe Gerry's calling to us, Julia. Guess her young man's arrived," and when Julia, with a little cry of surprise, rushed to the stairs, he managed to be right in the middle of them.

In the hall below were Gerry and Ned Stephens. She was standing quite close to him, looking up at him admiringly, but not too obviously. Gerry had her chin up. Nobody was going to dish her behind any potted palm this night.

She introduced Ned to her parents. Before Julia could say, "Oh, yes, my dear. I've known your mother since—" Mr. Hinsdale grabbed the reins and ran with them. He spoke loudly. "Good-by, kids," he said. "Have a good time."

He felt a little sick. It was as if she were walking out into the big cold world. It was as if he were saying good-by to her. And the boy! Such a fuzzy young peach, with the dew still on him.

"Good-bye, Mother!" Gerry called from the door.

In Fernie Andrews' very best manner, she blew a kiss to her dad.

"Good-bye, Duckpuss!" she called, and was gone. The door shut behind her.

Julia recovered first. "What did she call you?" asked Julia, and Mr. Hinsdale replied a little smugly that it sounded to him like duckpuss.

"Well really," said Julia, "I never saw Gerry in such a rush. It's almost as if she were ashamed of the young man." Her eyes rested thoughtfully on her husband. "John," said Julia, "John Hinsdale, what were you and Gerry talking about in her room before dinner?"

"I was helping her with her homework," said Mr. Hinsdale. "Julia, I think I'll lie down a little while. I've had a very hard day at the office," and he retreated to his room.

Now at last the house was quiet. Now at last Mr. Hinsdale could let the day fall away.

Relax, he said to himself, *relax.*

But it did no good. Mr. Hinsdale couldn't relax. All he could think of was Gerry, chin up, heading out into life. All he could feel was his affection for her.

This night was different from other nights. This was the night the rowboat goes by the iceberg and its wake turns over the submerged and greater part. Something kept trying to break the surface of Mr. Hinsdale's mind, something that had been lying quietly there for a long time. Whatever it was, Mr. Hinsdale did not want to face it. He kept poking it under. He was not going to try to think this night. Not after business hours.

He dug the newspaper out of the wastebasket. Europe was still in a mess. He tossed it back in. He lighted his pipe. That was it. He was smoking too much. Tomorrow he would start cutting down. He turned on the radio. All he got was some commentator worked up into a fine international frenzy. He turned it off.

The doorbell rang.

"Now what?" said Mr. Hinsdale fiercely. "Now what? Is there no peace in this house."

Minnie Mae had retired to her room. Mr. Hinsdale heard the tap of Julia's heels as she went to answer the door. He heard a murmur of voices. Then Julia's called up the stairs.

"John-n-n-n!" called Julia brightly. "John-n-n-n, dear!"

Mr. Hinsdale went to the door. "Yes, Julia."

"John, dear, the Huttons are here," and there was in Julia's voice that tone all well-trained husbands know which added without words, *The Huttons are right here in the hall beside me, and don't moan out loud, because they'll hear every sound you make.*

Mr. Hinsdale heard himself calling back brightly, "All right, Julia. I'll be right down."

Why, he asked himself desperately, *why, of all times, do the Huttons have to choose this night to call?* Not that he had anything against the Huttons. No indeed. They were nice people. A bit stuffy, perhaps. A little on the smug side. But nice, and Mr. Hinsdale remembered suddenly and with unexpected sympathy the little girl who asked God to make all the bad people nice, please, and all the nice people fun.

He changed his coat, knocked out his pipe. He had begun to feel a little vehement about the Huttons. Never before in his life had he felt vehement about anyone so harmless. He did not understand it at all. Mr. Hutton would get him aside and talk business all evening. Mrs. Hutton, a good woman whose sex appeal lay buried under twenty-five years of conservative marriage, would set her well-girdled end upon a chair, her skirt carefully pulled over her knees, and enter into a domestic huddle with Julia. There was nothing, surely, to fear from either. Yet Mr. Hinsdale felt some emotion very akin to fear.

Ridiculous, he said to himself and went downstairs, the lord of the manor, prepared to be nice and not show in any little way that he would prefer to go to bed. But this night Mr. Hinsdale performed this ritual with a difference, as if a little part of him detached itself and stood watching and listening.

He heard himself greet his guests, "Good evening, Sylvia. So nice to see you. . . . How are you, Albert?" Then a fine flurry of the best social cooing occupied the living room.

Presently, the amenities disposed of, the world situation was given the once-over lightly. The world was in a dreadful, dreadful state. Didn't Mr. Hinsdale agree? He did. Why, really, the newspapers were so discouraging that Mrs. Hutton simply put them down. And as for the radio, Mrs. Hutton simply turned it off. Didn't Mr. Hinsdale agree? And Mr. Hinsdale did, and began to squirm.

Finally Julia took Mrs. Hutton aside to discuss the servant problem, to preen herself because she had a Minnie Mae, and to listen to Mrs. Hutton groan because she hadn't. The two men settled down to talk business. Business was bad. Things in Washington were deplorable. Taxes were fierce and growing worse. Mr. Hutton wanted no large or local winds to blow upon him—not if they cooled his purse, his safety. Mr. Hinsdale, who was an honest man, had to admit to himself that he had often felt the same way. He began to squirm more than ever. He crossed and recrossed his legs.

John, said Julia's eyes, *stop wiggling. They'll notice.*

And just then a thought struck Mr. Hinsdale that was so horrible it kept him immobile at least a minute. Were he and Julia like the Huttons? Were they stuffy and smug? Were they self-satisfied? He denied it with that fierce denial we give only to the truth.

Go home, prayed Mr. Hinsdale silently. *Oh, do go home,* because the thought which had been rising in his mind was coming closer and closer to the surface.

But the Huttons showed no inclination whatsoever to go home. Mr. Hinsdale watched the clock, his eyes engaging in dialogue with Julia. *John, what's the matter with you? Don't you look at the clock again. Hear me?* And Mr. Hinsdale's eyes answered, *I can't help it. I can't stand these people.* And Julia's eyes replied, *Why, John Hinsdale, they're lovely people. We ought to be proud to know people like this. And anyway I didn't ask them. They just came.*

At last Mrs. Hutton gave Albert the we've-stayed-long-enough signal and stood up with that unmistakable small gesture which means a nice woman is dying to give her girdle a downward tug, but is too much of a lady to do so. The Huttons were leaving, thank God.

"So soon?" murmured Julia. But yes, the Huttons really must go.

Mr. Hinsdale, who wanted no scene with Julia, said quickly that if they must, he would get Lady and her leash, and accompany them a piece. He had promised Lady a walk. He went for Lady before they could change their minds.

Because he was a little ashamed of himself, he was unusually affable and talkative on the walk toward the Huttons' house. When he saw their front door safely shut upon them, his affability died. He started slowly back through the lovely evening, and he met old Mrs. Courtney strolling along in front of her house with her ancient poodle.

Mr. Hinsdale liked the old lady. Lady liked the poodle. They fell in step, the two dogs touching noses and sniffing at every bush.

"I see the Huttons have been spending the evening at your house," said Mrs. Courtney. "It was my turn last week. I thought they'd never leave. Such nice people."

Mr. Hinsdale made a polite noise in his throat.

"Such awfully nice people," repeated Mrs. Courtney firmly. "There's only one trouble with them." She chuckled softly to herself. "They're dead," she said. "They're dead and they don't know it."

Mr. Hinsdale felt sweet relief, the first fresh breeze of the day.

"You know something, Mrs. Courtney," he said eagerly. "I've had a miserable evening. I don't know why. I think it was because all the time the Huttons were calling, I kept seeing in them Julia and myself."

"Don't we all?" said Mrs. Courtney. "That's what makes the Huttons so devastating. They're all of us. They're all the very nicest people on this street reduced to the ultimate smugness. It's a little like meeting an essence of yourself."

Mr. Hinsdale laughed.

"Here's the world about to blow up around our heads," said Mrs. Courtney, "and all the Huttons want to do is keep the very best grade of American cotton wool pulled over their ears as long as possible."

"I guess we all want to hang onto our security," said Mr. Hinsdale.

Mrs. Courtney stopped in her tracks. "Security, Mr. Hinsdale?" she asked in a curious voice. "What security?"

And there it was, out on the surface—the thought that had been rising in his mind all evening. There it was—up at last. There was no security. Not now. Not anymore. A man thought so. It was part of his heritage. And then some fine night a series of little things came along that made him know it wasn't true.

They came to the corner and stopped. Mrs. Courtney prepared to turn back. Her old eyes swept the lovely street.

"It's a beautiful street," she said slowly. "But sometimes I feel I should have left it in cabbages. It's a dead-end street. That's the danger of the nice streets where the nice people live." Her voice lowered. "In another year we'll be in the war," she said, "and we'll come through it. When it's over, there will be two kinds of people left, I suppose—the quick and the dead. And do you know something? Even if I am seventy-eight, I intend to belong to the quick. . . . No, don't come with me. Its only a few steps. Good night, Mr. Hinsdale," and Mrs. Courtney went up the path to her door.

Mr. Hinsdale walked slowly home, little Lady following at his heels. He sat down on his own doorstep, Lady as close beside him as she could wriggle. This night he did not rest his hand upon her head or stroke her ears. He did not talk to her. He sat there motionless, looking out on the lovely street, bathed now in moonlight.

It seemed to John Hinsdale that he was seeing the street for the first time, and all the other streets like it in the big and little towns everywhere. It seemed to him that he was seeing all the other men like himself who had followed the pattern of their day, who had given of their hearts' blood to put their families on streets like this, confident that security could be won and held.

Now, with the breath of the war hot on his neck, he knew it wasn't true. No man could protect his children from the heartbreak. He could only build them strong enough to take it. And had he? Mr. Hinsdale didn't know.

He knew only that this night he seemed to be getting ready for some small war of his own, that he threw up his ramparts and raised his sights. He had heard it said that every man reaches the time when all he asks of life is a chance to retire honorably. Mr.

Hinsdale did not ask it. Like Mrs. Courtney he wanted to belong to the quick.

The lights were going out in the nice houses on the Street of the Impeccables. Mr. Hinsdale watched them. There was something a little pathetic about him, sitting there on his own doorstep with the little dog close beside him. Such a nice man! Such a successful man! And so uneasy on Easy Street.

The Street of the Impeccables went through the war as well as any street and better than most. Its heart ached at the same times. It worked, worried and sacrificed to the same needs. It cannot be said that it changed permanently in any large way. For a time, the life of everyone on it was greatly altered or subtly affected. Then, when the disease had spent itself, the scars grown white, and the memories begun to recede in mind, the Street of the Impeccables went back to being itself—quite a little better off in material things, and as lovely as ever.

On the day Julia Hinsdale came to her time of uncertainty, she was feeling unusually pleased with her own niche in this world. It was a late afternoon well after the war, and Julia was walking home from the bridge club, her mind, like her handbag, a jumble of odds and ends through which her thought was ambulating as happily as a cow in a daisy field.

"La-de-da," she hummed, "dum-de-dum." *Wonder where in the world Susan bought that hat she was wearing at luncheon. It looked like a vegetable plate with a poached egg on top. Well, it was becoming. I'll say that for it.*

She approached the Wilcox house and slowed. Sweet little Mrs. Wilcox had had no time to think about herself through the war, or to remember her pills, much less swallow them. She'd had her two daughters and five grandchildren for the duration and long after. They were gone now. The big house was looking lonely and bereft.

They say it's a perfect shambles, said Julia to herself. *Thank heaven I escaped that.*

Julia was a nice woman, and by no means a stupid one. How lucky she and her family had been. At the thought of it, she felt deeply grateful, almost humble.

Of course they'd had their bad times. Bill had enlisted in the Navy. Long after the war was over, he was bouncing around the Pacific, moored off some rubble heap. As John put it, the Navy had done nothing for Bill's spelling. Didn't Dad know an admirul who could get him out of this? Wasn't there some way he could get back to school? John didn't, and there wasn't.

Julia did not like to remember the day Bill's cable had arrived, announcing—three days after he was twenty-one—his marriage to a girl he'd met in Honolulu. But it had all come out beautifully. Mrs. Courtney knew the girl's mother and grandmother, and pronounced them lovely people. Bill was out of the Navy at last. After a short visit with his wife and baby, he was enrolled in a small California college, which was the only place that would take him. He was working hard and his family was flourishing. Julia liked to think of them out there in all that sunshine, in a nice little California bungalow with geraniums growing everywhere in that huge way California flowers seem to grow.

Then, of course, there had been the dreadful time when Ned Stephens was wounded. He was the boy who had taken Gerry to the supper dance so long ago. He was the one she loved. Ned had spent more than two years in an Army hospital a thousand miles away, which provided highly specialized treatment. While she waited for him, Gerry had finished college and found herself a job. But even this was coming out well. Ned was back at last, and only a little lame. He had to report twice a week to the nearby Army hospital while he awaited medical discharge. When it came through, he and Gerry were to be married.

Yes, they had been lucky indeed. Even John's stomach had survived, and his business was going well. And Julia and her bridge club had closed the sewing room they had run for the Red Cross, and were back at the card table. Life was almost normal again.

Julia was nearing home. She waved to Mrs. Courtney, who was surveying the street from her bay window, and went up the walk to the door. She took the key from her bag and slipped it into the lock. She did not turn the knob, because as she put her hand upon it, an unfamiliar voice sailed through the open living-room window. It was a city voice, male and young. It was a pleasant voice, but it bore the unmistakable mark of the alleys, of the narrow dirty streets across the tracks.

"Minnie Mae," it said, "by any shakes this is the best wild-blackberry pie I ever tasted."

Julia left her front steps and headed around the house for the side door. Her thought no longer ambulated through daisy fields. Emotion had taken over.

Oh, Minnie Mae, how could you? You knew I was saving that last jar of wild blackberries to make tarts for the bridge club. You knew it and you've baked it in a pie and you are serving it up this very minute to some absolute stranger—and heaven knows where you picked him up—proba-

bly sitting on my best love seat, contrasting beautifully with its yellow tapestry.

And how the bridge club would love it! The girls did not envy Julia her husband, her house, her children . . . not even her antique Wedgwood tea set. They envied Julia her cook. She was the only woman on the whole street who'd had the same cook for sixteen years. And now Minnie Mae, her trusted and dusky jewel, had fallen.

In the thirty feet from the front door to the side of the house Julia composed her speech of judgment.

"Minnie Mae," she would say, "if you think for one single solitary minute that I'm going to stand—"

No, Julia. That won't do. Use your head, Julia. This is just another one of those minor domestic moments in which a woman spends a large part of her life. If you say that, Julia, like as not, Minnie Mae will leave. Then where will you be? Right back in your own kitchen.

Julia threw out her speech and began another. Now, let's see: she would walk into the kitchen and she would say casually, "Minnie Mae, by any chance do I smell the wild blackberries I've been saving for the bridge club?"

She reached the side door. Little Lady rushed up to greet her.

"Go away, Lady," said Julia. "For goodness' sakes don't bother me at a time like this. You're a nice little dog, but go away."

Lady retired, her brown eyes reproachful and saying, *All right, Julia, I'll go. You'll need me yet. You'll see.*

Julia let herself in the door and walked down the corridor to the kitchen. Minnie Mae was entering through the pantry door.

"Minnie Mae," said Julia casually, "is that a pie I smell, made no doubt from the wild blackberries I've been saving for the bridge club?"

Minnie Mae beamed upon her. "You ain't savin' 'em anymore, Mrs. Hinsdale," she announced cheerfully. "Theyse bein' liquidated mighty fast in the parlor by a nice young gentleman."

"Well," said Julia, a little of the surety knocked out of her. "I'm certainly glad he likes it."

"Oh, he likes it, Mrs. Hinsdale. Yes-s-s-s, suh. He's sittin' on the love seat asmackin' his lips. 'Course he spilled a little of the juice on the tapestry, but I figured on gettin' it cleaned up 'fore you got home."

"Oh, you did, Minnie Mae?" said Julia with considerable sarcasm. "Well, I think I shall just walk in there and see if there is any little thing he needs."

Minnie Mae lost her beam and began to look worried. "Mrs. Hinsdale, I wouldn't do that if I was you," she begged. "Cap'n

Ned's in there, and Miss Gerry. . . . Mrs. Hinsdale you better not—"

It was too late. Julia had crossed the pantry and entered the dining room. Full of the most righteous indignation, she walked into the living room, straight into her time of uncertainty.

She came to an abrupt stop. On the floor with his back to the mantel sat Ned Stephens, the brace on his right leg showing a little below his trousers edge. Gerry was beside him, perched on the needlepoint stool, the coffee table in front of her.

On the love seat sat a young man, a first sergeant's stripes on his sleeves. There were crutches propped beside him, and his legs— even to Julia, it was apparent his legs were quite useless.

As Julia entered, they were relaxed and laughing. When she stopped, surprise and shock plain on her face, there was a moment of utter and appalling silence.

Gerry jumped from the stool, went over and put her hand on the sergeant's arm.

"Mother," she said, "this is Jimmy Devon. He was with Ned in the Pacific."

Julia did the best she could. She tried hard to make up for that moment of shock.

"How nice," she said cordially. "I'm so glad to meet you," and she sat down beside the young man on the love seat and became very animated and friendly.

As if motivated by the instinct that every mother has when she meets some other mother's son who has been less lucky than her own, Julia told Jimmy Devon all about Bill.

It did not go well. He listened politely, a patient, tired look in his wise young eyes. The glow had gone from the room. Somehow Julia had spoiled it. Finally there was nothing for her to do but excuse herself and make a graceful exit to the kitchen and Minnie Mae. It was outrageous of Minnie Mae to have permitted her to barge in like that. How could Minnie Mae have been so stupid?

And I shall tell her so, said Julie to herself, *no matter what happens.*

But Julia told Minnie Mae nothing. Minnie Mae was waiting for her just inside the kitchen door. For the first time in sixteen years Minnie Mae was mad.

"Mrs. Hinsdale, ain't you got no sense at all?" said Minnie Mae.

"Why, Minnie Mae, I certainly did the very best—"

"Here I've been standin' with my ear to the crack prayin' the good Lord to shut your mouth," said Minnie Mae, "and what did you do?"

"Minnie Mae, I can assure you I did the very best—"

"You sat there, Mrs. Hinsdale, showin' how sorry you was for Mistah Jimmy what'll never walk again, and all the time you kept agabblin' and agabblin'. My goodness, Mrs. Hinsdale, you told him all about what a terrible time Mistah Bill had in the Navy—all about him bouncin' around the ocean after the fightin' was done, doin' nothin' 'cept bein' mighty seasick and mighty safe."

"Now look here, Minnie Mae. I never thought—I had no intention—I didn't mean—"

"Oh, you meant well enough," agreed Minnie Mae. "All the nice peoples means well." She advanced upon Julia, her dark eyes bright with indignation. "Do you know what you is?" she demanded. "You is nothin' but a civilian. You is jest one of those awful dumb civilians."

Having delivered herself of the judgment, Minnie Mae turned her back on her mistress and became very busy at the sink.

"This kitchen ain't big enough for both of us, Mrs. Hinsdale," said Minnie Mae sadly. "You better go upstairs to your room while I struggles with my wrath. There's a letter from Mistah Bill on your chest of drawers."

Julia did not argue. She loved Minnie Mae and knew she had offended her deeply. She retired. No, she retreated. She went up the back steps so fast that she reached the upstairs landing puffing and had to lean against the railing to catch her breath and get her bearings.

The warmth and the glow had returned to the living room. They were all talking and laughing at once. Ned Stephens and Jimmy Devon seemed to be telling Gerry about something that had happened on a Pacific island with a queer name. Each was giving her his version. Suddenly there was a burst of laughter and an outraged howl from Ned.

"Why, you no-account cripple!" he yelled. "Don't you believe him, Gerry!" and this was followed at once by a prolonged howl from the sergeant, and a rapid flow of the finest, the smoothest-running invective.

Julia could make nothing of it. Here she stood, still out of breath and smarting from Minnie Mae's scorn for a blunder she hadn't even known she'd made, and downstairs those two were going at each other, insulting each other, hurling words at each other— words Julia had never heard in this nice house, and only read in the very newest books. Apparently the wounded could say anything at all to the wounded. Julia had lost merely a vermiform appendix, two tonsils and produced two children—with quite a little pain too. She didn't qualify. She simply did not understand it.

Then she heard Minnie Mae come in and ask, "Sergeant Jimmy, shall I make you some more coffee?" and she heard Jimmy Devon answer, "Yes, please, Mathilda." Julia thought he had mistaken Minnie Mae's name. Perhaps there was something a little wrong with his head.

She was thinking about this when the doorbell rang. It was Mrs. Courtney, who did not ask for the mistress of the house, but went right on into the living room.

"Oh, I'm so glad you're here, Jimmy," she said. "The postman just brought the pamphlets from the Government on how to start a nursery. Plants, my dear; not children. I could hardly wait for you to see them. I called the hospital, and somebody in the ward— Now look here—"

Chairs scraped. Evidently heads were bowed over the pamphlets. The voices were low and eager. Then there was a hush.

"You see, Jimmy," said Mrs. Courtney, "you can start with a small lath house. You can build the platform for the flats narrow enough and low enough so you can work each side from a wheelchair."

Julia heard Jimmy Devon say, "Gee, Mathilda, these are swell."

Mathilda again. Apparently he called every woman he liked Mathilda, regardless of age or color. It was too much for Julia, who went into her bedroom, shutting the door behind her.

She remembered Bill's letter, found it on the chest of drawers and opened it. It was addressed to her. The salutation was to John.

"Dear Dad," she read. "Tell Mother not to send any china for our annivursury present. We have no place to put it. Thank you for the check. We bought a secondhand washing machine, and I have been tinkering with the motor. It works fine. We are all well. There is a milk strike on, so we married veterans got together and bought a cow. Our wives won't let the children drink the milk because it is not pasteurized, so we drink it ourselves. I inclose my quarter's report, also a snapshot of the house. Tell mother it is not as bad as it looks. Much love. Bill. P.S. I hope you will notice that my spelling is improving."

The report showed one A and four B's. The snapshot showed a small boxlike structure of the variety willingly and gladly cast off by the Army. There were no geraniums anywhere. The earth looked cracked and baked. To the left of the door there seemed to be some forgotten and detached plumbing. To the right of the door was one flower—the tallest, largest sunflower Julia had ever gazed upon.

She laughed a little. She cried a little too. Then she heard a car draw up in front of the house and honk. She heard the front door open and Gerry call, "Jimmy will be right out!"

Julia went to the window. It was not pleasant to watch Jimmy Devon heave himself slowly on his crutches from the steps to the car. She bit her lip that such things must be. But Mrs. Courtney, Ned and Gerry, who walked along with him, seemed to think nothing of it. They sent him off in a flurry of laughter.

Ned and Gerry were to have dinner that night with Ned's parents. Julia watched them climb into Gerry's little car and drive off. She watched Mrs. Courtney cross the street to her big old house. She was confused now, and her head had begun to ache.

At dinner she placed Bill's letter at John's place, and waited anxiously while he read it. She watched him smile and listened to his low chuckle.

"Well, Julia," he said cheerfully, "at least he spelled a few words correctly. That's something. And his grades have certainly improved."

"John, don't you think we should help them get out of that horrible, that awful little house?"

John put down his fork and looked at her.

"No, Julia, I don't," he said slowly. "They're in a veterans' housing project run by the college. They're with a lot of kids in situations almost identical to their own. They're happy and they're well. They have budgeted their money. Bill knows I'll help him if he gets in a jam. He told me he had a chance to buy that old washing machine for thirty-eight dollars and I sent him a check. He learned more from fixing it himself than if I'd sent him the money to buy a new one. No, Julia, Bill's doing all right."

There was a note of finality about his tones that every wife knows. Julia let the subject drop. But after dinner, when John had his pipe lighted and was seated in his favorite chair, she approached the other thing that bothered her.

"John," she said, "this afternoon Ned brought a boy over from the hospital. He wasn't an officer. He was a nice enough boy, but—well, rather ordinary. I think he had a back injury. His legs were paralyzed. He was a sergeant."

"That must have been Devon," John said. "I wish I'd been here. I'd like to meet him. He and Ned were together in the Pacific."

"Yes, I know," said Julia, "but I don't understand. I mean I didn't think an officer and a sergeant were so friendly."

John put down his paper. "Listen, Julia," he said. "The fighting on that island was very bad. The men of Ned's outfit knew that if they came through, it would be on a litter. Ned and Devon were both good soldiers. They could count on each other. They went through the worst of it together, and each was badly wounded. Because most of the outfit was wiped out, neither knew the other was living until they happened to meet at the hospital the other day. It isn't unusual. It happens frequently. Now do you understand?"

"Yes, I do," said Julia. "My goodness, it must have been a relief when each came to in a field hospital between nice clean sheets and knew he was honorably out of it."

John put down his paper. "It was no relief," he insisted. "They were ashamed. They wanted to get right up and go back into it. They didn't think they had any right to be safely out of the fighting while the rest of the men were still sweating it out."

"But it wasn't as if—"

"Julia," said John Hinsdale cheerfully, "sometimes I wonder if women are members of the human race. There's no use trying to explain a thing like this to a woman. No use at all. It's a waste of time. No woman understands the bond that exists between men who've been through hell together. It isn't gratitude, and it isn't love or duty. It's stronger than any of them. Now go away and let me read."

This was the second time she had been ordered hence in one day. Her head ached clear to the brim. She wanted to ask Minnie Mae to bring her some aspirin, please, and warm milk. She went for them herself. Minnie Mae might be still struggling with her wrath. Something peculiar had happened to Julia. For the first time in all her married life, she felt like a stranger in her own nice house.

The feeling increased with the weeks. While he awaited his discharge, Ned came frequently to the house, and often he brought with him one of more boys from the hospital.

At first, stung by her defeat, Julia tried to make up for it. The reaction was the same. The boys were polite and reserved. They did not accept her. She was the outsider. She was the one who did not belong. After that she avoided them.

She could not avoid the sound of their voices. Whether she liked it or not, she grew to know them and considerable about them. They discussed everything, except their own injuries. Sometimes they discussed the boys back in the ward, the ones who would not get out. Then their voices held an unexpected note of tenderness.

For one—the one who hadn't the guts to make the fight to get well, who was hard on the wardboys and made it as difficult as possible for everyone else—they had no use at all. When they discussed him, their voices were hard as iron. They would do nothing for him, not if he were drowning, they said, except maybe poke his head under.

But mostly these boys discussed ideas. They hated sham and pretense. They took apart the best precepts and left them lying, bloody and mangled, around the living room. They were serious, and they were funny. Although they did not know it, they made Julia uneasy. They made her think, which is a hard thing to forgive.

Once, as she came home from the bridge club, she met Jimmy Devon coming out the front door. He said, "Good afternoon, Mrs. Hinsdale," the tired look again on his face. He turned and smiled and called out, "Be seeing you, Mathilda" to Minnie Mae, and swung himself off on his crutches, leaving Julia to nurse her small squashed ego.

Then one day Julia found herself back on familiar soil. Ned's discharge came through. His mother brought the news in a flurry of excitement, and the two women put their heads together, picked up their brooms and began to sweep, sweep, sweep the way clear in front of their children, which they considered to be part of the job of a wife and mother.

Mrs. Stephens said that Mr. Stephens was going to take Ned into the business at an excellent salary. He was going to talk it over with him tonight. The only thing that bothered her was where the children would be able to find a place to live after they were married.

Julia agreed. This problem had bothered her, too. Only this morning, by the most prodigious luck, she had heard that the Mumford house was going to be for sale.

"Not that darling little place with the green shutters," asked Mrs. Stephens, "right here on this very street?"

Yes, that was the place. Of course, the price was a bit steep, but Julia was sure that John would help the children buy it—that is, he would if properly approached.

Mrs. Stephens laughed and said, "I know you, Julia," and Julia laughed, too, and said why not; after all, men took a bit of handling, didn't they?

After Mrs. Stephens had gone, Julia walked around the house in a happy maze of excitement and anticipation. She had forgotten the wounded. Her ego was normal again, plumped and rosy.

So many things to think about. Her thought raced ahead of her like a little dog scampering through leaves. China and silver patterns to be chosen. The linen situation to be considered. Household equipment and furniture, and thank heavens she'd had sense enough to save those two old twin beds and the gateleg table. They were stored in the garage loft, and with a little refinishing, the children would be able to use them nicely. She would ask Mrs. Burke to help with the decorations for the church. Mrs. Burke was so clever about that sort of thing. And the very minute Gerry knew the date, she must call Mrs. Sablon, the caseress. There was nobody like Mrs. Sablon. Nobody at all.

Through all this pleasant meandering Julia had a vague picture of herself walking up the church aisle at Gerry's wedding.

And thank goodness, she said to herself, *I have counted calories. My rear view is still passable.*

After dinner she sowed the seed of the Mumford house in John's mind. She waited until he was fed and comfortable with pipe and book. John looked up, grunted and made no comment, which was satisfactory. She would pour a little water on the seed, now and then, and wait for its sprouting. It would come up by and by, and John, the dear, would think he'd planted it himself.

The next morning Mrs. Stephens telephoned to say that when he approached Ned on the subject of entering the business, Mr. Stephens had found his son strangely uncommunicative. Mrs. Stephens was upset. Did Julia know the children's plans? Could she find out?

Julia thought she could. She assured Mrs. Stephens that everything was going to be fine, told her not to worry, and prepared for a heart-to-heart talk with Gerry.

She had no chance until John went off to some civic meeting after dinner, and she and Gerry were alone. Then she told Gerry of Mrs. Stephens' anxiety.

"I don't want to be too inquisitive, dear," she explained. "It's just that there are so many things to be considered that I really feel you should let me know Ned's plans as soon as you can."

"But I don't know his plans," Gerry said slowly.

Julia was horrified. "But, darling, you must. You couldn't have gone along all this time without—"

"Oh, we've discussed them, Mother. We've done little else. But, you see, it's Ned's decision. He's considering it very seriously. He has to make up his own mind."

"But, Gerry, it concerns you too."

"He loves me, Mother. That concerns me. You know I've been thinking a lot lately. I want something of my own to do, something that's vital to me, that I like to do. It doesn't make any difference whether I do it wonderfully or not. It's just that I think the kind of women you see here on this street are pathetic. I mean when their children are grown they're so jobless."

"Gerry, dear," said Julia, "that's fine, but it's a long way off. Now, about Ned; a woman can't wait always for a man to make up his mind, as you call it. After all, every successful wife knows that men are little boys."

"But, Mother, Ned isn't a little boy."

"Of course he isn't, dear. I mean every man likes . . . has times of wanting his wife to be a bit maternal toward him."

Gerry stood up. "I hope not," she said firmly. "That's the last thing in the world I want Ned to feel for me."

"Gerry, you know perfectly well what I mean. Behind every successful man—"

"Mother, you're not going to throw James M. Barrie's *What Every Woman Knows* at me. Oh, Mother! That's too quaint. Anyway, it isn't true."

"But it is!" cried Julia.

"Oh, no, it isn't. History proves that for every man who has succeeded because some little woman subtly shoved him into it, there is another man who got there in spite of women. Now take Claude Bernard."

Julia couldn't take Claude Bernard. She did not know who he was.

"What a life he had, poor thing! And take Chateaubriand."

Julia couldn't take Chateaubriand either. She'd never heard of him. Why—why, she asked herself, does one educate one's children? At the most inconvenient moment they pick up their knowledge and toss it right smack back.

"I'll have to watch you, Mother," said Gerry, with a little ripple of laughter running through her words. "You'll be giving me a good old-fashioned talk on the flowers and the bees."

Julia stood up also. "Gerry, stop that. Stop talking to me as if I were an old dodo like Mrs. Courtney."

Gerry looked genuinely horrified. "Why, Mother," she said. "What a terrible thing to say. Mrs. Courtney is the most modern woman on this street. When I'm her age I hope I'm just like her. Why, Mother, Mrs. Courtney is the only older person I let see my syllabus on Marriage and the Family."

"Gerry, you didn't."

"Yes, I did. And when she got to the part where the professor discussed sex, do you know what she said?"

"No, and I don't want to. Gerry, I absolutely—I simply won't—"

From outside came a persistent honking. Ned had come for

Gerry. She grabbed her coat. She rushed to the mirror to look at her hair.

"Good-by, dear," she said. "If he's made up his mind, I'll wake you up and tell you."

She dashed for the door, changed her mind and dashed back.

"Mother," she said in the voice of an angel, "do you know something? You're sweet. A little dumb now and then, but sweet. I'm very fond of you."

"Thank you," said Julia.

"Mother, do you know something else?"

"What, Gerry?"

"I think older women—especially wives—are little girls."

And having dropped the atom bomb, Gerry was gone, the door closing behind her with a cheerful and loud bang.

Julia tottered out to the kitchen to Minnie Mae.

"Minnie Mae," she said fervently, "I don't see how any woman has the courage to bring a child into this world—especially a girl child."

Minnie Mae looked up from the sink where she was washing the last of the dishes.

"Me neither, Mrs. Hinsdale," she said, "but we keeps right on doing it. You shouldn't have tangled with Miss Gerry, Mrs. Hinsdale. That chile's too much for you."

Julia thought so, too. She sank down on the kitchen chair. Little Lady arose from under the table and sat down close to her feet.

"Yes, suh," said Minnie Mae. "That chile's gettin' away from you, Mrs. Hinsdale. She's got her head hangin' out of the nest, gettin' ready to flop out and fly. No tellin' where she'll land neither."

"Minnie Mae," begged Julia wearily, "make me a cup of coffee."

"After dinner, Mrs. Hinsdale? And you always talkin' 'bout how it keeps you awake. My! My! If Mistah Hinsdale knew that! But don't you worry none, honey. I won't tell him nothin'. No, suh. You won't be sleepin' much anyway. You'll be lyin' there atossin' and atossin' and awrestlin' with the universe. Do you good to have a warm spot in your middle."

She fumbled in her apron pocket and emerged with a letter.

"It came in the late mail," she told Julia. "I've been savin' it for you. I've been savin' it until you digested your dinner. It was a mighty fine dinner and I didn't aim to have it spoilt. Bein' from Mistah Bill, it's bound to be kind of upsettin' in an interestin' way. You take it upstairs and read it, Mrs. Hinsdale, I'll be along with the coffee."

Julia took the letter and went up the back stairs to her room. She permitted Lady to accompany her, which was most unusual. She sat down on the bed and let Lady jump up beside her, which was unheard of. Lady couldn't talk. Lady couldn't say, *I told you so*. She couldn't say, *Well, it took me long enough, but here I am right on the best bedspread*. Lady could only sit close to Julia, her brown eyes full of sympathy and understanding, and this Julia found comforting.

She opened the letter.

"Dear Mother," she read. "We are all well. We have had some very unusual weather lately. I enclose a snapshot of the house. Tell Dad one of the other veterans bought some chickens. They didn't lay well because none of us considered half past four a propitious time to wake up and turn on the lights in the chicken house so the hens would go to work. I connected a mousetrap with an alarm clock which goes off and turns on the light switch. It works fine. I am working hard. Love. Bill."

Julia looked at the snapshot. In front of the house was Bill's wife, with Julia's grandson slung on her hip like a sack of grain. Both were smiling. The detached plumbing and the sunflower were missing. They were missing in a sea of mud. It was California mud, and therefore the finest, the wettest, the thickest mud upon which Julia had ever gazed.

Julia read the word "propitious" four times. There was no doubt about it. It was spelled correctly.

Sitting there on the bed with Lady beside her, she felt no longer like a stranger in her own house. She felt as if she were the only, the one solid remaining rock in the universe. Everything else was shaky. The old, the safe, the dependable world was slipping away. And this night Julia Hinsdale was scared.

Julia went through the next week with a sense of foreboding. It was a waiting week. It was one of those weeks when a woman watches the clock, counts the days, fiddles with her handkerchief, and runs every time the telephone rings. When it rang, it was only Mrs. Stephens calling up to find out if Julia knew anything of the children's plans. Nothing happened.

Nothing happened until late Sunday afternoon. Julia was in her room when she saw Ned Stephens coming up the walk alone. She heard him tell Minnie Mae he had come to see Mr. Hinsdale, and she heard Minnie Mae say, "Yes, suh, Cap'n Ned. You go right on into the livin' room. I'll cotch him for you."

She heard John enter and greet Ned. Then she heard the words she dreaded.

"I've come to tell you good-by, sir," Ned said. "I'm leaving. I'm going to Europe. I have a chance to work with a construction engineer."

John asked slowly, "Are you taking Gerry with you?"

"I don't know. I want her. I told her I didn't want her to make up her mind until she had talked with you. She went with me when I told my parents just now. We had a bad time. They're very upset."

"Yes, I know," John said. "They said you were trading security for uncertainty. They said you had no right to traipse across the world with Gerry. They said you'd have no safety."

"Why, yes, they did, Mr. Hinsdale. They said it was foolish of me. They said I had some sentimental idea of helping build up what I helped tear down. I don't know whether I can say this, sir. You see, ever since I've been home, I haven't belonged. I can't repeat my father's pattern. It's gone stale. It's life warmed up. It isn't what I want to do. This job is."

"Then you must take it. That settles it."

Julia heard them go to the door. Through the upstairs window, she saw them go down the walk to Ned's car, still talking earnestly. They stood there quite a while until Gerry drove up in her little convertible. She saw Ned drive off, and Gerry and John come up the walk. She hurried downstairs to meet them.

When Gerry saw Julia, she said to John, "Does Mother know?"

"I heard Ned talking to Dad," Julia told her.

They went into the living room and sat down. For a moment, no one spoke.

"The Stephenses are terribly upset," Gerry said then. "They've planned for years that Ned should enter his father's business. They feel as if the bottom has dropped out of their world. They want me to use my influence to make him stay."

"They want you here at home nearby," Julia said, "where they can see you, where they know you'll be secure. Every parent wants safety for his children. So do I."

"But I can't urge him to stay, Mother. It isn't what he wants to do. He doesn't believe in safety. He'd like to, but he doesn't. I remember quoting to him that old bromide about daring to live dangerously, and he laughed and said, 'Try and live any other way.'"

"You've made up your own mind, Gerry?" her father asked.

"Yes, I'm going with him. But it scares me. I don't like going against his parents. And Mrs. Stephens had so much to say against it. She said I must remember that Ned isn't like other men. He's lame. He's crippled. That he can't take the chances other men could take. She said we wouldn't have a large salary, and if anything happened, if things didn't go well, if Ned's leg—"

Julia could say nothing. Mrs. Stephens had said it all for her.

Mr. Hinsdale got to his feet and took out his pipe. "Did Mother ever tell you about the days when we were first married, Gerry? We had a fine big wedding. I spent almost every nickel I had on our wedding trip because I had a splendid job promised me. The day I was supposed to go to work, it fell through. My employer died of a heart attack." He tamped his pipe and lighted it. "I rustled another job—a good one too. But it didn't start for three months. In the meantime, all I could find to do was some surveying for a lumber company that was going to build a spur into their high timber."

He chuckled suddenly.

"Julia was too proud to go back to her family," he said. "She came along. I remember we lived in an old deserted caboose. Julia fixed it up. She hung cretonne curtains and covered the table with oilcloth. It was beautiful country deep in the woods. There was a stream nearby, a rushing mountain stream, best water in the world. Julia used to catch fish for us, Dolly Varden and rainbow trout, and fry them with bacon on a miserable little kerosene stove that we had to nurse along like an incubator baby. . . . Remember, Julia?"

"Yes-s-s," she answered.

"We used to study Spanish in the evenings. Had some crazy idea of going to South America. We used to read a book called Amarillo, by Ibáñez. We were young and ambitious, and we were very much in love. Do you know something, Gerry?"

"What, Dad?"

"I'd give almost anything to be back there in that silly old caboose for a few days. God knows we weren't safe. We weren't comfortable. We were something more important. We were completely and fully alive. Every day had an edge to it, whetted and keen."

Gerry sprang out of her chair. "Will you go with me, Dad? Will you go with me when I tell the Stephenses I'm going with Ned? Dad, do you remember the first time I went out with him, when I was so scared? You took the part of the girl. You showed me just what to do. Oh, you were so wonderful, and so silly, and so ridiculous. Show me now."

"Well," said Mr. Hinsdale, "now let me see. You can be Mrs. Stephens and I'll be you. Now let me see. If I were you, I'd say something like this—"

Julia had had enough. She crept silently from the room.

When Gerry and John had gone to the Stephenses', Julia was alone in the house. Even Lady was not there to help her. Minnie

Mae had taken Lady with her to call on a friend. Julia was alone in her nice living room, surrounded by all the carefully chosen, lovely things with which she had built a setting for her life, which hitherto had seemed to symbolize her safety and protection, to insulate her from the cold ugliness of reality.

They failed her now. The house gave no sound, no echo. The lovely things were as inanimate, as comfortless as a shroud.

But Julia was a lady. She'd do the best she could. She would accept it. Tomorrow she would feel better. Tomorrow was the day she had the bridge club. She would wear her new black. No, she wouldn't either. It would look too gloomy. Not for the world would she have the girls know she was disappointed in any little way. She would wear her print, very gay and becoming. She would use her old Wedgwood. She'd use her best hand-woven mats. She'd order flowers sent up, big sprays for the mantel and exquisite small buds for the old silver epergne. She would use—

The doorbell rang. Since Minnie Mae was not there to answer it, Julia went herself. She opened the door on Jimmy Devon.

"Oh, Jimmy," she said, "I'm so glad to see you. Do come in. I'm all alone. Mr. Hinsdale's gone over to the Stephenses' with Gerry. Ned's going to Europe next week and taking Gerry with him. Had you heard?"

Jimmy was disappointed and showed it. "Gee, Mrs. Hinsdale," he said, "I'm sorry they're not home. No, I can't come in. I only have a few minutes. The Red Cross car is waiting for me. You see, I'm leaving tonight. Just knew it today. I'm going to my uncle's farm in Indiana. He's going to build me a little nursery. Gee, Mrs. Hinsdale, will you tell them good-by for me?"

Julia said, "Of course I will, Jimmy. They'll be so sorry they missed you."

She went with him down the walk to the street. As they reached it, who came strolling by but Mrs. Hutton—all the people of the street reduced to the ultimate smugness.

"Good evening, Julia," said Mrs. Hutton. "How are you, my dear?" and Julia said she was fine, just fine, and this was Sergeant Devon.

Mrs. Hutton saw Jimmy's crutches and his useless legs. Jimmy saw the look on Mrs. Hutton's face, and he stiffened, ready for what he knew was coming.

"You poor boy," said Mrs. Hutton, as friendly as she could be. "When I see you boys, it makes me ill that such things can be. How were you injured?"

Now Jimmy Devon was on the Street of the Impeccables. He could not lie like a trooper—not with Mrs. Hinsdale beside him.

He could not tell Mrs. Hutton that he had fallen down the steps on his way to the latrine, which was his stock answer. He modified it.

"Well, you see, ma'am," he said flatly, "a mule kicked me."

Mrs .Hutton smiled at him. "Oh, you boys!" she said. "You are such jokers. But you'll get well. You'll be just fine. We had the most dreadful worry with my nephew this year. He wasn't in the Army. Oh, he did his part. He had a high position with one of the airplane companies. They considered him absolutely indispensable to their war effort. On his way to work he was in an automobile accident and broke his leg in two places."

Stop her, prayed Julia. *Oh, do stop her. Don't let her go on.*

But only God could stop Mrs. Hutton, and he was busy with more important matters.

"And he's fine now, as good as new," finished Mrs. Hutton two minutes later; "and you will be, too, sergeant. Because after all"—and here she beamed on Jimmy Devon, who would never walk again and knew it—"there's nothing the doctors can't do these days, is there? . . . Good-by Julia. . . . Good-by, sergeant. So glad to have met you," and Mrs. Hutton sailed on down the street.

They watched her disappear into the evening. Neither spoke. Tears filled Julia's eyes and coursed their way down her cheeks— tears of humiliation, not for Jimmy or herself, but for all the nice people everywhere who mean so well and understand so little.

The tired, patient look went away from Jimmy's face. When he spoke, his voice was gentle.

"Why, Mrs. Hinsdale," he said slowly, "do you care that much?"

She couldn't answer him.

"You mustn't feel so bad about it. A guy gets used to it. I guess if a fellow learns anything, he learns to be tolerant, even of fools. And anyway she—she meant well."

Julia found her voice. "That's just it," she said fiercely. "That's what makes it so awful. All the nice people mean well. Oh, Jimmy, I'm so confused. I'm so mixed up. I don't know the answer anymore to anything. Do you?"

He grinned, took one hand from a crutch and gave her arm a little pat.

"Why, hell, Mathilda," he said, "I don't even know the questions."

Suddenly they were both laughing, and Julia had never felt so

close to any human being as she felt to this boy at this
moment.

Jimmy was still smiling when he hauled himself into the Red
Cross car and was driven off.

Dusk was coming to the street now. As she turned to go up the
walk to the door, Julia saw Mrs. Courtney rustling her ancient
poodle home before the dark caught them.

"Good evening, Julia," said Mrs. Courtney. "Lovely night, isn't
it? How are you, my dear?"

"Not very well," said Julia. "I think I have growing pains."

Mrs. Courtney came to such a quick stop she pulled her poodle
to a skid.

"Good for you, Julia," she said. "My congratulations. Some of us
girls never make it." She was off again. "No, no," she said to the
poodle. "Not that way. This way. No, no, I'm not going to argue
with you. This way."

Julia went up the walk to the house.

When John Hinsdale came home an hour later, he found her
alone in the living room.

"Why, Julia," he said, "what in the world are you doing sitting
here in the dark?"

"Thinking," Julia told him. "I was thinking about Jimmy
Devon." And she told him of Jimmy's call.

"I've been thinking, too, Julia. I realize that you set your heart
on the children living here near us. I know it's hard for you. I'm
not very good at making speeches, Julia. I just want you to know
I'll try to help. We'll be alone. We've been through a good deal
together. We've been through success, and success is not an easy
thing."

He walked to the front window and looked out at the street in
the gathering dark. Julia walked over and stood beside him.

"You know, Julia, I remember a time when this street scared me.
I thought it was a dead end, a one-way street. It isn't now. Not for
me. I like to think that it leads to a little nursery somewhere in
Indiana, to an ex-Army hut in California. Soon it will lead to some
rubble heap in Europe."

She looked down at the street, not this time as a good address, a
lovely place for nice people to make their homes. She looked at it
long and carefully. It cannot be said that she understood it or its
way of life. But because of her need to follow those she loved, she
saw the street in this moment as it seemed to John, saw it with an
instant's complete clarity.

Why, it was no good to him anymore, she thought. No place, no thing had any purpose anymore, unless it led straight into living and the world.

—*March 20, 1948*

GIRL NOT WANTED

They keep on coming, I notice—
the young hopefuls with that bright determination to make good
in this world. I see them sometimes hanging around the pressroom doors in the old cobblestoned alley where rolls of paper are
unloaded from the trucks and the air is filled with the cackle of the
linotypes and the smell of the hot lead. They always look so young
and vulnerable, and yet so sure of themselves in that arrogant way
youth has.

But the ones I watch for are those like Sally Blake who lose their
surety when they climb the stairs to ask for a job. They wait on the
bench in the hall outside the city room, and they yawn and lick
their lips and fiddle with their fingers. They're not afraid to be
afraid. They're willing to blunder and fail, to find out where they
belong on this earth. Oh, Sally was a nuisance, all right. She
amused and exasperated us, and she broke our hearts a little.
Maybe that's what makes her different from the rest.

She came on a doldrums day. The huge city room was heavy
with a kind of slow, forced activity. I was banging away on my
typewriter, on the theory that the more noise I made the harder I
was working. I was thinking I might as well give up and go buy
myself a new hat—something cheerful with posies on it. And just
then a lift went through the room. Heads lifted, eyes turned, and I
looked up to see our Golden Girl making an entry from the hall.
And in that instant before she shut the door behind her, I saw the
kid waiting on the bench and was amused even then.

She was small and cute as a new penny, and at the moment her
opinion of herself was of equal value—she was that scared. She
was sitting up straight, both feet firmly planted for anchorage. In
one hand she held a pair of gloves. She held them defiantly, as if
she were saying, "My mother brought me up right. I own gloves.
But nobody's going to make me put them on." She wore no
stockings and no hat. She wore a plaid pleated skirt, a plain jacket
and a crisp white blouse, collar turned out. And in her eyes she
wore that desperately serious and searching look of the youngster

155

who is about to grab the world with both hands, knowing maybe it will shake her off.

And I smiled to myself and wondered if the blouse was worn out under the sleeves, and the plaid skirt a little thin in the rear. Mine were when I sat there. Then I forgot her. The Golden Girl had shut the door and was approaching the city desk, which is next to mine.

She was out of Keats; she dwelt with beauty. You see girls like that any afternoon in the most exclusive shops. They float toward you wrapped in a dream of their own lovely young perfection of type, and they scarcely see you at all.

Her name was Allison Hunt, and she was the publisher's niece, who had to be given a job. When he'd heard it, Brett, our city editor, said he'd give her a job all right. "I'll stick her in the corner by the little girls' room," he announced, "where she can cry and bother no one."

I distinguished myself with a few loud remarks about society girls who make small flights into reality by slumming on newspapers.

But Allison Hunt had surprised us all. She was democratic and friendly to everyone. We'd had to forgive her for coming from a golden world where the doors stand open, and admit she'd been smart enough to walk through them graciously. It had been a severe shock to us all to find ourselves liking her.

She smiled at me now and called out a greeting. Then she sat down in the spare chair by Brett's desk. I could hear every word.

"Guess what, darling," she said. "I got the interview with the Queen of Egypt."

Her voice was the charming throaty variety so in vogue now and so monotonous. Her term of endearment was that form of address considered suitable these days for everybody from best friends to butchers.

Brett reached for his pipe and leaned back in his swivel chair. He looked less tired, almost young again.

"And just how did you manage it?" he asked, because in a month nobody had been able to interview Queen Mother Nazli of Egypt.

"It was too silly, really! I remembered a young man I met while I was in school in Switzerland. He's in the consular service here now. So I called him up, and he called up the Egyptian consul, and the consul called back, and I called Herbert—you know Herbert; he's in charge of the Cababacera room—and Herbert put me at a table next to the Queen's at luncheon. Just one of those things."

"If I had some bacon, I'd have some bacon and eggs, if I had any eggs," said Brett. "What did she say?"

"Not a thing," said Allison emphatically. "I have let you down badly. She wouldn't talk about politics. She wouldn't talk about Palestine either. She wouldn't even talk about her emeralds. She likes San Francisco. She wore a print dress and a silver-fox wrap. The two princesses were dressed exactly alike, and very attractively. They spent an evening riding on the cable cars, and the colored gripman played boogie-woogie for them on the bell."

"That's a good touch. Play it up."

"Oh, I shall." She sat silently for a moment, looking at him, her eyes smiling. When she spoke, her tone was very casual. "I'm warning you, Brett. When I finish the story, I'm going to drop in at the Demings' buffet supper with you in tow. I promised I'd bring you. Lucienne Boyer's going to be there, and she'll sing if we ask her nicely enough," and she hummed softly under her breath, *"Parlez-moi d'amour."*

I wished I were someplace else. I wished I hadn't heard it. He had never learned to play, and it was part of her careful charm that she could teach him and make it seem easy. And if she knew that he was married, she knew also he wasn't working at it, and in her crowd, if a woman couldn't hold a man, it was considered to be her fault, and he fair game for anyone. Besides, it was none of my business.

I ran a fresh page into the barrel. I put my mind strictly on the job. And just then Gladys, the girl at the switchboard in the hall, clacked in on sharp heels, and said brusquely, "That girl's still waiting, Mr. Brett. Did you forget about her? Her name's Sally Blake and she wants a job."

Allison Hunt stood up slowly, prepared to go to her desk and write.

Brett put down his pipe. "Gladys," he said, "you know as well as I do there are no jobs."

"Oh, I know, but I just can't tell her. It would be like smacking a puppy in the nose. She's the youngest thing, and she's so hopeful it makes you kind of ache, and it's funny too." And Gladys laughed a little ruefully, and she said, "If you don't see her, Mr. Brett, I'll be falling over her feet for the rest of my life. And besides, she'll just sit there and learn the dictionary."

"The standard desk size," asked Brett, "or the unabridged?"

"The big one. Honest she will, Mr. Brett. She's improving her vocabulary. You know what she says about you? She saw you when the door was open a minute, and she says you're very— very—*distingué.*"

Allison Hunt laughed with delight. "Good for her," she said stoutly. "I'm on her side." And I smiled, and Mike on police desk, who had come over to stick some copy in the basket, grinned.

"Did you tell her it was my ulcers, Gladys?"

"No, I didn't. I should disillusion her! Let her dream while she can. But you know something? She might do for the switchboard relief the Big Chief promised me. She'd be quick."

Brett said, "Okay, Gladys; send her in," and Gladys went out, and in a moment Sally Blake came in.

A queer little hush fell over that end of the big room. I saw old Mike's face soften a moment. There was something about the girl, I think, that took each one of us back a long way to a forgotten bit of ourselves, except for Allison Hunt, perhaps.

For a few minutes after he'd greeted and seated her, Brett was busy on the phone.

She sat there waiting for him. She had no seasoning. And yet she stood out so clear and true that you could see behind her into the small-town life that sent her here, and it was a typically American life and part of all of us.

Brett put down the receiver, turned and began the interview. I made as much noise as possible, so the girl could have a little sense of privacy. Presently the voices stopped and I knew it was all over. I kept my head down because I didn't want to see the look on the girl's face, but I listened now. Why not?

"I advise you to give up the idea," Brett was telling her kindly. "Go back to the little dairy town and marry the boy next door. It's a better life than you think. Believe me, the glamour of a career is greatly overrated."

The girl stiffened. Her parents, whoever they were, had done their job well. They had built self-reliance into her, and courage too. When she spoke, her voice was soft and a little shy.

"'Glamour'?" she said. "I wish that word had never been invented. And 'career' too. I don't want glamour and I don't want a career. I want a job." And then her voice lost its shyness, as if she had tossed away every last vestige of fear. "It's only the stupid girl who thinks she's going to choose between marriage and a career," she said. "The smart one knows better. Why, my goodness, there are millions of women who are needed economically these days as men, not as women at all. And it doesn't make any difference whether they like it or not. Did you ever think of that?"

Brett hadn't, and he hadn't expected any flank attack either. He had expected to get rid of her as nicely and easily as possible.

"Well, I can see what you mean," he said. "Perhaps you could get some experience on the home-town weekly."

This was just what she needed. She leaped on it. "How can a girl get experience when nobody will give her a chance because she hasn't any?" she demanded loudly. "It's the silliest thing I ever heard. It's ridiculous. And it isn't dairy country. It's prunes. And there is no weekly. And there's no boy next door either. Nothing but six girls. Disgusting, isn't it?"

Brett began to look annoyed, and I thought, loudly enough for her to hear, I hoped, *Go on, kid. Don't stop now. Go on.*

"Miss Blake," said Brett firmly, "I sympathize with you. There are, however, no jobs here. Much as I would like to create one for you, it is not within my power. As a matter of fact, we anticipate hiring no one in the near future, with the possible exception of a relief girl for the switchboard."

And I thought, *Don't ask for the world, youngster. Grab a toehold.*

"I'll take it," said Sally Blake.

"You'll what?"

"I'll take it. I'm a whiz on a switchboard. I helped work my way through normal school on a switchboard. I'll take it."

He looked at her exactly as if she were a superfluous kitten that ought to be drowned before it can grow up to be a nuisance. Then he sighed heavily and picked up the telephone.

"Gladys," he said dryly, "I'm sending out Miss Sally Blake. Give her a try on the switchboard."

She stood up. She couldn't believe it. Then a look of utter radiance went over her face.

"Oh, Mr. Brett," she said, I didn't—I mean I never—Why, it's stupendous! It's just simply stupendous!"

"Now don't thank me. And another thing. I am not *distingué*."

"Oh, no—I mean I wouldn't dream—I wouldn't dare—I mean of course not." And it was true. He was Sir Galahad now. Nothing less. When she walked to the hall she had one foot in the *Idylls of the King* and the other in heaven.

When the door shut behind her, those of us who had seen and heard it looked at one another and smiled wisely. The society editor came over by my desk.

"Oh, Martie," she said, "she makes me feel like one of Methuselah's oldest wives. She makes me remember when I was enchanted by life too."

And I said, "I know, pet. She makes me feel the same way."

Tough old Mike chuckled and knocked out his pipe against a metal wastebasket.

"I've got my own memories, gals," he said, "and darned if that kid doesn't stir them up. Makes me remember how I used to walk ten blocks out of my way to go by Simmon's Bakery. There was a girl worked there, and there was something about the glint of her hair—"

"But you never—never spoke to her," I said.

"Naturally not," said Mike indignantly. "Certainly not. That would have ruined everything. She'd have turned out to have a voice like a buzz saw or no teeth in the front of her face. You must never speak to them."

And we all laughed—not unkindly—we all laughed, except Brett, and I think right then I sensed why.

For the next two hours we were really busy for the first time that day. I had only a glimpse of the girl, head bent to the switchboard. In the late afternoon the society editor came over and perched on the edge of my desk.

"Do you suppose our little chickadee has a place to stay, Martie?" she asked casually.

I said firmly, "Nobody is going to get me out of my comfortable bed and back on that wretched couch. Nobody."

"Me either. I'm through with it. Absolutely. Every working woman in her own bed. That's my motto."

We both sighed, and the society editor took a nickel from her purse.

"Okay, Martie," she said. "Let's stop bluffing. Heads you look out for her, tails I do."

And when the nickel came up heads, she looked relieved and just a little disappointed.

"You know something, Martie?" she said. "You won't sleep on that couch. She will. And if she phones her mother, she'll leave a little stack of nickels and dimes all counted out right by the phone."

And so it was. I took the kid home with me, and the next morning I wangled her a room at Mrs. Miller's down the street. Before we left the office that night I gave her paper, an envelope and an airmail stamp. She sat at one of the empty desks and wrote vigorously. I knew what she was writing. What working woman wouldn't? "I have a job on a real city newspaper. Isn't it wonderful? On my first day too. Of course it isn't very big. One of the women on the paper is taking me home with her and going to help me find a room. You don't have to worry, Mother. She's nice, and I'm sure she's respectable because she's quite old." Probably she underlined the word "old."

We picked up her suitcase at the Ferry Building. We rode the cable car home, sitting outside of course. We passed Chinatown and clanged up the crest of Nob Hill. The cable car stopped to unload, and right in front of us, probably on their way to the Top of the Mark for a cocktail before the buffet supper, walked Brett and Allison Hunt.

"He's wonderful, isn't he?" the girl said softly. "And so-o-o distingué."

Her interest was not personal. It was hero worship. No more. He knew everything, and she knew nothing. Never—well, not for years, anyway—could she aspire so high.

"She's lovely, too," she said. "Is he married to her?"

"No," I told her. "He's married. He and his wife have been separated for several months. She worked on the paper once. As a matter of fact, years ago, when they were first married, Ann was—was quite like you."

She looked at me in amazement. "My goodness," she said. "Poor Ann! What happened to them?"

"Oh, just life. Too hard a time for too long. Too many problems and not enough youth left maybe to meet them. You know how it is."

But she didn't. She didn't understand at all. To her, if you loved somebody, you went right on loving. Of course. Naturally.

I suppose in a story Sally Blake would have shown some bright bit of genius within the week and scooped the town. She didn't. At first she was our errand girl. Nothing more. No big story fell in her lap, and she built herself every opportunity that came to her.

Oh, we all imposed upon her. You always impose on the willing one. She must have lost five pounds the first month, running up and down the back stairs to bring us damp galley proofs. And one afternoon when she was going from desk to desk begging matches for the Big Chief's pipe, Pete, on sports desk, looked up and said, "Hi, kitten, how's our little naïve one?"

She went over to the dictionary to look up that word "naïve."

" 'Artless,' " she read aloud. "I don't think I like that. Is it true, Martie?"

I smiled and said, "You're maybe a little ingenuous, kid. Just a trifle. But you'll outgrow it. It's one of the few things I'm sure of."

She loved to be sent outside on an errand, and she always came back with little pieces of local color sticking to her like filings to a magnet. Did we know that at the old church of Nuestra Señora de Guadalupe the services were still in Spanish? Did we know there was a Basque restaurant beneath Russian Hill where the sheepherders met and wine was poured from a goatskin bag held up over the shoulder? Wasn't it marvelous? Wasn't it wonderful?

We would smile and agree it was. We teased her a good deal, I'm afraid. The only one who didn't was Allison Hunt, who was sweet to her in her charming, seasoned way. And Allison was too busy to bother with her much. She was annexing Brett as her own. He didn't even know it, I think. He was just drifting along, thinking he was doing nothing, which sometimes can be the most positive action a man can take.

In three months Sally was on full time, mornings on the switch-board and afternoons in the city room at the dark desk in the back corner. Hers were the little odd jobs considered too petty for all our experienced heads. She was doing most of them anyway. Might just as well have a desk of her own.

The first time she wrote a paragraph for publication, she hung around hours to grab a paper as it slid off the press to see her own words in print. She had sent down the letters-to-the-editor that day. The public pulse was a little thin, I guess. There hadn't been enough letters to fill the space, so Sally wrote one herself, com-menting unfavorably on a hole in the street left by the water department and unmarked by light or sign. The morning the letter appeared, the water-department head appeared also, and very mad he was. The kid hid down among the linotypes for an hour, and when she came up, it was to find her first effort glued to the Mourner's Door, which is the back of the door to the morgue where the staff pastes its mistakes.

She made the Mourner's Door three times in two weeks, and the last time she said loudly and cheerfully, "Well, I guess that makes me president of the Green Pea Society. When bigger boners are pulled, Blake will pull them." Now who can help liking a kid like that?

Brett could and did. It was pathetic to watch—the girl so eager and willing, and the man so hard. He was fair to her. He was scrupulously fair. That was all.

Sometimes we'd hear his voice booming on the phone. "Orga-nize it," he'd say. "Organize it before you call it in," and old Mike would look up and sigh and give me a look which meant, "Well, Martie, the kid's getting her ears knocked down again."

Brett pulled no blows, softened nothing. If the kid slipped on some petty detail, she stood on the worn spot beside his desk and heard about it in front of the room . . . and loudly.

"Check it," he'd tell her. "Don't believe anything you read. Verify it first." And when she walked back to her desk, one of us would give her arm a pat and say, "Sit down, kitten. Your head will clear in a minute." And like as not she'd stop and say softly, "But he's right. I should have checked it." You see, she still thought he was wonderful.

One day Brett sent the girl to cover the Chinese New Year. It was old stuff to us. It was her biggest story, the pond which to youth looks like the ocean, and when she came in and sat down to write it, her fingers couldn't move quickly enough on the keys, and her eyes had a glow.

Her story had the glow also. It was about the Hour of the Rat, which is the last hour of the Chinese New Year. When you read it, you were there in the hour, with the popping firecrackers and the feasts with the cries of "Goong haw sen hay!" and the golden lion, Sze-Tse, gobbling lettuce leaves tied to the doors with currency. You were there with the dragon, which was more than two hundred and forty feet long, with its lighted head and tail and the relay teams of Chinese youths who gave it life.

I said, "Nice little job, Sally." Each of us said it, except Brett. He said nothing at all, and toward evening of that day I saw the girl approaching my desk, and I knew the moment had come which I had been dreading.

"I can't please him, Martie," she said. "Why not? What's so hush-hush about him? What is this thing nobody mentions?"

I said, "Sally, I'm no psychiatrist, and I don't know how to explain this to you. I don't understand it very well myself. You see, twelve years ago Brett married Ann. I've told you she was a girl like you—young and eager and—"

"And dumb?" asked Sally firmly.

"No, not dumb at all. Bright and young and very much in love and believing in him. We liked them both. They were our bright young romance. At first, things went well for them, and then they had a long streak of bad luck—sickness and family worries, and a long separation during the war. They loved each other, but somehow they didn't make it. I guess maybe they were getting a little older . . . and tired."

She just looked at me.

"You see, Sally, it's a kind of a transference. He sees in you the youth, the belief he and Ann had once, and I suppose he resents it. I think he's taking out on you a little of his own disappointment in life, without knowing it."

"I don't understand it," she said.

"Sally," I said desperately, "in your story you wrote about the Hour of the Rat. Well, it's the Hour of the Rat everywhere these days. That's what it is. It's a time when most of us are confused and disenchanted. We've lost our belief in life. I guess that's it."

It wasn't an easy thing to say. It wasn't an easy thing to watch how she took it either. It wasn't fair, but she was going to meet it somehow. I saw her looking at our Golden Girl. I knew what she was thinking. I'd thought it myself. Here were two girls, each with good intelligence and background. One of them had to prove herself every inch of the way, and against obstacles; and the other had to prove nothing, just walk ahead graciously.

"You have to admit one thing, Martie," said Sally stoutly. "He's a good editor. You have to admit that." And then she smiled a little and she said, "And he's so-o-o *distingué*," and she walked briskly back to her desk.

In the next two months she grew up a bit. We didn't speak of her anymore as "the kid" or "the kitten." Her hair was no longer a sleek, tossed mane. It was short and trim. She'd saved her money and bought a city suit, simple and well cut, all the details quite perfect. She wore stockings always, and on the street she wore gloves. But the look on her face remained unchanged.

You know how it is when you start in to learn a craft. You plug along awkwardly and don't seem to be getting anywhere. Then along comes some little thing that makes you realize you're up a step on a new plateau. You find out whether or not you're in the right peg. That's the way it was with Sally.

One Sunday morning she was on the switchboard, all dressed up in her new suit because she had the afternoon off and was going to the symphony. And this was the morning a little oil town up the bay caught fire. When the call came in, there were only Mike and one other reporter in the city room. But Gladys had forgotten something and dropped in on her way to church. Mike put her on the switchboard, left the other reporter on the desk and took Sally with him to the fire.

The tanks caught and the little town burned down. You know how it is at a time like that. Everybody on a paper seems to know it and gathers in.

When I reached the office, I found Brett already at his desk, taking the news of the fire over the phone.

I heard him say, "Okay, Blake; go ahead. . . . Yes. . . . Yes. . . ."

I knew Sally was phoning in the facts for Mike. Brett was calling her "Blake" and he wasn't yelling at her, and I knew she was getting the first things first, and the second things second.

Other reporters were sent over. There wasn't another word from or about Sally all day long. She was in the midst of it. That's all we knew. It was evening when she came in with Mike. Her hands were filthy. Her lovely new suit was smudged. She'd had nothing to eat all day long, and she was utterly exhausted, and didn't even know it. She had been there. She had seen it all. Wasn't it marvelous? The tanks had blown up and the town burned, and she had been there and had some small part in it. Wasn't it stupendous? She sat on the edge of my desk and told me all about it. She paid no attention to Brett. But he saw her. He had a curious look on his face, and I knew he was remembering the first time he'd felt the thrill—the thing that never lets a newspaperman go—the feeling of being a kind of instrument through which life flows out into the print.

"You know something, Martie?" Sally said with wonder. "Before we left, the people of that little town were starting to clean up and start over. Imagine!" And then, for the first time, she must have realized how tired she was. She said shakily, "It's hot in here. I feel sort of queer."

"Put your head down between your knees," I said. "Quick, Sally."

She did it, but it was too late. She kept right on going to the floor.

In the confusion, it was Brett's voice that stood out above the rest. His tone was one of complete exasperation.

"Darn little kid!" he fumed. "Ridiculous, silly little kid! Probably hasn't been eating properly. What am I supposed to be running, a nursery?"

But when he picked her up, it was as if he lifted something infinitely precious. It was as if he held all youth in his arms—ours, and his own, and Ann's.

He fussed and spluttered all the way to the hall, where he put her down on the old bench, and somebody put an overcoat over her, and somebody rubbed her hands. The office boy rushed out for some hot soup, and Mike called a cab. Pretty soon Sally came around—very apologetic—and Mike and Gladys wrapped her up and took her home.

We filed back into the city room, Brett in the lead, quiet and solemn. He sat down at his desk, and he didn't say one word. Finally Allison Hunt approached him.

"Don't be too tough on her, Brett," she said. "She's young. She'll learn. Poor little kid, she never has done anything quite right."

He looked up at her, and he said slowly, "Nothing but the most important thing of all. Nothing but that. Of course I'll be tough on her. You're always hardest on your own kind. She's going to make a newspaperwoman. You bet I'll be tough on her. She has it. I don't know what it is, but she has it."

For the first time there was a crack in the Golden Girl's seasoning. She was unsure of herself.

"What-t-t?" she said.

"The heat of life in the handful of dust," said Brett slowly. "That's what Conrad called it, writing of his youth. And whatever it is, most of us would give anything to have it back."

The big room was very quiet for an hour or so. When the paper was put to bed and the staff began to straggle out into the night, Allison tried again. She stopped by Brett's desk.

"You coming?" she asked, her voice a little sharp.

He didn't look up. "No, not yet. You run along. I'm not through yet."

He sat there by himself. He didn't look at all distingué. He looked almost middle-aged, and very tired and a bit nicked by life. I saw him reach for the phone, pick it up, put it down again. And I covered my typewriter and got away from there.

At the door, I looked back. He was dialing a number, and I knew he was calling Ann. I was sure of it. I knew it by the look on his face. It was the kid's look which he had recaptured for a moment out of his past.

Today, on my way to work, I saw a boy hanging around the pressroom doors with his head up to the cackle of the linotypes and the smell of the hot lead, and he had the look, too, with all its belief and its hope. You know the look I mean—the one we all had once and lost somewhere along our way.

—*May 7, 1949*

SWEET AND RUTHLESS

When Joseph took his place out-
side the great glass doors of the famous old hotel on Nob Hill, he
felt again the quickening and the expectancy.

This hour of nightfall was the best of all, when San Francisco
seems to toss off the work and worry of the day and slip back into
its zestful heritage. It was cool, the air invigorating, and it seemed
to Joseph that the girl who was approaching the porte-cochere had
been patterned and cut precisely to the hour and to the mood.

She was old enough to have been frightened by life, and young
enough to believe in it still. She walked with a kind of relaxed yet
eager purpose, her arms swinging a little, the hands free and
open.

The first time Joseph had ever seen this girl he had noticed her
hands. They were like the hands of a young boy—slender, lithe,
strong and shortnailed. Joseph had considered them out of place
in so feminine a person, until later, when he found out who she
was and what she was doing there.

She was a color consultant. In those months when the hotel was
being redone—most of the work at night, so as not to interfere
with the day's business—the staff had grown to know her well
and like her. It had been her job to harmonize all the colors used in
the new décor, right down to the linens, even the paper match
packets. "Color can speed up work in factories and offices. It can
make people happier," she'd told Joseph, and she'd proved it too.
Under her skill one drab corridor had turned into an invitation,
and the dining room into which it led had paid off in the hard,
telling cash.

She reached the porte-cochere now and came up the steps. On
her face was that radiant look only one thing gives a woman, and
it has nothing to do with work.

"Good evening, Miss Manning," said Joseph, and she looked up
with that nice friendly smile of hers and said, "Why, hello, Joesph.
Didn't I see you at the Firkusny concert the other night? How did

you like him?" and Joseph said yes she did, and wasn't Firkusny wonderful . . . and he opened the door.

But the girl hesitated. For an instant her radiance was replaced by something very close to fear.

"Well . . . here I go," she said a little breathlessly. "Wish me well," and she stepped inside.

He had no time to wonder about it then. The early diners were beginning to drift out into the summer night. But he did not forget her either.

Inside the door, the girl's eyes sought the clock. She was five minutes early. She turned left to the flower stand. The bird-of-paradise flowers were unusually beautiful, and the wild yellow Mariposa lilies. Everything was beautiful this night.

She had noticed it all the way up the hill from work. At Grant she had turned into Chinatown to buy some small gift for John's mother. When the old Chinese handed her the small brass box with the cinnabar top, he had said, "The lady is happy tonight."

She had answered, with the frankness one can use to a stranger, "The lady is in love." And she had stepped out again into the evening, past the children calling back and forth in their singing Cantonese, and on up the hill.

She looked at the clock again. It was time now, and she was afraid. Every change, no matter how happy, carries its thread of fear. Any girl is nervous when she's about to meet her future mother-in-law for the first time, isn't she? Even though John's mother could not be much of a problem—not with three thousand miles between them.

She walked to the house phone and gave the room number. The voice that answered was eager and charming. "Ann," it said. "Ann, my dear? . . . Oh, I'm so glad you're here. . . . I hope you're as frightened as I am. Isn't it ridiculous? . . . Come up." Her fear fell away. When she left the elevator and saw the slender, attractive woman waiting in the open door, she knew it was going to be all right.

They had only one hour together until John was due to take them to dinner. John's mother was flying home on the night plane, called from her trip by the illness of a sister. John was flying with her, and then on to New York on a job for his firm. When he returned, they would be married.

The hour matched the night. They had so much to say that each kept interrupting the other, and then they'd laugh, untangle and start over. Ann had to tell John's mother their plans, and how they happened to meet, and wasn't it amusing they'd been to the same college at the same time and hadn't known each other, and wasn't

it wonderful they had so many friends and interests in common?

The mother had brought some pictures of John to show her.
There was one of him upon graduation from high school—very
solemn. There was another at fifteen in a track suit—all legs. The
third was the best of all—a little curly-headed child sitting in a
tiny rocker.

"Wasn't he darling?" said his mother. "Did you ever see anything so sweet? And that was his little red chair. He loved it more
than anything else. Why, I remember—he couldn't have been
more than two—he came screaming to me and said the little red
chair had walked up and hit him. So we spanked it, and he
stopped crying and laughed and laughed. After that, when anything went wrong, he spanked the little red chair."

She gave Ann the picture to keep as her own. Then they heard
John coming down the corridor, and the hour was over. The
evening began to fly away, each one trying to hold it back.

Dinner at a table by a window. The air beacons on the bridge
running across the bay on bright red feet. John holding Ann's
hand across the table. And in no time at all a scramble for the
luggage and they were standing under the portico with Joseph
calling them a cab. And John was saying, "Now don't forget,
darling. You can always get me at the Hudington in New York.
Write every day, even if it's just a line."

Then the two women were in the cab, and as John climbed in he
said, "I'll be gone three months, Joseph. You watch out for my
fiancée," and Joseph smiled and said, "That I will, Mr. Davis."

This was the last thing the girl saw—Joseph's nice face as he
closed the door on the summer night.

Joseph watched the cab until it disappeared around the corner.
He liked things to come out right, and this was exactly right for
both of them. Davis was a fine young man. He felt very pleased,
almost as if he had brought this about himself. Then he heard a
sound behind him and turned.

It was the Burke girl. Only, of course, she wasn't the Burke girl
anymore really. Briefly she had been Mrs. Peter Paul Stuyvesant,
II. Later she had been Mrs. Ralston Chalmers, III. Now, since her
return from Mexico three weeks ago, she was technically Mrs. C.
Burke Chalmers.

In animation she was almost beautiful. In repose she was almost
plain. Her fingernails were very long and bright, her hands never
quiet an instant. He wondered how long she had been standing
there, and at once he knew.

"Touching scene, wasn't it?" she said, and Joseph said nothing and was as sorry for this girl as he had been happy for the other. "Best-looking man I've seen around," she said. "No doubt a bit dull." She laughed—a low, bitter, unhappy sound. "Who was it, Joseph, who said that there are only two kinds of men? The ones who make dependable husbands and bore their wives to death. And the others who fascinate women and never should marry at all."

"I don't know," said Joseph, and wished she'd go away.

"Well, Joseph, I've tried two of the second type. I think I'm due for a change."

"You—you know Mr. Davis?" he asked slowly.

"Oh, no; I've just been watching him. I've made no effort to meet him, here." And she laughed again.

Joseph wished he could dislike her, and could not, because he understood her too well, because he knew what had produced her.

Why, it was Joseph who had opened the door of the cab when they brought her from the hospital—two weeks old and coming home to the twelve-room suite on the top floor. During her early years it was he who had opened the door when her nurse took her down twice a day for a walk in the little park. It hurt to remember it. She had looked like a little flower in her pastel coats and matching bonnets, her hands in tiny white gloves as immaculate as his own, her voice soft and very shy—all her manners beautifully disciplined and quite adult.

She was like other hotel children Joseph knew—abnormally sweet when small, then too wise and precocious, but always, to him at least, ineffably pathetic. And he had wished for her a backyard, faded blue denims with patches on the knees, neighborhood children and puppy dogs and cats. And perhaps she had wished them also, because at five she had staged her first revolt. And it was queer that this incident should stand out above all else, because it had to do with nothing more important than a dollar wristwatch.

The watch was so big it kept falling down over her little wrist. It made such a racket you could hear it tick at fifteen feet. Every time the nurse brought her through the lobby some stupid grownups sidled over and said in that cooing, simpering tone reserved for the hurt or the very small, "Cecily, I wonder if you can tell me what time it is?" In five days they had ruined the thing she loved best. Then one woman asked it once too often, and the little girl had let the watch slide off her hand and thrown it in the woman's face and begun to scream uncontrollably.

Her parents could neither get along nor separate. As soon as she was old enough, they sent her away to school—one school after another, and none of them working out very well. In a time of warm reconciliation they brought her home for a huge coming-out party, the hotel's great ballroom decorated with silver trees blossoming white orchids. The next year they took their battles to court, and it was then that Cecily Burke had scandalized the whole city by eloping to Reno with a boy she'd known six days.

She stepped out of the shadows now.

"I hate these cold San Francisco summer nights," she said. "I like hot summer nights. I like fireflies and moonlight, thin clothes and long frosted drinks. That's what I like, Joseph," and she flicked a cigarette into the drive with a long bright nail. "Good-by, Joseph," she said, and went in.

He did not see her around for several days. When he asked the clerk what had happened to her, the clerk said she'd gone away—East, he thought. And hearing it, Joseph felt afraid for one of the few times in his life.

The first Ann heard of Cecily Chalmers was from John himself. He wrote every day. He missed her. He loved her. The weather was vile. He'd had one lucky break. He'd met a girl who was staying at the Hudington, and what do you think? She was from San Francisco. She even knew old Joseph. Her father had a suite on the top floor of the hotel. He remembered seeing her in the lobby there, but never met her. Of course, he'd told her all about Ann right away, and when she found Ann was responsible for much of the décor, she was very interested. She had included him on a Sunday sailing party on Long Island Sound, and he had met a lot of her friends. They had all been lovely to him. It would have been perfect if Ann had been along.

Later there were other references, each so casual that Ann's only reaction was of relief that he wasn't too lonely.

Then one day a friend of hers returned from abroad. She had seen John in New York and was eager to tell Ann all about it.

"He's fine," she announced, when they met for lunch. "Can't talk enough about you. He's a darling, Ann. He took me to a party with a group of people he's met there."

Later her eyes grew serious and she said, "But you know something, Ann? I'll be glad when John comes home. I don't know what's the matter with girls nowadays. A woman used to give a man at least the illusion that he was doing the pursuing. She ran gracefully ahead and stubbed her toe, so he'd be sure and catch her. But now—"And she laughed a bit ruefully. "But now a girl takes all the initiative."

"I'm not afraid for John," Ann said stoutly. "He's too smart."

"Oh, I'm probably being silly. Frankly, I didn't like that Chalmers girl. But then, it's very difficult for a woman who stands five feet ten and weighs one hundred and forty-five to be tolerant about the small helpless female who seeks counsel from the big strong male. I couldn't get away with it if I tried." And they both laughed.

That night Ann reread all of John's letters, noticing each mention of Cecily Chalmers' name. She didn't sleep quite as well, and the next morning she began to mark off the days that brought him nearer home. Then something happened to turn her worry into fear.

John's mother telephoned. Her voice was nervous and tense. Ann must come East right away.

"I went down to see John this weekend, Ann," she said. "There's a girl after him. Poor darling, he doesn't even know it. Her name's Chalmers, and do you know what I think? I think she followed him East deliberately. I tried to suggest it to him and he was almost sharp with me. He said he's grateful to her for being so kind to him. Ann, I'm frightened."

Ann explained that she couldn't come East; that she had contracted work which must be done on time.

That night Ann didn't sleep at all or work much the next day. And then there came along one of those small happenings so nicely timed that they seem planned. John's employer and his wife asked her to dinner. Oh, she had no intention of saying anything at all. Not a word. But they were such a nice couple, and so devoted to John and pleased about his engagement to her that somehow it spilled out. She half expected they'd laugh at her and announce firmly that John was too wise to be taken in by any woman at all.

They did not. The husband's eyes grew serious. John's a fine chap," he said. He was thoughtful for another moment. "We won't take a chance on it," he decided. "His work is almost done there. I'll wire him tonight. I'll bring him back."

John arrived two days later. He hadn't changed. He was the same sweet, thoughtful person. When he told Ann about his trip, the name of Cecily Chalmers came in quite openly—she was a nice girl; she and her friends had been kind to him; Ann would like her.

The third day after his return John telephoned Ann at her office. Cecily Chalmers was in town. She had flown in yesterday, called most unexpectedly by her father. She couldn't wait to meet Ann. She did hope they could come to dinner this very night.

Another couple would be there—friends of her father; the man a famous engineer whom John really should meet, since they were in related work. Her father had expected to take this couple to the theater, but they had already seen the play, so, if John and Ann wished, perhaps the three of them could go.

John obviously wished to go, so Ann agreed. She wanted to see this girl.

They had a cocktail first in the penthouse of the hotel on the hill.

Cecily Chalmers greeted Ann with great friendliness and introduced her in almost too flattering terms. Yet when they went down to dinner in one of the big dining rooms, Ann found herself seated between the two older men, with John across the table next to Cecily. The conversation was bright and amusing, but Cecily confined the talk almost entirely to her trip East. And when they left the dining room, Ann found herself walking out with the father. Cecily and John brought up the rear.

When the three of them waited for a cab, Ann found an unexpected ally in old Joseph. When the cab drew up, he opened the door, said, "Mrs. Chalmers" and put her in first, then Ann, then John. Ann thought he gave her a quick little look of warning.

At the theater, Ann took the offensive. She let Cecily follow the usher down the aisle, and when they reached the seats and Cecily stepped back, Ann said, "You go in first. We'll put John in the middle, so he can talk to both of us."

It was ridiculous. When the lights went off, Ann wanted to laugh, but, nevertheless, she neither saw nor heard the play. She was old enough to guess what Cecily Chalmers would try next. She would seek and seize any opportunity to drive the first small wedge between Ann and John. Ann told herself that never, never would she give Cecily Chalmers the opening she sought.

Ann's counteroffensive consisted in keeping John busily and happily occupied when he was not at the office. They spent the weekend looking for an apartment, and by the most miraculous luck found one. Of course, it cost too much, but the owner agreed to lower the rent if they would do the decorating. John was sure he could do the kitchen and the bath. Ann was equally sure she could do the hall and the woodwork in the bedroom. They were so busy mixing paints and climbing stepladders that it was almost as if Cecily did not exist. Ann wondered if she had exaggerated the danger.

Two days later she knew she hadn't. John came to her more upset than she had ever seen him. Why in the world hadn't Ann called Cecily for lunch, as she had promised? The poor girl had been hanging around the telephone every noon, waiting for her to call. She was terribly hurt.

"Really, Ann," he said, "I don't understand you. Cecily thinks you don't like her. I had a very hard time to straighten it out."

Ann explained that there had been no definite invitation. Cecily had said, "Call me for lunch sometime," and Ann had answered, "I'll do that."

It did no good to explain it. Cecily had convinced John that Ann had been very rude. He was almost cross with her. The only reason this incident didn't expand into a bitter quarrel was that Ann absolutely refused to let it.

"I'm sorry, John," she said. "I'll call Cecily tomorrow."

She did so. With considerable self-restraint, she said she was sorry she had been so negligent about their luncheon date—she'd been terribly busy—she did hope Cecily could go to luncheon today or any day this week.

Cecily's voice was friendly and charming. She'd been busy too. Perhaps if Ann called next week—

When Ann hung up, she no longer disliked this girl, she hated her.

The next three weeks were a nightmare. There was no avoiding Cecily Chalmers. She forced her way in through such plausible small doors. She dropped by one night to see how the apartment was coming on, and when she left, John wasn't sure if they should have painted one wall in the bedroom to contrast with the others. And he wasn't sure that the colors in the hall were quite right. Each day Ann found it harder to stay within the anger line, and each day she grew more afraid to precipitate a crisis. Once she said lightly to John, "You know, darling, I'm beginning to think Cecily would like to take you away from me."

John was offended. He stiffened to Cecily's defense. She was a lovely girl. She was straight as they come. How could Ann make such a remark, when Cecily had been so kind to her?

Ann had one thing on her side. She had time. The apartment would soon be done, and there would be no reason why they shouldn't arrange their marriage plans. Then this, too, was threatened.

John phoned one Saturday afternoon, his voice excited. Did Ann remember the engineer they'd met when they had dinner with Cecily? Well, he managed a couple of mines in South America and he'd just placed an order with John's firm. It was a big deal, and it had come through Cecily's father, who was part owner of the mines. The machinery would have to be taken apart and flown in, and there was some possibility that John would have to go down and supervise its reassembly. In that case they might have to postpone their wedding, since it was no trip for any woman. Well, they would meet that when it came, but right now could Ann come up to the penthouse? He had just finished going over some of the final details with the engineer and Cecily's father, and Cecily thought it would be nice if the three of them went out to dinner and celebrated.

And, oh, yes, one other thing. Cecily said to be sure and send her name up by the desk clerk, because some pest had been bothering her for two days.

For a moment she stood motionless. She had never before felt so angry, so outraged. All her life she had despised the things that only women can do to women, and refused to have any part of it. But she loved John, and she knew now she'd do anything to keep him. And she knew also that it was time for this shadow battle to be brought out into the open. But how?

She walked to the hotel. Under the porte-cochere stood Joseph in his fine uniform and his immaculate white gloves. When she started up the steps, he came forward. And she remembered suddenly that once before Joseph had been her unexpected ally.

"Good afternoon, Miss Manning," he said with his nice smile. "How are you today?"

She couldn't answer him. She couldn't keep the tears from coming to her eyes.

"Is it Mrs. Chalmers?" Joseph asked, and she nodded.

For a moment, his old face looked sad. "Her second ex-husband has been hanging around for more than a week," he said. "Did you know that?"

She shook her head.

"She won't see him. She won't admit anyone to the apartment unless she knows beforehand who it is. Every guest has to have his name sent up."

She said nothing.

"Mr. Chalmers is in the Chinese Room," he said. "He's been drinking," and he held the door open for her.

She didn't stop to think. If she thought, she wouldn't do it. She walked straight to the Chinese Room, and asked the first waiter she saw which man was Mr. Chalmers. She walked over and sat down on the next stool.

"I understand you've been trying to see Cecily Chalmers," she said, and he looked up and said, "That's right. What's it to you?"

"It's a great deal to me," she said. "She's after the man I love and am engaged to marry. She's up there with him now. They're expecting me. I'll talk to her on the house phone and you can go in my place."

He put down his glass, and said, "Okay. Let's go."

They went to the house phone, and she asked for the penthouse. Cecily answered, and when Ann gave her name, Cecily said with a little tone of triumph, "Come up, Ann. Isn't it wonderful about John's trip?" And Ann said indeed it was, and she'd be right up. When she turned, the young man was already on his way.

She went out the big glass doors. Joseph was waiting for her.

"I never thought I'd live long enough to do such a thing," she said. "I never knew I could hate anybody as I hate Cecily Chalmers."

"She was a nice little girl once," Joseph said slowly, and he told her about the child with the dollar watch and about her parents using her as ground for some of their better battles.

"I wish you hadn't told me," Ann said. "I don't want to understand her. It makes it harder."

When Ann reached her apartment she walked the floor and told herself that it would be all right now. Pretty soon John would call, and he would say, "Ann, when dumber men are made, I'll be it." They would make a joke of it, discussing it lightly without any blame. And then they would put it down and it would be as if it had not happened.

Finally the phone rang, and it was John. He wanted her to come over right away. He'd be waiting for her at the door and they'd go to dinner—just the two of them. He had something to tell her. She'd never believe it.

This time when she went up the hotel steps, she scarcely saw Joseph standing there. She saw only John.

He had never seemed so glad to see her—almost pathetically glad. He tucked her hand under his arm, and he never let go of it an instant until they were seated in a quiet corner of one of the smaller dining rooms. Then he began to talk.

"I just can't believe it," he said. "We were sitting there in the drawing room when the bell rang. Cecily answered it. It was Chalmers, and I couldn't help overhearing some of what was said. He was angry. It had something to do with the divorce she obtained in Mexico. He thought it wasn't valid. She took him into some other room, while I waited, growing more and more uneasy. And then she came back . . . alone." He stopped a moment.

"Yes, John."

"She was angry," he said. "Oh, not at me. She was angry at you. She said you had deliberately sent the man up in your place. Can you imagine that? And when I denied it, she—she lost her temper completely. The things she said about you! Why, she even attacked Mother. She accused her of trying to break up any friendship between Cecily and me. And when I defended you and Mother, she said I was the dumbest man she'd ever known in her whole life. She said when dumber men were made, I'd be it."

This was Ann's cue. It was her chance now to make a speech. It was her opportunity to admit she had sent up the ex-husband, and that she had done so in desperation because when it came to women he was dumb all right.

She said none of it. Any woman will know what she did say.

"Now, dear, don't be so upset. It doesn't matter, darling. Really, it doesn't. I don't care what Cecily said about me."

"But I care," said John, and started up again.

He talked and he talked. Oh, she had him back. He was hers. He was safe now. Only something spoiled it. Something queer was happening. It seemed to Ann that while she listened she was seeing a little boy and a little red chair, and hearing his mother say, "Spank it, darling. Spank the bad, the naughty little red chair. Spank it hard." And she knew that was what he was doing now. Cecily had become the little red chair. And she knew that she was taking the mother's role. She was helping him.

He wouldn't go to South America without her, he said. He was afraid this was the end of their friendship with Cecily. He was sorry, but what could a man do?

Finally John's ego was back to normal. His ruffled feathers were smoothed into place. They left the dining room. They walked through the lobby, through the glass doors and out into the night.

It was a night like the other—poignant and invigorating.

"Lovely evening, Mr. Davis," said Joseph.

"Isn't it? . . . No taxi, thank you, Joseph. We'll walk."

The night must be the same, the girl told herself. *Nothing must change.*

But something had changed, nevertheless.

Joseph noticed one thing. The hand by the girl's side had the thumb close against the palm, the fingers tight around it.

And when they stepped out into the evening, it seemed to Ann that she could hear some small voice deep within her, sobbing bitterly, and she knew it was the last of the girl in her who had been outgrown this night, and would not come again.

—*January 14, 1950*

THE WOMAN WHO MEDDLED

There was no more attractive or
charming woman in the town than Claribel Holmes. Everybody
said so. The mere mention of her name caused as definite a
reaction as a bit of radioactive material on a Geiger counter.

"Oh, do you know Claribel?" somebody always asked with
quick delight, as if this were a mutual bond. "Isn't she the most
wonderful person?"

And it was true; she was. Good fortune had attended Claribel at
birth and pursued her thenceforth. It had placed her on Easy
Street and kept her there, neither burdened by the responsibilities
of too much nor hemmed in by the bitter walls of too little. It had
given her good looks, good health and a husband who was a
natural-born monogamist. Claribel's William not only refrained
from climbing the fence beyond which the fields look greener; he
didn't even glance over its top. Together they had worked hard
and honestly, and they had prospered and produced two sound
children, neither a problem to anyone.

All this Claribel had accepted as due any nice woman . . . but
so graciously. She was generous. She was fine. She was fun. And it
is a tribute to Claribel that in the harmonious hum which responded to her name there was rarely heard a flat or even a minor
note.

Mrs. Twitchett intoned one, and loudly, at a tea. "I'm declaring
open season on charming women," she announced. "Last Saturday
I reached the butcher's so late his shelves were almost bare. I was
just leaving with some hamburger when in sailed our Claribel.
She smiled on the butcher and said, 'Why, Mr. Meek, surely
you've saved me some small soupbone,' and he—the idiot—nearly
fell over his feet rushing into the cold-storage room. And what do
you think he brought out for her—two fillets and a sirloin. Now,
honestly—"

The girls all smiled tolerantly, knowing well what was wrong
with Maud Twitchett. Poor dear. She had a beautiful mind in a
plain head.

Old Mrs. Courtney came out with a small minor chord once. At seventy-eight, Mrs. Courtney's own charm was as dry as her bones.

"Claribel is a thoroughly nice woman," she said. "It is inconceivable that she will ever dabble a toe in any of life's small mud puddles which beset less fortunate mortals. But sometimes I think there's a special danger that awaits the very successfully and happily married woman. And now that I'm older I've come to consider it one of the deadliest of them all . . . especially to other people." She was silent a moment, then chuckled. "But there's one thing. If Claribel falls into it, she'll never know it, will she?"

Mrs. Courtney was both right and wrong. Claribel tumbled into the deep waters, and for ten whole minutes knew herself to be both cold and wet.

It began one afternoon shortly after the marriage of Claribel's daughter, Susan. All was in order again. The best china was back on the top shelves. In the kitchen, Minnie Mae was ironing the last of the fine line. In the living room, Claribel was trying hard to make what the psychologists call "one of a woman's major adjustments."

How lonely was the house. For months it had throbbed with life and youth. Now—Susan gone to her new home, and Bill, the son, back in college—it seemed suddenly entombed with quietness.

Wasn't it unfair, she thought. When a woman's young and ignorant, her children and her husband need her desperately. But just about the time she matures a brain in the head, her children are gone, and her husband so well established even he doesn't need her quite in the same way—to go ahead sweeping the little walks clean, to stand behind, pushing him gently and very cleverly, of course, into success.

And then what does she do? What takes the place of those early, striving, zestful years? What gives life back its bright and cutting edge?

Stop dramatizing yourself, she said to herself. *Be sensible. Be brave,* and a sudden flicker of interest crossed her face. She had remembered something—a small incident that had been teasing at the edges of her mind ever since the wedding. She went into the kitchen.

Minnie Mae looked up from the ironing. "Bettah stop prancin' 'round, Missis Holmes," said Minnie Mae. "You's wearin' out the rug. Sit down and rest you' feet, honey. You can bawl if you want to. Won't bothah me none."

Claribel sat down. "Minnie Mae," she said, "when a woman's children are gone, there's only one thing for her to do."

Minnie Mae put down her iron with a thump. "Dat's right," she said positively. "When a woman gets middle-aged she's gotta keep her hands so busy she don't notice the dizziness in her own head."

"Minnie Mae, I don't admit for one minute—"

"No woman admits . . . 'ceptin' 'bout every othah woman," said Minnie Mae. "Now I tell you just what you do, honey. You go down to the store and buy you'self ten yards of apron material for the church sale. Missis Holmes, when you gets through cuttin' out dem aprons, you' poor back'll ache so you won't know you's got a head."

"I have a much better idea than that, Minnie Mae. Now listen carefully. Do you remember when Susan tossed her bridal bouquet straight to the maid of honor . . . do you remember the girl's face as she caught it?"

Minnie Mae reflected. "Yes'm'm'm," she said slowly. "I remember. I thought for a minute she wasn't going to try and cotch it. She looked mighty miserable."

"Exactly. So I was right. I didn't imagine it," said Claribel triumphantly, and she darted into the dining room, plucked the car keys from the buffet, and was back in an instant, heading for the back door.

Minnie Mae followed her. "Missis Holmes, you ain't gwine to reform nobody, is you?" she asked doubtfully. "Missis Holmes, all any married woman can do for any single girl is to ask her to dinnah with a hard-workin', good-lookin', unencumbered and absolutely unattached young gentleman. Dat's all."

Claribel was in the car now, and starting the engine.

"You bettah stop at the store," called Minnie Mae, "and buy dat yardage! Do you heah me, honey?" and the last thing Claribel saw as she drove off into her new profession was Minnie Mae's big, anxious face.

She drove happily, feeling somehow a little excited. She remembered again the wedding reception—all the nicest people gathered to pay homage to youth which must be served. And she remembered the girl's face in its unguarded moment, with its strange and haunting look, as if—and here Claribel thought it out carefully—as if her youth was not to be served, but must serve instead.

Oh, something was wrong. Gail Dearborn was to be married herself in a few weeks, and no girl in town deserved happiness more. It was years now since her father, a civilian engineer, had been caught by a Japanese patrol in the Philippine hills. There had been some mix-up about his insurance payments while he was hidden out and before he had been killed. Mrs. Dearborn had gone to work in her late fifties. Gail had finished college on a scholarship and taken a job teaching.

Now—after all that—something was wrong. Something big and threatening. Claribel was sure of it. And who better than she to help straighten it out, she who liked people so much, who wanted everyone to know the full and happy life.

She parked her car in front of the grammar school where Gail taught. The dismissal bell rang, and the children began to flow out into the street. Presently the teachers would follow. She watched and waited. For an instant she felt some small doubt.

This was no picture school bordered by trees and well-clipped lawns. It was drab and ugly, squatting here on the wrong side of town like some huge melting pot into which poured the lusty youth. And when the teachers began to leave, one by one, Claribel saw etched on their faces the battle's mark.

They were older, most of them. They were good, fine, conscientious women too. But so different. All their virtues hung below the hem. Theirs was the look of those whose convictions have collided with the realities.

Frustrated, said Claribel to herself with a wise little nod. *Why, I don't suppose most of them have really lived at all,* and then she forgot her doubt as she saw Gail Dearborn coming slowly down the steps. She touched the horn and waved, and the girl's pretty face brightened as she hurried to the curb.

"I've come to borrow you, Gail," said Claribel with her best charm. "My dear, I'm lonely. I feel exactly like some melancholy bossy who has lost her calf. Get in and I'll drive you home." And the girl laughed and climbed in beside her.

It was almost too easy. Claribel began talking of the wedding. How lovely Gail had looked. How determined Susan had been to toss her flowers straight to Gail, because it was she Susan wanted to be the next to carry on the pattern—the nicest tradition of them all. And how appropriate, too, since Keith Blake was due to arrive from Manila in a few weeks and carry Gail off.

The girl said nothing.

And that reminded Claribel. When Keith arrived, she wanted to give a supper party for the happy couple. At the country club perhaps. And it was high time she and Gail worked out at least a tentative date.

And now the girl had to speak. She said slowly that she was afraid her marriage was going to have to be postponed—perhaps for a long time—and Claribel said, "Oh, no, Gail," with all the sincerity of her big well-meaning heart, and tears rolled down the girl's cheeks as she told her all about it.

It was a trite story. Yet with her quick mind Claribel saw all its quiet drama unfolding before her. Doctor Peabody's nurse telephoning the girl the day before Susan's marriage, asking her to come in, the doctor wanted to talk to her, and perhaps it would be just as well if she didn't mention it to her mother. The girl hurrying to the clinic—scared, of course—and Doctor Peabody taking her into his private office. Claribel knew him. Such a brilliant man. Why, she could almost hear his words.

"Sit down, Gail. Your mother was in for an examination this morning. I sent her home in a cab and told her to go to bed. Now—now, nothing too alarming. With the proper care she'll have many good years ahead of her. Without it, she won't last three months . . . too much worry and strain . . . never work again . . . six months in bed . . . gradually let her up a little. . . ."

"I told him all about Mother's small income and my coming marriage to Keith," Gail said now. "And I told him about my brother, who lives in the East and has three children under five and a wife who hasn't been at all well since the twins' birth."

"Yes," said Claribel.

"He didn't say so directly, but I'm sure he doesn't think my brother's home would do for Mother. He was quiet a long time, and then he said a strange thing. He said no real problem can be solved, only outgrown."

"Oh," said Claribel flatly, who had never had a problem she couldn't solve, and who expected something better from Doctor Peabody.

"He gave me a list of rest homes," Gail said. "I telephoned my brother and he's sending a check each month. It isn't very much, but it will help. And every day after school I've gone to see one of the rest homes. There are several very nice ones, but far too expensive. There is just one left."

"It'll probably be exactly the right place," said Claribel brightly. "We'll go see it right now." And so they did.

It was a big old house set far back from the street, and the woman who answered the door wore a nurse's uniform and had a fine, kindly face. She quoted them a reasonable weekly rate and showed them the place, the rooms spacious and sunny, everything spotless. Gail's face was bright with hope. Then the nurse showed them the patients.

There was a sweet-faced woman in her nineties who was blind, and several stroke cases who couldn't speak. There was one little old lady who talked all the time. Oh, perfectly harmless, the nurse assured them; just a case of advanced senility.

They thanked her and left. When they were in the car again, neither mentioned the rest home.

"We'll get Minnie Mae to make us a pot of strong coffee," announced Claribel cheerfully. "Heaven knows we both need it."

When they reached home, and Claribel had lighted the fire in the small library, and Minnie Mae had set the coffee tray on the low table by the chintz-covered sofa, the house seemed no longer entombed with quietness. Life had back its bright and cutting edge. Here was the girl, so young, confused and vulnerable. And here was Claribel playing the vital role of the wise one. She went right into it like a large, white, benign hippo knocking down trees in a jungle.

"Gail, if a girl wants life, she must fight for it," said Claribel. "You mustn't be weak or sentimental. You must not let life turn you into a house mouse."

The girl looked up. "Mother's a dear," she said. "She's unselfish. She's wonderful."

"Exactly. And that's why she'll agree that you must send her to your brother's. He's had his chance for a normal life. Now it's your turn."

The girl said nothing. Claribel poked and prodded and banged away at her. Did she want to be a family martyr? Did she want to be thwarted and frustrated? Did she want to have on her face that queer look of those women who haven't lived at all? Did she want to end up as one of those dreadful career women who are trying to be men and don't know it?

And the girl said no, she didn't, and looked defenseless and horribly afraid, as if all her bright youth were in small pieces around her slim feet.

Claribel said all the things every married woman has ever said to any single girl, and she said them better and twice over. And yet in Gail there seemed to be some small, resolute and compact core she couldn't crack, couldn't even touch. When it was done at last, and the girl had promised to try to find some solution, and thanked her and left, Claribel knew that she had failed.

"What can I do?" she asked Minnie Mae, who had come in for the coffee tray. "If she doesn't marry Keith when he comes for her, she's sunk. What can I do?"

Minnie Mae did not look at her. "You can mind you' own business, honey," she said.

"But, Minnie Mae, this is my business. If I don't take an interest, who will? Life's going to trap her. Don't you see it?"

"I see it, and I heard it, too," said Minnie Mae. "Had my good ear to the crack. You atalkin' and atalkin', and poor Miss Gail, with her heart all busted, mindin' her manners. Lan' sakes. If she can taken that, she can stand anything. Dat girl's got spunk."

She started for the door with the tray.

"Missis Holmes, all women can't be just like you, even if you is nice. No, ma'am. And all women can't have husbands like Mister William neither. Dat man's nothin' but an angel put on this earth purely by accident."

"Nonsense, Minnie Mae. He's just as bad as most men. I've worked harder on him, that's all," and Claribel forgot Minnie Mae and went right to work planning her next strategy.

It was Claribel who took it upon herself to write to Gail's brother, explaining the situation and suggesting that he take the mother.

The answer was immediate. The brother was much concerned. But the children were noisy, the house small, the stairs steep, his wife's health poor. If Gail could just postpone her marriage for a year or two, perhaps then—

Wouldn't you know it? Wasn't that just what you'd expect? Claribel decided on a last desperate move. She had a long talk with Keith Blake before he'd even seen Gail, whom he'd come to marry and carry off to Manila. Such a nice boy, and so patient and cooperative. He thought Claribel was the most charming woman he'd ever met. He thought she was wonderful. He agreed there was only one thing to do—to put pressure on Gail; nicely, of course, but forcibly. To make her see that if she let life's train go by their station, it would probably never back up.

Even Claribel never knew quite what happened between Keith and the girl. Gail never said, and the next day the boy left town and never came back. The ring disappeared from the girl's finger.

Oh, tongues clucked from the North Side to the South Side. Poor girl! Poor duty-bound foolish little house mouse! Everybody had to admit she took it well. She simply kept her mother in bed and gave her the most precious possession age can have—to feel needed and loved.

"You know what will happen, William," Claribel said at dinner one night. "Keith will marry someone else within a year, and Gail will never marry at all."

"It seems to me it's a little early to write any epitaphs," said

William. "I've seen many very attractive single women who seem to get along happily without—"

"Oh, no, they don't, dear. They're just bluffing it out. What else can they do? But there's one thing for which I'll always be grateful to Gail. She's taught me where my interest lies. In people, William. People are my hobby."

What William was going to say to that, even he never knew, because Minnie Mae chose that moment to set his coffee down with such a thump it spilled over the white cloth. And the next morning when Claribel went down to breakfast, she was met by no aroma of coffee and toast. The kitchen was empty. Affixed to the table by the sugar bowl was a small note.

"Goody-by, honey," wrote Minnie Mae. "I just can't stand workin' for no happy meddler."

Claribel felt very bad about it. Minnie Mae was ignorant, of course, but such a lamb. And after all, who was she to hold ignorance against anyone?

In the next few years Gail Dearborn attained a kind of invisibility. After the first six months, Doctor Peabody let her mother up part of each day. She lived and stayed alert and happy, managing to be useful in innumerable small ways. The brother's wife died, so of course he couldn't help out much. Once in a long while Claribel saw Gail on the street, still pretty, but on her face the look of the convictions smacking into the realities. It always upset Claribel a little.

"If I had been wiser, I could have helped her to a normal life," she would say, and there responded always a loud and reassuring chord, "Nonsense, Claribel. You did everything you could. You were wonderful. We all know that."

Claribel and the friends of her own age were all busy adjusting themselves to the middle years, each in her own way.

Maud Twitchett had taken up the piano after long absence. It was said that when Maud practiced, the neighbors shut the windows and removed themselves to opposite sides of their homes.

"Poor Chopin," Maud told the girls. "I am slaughtering his nocturnes, one by one. But what a lovely time I have doing it."

The town's gardens had never looked so well, the gardening club having a large middle-aged attendance. Almost any spring morning you could see its members messing around with Mother Nature, ruining their hands. And almost any summer night you could see one or two out prowling the flower beds with a flashlight, happily plucking snails from the petunias.

But Claribel did not practice the piano, upholster the furniture, garden, learn a language or study political economy. Her hobby remained people. In a sense, she became a sort of amateur consultant. Just let some young bride get herself tangled up in a complicated marital problem, and Claribel, who had been so successful at her own marriage, could tell her exactly what to do, and usually did. But so generously.

Like most of the women her age, Claribel gave considerable time to charitable and civic affairs, and how natural that her charm and attraction should find their reward.

Maud Twitchett put it rather well. "Let this town have to raise thirty thousand for some good cause," she said, "and where are the rest of us? Out pounding the pavement, going from door to door, getting put off and sometimes even insulted. And where is Claribel? Up on the platform with orchids on her shoulder. Now, honestly."

And though the girls knew there was truth in this, they knew also that Maud wouldn't look half so well on the platform, even with six dollars' worth of orchids; and being modest, they weren't sure they would either.

Then one day the town found itself involved in a serious problem. The lusty youth on the wrong side of the tracks formed a gang of hoodlums, prowling the streets at night, stealing, smashing the best plate glass, and bloodying the noses of more privileged youth. It was said to be concerned with dope traffic.

The mayor tightened the curfew law and appointed an investigating committee—Claribel the only woman on it. The police enforced the law to the letter and maybe a bit beyond it, and the gang responded by waylaying and beating up three officers, and so skillfully that only one boy was caught who had tripped over a gutter. He was said to be one of the ringleaders.

The next morning, the police chief, the mayor, John Collins, the assistant district attorney, and the committee, complete with Claribel, questioned one Fernando Gonzales, aged fourteen.

Fernando said nothing. He wouldn't snitch. He sat there, silent and apathetic. Mr. Collins—an attractive young man—and the police chief conferred and brought in the boy's mother.

She sat beside him, a small woman with a face strained with worry. She took his hands, and she said in Spanish, "My son, I am your mother. Tell me everything." And the boy said nothing, and the mother began to cry over and over, "He good muchacho, he good muchacho—"

Mr. Collins and the police chief conferred again, and called the principal of the school that the boy attended, who promised to come right over. While they waited, Claribel asked if she might try. After all, she had a son of her own, and therefore knew all about boys.

Claribel went right at it. She questioned him persistently, making an excellent appeal to his better nature. But Fernando Gonzales only stared at her and said nothing. She kept on, more and more vigorously, until suddenly a voice said, "Stop that! Stop it this minute!" and there was Gail Dearborn. The principal had brought her along because, as the boy's counselor, she knew him better than anybody else.

She didn't look at all like the house mouse that Claribel remembered. She wasn't young and vulnerable and afraid anymore. She was thirty, still pretty and very mad.

"What are you trying to do to him?" she asked. "Frighten him to death?" And she brushed Claribel aside as if she had no importance at all.

"I want to talk to him alone," she told Mr. Collins, and he sent her and the boy, accompanied by a police sergeant, into a private room.

Presently Gail returned alone. She looked troubled.

"The police sergeant waited outside the door," she said, "and Fernando talked to me. But there's something wrong. His mother makes tamales for a small Mexican café, and every night Fernando delivers them. He said he did so last night, and was on his way home when he met the gang. That's all I can get out of him. He seems to be confused beyond that point, and he lied to me. I questioned him about things at school we both know well, and he lied when there was no reason."

She was silent a moment, her face anxious.

"He's not a liar," she said slowly. "I've always been able to count on him. That's what is so queer about it. There's something wrong with him. I want to take him to the hospital. I want Doctor Peabody to see him."

The police chief and Mr. Collins agreed.

It wasn't easy for Claribel to be brushed aside during all this, but Claribel was honest. If the boy was innocent, she wanted to know it. She was much concerned. And the next morning she telephoned Mr. Collins, who said he was to meet Doctor Peabody at the hospital at eleven to hear the results of Doctor Peabody's examination of the boy. Claribel had known Doctor Peabody for twenty years, so it was natural that she go also.

When Claribel reached the hospital the next morning, John Collins was there ahead of her. He was alone in a small anteroom, nervously lighting cigarettes and snubbing them out. He seemed very glad to see her.

"Miss Dearborn is a very attractive girl, isn't she?" he said suddenly, and Claribel, somewhat surprised, said yes, she was.

"Pretty, too, isn't she? Especially when she gets mad. She certainly lit into us, didn't she?" and Claribel said yes, she did.

"I hope she's right about this boy, Mrs. Holmes. By George, I hope so; and if she is, she certainly saved me from making a fool of myself."

Then Gail and Mrs. Gonzales entered, the girl saying good morning very politely, and all four sat waiting. John Collins and Gail pretended to be quite unaware of each other, neither missing the slightest move. It was a little warm in here, wasn't it, John Collins asked once, very formally, and wouldn't Miss Dearborn like the window opened? And Gail said yes, it was, and yes, thank you, she would.

When Doctor Peabody came in, Mrs. Gonzales stood up quickly, afraid to ask. All of them stood, and Doctor Peabody walked over to Mrs. Gonzales and took her hands, and told her gently that her son had a skull fracture. He was going to be all right; he'd have to stay here for a while; she could see him, but she must not talk, because he was resting.

Mrs. Gonzales cried as she thanked him and Gail, over and over. And when she had gone, the two men discussed the case in some detail, and both looked at Gail in a way Claribel didn't understand at all, in a way no man had ever looked at her. No, not even William.

"Well, girl," Doctor Peabody told her, "you certainly pulled one out of the hat that time."

Gail said quickly it was nothing. Nothing at all. It was just part of her job. And she thanked him and said good-by to them and was gone.

"If you'll excuse me, Mrs. Holmes," begged Mr. Collins hastily, "there's something I must say to Miss Dearborn. . . . Good-by, Doctor Peabody, and thank you. I'll call you in a day or two," and he was gone also.

Doctor Peabody walked to the window, Claribel beside him. They saw the girl come down the front steps very fast, and they saw John Collins follow her. He caught up with her on the sidewalk just outside the window, neither conscious of it. Claribel was going to step back, but not Doctor Peabody. He moved even closer.

"Miss Dearborn," Mr. Collins said, "I insist—I mean I hope you'll have lunch with me. I want to talk to you about—about Fernando Gonzales."

She hesitated. "I haven't very much time for lunch, Mr. Collins," she explained. "You know I'm a schoolteacher." She said it a little defiantly, as if he might as well get the worst fixed in his mind right from the start.

"My mother taught school," said John Collins. "Where shall we go?"

"But, Mr. Collins . . . you see, I take care of my mother, and I'm having lunch at home today. If you'd be content with a salad and a sandwich and a cup of coffee, perhaps—"

"I took care of my own mother for eleven years," said John Collins.

"You did?" she said doubtfully—and suddenly all her self-consciousness was gone. "You did? Why, how wonderful! And did anybody ever call you a duty-bound, meek, mild, wishy-washy little house mouse?"

"Miss Dearborn, you don't mean to say that some old hen—Not to you! Not really!"

And the girl laughed, nodded and made a small gesture toward the window to signify Claribel. John Collins, who was not stupid, got it too.

"No, no, no," said John Collins, and both were conscious for the first time that they were standing in full view of the window, and the man lowered his voice hastily, and he said, "Jeepers. Let's get out of here." They left like two children leaving the pantry cooky jar, all pockets crammed.

Doctor Peabody and Claribel turned slowly from the window, Claribel pink of cheek, Doctor Peabody smiling as if quietly pleased.

"You know something, Claribel?" he said. "I envy that young man. I do indeed."

Whatever Claribel had expected, it was not this. She felt a desperate need for a little quick rationalization. She faced him with all her nicest charm.

"I felt—I felt a little peculiar there for a minute, Doctor Peabody. You see, when Gail's mother was first ill and Keith Blake came to marry her, it was I who—who tried so hard to help her."

"Did you, Claribel?" he asked slowly.

"Oh, I did. I tried everything. I just couldn't bear to see her turned into one of those pathetic women, who are deprived of their chance in life, who never really live at all."

"I would say Gail has lived far more than most girls," said Doctor Peabody. "Not so easily perhaps."

Under his intent look, Claribel felt uncomfortable and flustered.

"Perhaps I was a little hard on her," she admitted doubtfully. Doctor Peabody spoke without censure, only with sadness. "Yes," he said, "that's what always happens, isn't it, when some nice, well-meaning married woman takes it upon herself to play Mrs. God."

From a loudspeaker a voice called Doctor Peabody's name.

"Good-by, Claribel," he said, "Nice to see you looking so well. Remember me to William," and he was gone, and she was walking down the hall, down the steps toward her car.

She was badly shaken. Never in her life had she felt so unsure. Was it true? In those middle-aged, leveling years when her own life lacked a vital edge, had she used the girl to give herself a vicarious importance? She denied it vigorously. She had wanted for the girl all good things.

And yet, now when there seemed to be an excellent chance that Gail might have them, Claribel felt a small resentment. And even a twinge of envy. She did not understand it at all, but she knew it had something to do with the way the girl had stood there—so quietly self-contained, as if, without any of the lovely fulfillment which Claribel herself most prized in life, she, Gail Dearborn, by her own strength had built a life strong and whole. Could she, Claribel, have done it? To this Claribel found no glib and ready answer.

She climbed into the car and started the engine. She needed William. She needed him as in those early years when she had committed some youthful blunder and felt his reassurance. It was Saturday. If she hurried, perhaps she could catch him before he started for his afternoon's golf. And she remembered that this was the day some of the girls were to drive by and take her to a luncheon. She had forgotten it.

She drove quickly. When she pulled into the drive, William's car was gone. When she entered the house, it was entombed with quietness, as it had been once long ago. And she wished suddenly and quite unexpectedly for Minnie Mae.

She hurried upstairs to change her dress and hat. She would take up a hobby, she promised herself. Yes, that's what she'd do. She'd study the piano again. Heaven knew, if Maud Twitchett could do it, she could. Maybe she'd take up gardening.

She heard a car stop in front of the house, and the girls coming up the walk, and the doorbell ring. She hurried down to let them in. For a few moments the hall was filled with a flurry of gay and affectionate greetings.

"Darling, we can't wait," one voice said. "Tell us what happened at the hospital this morning."

Claribel laughed, and she said, "Well, girls, I got my comeuppance. I was cut down to size this day. And guess who did it? Old Doctor Peabody."

Up came a loud and resounding harmony: "Claribel, not really!"

"Darling, how fantastic! What happened?"

"You mean to say Old Gimlet Eyes?"

And so, of course, Claribel told them all—well, almost all. They sat on the edge of the sofa and the love seat in the living room, and Claribel perched on the side of a chair and told them. It sounded very funny and amusing. She could see the accustomed response on their faces. She could see their faces lifting to her voice like little flowers turning to the sun.

And almost without knowing it, Claribel Holmes began to feel her wholly confident, her charming self again.

—*October 21, 1950*

GLAMOUR GIRL IN THE FAMILY

They saw her coming toward them down the great corridor, moving with that practiced and flowing grace which had helped build a legend around her name. It was the luncheon hour of a Saturday and the hotel was crowded. Everyone noticed her. Many knew who she was. No week passed that you failed to see her lovely face on the printed page and her name in the gossip columns; Candy Carlton modeling a gown; or a suit; or a hat. Candy Carlton seen at the Serrano opening with the young scion of the oil millions. Or the rubber millions. Or the steel millions. One of the most glamorous of them all, and as nice as she looked.

She saw them now and smiled, but her progress was slowed by minor triumphs. A debutante who had come out at last year's cotillion darted up like a bright minnow. A woman in blue mink with a worn face known on two continents delayed her casually. And a young man who had shot tigers with a maharaja, written a bad book, and gone through his father's money, greeted her a little too effusively and held her hand a little too long.

They waited patiently—these two who loved her, who were her deepest roots—as inconspicuous as the potted palms there where the corridor emptied into the quiet side street. The sweetfaced, graying woman who was her mother glanced down to be sure she had not forgotten to put on her gloves to hide the left forefinger where the heavy drapery needle had taken tiny bites of flesh. And the young girl ran a hand over her sleek short mane lest any stray lock shame the kid sister of one so fair.

Their eyes were proud and eager. Then worry flooded the mother's and she said quickly, "Betsy—if Candy doesn't seem to have much time for us anymore, it isn't because she doesn't love us dearly. You see, Betsy, I can't do much for her and—and, after all, a girl has to take care of herself. Do you understand?" And the girl nodded.

Now Candy was almost up to them. Just as they were about to speak, the revolving door from the side street turned, a man burst through, and his voice cried, "Candy—what luck! I've been trying to reach you all morning." He didn't even see them. He maneuvered her aside by an elbow. "Say, listen—is it true that Doreen Manning took an overdose of sleeping tablets last night?"

They both knew by Candy's face that it was true. They both knew she didn't want to tell him, because Doreen was her friend. Oh,—a silly one, a model like herself, and silly enough to fall in love with a married man whose wife didn't want him but wouldn't divorce him. They saw the pain on Candy's face. But what could she do? This man was a columnist on one of the city's best papers. He'd helped start the legend. He'd helped keep it shining.

She said, "John, don't ask me. I can't—I can't."

And the man said, "Why, Candy honey, you don't have to tell me. Just don't deny it and I'll know it's true." And so she did not deny it.

A moment later, when he had gone, they were leaning over a showcase where the hotel's gift shop displayed small luxuries locked under glass, and when they turned, no trace of what they had overheard showed on either face.

Now Candy was theirs—for a little while, for an hour perhaps. She was smiling. Her suit and hat were flawless, but she was more beautiful, more dominant than they.

"Oh, darlings," she said. "It's been so long—almost a month." And she laughed and she said, "Mother, what in the world have you done to that hat? You've set it on the back of your head and pulled it forward." And glancing around to be sure the corridor's end was momentarily deserted except for themselves, she plucked the hat, perched it over her mother's right eye, gave it a quick deft tug—and lo, the hat became smart.

"See?" she said. "That's the trick." And she opened her purse and removed a small box. "For you, Bett. A new perfume, and just right for you. Not too heavy. And don't put it behind your ears, sweet. The oil of your skin will make it acrid. Put a little on your slip or your hankie. And put a few drops in the last rinse water when you do your hair or your sweaters."

Betsy accepted the box with awe. At school she would demonstrate the hat tug and tell them about the perfume, and there would be no girl in her class thereafter who put perfume behind her ears, or whose sweaters did not smell—beautiful.

"I can't eat luncheon with you. I have a date later," Candy told them. "But I'll have coffee anyway. Bett—you run ahead, dear, to the Fountain Room. See if they have a table in the back where it's quiet and we can talk."

And Betsy knew that Candy wanted to talk to Mother about the young scions of this or that fortune who had a way of turning out mere honeybees. She went ahead like a page before a queen.

Then they were having luncheon in a big room with pink walls, and Candy was telling them about her new apartment which they hadn't seen yet. And the hour flew by. In no time at all their mother was putting on her gloves.

"It's an emergency order at the drapery shop," she explained. "Double pay. That's something. Now, Betsy, you go to the movie with your friends, dear. If I'm not home when you get there, you get your own supper." And to Candy: "And if it's a nice day tomorrow we'll drop over to see your new place. We'll telephone first."

Then she was gone, and Candy saying shakily, "Is she all right? Is she working too hard?" and Betsy assuring her that mother was fine—just fine.

"My date will be waiting. Bett, Here—you pay the check. With the change you can take a friend for a chocolate parfait after the movie. And, Bett—about tomorrow. I'm afraid I'm going to be tied up. Do you think Mother will understand?" And again Betsy was assuring her that of couse she would—perfectly.

Just as Candy was leaving, she gave Betsy a little hug, and she said, "You know something? I wish I were still young enough to think that a chocolate parfait was all one could ask of life."

Betsy lingered a few moments—because it had all been so wonderful. She paid the check and walked toward the hotel's main entrance in the hope of seeing Candy again. She was rewarded.

A man was with her at the curb. He was considerably older than she. Betsy was a city girl and she knew what kind he was. No blue-blooded scion. He was a red-blood who had battled his way up to success, and now for the first time could afford the fine clothes, the long, sleek car, the beautiful girl on his arm. Maybe he could even afford to marry her; and if he couldn't, Candy would send him on his way like the others.

They did not see her. They were waiting for a taxi, and Betsy saw the man slip a bill to the doorman, and when the next cab drew up, she saw the doorman step in front of the woman whose turn it was, and put them in, and send them off with smiles and bows.

All the enchantment went with them. Now Betsy was only herself. She walked slowly up the street. In the plate-glass windows she could see herself. Oh—never would she be one-hundredth part as glamorous as Candy. She was a nothing—an innocuous, smallish girl in a little green suit and Peter Pan blouse, fluffy bangs on her brow, hatless of course, her flat walkers making her feet look much bigger than they were. She was a nothing, and she had no shape. At school she did what the other girls did. She wrapped both arms around her books and held them tight against her, pushing her front up so as to make herself look larger than she was. Bookless now, gloved hands at her sides, she let down the whole female species.

She walked four blocks out of her way. Presently she came to the store where Candy modeled. Oh, not to go in. Candy had said once that the models didn't like members of their families to come there. Only to look. To stand at the entrance as if she were waiting for someone, to look in upon Candy's world of soft lush carpets, flattering lights, mirrored walls.

"All women can be glamorous," the store seemed to say to her. "Every woman is a rare jewel to be cherished and deserving these lovely things."

But it wasn't true. Just then a plumpish little woman with a rapt, preoccupied look dashed out, clutching one of the store's precious boxes. Obviously she believed it. But Betsy knew that whatever was in that box, when the little woman put it on she would still resemble nothing more glamorous than a squash.

It was true of some. It was true of Candy. It was true of a few girls at school. Betsy saw it every day. When the dismissal bell rang, out came a group of boys. Presently out came a group of girls. Then out came one lone girl, four or five boys clustered around her. And was she the prettiest? Sometimes. And was she the nicest? Not usually. Yet she had some precious and indefinable quality, and the other girls all knew it and were sure they'd never have it on this earth, and that was one rootlet growing from their self-doubt.

At the next corner Betsy caught the streetcar which would let her off in front of the neighborhood movie near the middle-class district where she lived and went to school.

In the seat in front of her sat two old women of at least forty-five. One of them was holding a newspaper, and between their shoulders Betsy could read its headline—TEEN-AGE GANG BEATS UP OLD MAN.

"Can you beat that?" one woman said to the other. "He was sitting there in the park feeding the squirrels and these crazy kids attacked him."

They discussed it earnestly. Behind them Betsy sat still, trying not to listen.

There were no gangs in her school, but the modern brashness was there nevertheless. You felt it sometimes like a rising wind.

One day in assembly the kids got so out of hand the principal had ordered the curtain rung down. One noon in the cafeteria a teacher had gone to pieces in a queer sort of way.

"They're brats," she'd said in a high voice like a scream. "They defy you to teach them anything. I'm tired—I can't take it any longer." And she'd begun to cry and laugh, both at once, and somebody had shushed her and taken her out.

Betsy did not want to think about the brashness. She had never been part of it. It was only lately she had felt it within her. In her homeroom she had cut up a little with the others, making a game of needling the teacher. Then last week something had happened she didn't understand—something frightening. She did not wish to remember it now—and did so.

Miss Hanson, her counselor and favorite teacher, had summoned her.

"Betsy," she'd said, "your work's slipping a little. I don't like it. You're a good student. If you start now, you can win one of our scholarships and go on to college. You can make something of yourself. Better think it over."

Betsy had looked at Miss Hanson and thought it over right then and there. Miss Hanson was the opposite of Candy. She had no beauty and no glamour. Miss Hanson was the nice little girl who works hard, develops character and grows into the nice big girl.

Suddenly Betsy had felt an impelling urge to say so. She'd wanted to say, *Why should I? Look at you. You did it. And what are you? You're an old maid. You're like the other teachers—scared to death you'll lose your job. Scared they'll fire you if you can't keep discipline. Scared to spend money because you have to save it so you can retire before you have to, if it gets too much for you.*

She had said nothing, sullen for the first time in her life, and Miss Hanson had looked at her thoughtfully from her fine, worried eyes, and she'd said, "All right, you may go now, Betsy. And by the way, how—how is your sister, Candy?"

Betsy had flushed to the ears, not knowing why, and she'd said, "She's wonderful—she's beautiful." She had thrown the words in Miss Hanson's face, and fled, feeling both proud and ashamed.

Now the streetcar came to her stop. She slid from it like an eel to the curb, to the box office and into the movie. She stopped in the foyer long enough to buy two bags of popcorn, and waiting for no usher, slipped through the doors into the blessed dark.

There were quite a number of girls from school this day, all sequestered in the last two rows. Lucy, her special friend, had saved her a seat. As she reached it, there rose a flurry of greeting.

"Hi, Sister Carlton."

"Hi, Sister Plummer."

"Hi, Sister Smith," and some grownup turned in the dark and said loudly, "Please be quiet," and was rewarded with the most infuriating of all sounds—the giggle.

Now Betsy was safe in the world she understood, whose protocol differs from month to month, from place to place. Of going steady or not going at all. Of slim wool skirts and sweater sets and kerchiefs. Of little white socks which must be rolled to the ankle bone. Of brushed and shining hair, frequently combed and perpetually tossed—a reflex left over from the longer mane.

Yet the brashness was here also. In front of Betsy sat three of the boldest girls in school. Betsy didn't know them very well or like them very much.

They were whispering sibilantly. After the show they were joining forces with kids from another school. They were going to the docks to get autographs from John and Julie Adair, who were sailing on the ebb tide. John and Julie Adair were the most famous acting couple in the country—the very essence of fame and glamour.

"Suppose they aren't nice to us?" one whispered loudly. "What'll we do?" and another answered, "We'll tear their clothes off," and all three squealed like little pigs.

It was a normal Saturday afternoon in any neighborhood movie. The double feature went on and on. The last bit of popcorn was loudly scrunched, the last piece of cellophane emitted its final rustle, and there began that squirming, wriggling search for some small spot which had not yet been sat upon.

Then it was over, the kids drifting out into the late afternoon, pairing off and homeward. Betsy asked Lucy to accompany her to the drugstore for a chocolate parfait, and over it she told Lucy all about Candy. And when they had finished the parfait to the last smidgin, she unwrapped the little box of perfume and they took turns smelling the bottle.

"My mother says it's queer Candy hasn't asked you to see her new apartment," said Lucy.

"Oh, but she has. We've just been too busy," Betsy answered and then said quickly, "I have to go now, Lucy. I have to go home."

But it was already too late. Betsy paid the check. They stepped out into the street, Lucy saying good-by and scuttling off home. And there by the drugstore entrance stood a metal rack and on it the evening papers. Across the top was a black streamer, BEAUTIFUL MODEL TRIES SUICIDE, and under it a picture of Doreen Manning. Betsy stood and looked at it, and although she did not even think it, she knew that somewhere in an inside column was a small item: "Candy Carlton, lovelier than ever, was seen yesterday—"

Now she felt the brashness within her, as she had before with Miss Hanson, only stronger this time and more demanding. She turned homeward. At the corner she saw the bold girls from school. There were other kids with them whom she didn't know, and they were all laughing and acting smartly.

"Hi, Sister Carlton," said one girl as Betsy passed.

And Betsy stopped, and she said boldly, "Hi, Sister Smith. You kids going somewhere?"

And Sister Smith recognized the boldness and she said, "To the docks for some autographs. I don't suppose—I don't suppose your mother would let you come."

And they looked at each other and Betsy said, "Why not? I can come."

Thus committed, she did not know by what process she had reached this place—only that she had been walking toward it for a long time, feeling at last some sweet relief.

It was wonderful. She didn't have to think at all. Only let someone think for her, to pile into a car with the others—everybody loud and giggling—and move swiftly through the dusk with the wind in her face. Then the car stopped in the shadow of a dock. Other kids joined them, and everybody quieted and listened while a bolder boy from a brasher school told the plan.

Like the others, Betsy lost her insecurity in the new collective daring. She saw the two celebrities drive by with a police escort. As their car turned to enter the wharf she saw two small and ancient jalopies dart directly into their path. In a moment the street was confusion. Taxi drivers swore, impatient passengers fumed, and policemen hurried to untangle the mess.

Like the others, Betsy slipped into the huge covered wharf, working her way toward the gangplank. A great crowd already waited. Through it wriggled Betsy, closer and closer.

Presently someone cried out, "Here they come. The police are bringing them. There he is. There's John Adair," and Betsy could see them, the famous couple, trying hard to be gracious and smiling and giving autographs.

Then a policeman called out, "All right—that's enough—let us through—let us through now."

The frustrated crowd surged forward. Sharp young elbows became wedges. Knees and shoulders became battering rams. An old man stumbled and fell. A woman screamed.

Betsy tried desperately to hold back and felt herself pushed onto the gangplank and up it. Ahead of her a girl snatched the hat from

Julie Adair's head, and when a ship's officer grabbed her, she kicked and clawed him like a wildcat.

When the police whistle blew, the brave bold leaders had already disappeared as if by magic, leaving the stupid little black sheep for the plucking, Betsy among them.

Then she was standing there on the deck with a boy and two girls she didn't even know. The other girls wore socks and kerchiefs, and they and the boy were still brash and smarty to the police. They enjoyed their limelight. They had succeeded. They had proved to themselves and others that they possessed one quality of vast importance. They had nuisance value. Only Betsy had failed.

The pocket of her little green suit was torn, and her sleek hair tousled. When she thought of Candy and her mother, summoned no doubt to the police station to take her home, her face was white with strain and fear.

It was still long before sailing time. On the dock the crowd was dispersed. Passengers and their friends were moving freely up the gangplank. The police were taking the kids' names, preparatory to taking them off, and people had stopped to stare. To one side stood the Adairs, talking earnestly to a ship's officer. Then they came forward.

"This one, officer," Julie Adair said in her famous husky voice, "surely you can see she doesn't belong with the others." She put her hand on Betsy's arm and turned to her husband. "John, isn't this the one to whom we were going to give an autograph?"

And he looked at Betsy carefully and said, "Why, yes—I believe it is, Julie."

Then Betsy was walking with them—Julie Adair's hand still on her arm—down one passageway and another, standing in the door of a *lanai* suite while the Adairs were thanking the police for all their courtesies. And then she was inside, the steps receding, the door shut and locked, and she was safe.

For a moment nobody spoke. The Adairs looked at each other as if they had fished a half-drowned kitten from a pail of milk and didn't know quite what to do with her.

John Adair said anxiously to his wife, "Are you all right?" and she laughed shakily and said she was fine—just fine—not a scratch on her, and his pipe and tobacco pouch were in his overcoat pocket, and while he was at it would he bring her knitting bag, please. It was in the top of the blue bag.

Very courteously she asked Betsy's name.

"Sit down, Betsy," she said. "Now don't be worried. There's plenty of time. We'll see that you get ashore."

Betsy sat down, and so did the others. John Adair stroked his pipe. Julie slipped one foot from its slipper, took a pair of large tortoise-shell specs from her knitting bag and set them on her nose.

"Now let me see," she said. "I simply have to finish this sweater before we reach Honolulu. Oh, yes, I remember. This is the row where I take off five stitches."

Something very strange was happening. The Adairs had set aside their glamour with the luggage. They had turned the *lanai* suite into a home, and somehow they had removed from Betsy her fear.

"Betsy," said Julie Adair, "find John an ashtray, dear. He'll have matches all over the floor," and it seemed perfectly natural that she should do it without self-consciousness or embarrassment, feeling no need for any explanations or apologies for anything at all.

John Adair had his pipe going.

"Thank heaven we're here," he said. "Did you two notice that tall girl with the dishcloth tied around her head? I thought she was going to pull my ear off."

"I noticed her," Julie told him. "She made me think a little of myself when I was that age."

"Julie—you never in all your life—"

"No, I didn't, dear. But I used to go to the Saturday matinees and sit in the front row of the balcony and drop gum on people's heads, and giggle horribly."

She laughed now gently. "It was all because of the bones in my neck," she said. "They stuck out. I was sure I was never going to grow into anything human. I expect the girl with the dishcloth feels the same way. When she grabbed your ear, she was just trying to come close to glamour."

John Adair took his pipe from his mouth.

"I hate that word," he announced loudly. "I loathe that word. I'm an enemy of glamour. When we retire to a place in the country and any silly females, young or old, hang over our fence in the hope of seeing those glamorous Adairs, I'm going to greet them. Do you know what I'm going to do?"

Julie Adair put down her knitting.

"I know," she told him. "You're going to take out your false teeth and wag them—like this." And she went through the motions, and Betsy could see it happening.

Then all was quiet for a little while, John Adair content and smoking. And then Julie asked Betsy about her mother, and did she have any brothers and sisters. She asked several questions about Candy, and in no time at all a voice was calling, "All ashore that's going ashore," in the passageway outside the door.

"So soon?" said Julie. "Why, we haven't even begun to chat. John—where are the pictures? We must autograph one for Betsy."

They found them, and took turns signing one. Then Julie signed another and without showing either to Betsy tucked them in an envelope and gave them to her.

"The big one is to show," she explained carefully. "But the smaller one, which is my favorite, is just for you," and to her husband, "Now John, be sure and have one of the ship's officers see that Betsy gets a cab. I don't want Betsy on the street after dark. Her mother wouldn't like it."

When Julie told Betsy good-by it was as if she were speaking to an old friend. And when John Adair escorted her to the gangplank, it was as if she were someone wonderful—like Candy.

In the taxi on the way home Betsy did not look at the pictures. She saved them as a child saves the best of the funny page until the last. There was no brashness in her now. She knew the Adairs had paid her the nicest of all compliments. With her they had been themselves out of some kindness she did not understand.

When she reached home, the flat was empty. It had seemed drab and unattractive after Candy had moved away. Now, with its white ruffled curtains and gay chintz, it had never seemed so homey or so nice. Betsy entered it as if she were seeing it for the first time. She hung her green jacket in the closet. Then she went into the living room and sat down on the old sofa, and opened the envelope which Julie had given her.

The first picture was large, impressive and carefully posed, the Adairs looking very glamorous and distinguished—and like strangers. "For our friend, Betsy Carlton," they had written and signed their names.

The second was small and unposed—a passport picture perhaps. From it Julie Adair looked directly at her. Every year of her life showed, and every line of her face, but the eyes were honest and intelligent—like Miss Hanson's. And across the bottom Julie had written, "Let those who will, be sugar-sweet, Betsy. You be spice. Julie."

Betsy wasn't sure what it meant. But she would know in time. That she knew. She put the pictures back in the envelope, and she placed the envelope under the paper that lined the bottom drawer of her chest, because not for this world would she show them to anyone or tell one word of the evening's happenings.

Yet when she heard her mother's key in the front lock, she raced to meet her, the words ready to spill forth. But it was not her mother. It was Candy; and the moment Betsy saw her there, lovely as always, she knew why she'd come. It was because Candy had seen the papers also, and her betrayal splashed on the page. She sought now the love and understanding she had outgrown.

Betsy spoke first.

"How is Doreen Manning?" she asked slowly.

Candy looked very much surprised. "I haven't seen her," she said. "But one of the other girls has. She says she's going to be fine. I tried to help her. I told her how silly she was. I—I want to talk to mother about it."

"Mother isn't home yet," Betsy said and led the way into the living room.

"I can't stay, Betsy. I'll have to run along. I just wanted to see Mother for a minute—about your coming over to see the apartment. You can come Tuesday for dinner. We'll have a fine evening all to ourselves, and you can see the view when the city's lighted after dark. It'll be just like old times. Don't you think that will be fun, Betsy?"

And now at last the tightly folded bud began to open.

"Mother can come," Betsy said, "but I can't. I have a test in school Wednesday and I have to study. I've been letting my work slip a little lately and I'm going to stop it. We have three scholarships in my school, and Miss Hanson says if I start now I can win one and go on to college and make something of myself."

It sounded very abrupt and rude, and Betsy felt somehow sorry for Candy, and felt the need to soften it.

"I know you'll understand," she said gently, as one woman of the world to another. "I know you'll understand, Candy, because, after all, a girl has to take care of herself."

—*February 10, 1951*

THE BOY WHO WANTED TO QUIT

When the world began again to shoot off sparks around his ears, Nathaniel Dorn felt so disgusted with civilization, if any, that he thought fondly of the day when he could turn in his tally and take his old bones up to the smelter.

It was natural that he should consider the hereafter in terms of his life's work; the mill blower filling the celestial air with its monotonous throb, the tram buckets casting their shadows upon the celestial clouds, the super going around with his nose to the ground counting up the tally, and not one Democrat in the place. On earth the Democrats had pegged the price of gold. Assuredly in heaven they would be dispatched down the flume with the tailings.

It was a thought which usually perked up old Nat considerably. This day it failed to mitigate his gloom. He sat on the porch of the fine old house where he'd been born, looking out upon an expanse of rough Western terrain which had produced a total of some twelve millions, and no man knew better than he that off the road leading past his gate to the mine on the hill's crest, under some ancient pine or lonely bit of scrub, lay long-forgotten graves of men—and women too—who had poured out their guts here to help build their country rich and strong.

Up there in the sun the Lone Jack, oldest gold mine in the land, was still running, and one mile under the ground men were still working in the dark and narrow stope. For many months now the miners had been drifting away, one by one. Not the Cornishmen, of course, who would stick to the last. The ones who had come west in the last war to work in the shipyards and, at their closing, on up to the mine. They were going back to the shipyards, drawn by higher wages—and some few of them by the hope that if they could establish themselves in so essential an industry they would escape the draft.

The gold was pegged and the guts were running out. That was the trouble, and the knowledge of it filled him with a kind of agony. Oh—he'd seen it coming. The blundering and the waste. The naïve assumption that the nation was a vast treasure house of easily won and quite inexhaustible wealth. The fools who voted solely for any candidate who promised to ladle the gravy on the plate.

And now the reckoning was coming too, and he was dog tired and useless. Couldn't take ten steps without his knees creaking like the hinges of Gehenna. Couldn't even get mad without his heart thumping wildly within him.

He saw a car now coming up the canyon road—and he got mad anyway. It was the first strange car in many a day, and, remembering the last war, old Nat thought of course it was driven by some whippersnapper from a government bureau, come to tell the mine what it could or could not produce.

He lifted his old bones hastily from the rocker and took them to the gate, creaking protest. But no—the car rounded a rocky bend with no careless disregard for the taxpayers' rubber. It was small and ancient. Yet when the sun caught it, its blue body and red wheels shone brightly, and it purred up the steep grade on all four cylinders as happily as a kitten full of milk.

It was a kid's car—well loved, well cared for. Some kid was coming to the mine when older men were leaving it, and even then Nat felt his surprise tempered by apprehension.

He waited. He could see the boy now. In his late teens perhaps, and so tall his knees cradled the little wheel. He was coming slowly, his eyes intent on the road. When he saw Nat leaning there against the gate, relief crossed his face, and he pulled to one side and stopped. Knew his manners. He didn't just sit and yell for directions. He climbed out and came over.

"I'm looking for the Lone Jack mine," he said anxiously.

There was a little wind within him pushing his words out, so eagerly did he walk into life. And when he spoke the name of the mine it was as if he spoke the names of all the famous old mines of the West—the Lone Jack, the Empire, the City of Scarry. Old Nat knew the sound. It was the sound of a kid in love with a profession he hadn't entered yet, in love with all he wanted to be and do in this world.

"You're right on the nose," Nat told him. "Just around the next bend you'll come to the little town. Turn left at the saloon."

The boy looked surprised. Probably he'd never met the word conversationally.

"Don't ask for the bar," Nat said. "Nobody'll know what you're talking about. It's been a saloon for a hundred years, including prohibition." And then quickly, before the boy could thank him and go, "You going up to work?"

"I'm going up to ask for it," and again the breath of eagerness ran through the words. Then he sobered. "Gee, do you think I'll have a chance?" he asked earnestly. "Oh—I know I'll have to start at the bottom. I expect that."

And do you know how far down is the bottom of a gold mine? thought Nat, but didn't ask it.

"I think you'll have a chance," he said. "The mine's losing men to the shipyards."

"I sure hope you're right," the boy said. "I'm in the School of Mines at the university. Just entered. I have to have practical experience in a mine to be graduated. I wouldn't be trying this so soon, but I'm expecting my draft notice pretty quick now. I want to get as much education as I can because—well, sir, a guy doesn't know just how much time he's going to have these days, does he?"

And Nat said no, he didn't, and walked with him to the car. When the boy had thanked him and driven on up the road, he retraced his steps and sat again in the rocker on the porch.

A nice kind of kid. A kid like so many others. Product of much thought, affection and expense. Product of the soft living of his day.

Old Nat didn't have to ask what kind of home had produced this boy. He knew. Probably the biggest heartbreak he'd suffered so far was the time his little dog was run over, the whole family trying desperately to make him eat. Probably the hardest physical pain was having his tonsils or appendix out, his mother at the bedside when he came to, his father eager to rush and buy some ice cream the very moment he wanted it.

Kid jobs and summer jobs of course. A paper route. Cutting lawns for the neighbors. Waiting on table to help himself in school. Or rustling luggage at some summer resort. All the years a preparation for the future.

Yet here he was. With one last summer to grow—to get himself ready for his country's quick and vital need. Here he was, still hanging onto his dream, come to earn his manhood in one of the toughest jobs of them all, and no real inkling of just what a battle it was going to entail.

But old Nat knew, and the knowledge amused him a little and made him a little sad.

He sat there on the porch in the sun, knowing that if the boy didn't land a job he'd be back. Behind him the house seemed to wait also. He was alone in the house now, and to break the silence he had set the many Victorian clocks twenty minutes apart. All afternoon the clocks struck—bing-bing—bong-bong. But the little blue car did not come back down the road.

The next two days Nat paid no attention to the road whatsoever.

"If he folds up the first two days, he's not worth saving," he said to Pansy, the cat.

On the third day there was not a moment when his ears were not listening for the purr of those four cylinders, or an hour when his mind did not descend into the dark honeycomb beneath the sun-baked earth. On the fourth afternoon—and no sign of the boy yet—he couldn't stand it another minute.

He made up the bed in the guest room. He set a large bottle of chloroform liniment on the guest-room table. He shut Pansy in the kitchen, and backed his big black car out of the garage. He did so without benefit of license, the motor-vehicle department having recently pronounced him too rickety to drive a car. Old Nat was certainly not going to let a thing like that stop him at a time like this.

He headed up the road. Behind him rose the dust. Ahead of him a hen flew for her life. He was in a hurry and worried too. He might have quite a time finding the boy. The mine's bunkhouses were closed now, and the miners lived in the nearby villages. And besides, he didn't even know the boy's name.

His name was Jim, but sometimes even yet his mother forgot and called him Jimmy.

The first morning when he reported for work at the drying shed, the shift boss said, "Hang your forth-and-to'y clothes on a hook, kid. I'll be waiting for you at the collar."

He didn't know what his forth-and-to'y clothes were, and he didn't know what the collar was either. The superintendent had used the word when he'd given him the job.

"We pay collar-to-face here," he'd told him, and he'd looked at him carefully with something wise and speculative in his eyes and added, "Well-l-l, good luck."

But the super had told him what clothes he'd need. Now in the drying shed the other men were changing theirs, hanging the clothes they'd worn to the mine on a hook; so he did too. He watched the others. They were the strongest-looking men he'd even seen. They were short-legged and barrel-chested, and although he'd always been confident of his six-feet-one, and hundred and seventy pounds, now he felt unsure of his own strength.

The long-legged wool underwear seemed strange for a warm summer day. His feet seemed even larger than usual in the sturdy shoes with the metal on the toes. And his head felt heavy in the hard-boiled hat with its miner's lamp. Then he was dressed and following the others out of the drying shed to the place where you entered the mine, which must be the collar. Then the other men were taking their places on a little car on a track, and the shift boss was motioning him to take his. He did so awkwardly, his knees fitting closely around the shoulders of the man in front. Then the car slipped down the track, and the daylight was gone and the dark took them.

It was a little scary moving so fast into the deep earth, and he hung on for all he was worth. When the car stopped at last, they were a mile under. The air was cold and musty. There was no electricity in the old mine, and the boy could see his breath, white in the light on his hat. He walked into the dark labyrinth beside the shift boss.

They walked and they walked. Then they climbed down a ladder and walked on a second level, and down a second ladder, and walked on a third level. And the shift boss grinned and said, "Cheer up, kid, you're being paid for this. You'll come out on your own time."

They walked, the boy thought, about a mile, coming finally to the place where he was to work. The shift boss explained the job carefully and showed him how to pick out the white quartz from the black shattered rock and dirt.

"We're a tally-happy mine," he said. "You're to fill thirty ore cars a day. Any questions?"

There were no questions. For a moment a speculative gleam flickered in the shift boss' eye. "Well-l-l-l, good luck," he said, and was gone.

Thirty men were working on this level, but no man close by. The boy was alone, detached from all he had known. Susan, his girl, was back there somewhere in another world, and his parents, and the white house with the green trim.

He was determined to make good. He picked up the shovel and went at it as if he were killing rattlesnakes, knocking himself out with huge bursts of effort, and then leaning on his shovel to rest.

Once during the morning a huge miner from Oklahoma came by, carrying a piece of machinery that looked as if it weighed three hundred pounds and probably did.

"Harder'n books, ain't it, kid?" he said, and the boy answered
fervently, "Yes-s-s, sir."

He ate lunch with the other miners down in the mine. He was
there. They accepted him. Yet he was conscious of the gulf
between them and him which somehow he must cross.

The rats were very friendly. He almost had to knock them off
his lunch pail with a shovel. They were such big thin rats, and he
felt for them a kind of sympathy. He couldn't figure out how in
the world they got down there, and he was beginning to wonder
how he did.

After lunch he went back to work, and now something very
strange happened to time. Time stood still. When he was sure it
was two, it was one, and when he was positive it was three, it was
one-fifteen.

In the middle of the afternoon an older miner came along.

"Got to work steady, kid," he said. "Got to work steady. Let me
show you," and he took the shovel, placed it at the bottom of the
pile—and lo, the ore seemed to rise by a flowing movement all its
own. He did it again and walked off.

Then the boy tried it. He did it exactly the same way. He placed
the shovel at the bottom of the pile—and hit a rock and couldn't
budge it.

When it was quitting time he thought he'd never reach the
collar. His arms and legs ached, and his hands were badly blistered. When he reached the shabby little hotel where he'd found a
room, the first thing he did was telephone his dad.

"How did it go, son?" his dad asked so quickly that the boy
knew he'd been sitting by the telephone just waiting.

"Okay, Dad," he said. "It's hard work, but it went okay."

There was still the breath of eagerness in his voice.

The second day was much like the first—only more so. The boy
nearly killed himself and filled only twenty ore cars. He dropped
a tool down a shaft and had to go down after it. He knocked his hat
off and put out the light. Yet already he had learned to dip his
hands in the tallow like the others and his work had begun to
level off a little.

In the morning he laid off his own work a few moments to help
another miner get a piece of machinery up a ladder. In the afternoon the miner returned the favor. He came by hurriedly.

"Muck 'em up, kid," he said. "Rattle 'em up. Here comes the
super with his nose to the ground."

The boy made as much noise as possible, and he made the dirt
fly through the air. And sure enough—the super was coming, all

right. In fact he was firing a man somewhere up the dark tunnel, and he did it like this:

"Take your blankety-blank face up to the blankety-blank sun," he said, "because I'm tired of looking at it." And though the boy admired the beauty and dispatch with which it was done, he shivered in his shoes, knowing his turn was next.

But when the super reached him and learned how many ore cars he'd filled, he made no comment at all. He simply put his tongue behind his upper teeth, let out a faint clucking sound, and shaking his head sadly he disappeared into the dark.

That night the boy was more tired than he'd ever been in his life. He wrote a short note to Susan, his girl. The job was okay, he wrote, but hard. He would write more tomorrow. He loved her.

He was in bed at six-thirty, and he was asleep at six-thirty-two.

The third day he helped an older miner blast the rock in the dark and narrow stope. He held the fuses while the older man lighted them. He learned to hurry to a place of safety and to wait for the rush of air, for the ominous crack-crack—for the rattle and shake, and the flickering lights.

That night the boy was too tired to eat well. There seemed to be something wrong with his stomach. It was tied into knots, and now there was part of him that hoped he wouldn't be sick, and there was another part of him that hoped he would.

He had scarcely reached his room before his dad called.

"How does it go, Jim?" his dad asked, and the boy said it went okay. He'd upset his stomach a little. He thought it was the water in the mine which didn't agree with him.

He didn't know it, but the breath of eagerness was gone from his voice.

The fourth day the boy mucked ore. The stope slanted upward, following the vein, and he worked on his knees in a space not three and a half feet high. The day was endless and at quitting time he could hardly get to his feet, and when he reached the collar he blinked at the sun as if he had been down a lifetime.

On his way to his little blue car he met an old Cornishman he'd seen in the mine.

" 'Ell of a 'ole, ain't it, kid?" said the Cornishman cordially, and the boy was so pleased that for a moment the eagerness was back in his voice.

"Gee, yes," he said. "Yes-s-s, sir."

But it didn't hold. When he reached the hotel he had the coins ready in hand to call his dad. He shut himself in the phone booth and dialed the operator, and when he deposited the coins as she directed and heard them ring, he tasted something salty in his mouth, so bitter was defeat.

Then his father said, "Jim? That you, son?" and he knew his dad had been there waiting and worried, and he heard his own voice saying, "Dad—it's not going well. Dad—I'm afraid I can't stick it."

Then there was silence—the boy desperately wanting his dad to say he could quit honorably, and the father wanting to say it. Then his dad spoke, his voice very gentle on the wire.

"It's your decision, Jim," he said. "I expect the other miners are betting you won't show, about tomorrow. I think I'd show if I were you."

And presently the boy was going up the stairs to his room. He wasn't standing very straight and he wasn't walking quite straight either. He dragged himself up the last few steps and started down the hall, and there, sitting in a chair in front of the door to his room, was the fierce, fine-looking old man he'd met on the road.

Nat stood up slowly, as one man to another. One look told him everything he wished to know. The boy had lost several pounds. On his face was the beginning of the pallor that comes from working underground. Across his brow was a row of eruptions which were going to end up boils, where the abrasive quartz dust had cut the flesh beneath the sweatband of his hat. In his eyes was the hideous self-doubt.

Nat wasted no words. "James," he said loudly—it was one of the few times anyone had ever used the word—"James, what you need are some pasties and some heavy cake. Where have you been eating?"

The boy told him.

"Food there doesn't stick to a man's ribs," said old Nat. "Wait till we get some Cornwall meat pies into you. Then the dirt'll fly."

The boy said he guessed he was too tired to eat anything right now. He was so glad to see the old man he didn't trust himself to look him in the eye.

"I'll tell you what we'll do," Nat said. "You can come home with me for the night. You can stay if you want to. After a few hours' sleep you can go down to the kitchen and fix yourself some grub. And tomorrow we'll fix you up at the boardinghouse of the Cornish widow."

The boy brightened. He'd like very much to have a room at Nat's, he said. He was sure it would help a lot. Together they packed the boy's things, and while they did it, Nat learned all he wanted to know. The boy's father was judge on the superior bench. He lived in a coast city.

When they reached the house and the boy was established in the guest room, Nat waited just long enough for him to fall sound asleep. He knew what he had to do. Down there in the city the boy's parents were looking, no doubt, almost as doubtful and white as he did. Probably this very minute they were discussing driving up to see how their Jim was getting along. And if they saw him with the fatigue on his face and that row of boils, they would snatch him home. They wouldn't want to, but they'd do it sure. And it wouldn't do. Not for this boy who had come here with his heart. If he failed now, then next year in some far corner of the world perhaps there would be another kid with his own inadequacy deep within him.

Old Nat called the long-distance operator and asked her to get the boy's father. Presently she called him back.

"Judge Mason's ready, Mr. Dorn," she said, and Nat felt his heart thumping wildly within him.

He began by introducing himself. He told Judge Mason he'd been around mines for forty years and managed a few in his day. He gave some references. He told him how he'd happened to meet the boy that first day, and just what he'd done.

"He's a mighty nice boy," he said, "and he's having a mighty hard time."

Then he heard a woman's voice saying, "Is it about Jimmy, dear? Is he all right?" And Judge Mason was thanking him. They'd been worried to death, he said. As a matter of fact they'd just been discussing driving up to see for themselves how Jim was getting along. They'd been afraid the job was too hard for him, that he was too young for it.

"James will be mighty glad to see you when you drive up," said Nat. "Why don't you plan to drive up over the Fourth?"

The Fourth of July holiday was two weeks away and the old man stressed the word James heavily with a new dignity in his voice.

"I see," said the judge slowly. "Mr. Dorn—has Jim arranged to pay you for the room?"

"James and I have not yet discussed it, Judge Mason."

"Well-l-l-l, don't you think you had better plan to take a bite out of his first paycheck?"

"James and I will consider it."

"Well, how about linen?" said the judge with some desperation. "Don't you think perhaps we should send you some towels and sheets?"

"When it becomes necessary to shovel James in and out of the sheets," said Nat, "I'll change them."

"I understand," said the father—a little shakily. "We'll stay away until the Fourth. But if James needs us, if there's anything we can do—" and Nat promised, and thanked him, and hung up.

As he hurried to the kitchen, he felt sorry for all parents. On the kitchen table he placed six eggs, two quarts of milk, a loaf of bread, and a large quantity of cold meat, cheese, jam and fruit. There was no sound in the guest room when he went to bed, but when he awoke in the morning he could hardly wait to get downstairs.

The six eggs, the two quarts of milk, and half the loaf of bread were gone. So was much of the meat, cheese, jam and fruit.

Then Nat remembered something and hurried back upstairs as fast as his creaky knees could carry him. He entered the guest room and approached the disheveled bed. He leaned over and placed his nose close to the sheets. They smelled strongly of liniment. He'd been a little worried about that. He'd been afraid the boy would think it was something to drink.

After that, Jim ate pasties and heavy cake at the boardinghouse of the Cornish widow, and every late afternoon he dragged what was left of himself home to the fine old house by the side of the road. Sometimes Nat rubbed his shoulders and his aching back, and they discussed whether he should stick it out one more day and always concluded that he should.

"Not that it matters much," Jim always said, halfway between hope and dread, "because I'll never live long enough to fill thirty ore cars a day. Tomorrow the super will fire me sure."

And he was right in part. He never filled more than twenty-three ore cars. Yet when the super came around with his nose to the ground and heard the tally, he contented himself with that same odious cluck of the tongue and disapproving shake of the head.

The boy harbored strong emotions about the super. The super had become the last of a long list of juvenile dislikes, once headed by castor oil and spinach. This old Nat understood. Oh—the super was a tough man, he agreed. He was a hard customer all right. But he was fair. He was a good judge of men. You had to admit that for him.

The job grew no easier. But very gradually the boy began to harden to it. His pallor increased, but his fatigue was no longer cumulative, and he gained back the weight he'd lost. Every night he spoke harsh words of the super while Nat agreed with him, but now when they discussed whether to stick or quit it was on a weekly basis.

On the Fourth of July holiday every house in the old town had a flag flying from its porch in the old-fashioned way, and Jim's parents drove up to see how he was getting on. And though they swallowed a little hard at seeing him, they backed him up. They encouraged him.

At night the boy was always too tired to do anything but sit around and chat a little before going to bed, and the talk was always of mines. Slowly the old man was building up the back lore of the boy's profession. His vocabulary had altered greatly, filled now with mining terms. One Sunday as they strolled down the main street of the old town, they met some of the older miners, and Nat observed that they greeted the boy as one of them with no speculative gleam in their eyes. He was crossing the gulf.

The little eager breath ran through his words when he spoke of Susan, his girl, and one other thing, the engine that drew the ore cars, which was apparently the only new object in the old, old mine. Never once did he describe the engine in technical terms. Instead he paid it the highest compliment a man can give an inanimate object. He imbued it with sex.

"Gee—she's a pretty thing," he'd say with his eyes glowing. "Gee—she's a beaut. Do you think the super will let me run her—just once?" and Nat would remind him that the super was a hard man and a tough customer, but he might—he just might.

At the end of some weeks the boy took an extra day off and drove down to see his girl. When he returned, he had changed.

He was restive and solemn. Even the little engine inspired him to no rapture. He said no word of explanation, and Nat asked no questions, knowing very well what was wrong; Susan was in revolt. Susan thought this was the worst summer any two young people had spent upon this earth. Susan thought he was ruining his health. Susan wanted him to quit.

Nevertheless the boy stayed on, and then one afternoon Nat saw a car pull up at the gate and a girl climb out and come toward him slowly up the path.

She was a girl like so many of her day—small, slender, with a pretty, intelligent face. When she reached the porch, he was standing to welcome her, and he saw then that her eyes were curiously watchful and resentful.

He spoke first. "You must be Jim's girl," he said. "You must be Susan. Jim will be delighted to see you. I'm glad you've come."

He welcomed her as if he were welcoming Jim himself. She could stay here in the house. She could have the bedroom and bath downstairs. He was an excellent chaperon and the whole county knew it. It would do Jim good to talk to her. He was having a mighty hard time.

The girl bit her lip. "There's no use being nice to me," she said. "I know you've been kind to Jim and I appreciate it. But I think it's only honest to tell you why I've come."

"I know why you've come," Nat said gently. "And I don't blame you. If you think Jim must quit his job, you must tell him so. You must urge him to do it."

She was surprised. She hadn't expected this.

"It takes a heap of backing to make a man," he said slowly. "A boy doesn't do a thing as hard as this job just for himself. He's got to be backed up. If you're going to be a mining man's wife, you'll have to learn that."

"He wants to quit," she said quickly. "He's told me so."

"Oh—he wants to quit, all right. He talks about it every day. He dreams about it every night. He wants to quit the way the boys overseas want to come home. But I don't think he'll do it."

Jim took Susan out to dinner that night, and in the evening Nat retired early to his room so they could have the downstairs to themselves. He couldn't sleep. He could hear them talking for hours, and then the boy coming up to his room.

In the morning he hesitated to go down, wondering if the boy had gone to work or would be waiting for him in the kitchen with Susan, his face a little ashamed, a little defiant. But when he went down the stairs, Susan was alone.

She was busy at the stove and when he entered she said briskly, "Breakfast's ready," and she carried over the coffeepot and poured the coffee.

She did not look at him directly. She was very busy, making the toast, scrambling the eggs. It was not until he'd had his second cup that she spoke.

She sat down then beside him and she said, "Well—I did it. I urged him to quit. And you were right. He wouldn't do it. He said his father would be so disappointed. But mostly he said he couldn't quit because of you. He said you'd think the country was in the hands of infants. You'd think the country was doomed."

Old Nat made no comment.

"Oh—I knew he should stick it out," she said. "I knew it all the time. But don't you see? We may not have another summer. We may never have the lives we've planned, because the older people have made such a mess of this world that it looks as if the lives of our generation are going to be all loused up."

She chose the crude word deliberately, and she threw it at him, and then she began to cry.

Nat sat there patting her hand, and he heard himself telling her that his own life had been ruined—oh, utterly loused up at least two or three times—yet it had been a good life and more meaningful perhaps because of its dangers. His words seemed very inadequate, and he heard himself telling her she could come up weekends and that before the summer was done she and Jim would have some time that was their own.

Thus the summer passed. It was the longest the boy had ever known, and to the old man the shortest. Susan came up several weekends, and twice the boy drove down to see her and his parents, and every afternoon Nat sat on the porch in the sun just waiting. And then at last it came.

The boy came toward him up the path, carrying his draft notice in his hand.

"I'm going to quit now," he said. "I have two weeks before I report and I want to spend them with Susan. Do you think that's all right?" And the old man said he thought it was fine.

It was the super who bothered the boy. What would the super say? He dreaded telling him, and Nat announced that in that case there was no use putting it off. Jim had better do it right now, and he'd go along for the ride.

They climbed into the little blue car and started for the mine, up the dusty road and through the old town, neither speaking.

When they reached the mine, the boy parked the car in front of the office and went in by himself, while Nat waited.

The door to the office was open, and the super evidently seated at his desk, because Nat heard him say, "Yes, Mason. What is it?" and he saw the boy standing there in the door and he heard him say, "I'm quitting, sir. I've got my draft notice."

The super said, "So you're quitting?" Just that. Followed by silence.

"I hope my work was satisfactory," the boy said slowly.

"If it hadn't been, I'd have fired you," said the super. His chair scraped on the floor. Nat saw him come to the door with the boy.

"I put you in the damnedest hole in the mine," said the super slowly, "and you never groused once. As a matter of fact I was going to give you a better job next week. I was going to let you run the little engine."

And that did it. There came from Jim a completely adult and grown-up roar.

"A fine thing," he said, "to tell me that at a time like this when all summer long I've been dying to run her just once. And she's such a beaut too." And then he laughed, and to Nat it was one of the most poignant sounds he'd ever heard, because he knew that with it went the last of Jim's boyhood.

Presently—the good-bys said—Jim came toward the car to drive away for the last time. Even his shadow on the sun-baked earth had changed, and it seemed to Nat that in it he saw the shadow of thousands like him.

The weight was off the seat now and on the back, where it belonged.

—*June 30, 1951*

LEADING LADY

He walked slowly past the big yellow tent of the Music Circus which the workmen were mooring to the stanchions, and he came to the door of the wooden annex where the tryouts were about to begin, and stopped, hand on the knob. Kovach Varga was from Vienna, and even now, after thirty years' directing light operas and musical plays in six countries on two continents, he still felt humble before the bright and eager hope that awaited him within this door.

Each year they looked younger—the kids gathered around the dingy upright which, miraculously enough, sometimes turned out to be in tune. Usually they were laughing and talking—their voices too loud, too shrill, because they were afraid; but when he entered, sound would cease and for a naked instant they would find and fix him with eyes pathetically vulnerable.

These kids would be strangers, yet he knew them well. The boy who had ridden the bus all night to reach here. The small, sure blonde with the small talent so highly polished as to look bigger and better than it was. The fortunate two perhaps, destined to reach the sound secondary and supporting roles—and go no further.

But only a few times had he met the girl who was among them today—the one who has it and doesn't even know it, the gift so rare it can take her into the limelight and the fame, and keep her there. He remembered what Madame Alba, his old friend, had said about her.

"Oh, Kovach—such a tonta! Such a sweet, foolish little one. Can you believe it? In this crazy country of bathtubs and washing machines she is not even sure if she wishes to leave her father's plump sugar beets and develop her talent and give it to the world." And Madame Alba made a noise of utter exasperation. "As yet, Kovach, she has made no—no act of commitment."

He opened the door and went in. The chatter stopped. The Italian music conductor hurried forward, accompanied by a string

217

bean of a woman topped with a plain but lively face. Sadie Hibbs, the wardrobe mistress. Supporter of the timid, deflater of the smug. Good old Sadie, on whose bony shoulders the failures and successes of two generations had wept their tears of joy and disappointment.

"Why, Miss Sadie," said Kovach, "how long has it been?"

And she said, "London—1937," with such warmth in her voice that the kids gathered around the piano in the corner relaxed again and began to joke and laugh.

There was a quick conference.

"O.K., kids, break it up; break it up," cried the music conductor. "We'll warm up on a chorus. All together now—you all know it," and the tryouts began.

Kovach picked them out, one by one, listened, talked, advised, hired and dismissed, until only one girl was left.

The others had all had some experience and showed it in their clothes, their manner, their talk, in a hundred little sureties they didn't know they possessed. This girl showed nothing.

She was seventeen; a little older perhaps. She was rather small, but sturdily built, which was fortunate. She had soft dark hair, shoulder length, and she wore a light blue linen dress and a cashmere sweater exactly the same shade. And under the thin nylons Kovach could see the white bars left by the straps of last summer's sandals and knew she had run long and bare-legged in the sun.

"Did Madame Alba send you?" Kovach asked gently, and the girl said yes, Madame Alba was her teacher, and Kovach saw she was frightened.

"She called me about you," he told her. "Did you bring some music?" And the girl said yes, she had, and handed him several pieces.

He picked one quickly.

"This one," he said, as if he were very much pleased and surprised. "This Strauss. What a lilt it has to it."

And he seated himself at the piano and began to play it and to sing, too, in his old creaky voice, motioning the girl to join in. Then when she was confident he dropped out and left her singing alone.

When she had finished, he did not speak, and the girl looked at him anxiously and she said, "Was it all right? Did—did I do it well enough?" She spoke as a child says to its mother, "Didn't I do it well?" and the mother answers, "You did beautifully, dear. Mother's proud of you. Now run along and play. Mother's busy." And there was something so young, so naïve about it that for a moment Kovach had difficulty replying.

"You were excellent," he said. "We'll be pleased to have you with us."

He discussed the details, told her when to report for rehearsal, and walked with her to the door. When she had gone, he stood with Miss Sadie and the musical director and they saw a small convertible draw up to the curb and a boy climb out to greet the girl, while a second girl waited in the car.

"That's her best beau and her best friend," said the musical director dryly. "They'll celebrate. They'll have a double chocolate soda—maybe a banana split." And they all smiled and none said what was uppermost in his mind.

Why did it have to be this one? This child of plenty? Even if Madame Alba hadn't told him, Kovach could see the life she came from. The prosperous ranch in this rich valley. The long, low rambling house. The swimming pool on the place next door. The loving parents. No necessity. No harsh need to impel up the long rough road she must travel.

It was Miss Sadie who put it in words. "That wonderful glorious voice," she said, "and no wolf at her heels."

Then Kovach spoke.

"When I was a little boy in Vienna," he said, "my mother made our bread. She mixed it in the evening and placed it to rise beside the big kitchen stove, and the next morning when I peeked under the blanket which covered it, the dough was like this girl, all light and new with no mark on it. Then my mother did something I did not understand. She made a fist and hit the dough hard, and knocked the air out of it, and she said this must happen before it was fit to be kneaded into any shape at all. Maybe life will make for this girl a fist," and he shut the door.

They sat close together—the three young ones—Laird in the middle between Jim and Fran, and the moment the car was away from the curb the others questioned her in quick excited voices. Did she get the job? Had she been scared to death?

Oh, it was wonderful to share her triumph first with them. With Jim, the boy she liked best of all, the one she was sure someday she'd grow up and marry. And with Fran, her oldest, her closest friend. Jim was all any girl could wish, and she and Fran, living on adjoining ranches, had known each other all their lives.

She told them everything. Because she had been so nervous, relief was very sweet. She elaborated it just a little, spun it out as long as she could.

"I have to stop by Madame Alba's," Laird said finally. "I promised," and the others groaned loudly, and Fran said, "How do you stand her? That queer old fuddy-duddy. She's depressing."

And Jim said, "We'll humor her, Fran. We'll take her. We'll even wait for her, but if she doesn't come out in ten minutes, we'll honk like crazy."

When they reached the white house, Laird ran up the walk, slipping quietly through the door so as not to disturb the lesson Madame Alba was just finishing. And Fran had been right. Depression waited here.

From the hall she could see the studio, almost filled by a huge concert grand, every desk, every tabletop, every foot of wall space covered with pictures of the great concert and opera stars, most of them long-retired, some of them forgotten.

Each picture was signed in big, bold, egotistical handwriting: "To Madame Alba with undying admiration," "To Madame Alba, greatest soprano of all time."

Laird admired Madame Alba, but she didn't like her very much. She could never please the woman. When she sang a solo at the church, Madame Alba fussed at her as if she were making a debut at the Metropolitan, and if she was careless about any little thing, Madame Alba pointed it out with sometimes pointed scorn.

Today there was no scorn. Madame Alba dismissed the other student and came to Laird with her hands outstretched.

"I do not need to ask if you were given employment," she said. "I can see it in your face. You will learn much. Perhaps by the end of the summer you will be given a small part. You will learn and you will be hurt too."

The girl stared at her.

"I have been too hard on you, I think," said Madame Alba. "It is difficult for me to understand abundance. But we are alike in one thing. When I sang my first concert in Madrid, I did not really know I had a voice, and you don't either. But you will find it out now and what it means, and you will work hard and someday you will sing like an angel from heaven."

Then there was silence and they heard Jim honking the horn repeatedly.

Madame Alba smiled. "Go to him while you can," she said, and went with her to the door, and the girl, confused and greatly relieved, got away quickly.

They took the river road home, chatting of their plans for the summer. Lazy Sunday breakfasts on the terrace. Swims in Fran's pool. And in the fall, college for Jim and Fran, with Laird entering

after Christmas. And did they want to join a sorority and a frater-
nity, and if they did, would they be asked?

The river road home was like life itself—smooth and beautiful
in the early summer's sun, stretching ahead like a ribbon of
enchantment. Then they reached the ranch of Laird's parents, and
the good-bys were said and she was running to the house.

The house was low, rambling and attractive, sound evidence of
prosperity. It had not always been thus. Once, before Laird was
born, her parents had been through something called a depression, and her father had given her mother two hundred old ewes
to lamb out, and her mother had bought one hundred feeder
lambs in the spring, and she had trimmed hoofs, branded, sheared
and made camp for the herders. When she mentioned it, Laird
always felt proud—and a little ashamed.

She found her mother in the kitchen. She told her everything,
and the mother listened thoughtfully.

"Isn't it wonderful?" the girl asked. "Aren't you proud of
me?"

The mother said it was very nice.

"And wasn't it thoughtful of me to go by Madame Alba's?" the
girl asked.

And the mother turned slowly and she said, "You don't do
things in this world for praise, Laird. You do them because it's
right. You do them because they deserve to be done well. You
must learn that now."

But the girl wasn't listening.

Rehearsals began the next Monday and with them a life altogether new and wonderful. The girl had nothing to lose, everything to learn. She was the youngest in the company. By comparison, the others seemed to themselves vastly wise and experienced, and so of course they were kind.

"Watch out for the chickadee," they said to one another. "Don't
let her fall off the stage."

And when she asked Miss Sadie, the wardrobe mistress, to take
in one of her costumes, please, to make her appear even more
slender, Miss Sadie did so with scarcely a smile.

"I'll just baste it, kitten," she said. "After the opening night
you'll ask me to let it out again so you can sing."

Then the Music Circus opened with *The Student Prince*, the big
dressing room tense with waiting and excitement. It was Miss
Sadie who caught Laird putting on her first makeup, or trying
to.

"Take that goozlum off your eye winkers," she cried, grabbing a towel. She did it herself and remade Laird's face, as if she were plucking a kitten from a pan of milk, and holding it up until its whiskers stopped dripping.

Then the girl was running with the others of the chorus through the dark to the tent. She was part of the excitement, of the lilt of the music and the laughter, of the applause that came from the circle of dark faces.

Each week the show changed. They did *The New Moon, The Chocolate Soldier, The Red Mill* and *The Merry Widow*, the girl hopping blithely with the rest from one mythical kingdom to another, always hurrying, always on the run, attending rehearsals each morning, and returning each night to the Y.W.C.A., where her mother had found her a room. She was grown up, and sure of it. She was independent and on her own, and every Sunday her father or Jim picked her up and drove her home for the day.

Five weeks had passed when Mr. Kovach gave Laird a tiny part with three whole lines to speak and one song all her own, and at once the summer shifted and all that had been wonderful became a nightmare.

The leading lady for this week's production, and the three following it, had had some success on Broadway. She was older now and waning, bracing herself against the long slide down. She fought with the leading man, with the photographers, the music director. When the show opened and she saw Laird, so young and lovely, and heard her sing and the applause which followed, she saw in the girl all she herself had wanted and failed to be.

After that, nothing Laird did pleased her.

"The little dumb cluck spoiled my entrance," she complained to Mr. Kovach. "She is a moron. She knows nothing. She belongs home with the chickens and the cows."

Not once in the next month did she cease her sniping, teaching Laird her letters in the primer of cruelty, trumping up excuses to find fault with her until some of the more timid members of the company, fearful lest they, too, fall under this wrath, avoided the girl.

One afternoon, shortly after this began, Sadie Hibbs found Laird alone in the dressing room, gathering together her possessions and packing them.

"I'm going home, Miss Sadie," she told her. "I've had enough of this. It's outrageous. It's simply outrageous."

Sadie took over the packing.

"Can't say I blame you," she said. "She's a mean one, all right. Most cantankerous female I've seen for months. She'll be awfully pleased to hear you're quitting; probably throw a party for the whole company. The rest of the company will be sorry, if that's any comfort. They've been betting you'd last another week."

"I don't care."

"That's what I say. What do you care how pleased she'll be? Some people just don't belong in the theater, and you're smart to recognize it. Must be all those sugar beets your dad raises. Life's too easy. Just no salt in your veins. No vinegar, no iron."

The girl flushed. "I'm going home, Miss Sadie," she insisted. "I don't feel very well. It isn't as if I had done anything to deserve this. I've been nice to everyone. You know that's true. What did I do to start this, to deserve this?"

"Nothing," said Sadie. "Absolutely nothing, and that's a fact, honey—'cept maybe being young and pretty, and having a voice that six million women in this country would give anything in the world to possess."

She closed the suitcase with a snap.

"There we are," she said cheerfully. "You're all packed, neat as a pin. You can go home to your mother now. You want me to phone her? She'll be mighty upset if you just run in like a puppy with its tail between its legs. Better let me prepare her some. She got any salt in her veins?"

The girl remembered the depression and the old ewes, and the feeder lambs.

"Yes," she said hotly.

"Then I'll break it to her easy. I'll tell her you're sick. That won't worry her half as much as finding out you haven't the spunk to fight out your first battle."

She picked up the suitcase and started for the door, when the girl stopped her.

"I hate you, Sadie Hibbs."

"You can kick me around like a football, kitten. I don't mind. I'm used to it. That's what I'm here for. And don't think the sniping soprano is going to change. She isn't. There's so much bitterness and hatred inside, she can't. She doesn't like herself. It's you who'll have to do the changing. Don't let her know she gets under your skin. Might try making a joke of it." And she opened the suitcase and started unpacking.

The girl didn't go home—not even for a weekend. She knew if she did, she'd tell her mother, and her mother would tell her father, who wouldn't let her come back. And Sadie Hibbs was right. The jealous soprano did not change. Only somehow now her sniping did not hurt quite so much. The days slid by, and the

Margaret Craven

month, until the soprano had finished her last role and gone. Then again everything shifted, and the summer changed completely. Mr. Kovach gave Laird the role of Dorothy in *The Wizard of Oz.*

At first, Laird was too pleased and flattered to be afraid. Then she was too busy. Madame Alba helped her with the songs. She spent hours learning her lines, too busy to do more than talk to her mother and Jim by phone.

It wasn't until the day *The Wizard* opened that she felt something tight and cold within her, that she found herself beset by doubts. She would fail. She was sure of it. She would forget her lines. She would disgrace the family. She would ruin the production. She would disappoint Mr. Kovach. And as for Sadie Hibbs— the thought of what Miss Sadie would say to her was too awful to face.

When the final morning rehearsal was over, Laird stayed in the dressing room going over her lines, fearful that Sadie would find her hovering there, and in some strange way wishing she would.

But Miss Sadie did not appear, and the girl walked to the Y.W.C.A. and tried to rest. She couldn't rest. She couldn't eat her dinner. She couldn't even call home for assurance, fearful she would break down like a child.

Then she was walking to the theater, an hour too early and time crawling. When she entered the dressing room, Miss Sadie was waiting.

"I have some fresh coffee all made," she said curtly, "and some nice hot toast. After the performance you'll want a steak."

"Oh, Sadie. I love you."

"You'll hate me before the night's out. Drink your coffee now, and then we'll do your face."

"Sadie, I'm scared."

"Sure you're scared. Every night you'll be scared, and especially opening nights. When you aren't, look out."

"Sadie, maybe I'll—"

"No, you won't. Nobody faints unless he's sick. You won't forget your lines either. When the music starts and you see all those people waiting in the big dark tent, you'll be all right. Finish your coffee now and hold still."

Miss Sadie spent so much time on the girl's makeup that when she had finished, it was time to dress. The others arrived, and excitement and suspense picked up the girl and sustained her until the show began.

Now for the first time Laird realized her gift. Something alive reached from her to the people in the tent, something she could project to them and make them laugh, make them wait.

It was so heady it gave her a feeling of power and elation. She was so pleased with it and herself that during the first costume change, while Miss Sadie was peeling her out of one dress and into another, she tried to put it into words.

"It's going well. Can't you feel it?" she said. "Don't you think I'm doing well? Aren't you proud of me?"

"Part fits you like a glove," said Sadie. "Nobody but you could do it. You're the only one young enough, or naïve enough—or dumb enough."

"Sadie, I hate you."

"Make up your mind."

When it was over, and Laird's family and friends were backstage congratulating her, she felt no longer quite so pleased. And when Mr. Kovach told her she had done nicely, she said, "The part suits me. Ask Miss Sadie. I'm just young and dumb enough," and she smiled; and he also.

Then her week's prominence was over. She was back in the chorus, and the summer shifted to the final time.

The Music Circus presented *Die Fledermaus* for the last two weeks with a famous young star of the Metropolitan in the lead. The company was awed by her attainments and quite sure she'd be difficult. Instead, the Metropolitan star was friendly and without pretension. She worked harder than anyone else. She was meticulous. When Mr. Kovach asked Laird to sing for her, she was impressed by the girl's voice, freely promising any help she could give, and taking the trouble and the time to tell Laird of the years of work that had gone into her own training.

Laird listened to her smallest words with fascination and a growing doubt.

"No, thank you. I don't smoke. Makes my voice husky."

"No, Mr. Kovach, I haven't been home for two years. It's so hard for me to leave. I'm so devoted to my family that my affection interferes with my work."

Then the last two weeks were over. The Music Circus gave its final performance of the season. The next morning Laird went down to the station to see some of the principals off.

"When you come East," said the Metropolitan star, "I'll see you."

"You have a date with the world," said Mr. Kovach. "Remember that."

But Sadie Hibbs just smiled dryly. "Good-by, kitten," she said. "Don't wear your voice out hollering in the bathtub. Practice two cadenzas each morning and do the rest in your head. You still hate me?"

And the girl said chokily, "Sadie, I love you."

And Miss Sadie laughed and said, "That cantankerous jealous soprano and I did our best for you, kitten. We kicked you up the first rung of the ladder. You can haul yourself up the rest of the way."

Then the girl was waving from the platform, walking slowly back to the Y.W.C.A., packing her things, waiting for Jim and Fran to come for her and drive her home. The summer was over.

She sat in the middle between Jim and Fran, and it was as if the summer had never happened.

They drove the river road home, Jim and Fran keeping up the old gay banter. Fran was going to college in the fall, and Jim to the state university. Would the sororities and fraternities bid them, and if so, did they want to join? And the girl listened and tried to join in with the old keen interest, her mind slipping away from them to the circus, to the people who had been so good to her, to the jealous soprano who had made for her a wall against which to strike—and above all else to Miss Sadie.

"Aunt Susan says she gave two hundred dollars toward the new roof on the sorority house," Fran said. "She's sure there will be no problem at all, and when you come, after Christmas, Laird, I'll be there to help you," and Laird heard as if from a long distance.

When they reached home, Jim set her bags in the door, and she promised to join them for a swim as soon as she had seen her mother.

She went in the door, and stood looking. She had never been away from home so long, or emotionally so far. It was as if she were seeing all the old familiar things for the first time, the colors deeper, richer than she remembered, everything more precious to the heart.

She walked through the open door into the patio, and she saw her mother sitting in the sun watching the birds pecking at the bread crumbs she had placed on the feeding platform. She waited until her mother looked up.

"Why, Laird, I didn't hear you. Why, darling!" And the girl went to her slowly, sat down beside her and began to cry.

The mother waited, saying nothing.

"I loved the summer," the girl said, "and I hated it. It was fascinating. It was hard work. It was marvelous, and it was cruel."

"Like life itself?" said the mother.

"Yes, I suppose that's it. Like life itself. I could hardly wait to come home to you and Dad, and to Jim and Fran. And then when they came for me and drove me here, I wasn't part of it any longer, I didn't seem to belong because—because—"

"You've grown up," said the mother.

"Yes—and I can't bear it."

"When Madame Alba called me and asked me to send you to see Mr. Kovach and try out for the Music Circus, I thought I couldn't bear it," said the mother. "It would have been so easy to have kept you. I'll never forget that morning. It was the day the mother sparrow taught her fledglings to fly. I could hear her scolding and clucking at them. I did something I've never done in twenty-two years of marriage. I left the dishes undone, and the beds unmade, and I came out here to the patio and waited and watched."

"You did?"

"Yes, Laird. The first two little birds were no problem. But the last one didn't want to go. It hung over the nest while the mother scolded, and finally the mother bird shoved it out, nest and all, and pretty soon it was flying better than the others."

The girl was silent.

"Then there was that horrible woman who was so jealous of you. Oh yes, we knew it. We saw it in her face the night you sang your first song. I don't think I slept well that whole month, and I know your father didn't. We wanted to go and snatch you home. Miss Sadie wouldn't let us. She called every day to tell me how you were working out your own problem, and for a little while I think I—I almost hated her."

From beyond the old olive trees they heard Fran and Jim calling to Laird to join them in a swim.

"They'll grow up too," said her mother. "You'll find them again in the old way," and the girl answered nothing, and went to her room to put on her suit.

When she came back, she was smiling.

"If Madame Alba calls and wants me to sing a hymn in the church next Sunday, be sure and ask her which one."

"Yes, dear."

"And tell her not to worry, I'll practice it."

"Yes, Laird."

"And tell her I'll be over to see her tomorrow. I'm going into town to buy her a present, and one for Sadie Hibbs too. Something special. And I'm going to pay for them myself out of the first money I've earned."

"I see," her mother said and waited.

Would she say them now, the old words? "Isn't that nice of me? Isn't it thoughtful of me, Mother? Aren't you proud of me, Mother?"

For a moment their eyes met, and a little look passed between them. But the girl didn't say the words. She turned, smiling, and started across the grass for the pool beyond the trees.

She was gone, and in a sense she would never be back. Yet the mother watched her go with pride.

—*September 5, 1953*

Campus Cinderella

The pretty girl whom the student committee had expelled for cheating had shed the last and futile tear. She rose to go, sullen now and petulant, and the dean rose also.

It was all the university's fault, the girl said. The boys were cheating to keep up their grades and escape the draft. It was natural for the girls to cheat too.

The dean walked with her to the door, trying hard not to show her desire to shake this girl, to snatch the opportunity cast aside so shabbily, and give it to the next. Then she returned to her desk to wait.

The chimes struck five. From the biology and chemistry labs and the huge gray libe, students began to filter out into the quadrangle, weary and drifting homeward to the noisy fraternities, the ancient, inadequate halls, the lonely rented rooms.

To the dean all the girls were her girls, and because they were young and therefore conformists, they were look-alikes. White bucks or saddles. Blouses, sweaters and skirts. Bobs, bangs and poodle cuts. Books cradled in the left arm. It was only in the big and hidden things that they differed radically, in what lay deep in their bright young heads. Then she saw the next one coming slowly up the walk toward her office, and she remembered how great that difference could be, and felt a twinge of conscience and defeat.

This was the girl—whatever her name—who disturbed her nights. Not the cheat. Not the girl of the six percent who still go to college in a prom trotter's dream. Not the one of the sixty percent who work hard and play hard, too, who come back to reunions laden with pictures of their offspring, to greet one another with yelps of middle-aged glee, eager to relive the old, the happy times.

It was this girl who would never come back because she'd have no carefree college days she'd wish to relive. Only a desperately serious ordeal to be passed through as quickly as possible and consciously forgotten.

Yes, there were exceptions. The famous actress had come back last year. Her class of '26 had given a reception in her honor, and people who had never more than said hello on campus had come from many miles to call her by her first name and remember her when. And when it was over, the actress' eyes had sought the dean's and she had laughed and said, "And now I have a chance to know them." Then she'd sobered and said wistfully, "I shouldn't have come. It makes me remember that funny, broke, lonely kid who put up such a battle to get through this place and in a sense never came here at all," and the dean had known exactly what she meant.

There was a knock at the door.

"Come in," the dean called. "Come in, Miss Hoyt. It's nice to see you again," and the girl entered and sat down by the desk.

She was pretty too. She sat very straight and a little watchful, as if she asked no quarter and intended to give none. There were generations of thoughtful gentle living behind this face, and honesty in the eyes, and courage in the lift of the chin. And surely, if pricked with a pin nothing would flow forth but character. The best kind. Enough for a platoon. All good things. And too much of them, unleavened by anything lilting, light and spontaneous.

"Well, Susan," said the dean, "tell me how it goes," and the girl sat up even a little straighter, and told her.

Not a new, not an unexpected word. Yet as she listened the dean felt herself burning in shame for her own sex. It was a familiar story. With tuition high, there were more students working all or part of their way. With enrollment higher than it had ever been, there were no new halls where girls like this could hash for their board and room and have fun together. They worked for private families who lived on or near the campus, and although the university tried to screen these homes carefully and prescribed the hours of work, there was always that clever opportunist among the housewives who found it easy to impose upon girls so naïve and inexperienced.

"Susan, when you come home from classes today would you do the ironing? There are only a few pieces," and the girl unwrapped the bundle and found four blouses, three slips, eight napkins, two luncheon clothes, six shirts, three house dresses, two aprons—

"Susan, when you finish the dishes, would you put the children to bed? We won't be late." And it happened four times a week, and when the girl had done the dishes, put the children to bed and kept them there, answered the telephone three times and the doorbell twice, paid the paper boy, and quieted two quarrels, it was ten-thirty and three hours' studying to do, and a head too tired to think.

"Spare me any more detail," said the dean dryly in the middle of the girl's speech. "We'll find you another place."

She went to the files and returned with a folder. There was no sound in the room, the dean checking the list, the girl waiting.

"Well, here's one," the dean said thoughtfully. "Professor and Mrs. Peter Vargas—no children—1216 Elm Drive. I believe that's the old Pierson home, a nice big house in an old-fashioned sort of way."

She put down the folder.

"Professor Vargas was once in Prague, or perhaps it was in Vienna. England gave him refuge before the last war. Then when American universities did their bit to find berths for some of the best displaced brains of the world, he was brought here. He's in nuclear physics or some such."

She smiled thoughtfully.

"I can't tell you much about his wife," she said. "She's like many professors' wives. She's not ambitious for herself. You see her in the market sometimes buying the family turnips. And always at the president's reception. She's the one in the corner in the old black lace. And that reminds me. I must send my own old black lace to the cleaners."

For the first time the girl laughed.

"She's a lady with a broom," the dean said. "She sweeps, sweeps, sweeps the way clear of all life's little obstructions so that her husband can walk smoothly ahead. In a sense, she has little identity of her own. I might say the type is confined to no campus."

"If there's a quiet place to study," the girl said quickly, "that's all I want."

"Then I'll call her. If she's willing, you can move tonight. I will call the house where you've been living. It will be easier for me to explain the change."

And so it was done, the girl touching in her gratitude.

When the girl left the dean's office she walked with hope. She crossed the quadrangle into the tree-lined sorority row. In one big house lived a girl from her home town whose parents had been friends of Susan's mother and father when they were young and alive, long before she had gone to live with Aunt Eleanor. This girl had asked her here to lunch once, and all the girls in the big house

had been lovely to her, yet she had left with deep relief, feeling
not envious, only horribly aware of a whole college life of which
she was no part.

Tonight she did not feel apart. When she reached the edge of
the campus, she came to the house where she had been living, and
she hurried up the steps and in the door.

The family was having dinner. When Susan entered, there was
an awkward silence.

"You don't need to explain," the housewife said. "The dean of
women called me. Just pack your things and go."

She was a nice enough woman really. It was just that she lived
in a college community. Her husband had been to college. Her
friends also. She had not, and she resented it; or rather she
resented the fact that she had not had the courage to sacrifice and
go herself, and unconsciously she had enjoyed taking it out on
Susan, who had that courage.

The girl knew this, yet it did not make the relationship less
painful. She ran upstairs and packed her things quickly. She
carried them to the porch, the young husband at the dinner table
looking ashamed and wishing to help her, and not daring for fear
of a rumpus with his wife.

When the last load was out, the girl called a taxi and approached
the dining table.

"Here's the money for the long-distance call I made to my
aunt," she said, "and for the dress I had cleaned."

No one told her good-by. But it didn't matter. The minute the
front door was shut behind her, it fell away. She helped the taxi
man carry her stuff to his cab and all the way across the campus
she had a feeling of expectancy. Then the cab stopped in front of a
big brown shingle house set back among trees, and she was on the
porch with her luggage.

She rang the bell. It was like the moment when the curtain goes
up. It was wonderful and tense with waiting. Then footsteps
sounded in the hall and the door opened.

A man stood there. He was fifty or more, and he looked gentle
and rather shy. He wore an ancient smoking jacket and he had a
pipe cradled lovingly in one palm.

"I'm Susan Hoyt," the girl said. "The dean of women sent
me."

He looked surprised, confused, then cognizant.

"But of course," he said quickly. "We have been expecting you."
He pronounced each word correctly, yet something clipped and
piquant flowed in his voice. "Come in, girl—don't stand there in
the cold," and he picked up the nearest suitcase and the looseleaf

notebooks she had placed on its top, and followed her into the hall. Then he did something which amazed her. He lifted his head. "Lili, fairest of women," he called loudly, "come quickly," and one of the notebooks slid from his arm and disintegrated. They were both on their knees scrambling after its contents when the woman came in.

She was not the fairest of women. There was about her no assemblage of careful detail which indicates that a woman puts herself at the top of all that is important in the universe. She was middle-aged and gray, and her hands were long, lithe and well used. She looked down at them, smiling.

"Peter, my dear," she said gently, "it isn't necessary that you prove your affection for me before our new friend by kneeling."

The professor scrambled up—the girl also—and he said, "Lili, there is something wrong with the construction of these notebooks. At the least provocation they have a way—"

And she said, "I know, dear. You go back to your reading. John will bring in Miss Hoyt's things."

He departed, happy as a small boy dismissed from school.

"You have had dinner?" the woman asked, and Susan hesitated, ashamed to say no because of the lateness of the hour.

"No, of course not," the woman said quickly. "You must be starved," and led her to the kitchen.

At the sink stood a young man washing dishes. He had a plastic apron tied around his middle, his sleeves rolled up, and sufficient soapsuds in the pan to wash all the dishes of a small hotel. He was going at it as if he were killing rattlesnakes.

"Susan," the woman said, "this is John Miller. He has the room over the garage, and drives the car and helps with the garden. He is being retired from dishwashing. He breaks too many. John, this is Susan Hoyt, your relief. Her luggage is on the front porch. Would you mind carrying it to the downstairs bedroom, please?"

The young man said he wouldn't mind. He flipped the suds from his arms, wiped them carefully on the tea towel, and departed. The woman asked Susan to sit down while she brought her some dinner.

All her movements were deft. She took the dinner leftovers from the refrigerator and heated them. She poured the milk.

When the plate of hot food was set before her, the girl was suddenly very hungry, and when she took the first bite, nothing had ever tasted so good.

"Borjupaprikas," Lili Vargas said. "I learned to make it as a child. When you are poor you put in many noodles and little meat.

When you are rich you put in much meat and little noodles. This is medium borjupaprikas," and she smiled. "John will finish the dishes. I'll be in the living room to show you your room."

Then the girl was alone with no one watching, and she ate quickly until the boy came back. She did not speak. She did not know what to say to this boy. Life had given her no pleasant buoyant springboard from which to leap into easy casual acquaintance.

The silence became intolerable.

"When I carried your things to your room," the boy said, "I looked inside your notebooks. So you're going to be an architect?"

"Yes, I am."

He looked at her carefully.

"Only two kinds of girls come to this university," he said. "The ones who are so plain they have to educate their heads, and the ones who are here to find a husband. I suppose that's what you're after."

"It isn't true," she said. "You boys think a girl won't look at you unless you have a car and can spend money on her. You turn into lone wolves. You stand on the sidelines and drool when the campus queens go by, and you never look at anybody else. You're egotists. That's what you are. You're snobs."

She was not going to leave without the last bite of borjupaprikas. She put it in her mouth, washed it down with the last gulp of milk—and fled.

Professor and Mrs. Vargas were in the living room. They had heard her outburst and they did not pretend they had not.

"Good girl," said Professor Vargas. "It will do the lad benefit. He is one of my best students, not very prepossessing at this stage perhaps."

And Lili Vargas said quickly, "Now, Peter, what boy of his age is really prepossessing? A girl chooses a boy because she sees in him what he can become, and she goes to work on it. Susan knows that."

"Indeed? And is that why you chose me?"

"But of course," she said. "Come on, Susan, I'll show you your room."

It was a pleasant room, and in a corner was a huge rolltop desk.

"I thought you'd like it," Mrs. Vargas explained. "It has such fine pigeonholes."

She told the girl what time they had breakfast, and left her to unpack her things.

When all the clothes and books were in place, the girl put on her ink-stained bathrobe and tried to study. It didn't go well. There was too much to think about. She closed the syllabus and scribbled a note to her Aunt Eleanor.

Aunt Eleanor was unmarried, a schoolteacher, and a worrier. Aunt Eleanor worried because she could not give the girl more aid. She worried for fear the girl was working too hard, and not having enough fun. It had always been necessary to fib a little to Aunt Eleanor. But not this time.

"I have a wonderful new place to stay," the girl wrote. "Professor Vargas is the sweetest old lamb you ever saw. At first I thought he was a little stupid, but I don't think he is really. His wife is very calm and serene, and she can cook. There is a student—male—who lives over the garage. Utterly obnoxious." She underlined the word "obnoxious."

There was a knock at the door, and thinking of course it was Mrs. Vargas with an extra blanket or an armful of towels, the girl called come in.

It was the boy, carrying a plate with a tall glass on it.

"Mrs. Vargas made you an eggnog," he told her. "She thinks you're too skinny." Looking frantically for a bedside table and finding none, he set the plate firmly on her middle—and bolted.

The eggnog was excellent. When she had finished it, she added a line to her letter.

"The student—male—just set an eggnog on my stomach," she wrote. "It is possible that he is not so obnoxious as I thought. After all, Aunt Eleanor, a girl chooses a man for what she sees he can become."

When she was ready to go asleep, she lay in the dark, listening to the night sounds of the big old house. She did not know at all that she had met the boy she was going to love. She did not even imagine that already the lady with a broom had placed a gentle hand on her shoulder which she was to feel resting there all the days of her life.

Now began a time of blossoming. It was so natural and so gradual that the girl was unaware that she was beginning to tear down the little defensive walls she had built around herself. It was as if she stood now on a stone and felt—without thought—it firm beneath her feet.

When she came home from classes on the nice days, Lili Vargas was apt to be working in her garden, and sometimes the boy helping her. She would smile in that easy friendly way and say,

"Susan, he's starving again. Would you slip a sheet of cookies in the oven?"

The girl would hurry inside to take the roll of dough from the refrigerator and slice it quickly, eager for the boy to twine his long legs under the breakfast table and talk.

It was a good house for talking, and the talk was always wonderful and the talk was free. It never dealt with what people had, and seldom with personalities. It dealt with what people thought in their heads and did with their hands. Often some of the professor's more advanced students dropped by on some pretext or other, and they were all alike—very earnest, often confused, and always hungry.

Susan had always looked with distaste upon those girls who were clever and often unscrupulous in maneuvering attentions, and she had envied them secretly because she couldn't do it herself. But here there was no need for maneuvering. They were all young and most of them broke, and they liked to laugh and have fun. It was as natural as that, and for the first time the girl began to feel attractive and to know she was a woman.

Mrs. Vargas was always kind—but so unobtrusively. She did not dominate anybody or tell the girl what to do. She gave advice only when asked, and then cautiously, offering only suggestions.

"There's something different about these two, Aunt Eleanor," the girl wrote. "They're friends first. They like each other. Mrs. Vargas is not ambitious. She's just content to sweep, sweep, sweep ahead of her husband. And it's a good thing, too, because the poor dear is so absent-minded he'd never amount to a hill of beans if she didn't. He isn't stupid, Aunt Eleanor." She underlined the word "stupid."

One day when Susan was dusting some books, she pulled out a leatherbound parchment in a language she didn't know and she puzzled out enough to know it was a graduation diploma awarded to Lili Mueller from a Prague music conservatory. Then she knew why she always stopped studying to listen on those evenings when Mrs. Vargas played the Chopin études and nocturnes.

"Did you ever plan to make music your profession?" she asked.

The professor answered, "She did indeed, Susan. She was ready to give her first concert when she met a lonely, ungainly student and gave it up."

Mrs. Vargas had smiled. "But look what I got instead, Susan," she said, and she took hold of her husband's top hair and twisted it into a peak. "Doesn't he look just like Foxy Grandpa, Susan?"

He cried, "Lili—stop that," in the way men do when they like something, but feel impelled to protest loudly.

Every Saturday morning the boy brought his dirty clothes from the room over the garage, and Susan dumped them in the washing machine along with her own. There was something very intimate about their clothes swishing together in the hot suds, and while they waited, they talked. Especially the boy. The girl learned to listen.

She knew he was going to be one of those men whose work comes first, who give to it a kind of dedication. His talk was of his work. Would he ever be good enough? Would he live long enough to earn his advanced degree? And Susan found herself listening and saying, "Of course you will. Of course you can."

They did not speak of love. Its fulfillment was too distant for utterance. They joked about that sometimes.

"I would never do for you," Susan told him. "I'll never know enough about physics to understand one tenth of what you're doing. If I married you, you'd have to type out a statement of what you were doing. Then when someone asked me what my husband did, I would hand it over and let him read it for himself. How would you like that?"

The boy said, "I wouldn't mind, Lame Brain."

As the girl blossomed, so did her work. She was no longer content to be merely a straight-A parrot who could memorize easily and retain just long enough to spill her knowledge in a blue book. She was more ambitious now and in Judith Baird, who taught architecture, she saw all she hoped to become.

In the architectural department all the women students looked upon Judith Baird with awe, cherishing every word she said, and wishing to be like her. She was a legend. She had everything. She was lovely to the eye. Houses she had planned were pictured in the fifty-cent magazines. She taught modern design and had an office of her own. She was married to a professor in the biology department and had a child.

The girl watched her, but never mentioned her at home. In her mind she made no odious comparisons with Lili Vargas, who was so kind—and colorless.

In class, Susan's work grew more confident, developing an originality, a mark of her own. Several times Mrs. Baird complimented her. So the months passed.

Then one day this firm growing spot became a thing of passing. Professor Vargas obtained leave for the fall quarter to do research abroad with a European physicist, and two days later Mrs. Baird suggested to Susan that she submit her name for a much-coveted scholarship, and when the girl agreed and said she was looking for a new place to work for her board and room, she offered Susan a chance to live and work at her home.

It was as easy as that. One good thing passing and in its place an opportunity even more promising.

On the day Professor and Mrs. Vargas left, John and Susan went with them to the station, everyone trying hard to be bright and gay.

"You must not let the professor handle the tickets," Susan cautioned. "He'll lose them."

"And don't let him out of your sight," John said, "or he'll stick his nose in a book and forget where he is." And the professor smiled in his gentle way, and his wife promised.

When it was time for them to climb on the train, Mrs. Vargas kissed the girl good-by.

"If you are not happy in your new place, you can come back to us. You are beginning to know yourself. I do not need to worry."

When they had gone, John and Susan drove home in the professor's old car. The big old house had become a shell, empty of all that had been warm and tender. When John had packed her things, ready to take her to Professor Baird's, she had a moment of faltering, and they clung to each other, promising to be patient, promising to wait. Then he drove her to the new place and left her there, and the time of blossoming was done.

Surely now began a time of flowering. It was all new, and different and exciting. Even the house was different, a house for moderns and extroverts with glass walls, open, fluid rooms, and a garden so skillfully lighted at night that the indoors and the outdoors became one.

Oh, Susan missed Peter and Lili Vargas of course, and she was grateful. When she received their first postal, mailed from the boat, she felt homesick, and wished for some secluded, badly lighted corner of the mellow old place where she could be with herself. And she missed the afternoons when she had baked cookies for John, and the easy evenings when students had dropped by on some excuse or other and stayed to talk.

People did not drop by this house. They came only when invited. It was too busy for casual entry. Cookies weren't baked here. They were bought. A Filipino boy put the dishes in a dishwasher, and once a week he washed the glass walls with a storewindow squeegee until they were so clear that in her her own room Susan had to place a chair in front of the full-length window lest she bump her nose.

Each morning Judith Baird made a list of Susan's duties for the day, many of them pertaining to Nancy, the ten-year-old daughter.

Nancy to the dentist. To music or dancing lessons. Groceries to be bought. Cleaning to be picked up. As Mrs. Baird found the girl apt and ready, she extended these duties to include errands pertaining to her own business, sometimes important and very interesting, so that gradually Susan became her little-girl-Friday.

"You have the talent, Susan," Mrs. Baird said to Susan one day. "You have the self-discipline which is so unusual. If you are willing to sacrifice—" And she said the scholarship was practically assured, and suggested the possibility of a job in her own office when the girl was ready for it.

Now Susan had a flame within herself. She had her dream of glory; and the future, once so nebulous, seemed safe in the palm of her hand.

She blinded herself to small moments of uneasiness. Twice she found Nancy, a shy, sweet little girl, shut in the dark closet of her room, sobbing bitterly, and she scolded her. Even if her mother didn't have time to be with her very often or very long, wasn't it a fine thing to have a mother so lovely, so successful? Wasn't it?

She noticed that Judith Baird did not have friends of her own sex. Many acquaintances? Yes. Great admiration from younger women? Yes. But not friends. She was too critical. She did not like women. She liked men, and this of course was because other women were jealous of her.

There was just one thing to which Susan could not blind herself. The first time Mrs. Baird met John she said, "I'm sure he's a nice boy, Susan, but a little gauche, isn't he?" and Susan explained quickly that John was one of Professor Vargas' best students and that she had met him at the Vargas home.

"What kind of a woman is Mrs. Vargas?" Judith Baird asked, and Susan said she was a lady with a broom who swept the way clear in front of her husband, and a good thing, too, because the poor dear needed it. And Judith Baird laughed.

Susan looked up the word "gauche." Clumsy. Awkward. It was true, John was awkward in this house; and after that she met him elsewhere.

One day Professor Baird met him also on campus. He was a good-looking, quiet man who never had much to say.

"I like your young man, Susan," he told her, and Susan said she did, too, and added and could not stop herself, "I know he's not prepossessing. I know he's a little—gauche."

He had looked at her shrewdly. "My wife said that, didn't she?

It's true. It's true of most young men, who are still groping, who know they have much to learn." Then he said a queer thing. "If she must, a girl can work *with* a boy she loves, or *for* him, Susan. She cannot work first for herself, because this is to work against him."

She did not try to figure out what he meant. She did not wish to know. In her mind she was loyal to John, yet when they met, something had changed. He was lonely these days and easily discouraged, and when she said, "You can do it; of course you can do it," she was thinking first of herself. But as the time of Peter and Lili Vargas' return drew near, John brightened. She would come back to the old house, he said. They would see each other often again. It would be as before, and Susan thought of leaving her warm spot of promise—and said nothing.

One morning Mrs. Baird greeted her at the breakfast table with a cry, holding up the paper for Susan to read. Peter Vargas had been awarded the Nobel prize in nuclear physics.

"All those brains walking around on the hoof right under your nose, Susan, and you never guessed it," and she laughed, and her husband smiled.

It was amusing, and to the girl somehow appalling.

The university had never before had a Nobel-prize winner. All day long the campus was agog. Nobody talked of anything else. Wasn't it wonderful, they said? Professor Vargas was so modest, so shy. At the very end would come a pause.

"What kind of a wife has he?" somebody would ask, followed by a blank stare.

And someone would answer vaguely, "You never see her around very much; nice enough, I guess."

At noon John was waiting for Susan at the campus sweet shop where she had her lunch. He had a telegram from Professor Vargas that they would be home this evening, they would take a cab from the station, and would John please not mention their arrival, and have sufficient food in the house for breakfast?

"They're going to slip in quietly and miss the rumpus," he said. "Isn't that like them? Susan, help me make a list. Coffee— bacon—eggs—"

"And bread and cream," she told him. "And orange juice; and don't forget the butter."

They bought the supplies together until it was time for classes, the girl hurrying, and the talk beginning again, and the pause and the question the same.

It was late when she reached home that afternoon. The living room was full of people. The Bairds were going to a campus faculty dinner, and Mrs. Baird had asked some of the guests for a cocktail first.

Susan prepared trays of dips and dunks in the kitchen. But when it was time to carry them in, she was afraid. She could hear the guests talking and laughing out there in the lovely spectacular room which was a room not for the wise and gentle words, but the witty ones. She went in.

Someone was telling an amusing anecdote about Professor Vargas. And another. And another. All funny, and flattering and admiring.

Susan passed the spreads, waiting and listening, and more afraid. Then came the pause.

"What's his wife like?" somebody asked. "Does anybody know?" and there was a lull and a silence.

Mrs. Baird put down her glass.

"I can tell you," she said gaily. "You see her every day on the radio. She's the dreadfully drab little woman the emcee fishes out of the audience, and he flatters her and he says, 'Madam, what do you do?' and she says, 'I don't do anything. I'm just a housewife.' "

Her imitation was so good, everyone laughed.

"She's a lady with a broom," said Judith Baird, "who sweeps, sweeps, sweeps ahead of her husband. At least that's what Susan says, and she lived in their house for months. It just proves something I've always contended; that nothing can stop genius. A man like Peter Vargas goes straight to his goal no matter how he's handicapped, no matter how dull a wife is draped around his neck."

She looked up and saw Susan's stricken face.

"Isn't that what you said, Susan?" she demanded. "Isn't that what you called her? Didn't you say Mrs. Vargas was a lady with a broom?"

The girl set down the tray carefully. "The dean of women said it first. I repeated it," she said slowly. "And it's true—but not as you mean it." She hesitated, choosing her words carefully. "When she met Peter Vargas, she was ready to give her first piano concert. He was a broke, gauche student. She must have seen in him what he could become, and how much he needed her; and after that nothing else mattered."

"Really?" said Mrs. Baird. "Go on, Susan."

"They're friends," Susan said. "They can play together like—like children. Their home is a place to be shared, where students like me—the lonely ones—can find themselves."

She picked up the tray. "She's content to be just what she is—a woman. She can let her hair turn gray. She can be middle-aged. It doesn't matter, because they're both so sure of what they have built." And seeing the look on Mrs. Baird's face, she knew she had no future in this house, she had thrown it away, and as she carried the tray to the kitchen, she knew also that it didn't matter.

She waited until the guests had finished their drinks and left for the dinner. Little Nancy was spending the night with a friend. The Filipino boy had his day off. The house was suddenly very still.

She knew now what she must do. She put away the food, carried out the glasses and washed them. When this was done, she put on her coat and went out into the evening, almost running toward the old house. When she rang the bell, John answered it, and they stood looking at each other for a long moment.

"I knew you'd come," he said, and she went in.

"We must hurry, John. They'll be hungry, but they won't stop for dinner. They'll come straight home. You lay a fire and start it, and don't forget to put the screen in front. I'll set a card table. I'll get supper started."

"Borjupaprikas?" he asked, and she laughed, and said bacon and eggs.

"But it's a good dish," she admitted, "especially for the young. You can make it with lots of noodles and little meat."

And John agreed it was a fine dish and someday they'd eat lots of it. That's all they said between them.

When everything was ready, they put out the lights in the front of the house and waited in the kitchen. They heard the taxi stop, and steps coming up the walk. They heard the door open and Peter and Lili Vargas come in, and snap on the lights, and they knew they were standing there—the two of them—seeing the fire and the table by the hearth.

Then they heard steps coming to the kitchen door. It opened and Professor Vargas stood there smiling.

He set down the bag he was carrying in his left hand, and he lifted his head.

"Lili," he called loudly, "Fairest of women. Come quickly, Lili. Our children are here to welcome us."

—*February 6, 1954*

HALFHEARTED WIFE

They sat close together—father and daughter—saying little and driving slowly through the golden hills and the dark live oaks toward the forgotten towns of the Mother Lode. The depression was behind them now, with its scare headlines, its queues of jobless men waiting at the soup kitchens. The house in the East was three thousand miles distant, and the woman who had told them good-by from anxious eyes.

Mother had no need to come west seeking her roots. Her taproot lay east in home, family and friends. She did not like the west or know it.

It was Father who had been hurt and who sought like a dog the hidden home place to rest and lick his wounds until he should be strong enough to strike out again. To the girl it was still too wonderful to believe—that suddenly he was no longer the successful and solemn man who came home from the office each night, world-weary and taciturn; that for the first time in her sixteen years he had a chance to know her and needed her.

It had been hard at first. Crossing the continent, gloom had pursued them. Then in San Francisco they had ridden on a cable car, and on the steepest hill all the passengers had slid down to one end and begun to laugh and chat. Father had taken her to dine at a restaurant he remembered as a boy. No velvet hangings. No crystal chandeliers.

"It hasn't changed, thank heaven," Father had said, and ordered the dinner with great care. And when the old waiter had brought it, he had bowed to the girl and asked, "Will madam have wine also?"

Nothing so grownup and wonderful had ever happened to her before, and surely never would again. And then it did. Father had leaned across the table, smiling and relaxed for the first time in many months, and he had said earnestly, "Do you know something, Muffie?" as if he had just discovered it. "Do you know something? Daughters are fun."

They drove slowly, the girl sitting quietly beside him, happy and proud. Several times on the day's long ride she glanced lapward to be sure—to be absolutely sure—the old bulges had rearranged themselves at last. Such a plump little girl she had always been. So clumsy. So slow and awkward. It was no wonder Mother thought daughters were work.

"Hurry up, Muffie." She had heard it all her life: "Stand up straight, Muffie. . . . Put your shoulders back. . . . Pull your stomach in. . . . Keep your hands away from your face. . . . Hurry up, Muffie."

It was only this year that the miracle happened. She had sprouted up and thinned. It was only very recently that she had felt sure—well, almost sure—she was going to make a woman and perhaps even a pretty one, at least one that would not let Mother down too much.

Now the country was changing, strange rock formations dotting the tawny fields. Now Father drove faster, a look of eagerness on his face.

"You'll love the names, Muffie," Father said. "There's Fiddletown and Tuttletown. There's You Bet, and Rough and Ready. And Whiskey Slide and Shirt Tail. Used to be a little place called Slumgullion. Thank heaven, my grandfather didn't start his diggings at Slumgullion. With her Eastern background, Mother would never forgive it," and he laughed, then sobered.

"A river of gold flowed through these foothills," he said. "It was a mile wide and almost a hundred and fifty miles long. They say old Abe Lincoln paid for the Civil War with gold from these hills. It changed us into an industrial nation. It helped make us great. It affected the whole world." And just then they came to the first town. Afterward she was never quite sure which was the first, or even of the exact route by which they reached it.

They rounded a bend and up a gentle hill through old trees casting deep shadows against the summer sun, and there on each side of the dusty little road lay what had once been a rip-and-roaring camp. All strife and greed were long gone, leaving only the tranquil beauty, softened, mellowed and appealing. And the girl stared at the old tavern with its veranda overhanging the street, and at the old stores with their heavy iron shutters still standing guard against bullets and fire. And they slipped through the town and on to the next and the one beyond it, until all she saw blended in her mind—Mokelumne, San Andreas, Angels Camp—until it became part of this day, which lies for everyone between childhood and maturity, when for the first time she fell in love with life itself and felt she could last forever and do anything at all.

It was late afternoon when they reached Columbia, and Father went into the little store for the key to his grandfather's house. A woman produced it.

"Your third cousin twice removed said you was comin'," she told him. "Mighty sorry he couldn't be here to welcome you. I sent Josefina over to clean the place up. Kindlin's cut. Beds is made. You need some groceries?"

Father said he did, and bought them.

"Biggest sale I've made this month," the woman said. "See those old men across the street, sittin' in the sun? They're pensioners. Live in cabins in the hills and eat sourdough and sowbelly. Don't buy nothin', and my taxes gettin' higher. Ten dollars they was this year. Times is bad, mister."

Father agreed and promised to come back tomorrow, and they drove on.

"I hope the old place hasn't changed much," Father said. "I used to spend the summers here as a little boy when my grandmother was alive. Somehow I've always thought of it as home."

They drove slowly through the lovely little town—all but deserted—and just beyond it, set back from the road in a grove of Digger pine and catalpa, stood the house. Red brick it was, and trimmed in white; the old bricks faded now to a muted tone. It was not a big house, but carefully made with walls eighteen inches thick and built to last. It belonged here in this setting, as quiet, as peaceful as the day, and they left the car and started up the path, neither speaking.

In the center of the path, halfway to the house, a young man sat on a campstool, painting. In front of him was a folding chair. To its back was a canvas. On the seat of the chair was an open paintbox and palette. He was working as slowly as a child who learns something very hard and more important than life itself. He did not hear them, and as they drew close they could see he was painting a picture of the old house.

Then Father's foot snapped a twig. The young man turned and stood up, still holding a brush by the end. He was nineteen, perhaps, and from the first look Muffie liked everything about him, even the place on his brown head where the hair wouldn't stay down, and especially the look on his face which was so much like the look on her own—a little shy and uncertain, as if he, too, found growing up none too easy. But Father only saw the picture.

"Not bad," he said, his voice warm and surprised. "Not bad at all. You've done the house nicely. You've caught the color exactly."

"I put a little orange with the red," the boy said shyly, "and a touch of yellow ocher for the sunlight."

"The Digger pines are excellent," Father told him. "I like the way they reach out. It gives a kind of motion. And you've caught that smoky blue-green."

"It's viridian green," said the boy, "with cerulean blue."

"But the hill back of the house," Father said slowly, and the boy's face fell.

"It's not right," he admitted. "It belongs farther back. It's not right at all. I tried adding yellow ocher and it doesn't work." He looked hopefully at Father and he asked, "Would you know how to make that hill move back, sir?" And because she knew Father didn't and because she wanted the boy to like her, Muffie spoke quickly and without thought.

"Why don't you gray it?" she said, "and add maybe a little white?"

For the first time the boy looked at her closely and said why not, he'd tried everything else.

He washed his brush and wiped it carefully on a horrible old cloth. Then he took the cap from a little silver tube and squeezed some paint onto his palette, and as he worked they saw the hill recede until it was right.

Father spoke first. "Muffie, how in this world did you ever—"

And she blushed and admitted she didn't know; she'd said the first thing that popped into her head, and wasn't it wonderful? And they all laughed, and Father explained that this was his grandfather's house and they'd come to spend a month, and he asked the boy if he would like to see the inside; and the three of them walked to the door, which Father unlocked, and they went in.

On the wall facing the door was a picture of General Beauregard, and over it a small Confederate flag. Beside the picture was a poem, framed, dated and handwritten in fine old script, entitled "When the Flag Came Down."

Father walked over and read it to himself, and he said a little chokily, "My grandfather was a good man, but I'm afraid he was a little emotional as a poet," Then he sat down on the old rosewood sofa.

"To see if it's stuffed with the same horsehair," he explained, "and it is, and it still prickles."

They walked through the old rooms, looking at everything carefully—at the fine old sconces, the marble mantels, the furniture that had come around the Horn. The boy helped carry in the luggage, and he built a fire in the kitchen stove.

His name, he said, was Jon Evans. He lived in a valley town and had been two years to art school in San Francisco. It was tough going, because his father wanted him to go into business. He had a little rented room in Columbia and an old rattletrap car. He was here because he liked the country. He was just painting.

Father asked the boy to stay to supper, but he declined. He would like to come again tomorrow and finish the picture, if he wouldn't be a nuisance.

When he had gone, Father made coffee, and Muffie cooked bacon and scrambled eggs.

"Do you think he's nice?" she asked anxiously, and Father said of course he was nice, didn't she think he knew a nice boy when he saw one?

"Do you think he likes me?" she asked, and Father said of course he liked her, and they'd probably be tripping over him the whole month.

When nightfall came, the dark took them. There was no light anywhere. No car moved on the dusty road. Yet it seemed to the girl that the night sounds in the old house were touched by a kind of magic. And this was the first day of the lovely summer.

It was a sweet summer and innocent, made up of simple things, freely given and gratefully accepted. Father rested and grew strong again. Each morning he cut a little kindling or walked to the store for groceries, and every three or four days he drove into Sonora for an armful of books. He steeped himself in the old tales of the gold rush and regaled them with fierce and heady bits of history over dinners made pungent by those two members of the lily family upon which mother looked with a prejudiced eye, the onion and the garlic.

Each morning the boy painted, the girl beside him. Oh, he was clever. There was no doubt about it. Muffie was sure he was destined to be the finest artist God has yet put upon this earth; and she said so, but Jon demurred. He said he just wanted to be a good craftsman, if it took him twenty years, and it would.

The first week Muffie learned that even a very young artist spends as much time cleaning his brushes as he does painting, and in this process uses innumerable paint rags. It was her job to provide them. The towels disappeared one by one, and presently Father put a hand backside every day or two to be sure his shirttail was still intact.

"We'll have to leave before the sheets go," he said cheerfully.

The young couple rambled through the little old towns in the boy's aged car, painting whatever appealed to him.

One day he was painting in a meadow—the girl reading aloud—when he reached for his paint rag, which he had placed carefully on a handy bush, and missed it, and turned to see it disappearing slowly and very surely into a cow, attracted by the smell of the linseed oil.

Muffie was sure the cow would lie down and put up her feet, and the boy was sure that if she did, she would turn out to be the most valuable cow in the whole state. They left hurriedly, and every day for a week they drove by the meadow to see if the cow was still able to look at them with her big soft eyes. And she was, though Father insisted her milk must be flecked with viridian green and burnt sienna.

One Sunday morning Jon was painting the lovely little red church at Murphys, the girl helping clean the brushes, when an old man came up to watch. As he was leaving, the old man dropped a paper bag and a bottle fell out and broke, and he wept loudly and ambled off. And just then Sunday school let out, and the children filtered out into the sun and came over to watch, the teacher and a stray mother or two hastily snatching them out of the way.

"They're artists, all right," said one mother indignantly. "Did you see them, sitting there, painting in a pool of whisky? And so young too."

They did not return to Murphys for quite some time, and when they saw an old man basking in the sun thereafter, they looked upon him with a certain cynicism.

A rancher who lived nearby lent them two horses, and sometimes Jon renounced painting for the day and they rode far from the roads through manzanita and pine, through aspen that grew in the creek beds.

Now, in the depression, men were panning gold once more, and they came on them sometimes, bent to their labor. Once they tied their horses and stopped to eat lunch at what they thought was a deserted shack, and a miner came out to greet them. They shared their lunch with him, and he lent them a pan and showed them how to use it, and after what seemed hours and hours of prodigious work, they could see a few tiny flakes of gold shining in the black sand.

Then one day Mother wrote that she was lonely, and Father had a letter from his office that business was stirring again. The boy left first. On his last afternoon he and Muffie walked through the town, hand in hand, like children, for a last look at Papeete, the hand-pumper fire engine, whose hoses were said to be made of buffalo hide. They looked at all the old stores and buildings, at St. Anne's on the hill, and they walked to the shed back of the old red house to see the surrey which had been great-grandfather's pride. They even climbed through a broken back door into the old Fallon Theater and stood on its shaky floor in the dusk, the bats flying overhead.

They were full of fine plans and big hopes. They would write every week. When the boy went to Paris to study, the girl would meet him there. When it was time for Jon to go that night, he shook hands gravely with Father. Muffie walked with him to the road, and he kissed her good-by. It was the first time any boy had kissed her. Yet this night the sounds of the old house were restless, untouched by magic. The summer was done.

When she saw them, Mother thought Father looked splendid. So rested and relaxed.

"But what have you done to your hair, Muffie?" she asked. "It looks like hay. I'll make an appointment for you in the morning. Perhaps we can work it in with our shopping. Now hurry and get ready for supper, dear. And put your shoulders back."

It wasn't Mother's fault really. Mother's life had followed the old pattern—school, plenty of nice young friends, college, perhaps a bit of travel, and marriage to a fine young man. It was a good pattern. Probably it was the best pattern, and Mother knew it and wanted Muffie to have a good life. And she knew also that Muffie had not one shrewd and designing trait to help her, and was not one of those glamorous girls who have young men tripping over each other on the front stoop without the help of anyone. No doubt about it. Muffie needed aid, and Mother was going to give it—even if it meant keeping her so busy she forgot the romantic, impractical boy she talked about so much just at first. No doubt his own parents were working hard, too, maneuvering him from the vagaries of art into the safer shoals of real estate or dentistry.

Muffie herself never knew quite how it happened. Life just seemed to take her and carry her away. She wrote Jon frequently at first. But this was her last year at Miss Potter's—all the more fortunate girls in her suburb went to Miss Potter's—the entrance-board exams poised over her head. And the next year was her first in college. So many important things to do. To choose the right clothes. To make the right friends. To belong to the right sorority. Oh, Mother had to work on that one, but it paid off, and then, instead of Mother, the house was pushing her into activities, making her keep up her grades. And the letters dwindled gradually—and stopped.

So the months slipped into years until one June day Muffie was married to Stephen Strong, a nice boy from a fine family, with Father feeling sad and trying to look happy, with Mother feeling happy and trying not to look smug, with Muffie feeling very happy and just a little scared, because already she was beginning to realize that a fine wedding is not the end of anything at all, but only the merest beginning. And thus the pattern began over again. From blended muskrat to mink. From the small apartment to the nice little house to the much nicer, much larger house.

In the town where her husband was in business with his father, Mrs. Stephen Strong produced a boy and a girl, worked for the Charity League and the Crippled Children's home, ran her own household and belonged to a study club. She was both capable and attractive. She grew into one of those smart young matrons who drive up to the supermarket in shiny station wagons, wearing crisp blue cotton with cashmere sweaters to match, hurrying through the crowd, poking avocados and hefting crabs, their nice faces preoccupied and a little tense.

Stephen progressed, and each step forward brought innovation and change. The muskrat gave way to the Japanese weasel. Mother's nice old Orientals went out and the soft-green carpeting came in, and after a time the soft-green carpeting went out and the lush off-white rugs came in.

Sometimes when friends were gathered—this was in the Persian-lamb phase of progression—and spoke nostalgically of their youth, Muffie mentioned her great-grandfather—never forgetting, of course, to point out that he was a Southerner who had chosen the terrors of the gold rush to living under the Northerners, and she told about the cow that had swallowed the paint rag, and about the old man who had dropped the whisky bottle.

The cow never failed to make a small conversational hit and, when the chuckling had died, someone always asked what happened to the young painter, and Muffie had to admit she didn't know, she'd lost track of him years ago. And the someone always laughed and said probably it was a good thing; no doubt the boy was happily employed now in wholesale produce or hardware; and the assembled guests smiled with the tolerance which middle age bestows upon something which happened in youth and is therefore unworthy of anything but humorous allusion.

When Muffie's daughter, Susan, was sixteen, it became evident to her mother—precisely as it had to Muffie's mother—that daughters are work.

Susan was a rebel. She absolutely refused to go to the town's equivalent of Miss Potter's. In the public high school, she chose for her best friend the most beautiful and giddy girl in her class. She talked about her all the time, waited on her every whim and convinced herself that by comparison she, Susan, was hopelessly plain, if not downright ugly. It did no good to tell Susan that she was a nice, sweet, intelligent-looking girl. She considered such a description insulting, and moped around the house, her hair lank at the neck.

Then one day Susan acquired a beau. She acquired a solemn young man who wanted to be an ichthyologist, as unprepossessing as a littly guppy. Maybe she'd get over him, but Muffie was taking no chances. When summer came and the young man took a job at Cape Cod, Muffie maneuvered Susan into spending six weeks as assistant swimming instructor at a girls' camp five hundred miles distant.

This accomplished, and weary from much work and worry, she accompanied her husband to San Francisco on a business trip, and it was there that the lovely forgotten summer stepped slowly out of the past and rejoined the present.

While Stephen was with her, there was no time to be reminiscent. Then he found it necessary to fly to Honolulu with local representatives of his firm, and as the others did not take their wives, he left Muffie to spend a week by herself.

It was the first time in all her married life that she had been alone for a week, without responsibility, in a city she had not visited since girlhood, and it was surprising how long, how lonely were the days and how inadequate were her own resources.

She rode on the cable cars by herself and remembered her father. She sought the old restaurant on Pine and found it, still unchanged, and she remembered that it was here that her father had said, "Daughters are fun."

The next day she went to the park—very smart in her simple summer suit, well-armored with all the little sureties that come to a woman secondhand from the success of her husband. She ambled through the aquarium, then to the museum, and seeing a placard announcing the annual exhibit of the Society of Western Artists, she went in.

She was not looking for any one picture. Yet shen she came on it, it was without surprise, as if it were waiting there for her to find it. *Seascape* by Jon Evans. She stood looking at it for a long time, and then she walked quickly toward the receptionist at the desk by the entrance.

"I want to ask about Jon Evans' picture," she said. "The seascape."

The woman's face brightened. "Wonderful, isn't it?" she said. "Of course, he's a fine artist. It's the best picture in the show, I think. It wasn't given an award, because Mr. Evans was one of our judges this year. The work of the judges is jury-free."

"I'm interested," Muffie said, "because I knew a Jon Evans when I was a young girl at my great-grandfather's house at Columbia."

"Well, it must be the same man," the woman said. "Mr. Evans has made something of a specialty of Mother Lode pictures. He's retired from teaching at the university. He's just painting now, and he's at Columbia for a month or so. He loves that country and tries to go there each summer. Of course, you know that Columbia is a state park now?"

"No—no, I didn't."

"Yes, and the old Fallon Theater has been repaired and is active again. The College of the Pacific puts on the old plays. They're very good. You're just visiting?"

"Yes."

"Well, try and go up. It's worth the trip. It's something you'll never forget."

Muffie thanked her and left. She did not even have to think about it. Of course she would go. She would go as her father had gone, because her roots were there, with the same eagerness, the same fear that it might have changed.

The next day she went to Sacramento by train, and the following day she rented a car and set out. She could not remember the route they had traveled that first time. She drove through the valley towns, properous now and busy, and stopping once for a cool drink against the heat of the summer, she entered a café, to be met by the blare of a jukebox.

The golden fields were the same, dotted now by fine cattle, and she kept looking for the bend in the road up the gentle hill and could not find it. She was anxious now, a little frightened.

Then the road climbed, and strange rock formations appeared on the hillsides, and she came not to the first little towns she remembered, but to Sonora. It had grown, too, but she remembered the lovely little red church called St. James, and sought it eagerly and found it.

She registered at the hotel, and that night, with other guests who were there for the same purpose, she drove the three miles to Columbia to the Fallon Theater. In the early evening the lovely little town was as she remembered it, mellowed and sweet. The old theater was alive now and lighted, and when she went in, she could see that in repairing it they had spoiled nothing at all. The play was one which had been produced here in the days of the gold rush, and the college students who appeared in it were young and eager, as if life for them, too, held its magic. Between the acts, when the audience sauntered through the old taproom into the soft night, her eyes sought one face and did not find it.

The next morning she checked out of the hotel and drove again to Columbia to find Jon, to see her great-grandfather's house.

"Yep, he's here," said the man in the store. "Saw him go by half an hour ago. He's painting some trees down the road a spell. You can't miss him, lady."

She drove on, and presently she saw him, and she parked the car and approached slowly. He was working in the shade of a tree. He was painting very slowly and carefully, as a boy who is learning something new, and very hard, and more important than life itself. He was sitting on a campstool, a folding chair in front of him, his canvas resting against the back. And on the chair seat was his open paintbox and palette, and the little bottle of linseed and turpentine—and, of course, the paint rag.

Then he turned and saw her. He hadn't changed very much. "Yes-s-s?" he said, very politely. "You are interested in painting?"

"I—I believe I saw one of your pictures in the show at the De Young Museum, in San Francisco," Muffie said slowly. "It's wonderful," and she waited.

"How nice of you to stop and tell me," he said. "An artist appreciates that. You're just driving through?"

"Yes. As a matter of fact, I'm looking for the old Pembrook place." And she was sure now he would guess, he would know.

"It's farther on. You'll know it by the fine old catalpas and the Digger pines. They're still standing."

"You mean the house—"

"No," he said; "you know how it is. It was a brick house, and the brick had faded to a lovely muted red. Brick's valuable now, and everybody is building barbecues and patios. Somebody pried loose a few bricks, and others pried out the fine old woodwork and the marble mantels. About a year ago there was one wall still standing."

She could not speak.

"It's sad, isn't it?" he said. "We build, and then we destroy, and when it's too late, we try to put back what is gone. They're talking of reconstructing the old house, and all they have to go by is a sketch I made years ago when the grandson of the original owner and his daughter were here."

"You knew them?"

"Yes, I did. I was just a boy beginning to paint. The father was very kind to me, and the daughter was the sweetest girl I ever saw. I've never forgotten her."

And she knew then she could not tell him who she was, and she thanked him and returned to her car, and drove on to the house. The trees still stood, but there was nothing left of the house except a few heaps of broken brick so badly rubbled as to be worth nothing to anyone. When she turned to go, she was crying.

On her way back to San Francisco, Muffie sat very still and thought very hard. It was difficult. For years she had read only those books which the best reviewers pronounced worthy of her time. She had listened only to that music, attended only those plays carefully screened by expert opinion. Now she drew a line under the figures of her own life, and she added up the columns by herself. She was not pleased with her conclusions, and she was convinced that there were two things she must do. When she reached the hotel, she found a note from Stephen, who had returned that morning. They were to fly home tomorrow. Tonight they were to meet the Grays and the Dunbars—business associates and their wives—for cocktails at the Top of the Mark and dinner.

It was a note like many others, but this time it did not seem important, and she read it hastily and hurried up to her room. There she placed a long-distance call for Susan, but when the call went through and she heard Susan's voice at last, she found it hard to speak.

"Darling," she said, "it's Mother."

"Are you all right?" Susan asked. "Is something wrong? Is Dad ill?"

"Nobody's ill. We're fine. We're flying home tomorrow. I just wanted to tell you something. I thought perhaps when you finish your job there, you and I might go up to Cape Cod for a few weeks if—if you'd like that."

"Oh, Mother, could we?" The voice was all life and eagerness.

"Of course, dear. And, Susan, there's something else I want to tell you. I—I maneuvered you into that summer job. Oh, yes, I did. I did it deliberately, and I was wrong. I was wrong because your life belongs to you. I know that now."

"Why, Mother—"

"I know, dear. It surprises me too. I'll write you as soon as I get home—and, Susan—"

"Yes—"

"Are you standing with your toes pointing in and your shoulders slumped, because if you are, go right ahead. I'm through with that too." And they both laughed and said good-by. The first thing was accomplished.

As she dressed to go to dinner, she thought only of Stephen and of what she intended to say to him. It seemed to Muffie that for years she had been walking slowly toward this moment, ground as fine as a crystal lens.

Then a key turned in the lock and Stephen had come. He talked first, of course, full of his flight to the islands and the plans for the evening. And she listened, hiding her impatience, waiting for him to finish.

"And what did you do, Muffie, while I was gone?" he asked at last.

And so she told him. She told him of going back to the Mother Lode, of finding Jon painting in the shade of the tree. She told him of the old house which had been destroyed by people prying loose the muted bricks to build something new in the name of progress.

"Jon didn't know me," she said. "And I couldn't tell him who I was because he's changed so little and I so much. He's just the same sweet nice person. Only older. He's done what he planned. He's put down his roots deep in his own country. As soon as I saw him, Stephen, I knew that I'd met a happy man."

He said nothing.

"What happens to most of us, Stephen? We don't mean it to happen. Those people who pried loose the first bricks didn't mean to destroy the old house. We're like them. I'm like them. We want everything that's coming and everything that's new. We keep going faster and faster until we destroy ourselves. What happened to that girl Jon didn't know, because I want to find her again?" And it was the girl who spoke. It was the girl who sought his face so earnestly. And just then the telephone rang, and Stephen answered it.

"Yes?" he said in his nice voice. "Oh—Barclay? Glad you called. . . . Yes, I flew over and I can give you the situation in a nutshell. Excuse me a minute, Barclay. Just a minute," and he turned from the phone to his wife.

"Muffie," he said, not unkindly, "we have to leave here in four minutes. If we're late, they won't hold the table. Now put on your hat and ring for the elevator. I'll join you there. We'll talk about it later. You've been alone too much. It'll do you good to get out. Now hurry up, Muffie."

He turned back to the phone. "Barclay?" he said. "No, no problem. Nothing serious. Just a slight hassle with the little woman. She's a little slow tonight getting organized."

—*May 22, 1954*

AMBITIOUS MARRIAGE

It was a Friday, the busiest day of the week, and like all Fridays it began at six. The street lights were just blinking out when the car turned into the driveway of Quality Cleaners and came to a stop in the rear. The owners, Franz and Gretchen Muller, slipped from the front seat, and without speaking walked to the door.

The man took out his key, his thought hurrying ahead to check the valves of the boilers, because if the boilers didn't work there would be no steam, and if there was no steam there was nothing.

He turned off the burglar alarm, unlocked the door and went in first to snap on the lights in the big workroom, his wife two steps behind. As he touched the switch, he hesitated. Every day it was the same. Every day when the lights went on they saw each other pitilessly revealed—worn before their time, Gretchen's shoulders weary from the constant reaching, Gretchen's ankles swollen from standing through the terrible summer heat; and on his face the patient look of one who died a little long ago, leaving behind everything he was and had a right to be, to start anew in another land where he had nothing, where he was nobody, where even the words would lie forever strangely upon his tongue.

He turned on the lights. For an instant their eyes met, and each saw the other was afraid. Never in this country in all the twenty-two years had they been afraid. Not of the work. Not of the sacrifice. They had forgotten the dryness of the throat, the desire to yawn, to swallow. They felt them now.

"Papa, I go to work," said Gretchen Muller, and there was something so steady and gentle in her voice it was as if she picked up her husband and gave him a lift into the day.

He hurried to the boiler room. She walked to the huge canvas cart from which last evening she had lifted the warm, sweet-smelling clothes, fresh from the tumblers, placing each garment on a hanger and each hanger on a rack. And she reached up now and began to sort these hangers so that when the employees came

257

at seven they should have sufficient work to start the morning. Not too much, lest they be discouraged. Not too little, lest they set the tempo too slow. This done she climbed the steep stairs to the little flat above the workroom, and made coffee—made it strong— putting the pot to boil. And when she heard her husband coming, she poured the coffee, and they sat down side by side. The time had come to speak.

But what to say with the past pressing close about them? This flat had been their first home in the new land. The Lutheran pastor had brought them here in the hard days of the depression, and old Heinrich Mann, who owned the cleaning plant then, had given them their start. Here, Johnny, their son, had been born. Here they had put aside their own fine hopes, and worked, saved and sacrificed. And every moment had been one of thanksgiving, because it was all for Johnny, whom this day they must lose.

Gretchen spoke first.

"When children are little, they step on your toes," she said. "When they are older, they step on your heart. I remember my grandmother saying it, Franz, but I didn't know what she meant."

"Mamma," he said quickly, "we must not expect gratitude from Johnny. No parents can ask it, and few young people can give it. Not until they are older and have children of their own. I have read somewhere that the first duty of parents is to know they are expendable."

"I do not want to be expendable," she said. "Papa, I do not think I can go to the wedding."

"I do not think I can go either, but when the time comes this afternoon, Gretchen, I know we shall go together. The waiting is hardest."

They did not speak more. The employees had come to work now and the day had caught its rhythm. Steam filling the air with its insistent hiss. Hands reaching for the presser heads, the thick pads and the brushes. Hands lifting, turning, caressing the garments into shape. Above all other sound they could hear the sharp staccato report of the steam gun, and they remembered Johnny working summers to earn money for college, his feet on the pedals, the steam gun in his hand. And they could still hear him whistling as he worked.

As they descended to the workroom, the rhythm broke. The silk finisher, the fancy spotter looked up. The mender lifted her head from her needles and her button boxes. And all the eyes were curious, and all the eyes were sad. Franz went to the washing rooms. Gretchen inspected the finished clothes, checking the buttons and the belts, flipping a trousers leg to be sure the men's presser had left no crotch wrinkles to save a lay. And the day passed until it was time to go.

They dressed in the flat above the workroom, and at three the steam went off, and the plant was starkly quiet. But when they went down, two of the women employees had lingered to be sure Gretchen's hair was just right, and not a wrinkle in her fine new dress. And when they went out to the car, they found the fancy spotter polishing it vigorously, and when they drove away they could see their faces, all smiling and trying hard to look happy, because they loved Johnny too.

They drove too fast, then too slow. They drove thirty miles to the fine suburb near the big city where the neat small plots gave way to sweeping lawns, large, impressive houses.

Gretchen sat quietly, hands clasped in her lap. Franz drove carefully, eyes held to the road. When they reached the church, a traffic officer directed them to a parking place which had been reserved for them, and when they went up the walk through the trees, they saw that a large crowd had gathered.

The voice of a bobby-soxer roared above all others.

"Johnny's a doll," she cried. "Oh—he sends me. He's one of the greatest football players of all time. I'd rather have him than the Duke of Edinburgh," and she squealed like a little pig.

They hesitated, seeking some other entry. But it was too late. Too many people pressed behind them, and a policeman was pushing the crowd back to keep the walk open ahead. As they started forward a man stepped in front of them from nowhere, an ingratiating grin on his face, a microphone in his hand.

"And here are the parents of the groom," he said, and the crowd gasped, stared, and let out a sigh of disappointment, hoping for something much more quaint and picturesque than this patient, tired-looking man in a dark suit, and the middle-aged woman clutching his arm.

"I bet you two are just about the happiest people in all this world," said the man. "And you have a right to be. Indeed you have," and he stuck the microphone in front of Gretchen's face. "*Sprechen Sie Deutsch*? Oh—come on—just a little—just a little for the folks to hear," and his tone was that considered suitable for pussycats, infants, idiots and the senile old.

"Thank you," said Franz quickly. "We are very happy. Thank you very much," and somehow they went on and up the church steps.

Inside the door Gretchen stood trembling a moment. Then an usher came forward and showed them to the vestibule. People hurried in and out, whispering in hushed, excited voices until the usher said it was time, and offered Gretchen his arm. Then they were walking up the aisle of the big crowded church, Franz following, to the first pew on the right.

They sat very straight and under the fold of Gretchen's skirt they held hands tightly. When the bride's mother entered, she bowed to them graciously, and when she was seated, the clergyman entered from the chancel, followed by Johnny and his best man.

They saw only Johnny, who did not see them at all. How fine he looked. How tall he stood, his head lifted, his eyes shining and fixed beyond them down the long aisle where his bride would come.

"Mamma, I have met the girl I am going to marry. Oh—not soon of course. Not until I go through law school and am started." He had said it three months ago, and they did not know just how this wedding had happened, and they were not sure Johnny knew either.

Now the processional began. Everyone rose. Friends of the bride and her family. Friends Johnny had made at the university. They were the strangers.

When the ceremony began, they watched the bride's mother carefully to know when to stand, to sit, to bow their heads. They saw it as if it were not real. They heard it as if from some great distance. They were giving him up completely, and they knew it and were doing it as well as they could.

When the recessional began, the music joyous, they followed the bride's mother down the aisle, and presently they were back in their car, following her car to the home reception.

"Mamma, we lived through it," Franz said. "I do not see how we did it."

"Papa, my new slipper hurts, and I think my back hair is coming unpinned," Gretchen said, and she slipped her heel out carefully and she felt her hair and found it pinned tight. They both knew the hardest part lay ahead. This they did not mention.

The reception was held informally in the garden, the bride and groom and her attendants receiving on the terrace. Franz and Gretchen Muller stood together at one side. Many people spoke to them, and all were charming.

Did they know, asked the bright gay voices, that they had a perfectly wonderful son? How proud they must be of him. Such a fine athlete and a good student too.

"Thank you. We are very happy," said Franz Muller.

They had little chance to speak to Johnny.

"Isn't she beautiful?" he asked them. "Aren't I the lucky one?"

And they looked at the lovely stranger and said, "Yes, Johnny. We are so happy for you." That was all.

The garden was filled with talk and laughter, the women's dresses like flowers, the caterers moving expertly about.

Then the bride tossed her bouquet from the balcony above the terrace, and soon the guests were leaving the driveway to see the happy couple on their way, the good-bys spoken, people drifting away through the late afternoon.

The bride's mother asked the Mullers to join her family on the terrace. They did so.

"Johnny just completes our family," she said to Gretchen with great complacency. "The first time I saw him I knew he was the one I wanted for my daughter."

"Johnny is a good boy," said Gretchen.

On the far side of the terrace the bride's father was speaking to Franz.

"I hope you don't mind that I have found an opening for Johnny," he said. "It takes so long for a young lawyer to establish himself. There is no money in law."

"Johnny has always wanted to be a lawyer," Franz told him. "It is his decision."

They did not stay long after that, and when they left, the bride's parents walked with them to their car. They must see each other soon. When the children were settled perhaps.

Then it was over. They were alone at last and on their way home.

No—not quite home. First they must return to the plant to tend the chores they had left undone. When they reached it, they took off their new clothes in the little flat and put on their old. Franz hurried to the washing room. Gretchen went to the canvas cart to hang up the last cleaning. Only when this was done, and it was time to go home to the neat small house on the nice little street did Gretchen cry a little.

The big words, the important words, nobody had spoken. "Thank you for raising such a fine son. And now, if you'll just step aside, please, we will take him over completely." No one had spoken them. They did not speak them now.

"No one can take Johnny from us, Mamma," Franz said. "We must wait. We must be patient."

Johnny Muller did not know he had a problem just at first. Like many a young man born with no silver spoon handy, he was serious, hard-working—and naïve. He was grateful for whatever success he'd had in football, but not overly impressed by it. It had provided some fun, much work and two athletic scholarships which had helped a lot. He had earned them. He was a good student.

When he first met Kay Dearborn, he had shied from her. She had so much and he so little. What could she see in him except a serious young man who wanted to make something of his life, who was determined not to end in some small, safe alumni job where he could relive his gridiron triumphs and be exhibited at the big-game rally each fall? Johnny knew nothing of the surety of the world in which silver spoons are taken for granted.

When Kay bobbed up—not too often—wherever he happened to be, he thought it was coincidence. When he fell in love with her and explained carefully he wouldn't be able to marry for some years probably, he thought she'd wait for him. She said so.

It was Kay's father, Mr. Dearborn, who pronounced waiting ridiculous. He and his wife had waited to marry in the early days of the depression. An unhealthy, stupid waste! Why not take a job for a year or two? He could provide a good opening for Johnny. Only a stopgap of course. If Johnny still wanted to go on with law, there would be a right way.

Johnny said he'd have to talk it over with his parents, and he did so. But when he returned to the university, it was to find Kay much upset. The news had leaked out and the campus was talking of little else, assuming the marriage would take place soon. She took all the blame upon herself, and he was so in love and eager that—well, it was easy to go along. Nobody waited to marry any more. It was old-fashioned and stodgy.

After the wedding reception was over, Kay and Johnny drove to the little city apartment which was to be their home, and on the way Johnny thought of his parents with affection and gratitude.

"I don't want Mother and Dad to feel lonely or neglected, Kay," he said, and she agreed. Absolutely!

As they were unpacking the wedding presents, Kay circled the dates on the calendar of the new desk set which no good daughter-in-law must forget, and if she did not put a ring around the Mullers' wedding anniversary, it was only because Johnny couldn't remember it himself.

Then they unwrapped the hand-crocheted bedspread which Gretchen had sent Kay. It was so beautifully made it belonged in a museum, but it looked strangely out of place with the modern decor. Even Johnny saw that, and agreed that until they had the right place for it, the bedspread would have to be sent to the top shelf with those other wedding gifts which are gratefully acknowledged and hastily brought out for display when the donors come to call.

This was not difficult, since Johnny's parents were too busy to visit anyone. Johnny telephoned, of course, and he tried to write frequently at first. As life led him along new roads, the letters turned into notes, and the notes became less frequent.

Johnny and Kay saw his parents twice the first year. They had so much to do and so little time, that each visit was a rush affair.

Everything was pleasant. The Mullers couldn't have been nicer. A little quiet perhaps. Each time Johnny came away with a vague sense of relief, unable to shut his eyes to the differences in their life and that of Kay's parents. And each time his mother said, "Are you all right, Johnny?" and he assured her he was fine. Everything was splendid.

They saw Kay's parents often, which was natural. Mr. Dearborn was on the board of the big city company for which Johnny worked. He came frequently on business. Furthermore the Dearborns had both leisure and money. They waited for no opportunities. They made them. Scarcely a week passed without some tangible evidence of their thought and generosity.

Whatever his little girl wanted, Mr. Dearborn wanted Kay to have. This was natural, wasn't it? It was normal for parents to want their children to enjoy the things which made life pleasanter and easier.

Yet when Mr. Dearborn had a shiny new convertible delivered on their first wedding anniversary, Johnny did not drive it. He left it for Kay's use, and continued to drive the old car his father had given him when he bought a new one.

So the first year passed, and when friends dropped in of an evening and the talk turned to the difficulties of inlaws, Johnny and Kay listened sympathetically, and it was Kay who always said proudly, and a little complacently, that Johnny's parents—bless their good hearts—were no problem at all. Such wonderful people. And so courageous. They had left all behind them to come to this country to escape the Nazis. Kay never mentioned the little cleaning plant, and Johnny listened and felt uncomfortable, glad when the subject changed to other fields.

His awakening came gradually, pricked by instants of perception and awareness. The firm in which he worked dealt with corporations in figures so huge it was hard to believe that behind them were people who lived and hoped. Around him Johnny saw other young men in love with the power and mystery of finance, which he did not feel.

He admired Kay's father. Mr. Dearborn was a strong and dominant man, kind to his family and his friends, implacable to his enemies. Sometimes in those wakeful hours of the night Johnny saw himself as he would like to be. Not so much a big successful man as a deep one. And always in a law office that smelled of musty books. And he pictured himself walking to work down the streets of some smaller town where the roots grow deep, the townspeople stopping him to chat, the family dog tagging by his side, because the children were in school and he was lonely.

Once he mentioned to Mr. Dearborn that he thought sometimes of going back to study law, and his father-in-law smiled and nodded, and pointed out carefully how long it takes for a young man to establish himself in a profession so slow, so precarious. Johnny had taken on new responsibilities now. He must remember that.

Johnny was not likely to forget it, because in the second year of their marriage Kay expected a baby, and this changed everything and left no time for dreaming. Kay insisted they must find a larger apartment. Something with a fine sunny room for the newcomer. Perhaps even a house. And when Johnny insisted they couldn't afford it, Kay's father smiled again, and said it could be arranged. There would be a way.

Anything could be arranged, if Kay wanted it.

All the nice and pleasant things could be arranged, and so easily and smoothly. All Johnny had to do was be Kay's husband, to work hard and behave himself, to be grateful, to follow the path carefully laid before him; and to disagree with Mr. Dearborn on no large and pertinent issues.

But something was wrong. Something was missing. He had lost the right of choice. He was not free to make his own success or his own failure.

At the office he saw other young men who envied him, and showed it. Once when several of them were discussing raises and promotions, Johnny expressed some doubt as to his future.

"You don't have to worry," one of them said. "Oh—you'll have to work as hard as the rest of us. No doubt of that. But every time you're ready for the step ahead, the spot will be waiting for you." And though he did not say so, there was a tone to his voice that implied another young man with no influence might easily be sidetracked while Johnny moved ahead.

He worked harder than ever. He telephoned to his mother occasionally to report Kay's progress, and he planned to see his parents. When the opportunity came, he avoided it.

"Are you all right, Johnny?" his mother would ask, and what could he say? To speak at all seemed disloyal to Kay.

One late afternoon when he returned to the office from a business conference which had kept him away all day, he found Mr. Stebbins, the bookkeeper, waiting for him.

Mr. Stebbins had been with the firm for thirty years, a wise man and a kindly one.

"Your father was in," he said. "He came to the city to order some new equipment for his cleaning plant. He was disappointed not to see you, and so I asked him to lunch."

"I hope it was no trouble," said Johnny quickly.

Mr. Stebbins looked surprised, then thoughtful.

"It was a privilege," he said. "Your father told me a little about himself. He's a fine man."

"Yes, he is. Dad's tops."

"You've never told me about him," said Mr. Stebbins. "You don't really know him very well. We never know our parents well. We take them for granted. We give up the very things for which they've battled out their lives, and when it's too late, we have to earn them back," and he turned and walked quickly away.

But Johnny remembered what had been said, and for the first time in his life he began to think about his parents. Mr. Stebbins had been right. He knew them too little. When he was growing up and the war on, he had been ashamed of his Teutonic ancestry. In school the boys had teased him, calling him a Nazi and he had punched noses to stop them, coming home battered and triumphant. He had sensed that in their past were issues so deep his parents could live only if they could put them down completely. They had wished to forget, and he had been content never to know. He wondered now, and in him grew a new and slow curiosity.

When the baby arrived, it was a boy, and on the day Kay came home from the hospital, the head of the firm called Johnny into his office and told him they were transferring him to a better job in the city where Kay's parents lived, and at a substantial raise. Johnny had earned it, he said. The firm was much pleased with his progress.

That night when Johnny told Kay, he realized the news came as no surprise. That's why nothing further had been said of changing the small apartment for a larger.

"We'll move as soon as I'm strong enough," Kay said. "Mother wants us to stay with her until we find a place of our own. Oh, Johnny, just think. We'll be nearer your parents also."

"I want to see them," Johnny said. "I want to see them very much," and Kay said of course they would see them. They would ask them for dinner as soon as they arrived. Her parents would want to see them too.

And so it was arranged. Yet when Kay and Johnny had made the move to the Dearborns', he dreaded his parents' coming. He wanted it, and he was afraid of it.

Franz and Gretchen Muller drove to dinner on a Sunday. It was the first time they had seen Kay's family since the wedding, and again everyone was kind. This was a duty occasion to be marked by pleasant, if empty, amenities, to be done nicely and accomplished with relief that it need not be repeated soon—in a year or two perhaps. Only now Johnny was aware of this. He was no longer quite so young or naïve. He could look at his parents objectively, almost as if he were seeing them with the eyes of a stranger.

How gentle and self-contained they were. Just once some fleeting and poignant look crossed his mother's face. When Kay placed the baby in her arms, Johnny saw her bite her lip as if she were going to cry.

But no—she smiled instead and she said to Kay politely, "He looks like you. He is a lovely baby. He has my Johnny's ears." And then as if she were suddenly aware that she had used the possessive pronoun, she added, "Papa, don't you agree? Don't you think the baby has Johnny's ears?"

At dinner Johnny kept watching his parents. They were working hard and they showed it. He could see them driving to work before the town was awake, starting the pattern of their day, which was always so much the same, and never quite the same. In a business where the employees have itchy feet, they must be ready to substitute for anyone at all, and they must work harder and longer than the others. He could see them driving home at night to the neat small house his mother loved and in which she had so little time to spend. Compared with the lives of Kay's parents and their friends, the life of his parents seemed rigid and brittle. Yet they seemed happy. Between them lay some sound and deep content. It was only when they looked at him that doubt showed in their eyes, as if they knew—as if they had known from the first—that he was caught in a silken trap. And Johnny remembered what Mr. Stebbins had said, and he felt the questions rising which he had never asked about the past of which they had spoken so little and so seldom.

Presently when the Dearborns and his parents were gathered in the living room around the fire, Johnny could contain his curiosity no longer. He had to know. He had to find out, and he waited for a lull in the pleasant, desultory talk.

"Father," he said then, "I want you to tell me something. When you came to this country, what was it that caused you to leave? What was it that made you decide?" and there was something so imperative in his voice that, after he had spoken, there was an instant's utter silence.

"I went to Heidelberg from Vienna, and there I met your mother," Franz said. "She was a student at the university also. Oh—we had fine hopes for ourselves. I was going to be a fine scientist. We were married and continued our studies. You remember, Mamma?"

"Yes," said Gretchen. "And you were so handsome, and I was so proud of you." And she looked at him—gray now and worn—and smiled.

"When the Nazis first began to come into power, it was in the universities they first showed what they intended to do. I remember a Jewish professor whom we admired—who was a fine and honest man—was stoned to death."

"Johnny," said Mr. Dearborn quickly, "I am sure your father finds this a painful subject," but Franz said, "No, I will tell him. It will not take me long."

He turned back to his son.

"We saw the plague growing around us," he said quietly. "At first we thought we could be so quiet and so meek, we could escape it. We could shut our eyes to it and it would not exist. Then Gretchen's brother became prominent among the Nazis, and we knew we must cooperate or leave. Do you remember, Mamma?"

"Yes," said Gretchen, "I remember. We knew a child was coming, and this was what decided us. And when we arrived, there was no work anywhere, and the old man let us have the little flat above the cleaning shop, and you swept the place and kept it clean, and we were happy because we had each other and were safe."

"You did not mind working so hard?" Johnny asked slowly.

"If you want freedom, you must pay for it," his father said. "We made only one mistake. We thought we could earn it for you also. But one cannot assure freedom for his child. In his own time and in his own way he must earn it also."

No one spoke. Then Gretchen said it was time for them to go, and said good-by.

Johnny and Kay walked with them to their car. Gretchen did not ask her son the question she had always asked, "Are you all right?" She said good-by almost impersonally and Johnny knew that she and his father had done the most difficult thing parents can ever do. They had released him completely. They had let him go. They had given him the freedom for which they had sacrificed. He could choose his own life.

When his parents had driven away, Johnny and Kay returned to the house. Johnny carried the baby upstairs for Kay, and put him down gently on the bed. He stood looking at him, so quietly and so long that Kay drew silently and a little fearfully to his side.

"What is it?" she asked. "Is anything wrong?"

"Being a parent frightens me," Johnny told her. "It makes one vulnerable all the rest of his life. Anything that hurts one's child can hurt the parent so much more. How do you suppose we'll feel when—if some pretty girl plucks him away from us—completely away from us and from all we've worked and hoped for him?"

"As I did you?" Kay asked.

"It was my own fault," Johnny said.

"No, it wasn't. I did it. I admit it. You were the one I wanted, and I was afraid if we waited, you'd get away. I thought it was very clever of me to ask Father to help me. I thought I was the smart American girl who always gets what she wants from any man. Only you haven't been happy in your work, and you've never said so. You've never talked about it, and you've never blamed me. And I can't bear it, because I love you."

And they stood looking down at the sleeping child, silent—and close.

One afternoon, a month later, Franz and Gretchen Muller were busy in the workroom at the rear of their cleaning plant. The sharp staccato report of the steam gun had ceased. The employees had gone for the day. Gretchen was working at the big canvas cart, lifting the sweet-smelling clothes, fresh from the tumblers, placing each garment on a hanger, and each hanger on the rack. Franz was checking the clothes that had come last from the pressers, flipping a trousers leg to be sure the men's presser had left no crotch wrinkles.

When the door opened and Kay and Johnny came in, they did not hear them at first. When they turned, they were surprised and a little appalled. Kay had never been here at the plant. They were ashamed that she should find them like this—hot and weary toward the end of the day.

They couldn't stay long, Johnny said casually. They'd just dropped by to tell them the news. He had a new job. He was going to help the freshman coach, back at the university, and it wasn't too much of a job, but it would give him time to study law, and heaven knew he would probably be baldheaded by the time he was ready to go into practice. And furthermore they'd found a nice old house on the edge of the campus, and just as soon as they were moved they wanted them to come and see how well the crocheted bedspread looked on the four-poster Kay had found in a second-hand store. And anyway Kay wanted to learn to make kartoffel suppe, and maybe even apfelstrudel if she was smart enough, which she doubted.

Then—so soon—Johnny and Kay had gone. Franz and Gretchen Muller watched them go from the door, and then they went back to their work—Gretchen to the big canvas cart, and Franz to the checking rack.

"We will not see them very often, Mamma," Franz said, "but it doesn't matter."

Gretchen picked up the next garment and placed it on a hanger.

"It does not matter at all, Papa," she said, "Johnny is our son again, because he belongs to himself."

—*January 8, 1955*

SUSANA AND THE SHEPHERD

All the passengers on the big transcontinental plane were interested in the young Basque who occupied the rear seat. He was a good-looking lad with his dark eyes and his proud, inscrutable face, tagged on the jacket with a check badge like a piece of luggage because he couldn't speak an English word.

"He's a sheepherder from the Spanish Pyrenees," the stewardess replied to an inquiry. "The California Range Association is flying over many of them. Usually three or four come together. He's the first to come alone."

Several of the passengers tried to be friendly, but the young Basque only stared at them, too bewildered and confused to smile, and finally a sure blonde, who had traveled in Spain, said she'd draw him out. She'd toss a little Spanish at him. She'd just go over and sit on the arm of his chair and give him the good old American *bienvenida*.

So she did it, and the young Basque fixed upon her a pair of scornful, suspicious eyes and ignored her.

"You know what I think?" said the defeated blonde to the stewardess. "I think his mother warned him to have nothing to do with American women. They'd eat him alive." And she was wrong; it was his grandmother who had warned him.

"Oh, he's a strange one," the stewardess told the navigator. "They're all silent, but this one wouldn't even talk if he knew how. I hope somebody meets him in San Francisco. I have strict orders not to turn him loose unless he's met."

The navigator was wiser. "He's from some small village, probably," he said. "Never seen a big city. Never been in a plane. If he's afraid, it's the kind of fear only the brave know. Otherwise he wouldn't be crossing an ocean and a continent to herd sheep for a stranger in a land he doesn't know. Let him alone. He's a kid with a dream."

And after that, across the plains and the mountains, the boy sat undisturbed, holding his dream, and his was the old dream many

Basque boys have held in their hearts. Their land was not big or rich enough to support all. By custom, a family's land was left to the eldest son. The younger sons, therefore, must emigrate; their only hope of keeping the land they loved was to leave it—and come back rich.

It was possible. From his own village in the Valle de Arce in the province of Navarra several had done it. Felipe Lacabe had done it. He had herded sheep for six years in a place called Nevada. In all that time he had learned no more than fifty English words, and been to town twice, and spent not one coin on drink, smokes and girls. He had come back with twelve thousand dollars—a fabulous fortune—and he had bought himself a band of fine sheep and married the prettiest girl in Uriz.

Many had come back, and more had not. Whenever American tourists came to the remote villages of the Pyrenees some Basque father, prodded by his wife, said slowly, "If you have been to California, is it possible you know our son, Bonifacio?" or Fermín. Or Esteban. But they never did.

He, Juan Varra, was going to be one of the lucky ones. He had made up his mind. The American consul at Bilbao before whom he had appeared for his sheepherder's examination had praised him. The doctor who had given him his physical had spoken of his strength. And while he had waited the long months for the completion of his papers, the priest had strengthened him.

No Basque had ever been remembered for his words, the priest had said. Only for deeds and for courage. And if the ignorant thought he had a mist in his head like the mists of the mountains he loved, what of it? The thing to do was to be strong.

Yet when it was almost time to land, the boy found it hard to be strong. He reminded himself that an unknown *Americano* had paid seven hundred and eleven dollars and ten cents for his passage, sight unseen, and why? Because he knew—as who does not?—that for two thousand years the Basques have been famous for their skill with the sheep.

He thought hard on *abuelita*, his little grandmother. How confidently she had smiled at him as she had prepared his favorite omelet for his last supper at home. With no teeth, she had looked like a little old baby, and he vowed now that with his first wages he would send her enough money to buy a set of shiny white store teeth, so she could walk through the village, head high and smiling.

Also he thought of his little brother, who had begged to come along, who must emigrate, too, when he was older. He must set him an example. He must not fail.

Then the plane landed. The passengers began to file out slowly. He followed them. Surely el Cid, the bravest knight in all Christendom, never went forth to battle more staunchly than Juan Varra left that plane, the little stewardess at his heels, praying fervently somebody would meet him and ready to grab his jacket tails if no one did.

He was the last to pass the gate, and as he stepped through he saw the most beautiful sight possible to any Basque far from home. He saw another Basque. He saw a browned face, no longer young, which was smiling and showing some splendid gold teeth. And the voice was speaking his own dialect and it said, "Welcome, Juan Varra, and are the girls still as pretty in Navarra?" And this was Ancelito, thirty years from home and as much of a Basque as ever.

Ancelito collected his luggage and led him to the pickup truck. When they had left the confusion of the city, and were driving through the great wide green Sacramento Valley, Ancelito dropped pleasantries and began to speak so slowly and seriously in Spanish that the boy knew he must remember every word.

Now in early May the alfilaria was already dry. The corkscrew spirals on the wild grass that can work their way into the sheep's hides had already formed. It was vital, therefore, that the sheep be moved at once from the low range. Separated into bands, sheared and branded, they had been driven to a central campsite, the trailer houses of the herders accompanying them. At the campsite, freight cars waited. The rich *Americano* who owned the sheep had rented a whole train, and this very moment he was supervising the loading of the sheep bands into the cars. Tonight the train would carry the sheep across the great mountains into Nevada, where the long summer drive would begin at dawn.

Usually, said Ancelito, a youngster from the homeland was kept on the valley ranch for several weeks to accustom him to the strange American ways. But now they were desperate for herders. Last year they had lost two older men from heart attacks. The camp tender had found them at eight thousand feet, stiff in their blankets. It would be necessary for Juan Varra to go with them to Nevada and to start out at dawn with a band of two thousand sheep. Every other day a camp tender would bring him supplies and tell him where to find water. He would have a burro, of course, and a dog which Ancelito himself had trained.

"There is nothing to fear," Ancelito told him gravely. "The dog will know what you do not."

The boy said with dignity, "I have no fear."

Ancelito questioned him carefully, and in response the boy told him, shyly and briefly, a little of his dream. After four hours' driving, they came at last to the campsite.

In the trailer house Juan Varra ate a quick meal while Ancelito checked the clothes and the bedding he'd need. Then it was time to go, and they walked together through the dark to the train.

"You will go in the caboose," said Ancelito. "You will sleep better, and tomorrow you will need that sleep. I will go by truck with the others, and I will see you at daybreak."

Once, at night in his bunk, the boy woke and felt the train moving under him and the cold air on his cheek, and he could hear the hard pull of the engine, and knew they were crossing the mountains. When he woke again, it was to the smell of coffee and the touch of a trainman's hand on his shoulder. He put on his shoes and his jacket and drank two cups of coffee. When he left the caboose, he stepped out into the clear dawn and such a sight as he had never seen.

Already the sheep were being spilled out into the sage, each band at a time, its loaded burro, herder and dog waiting to drive it away.

Because he was new, his band was the last. Then it, too, was spilled into the sage, and his burro and dog and a sheep tender drove the band away from the tracks as Ancelito motioned him to wait.

The train moved on, the boy waiting by the truck while Ancelito talked earnestly to the *Americano* who owned the sheep, and though they spoke English and the boy could not understand a word, he knew the *Americano* was worried.

"Andy, I'm scared to death to send him out. Can he do it?"

"Yes, He's used to hardship. He is not an American boy. He does not put his manhood in a car that can go ninety miles an hour. It is in himself."

"I know. He'll have the inbred willingness to endure."

"He has something else. He has a dream."

"All right. Let him go."

Then Ancelito gave the boy his directions and told him where he would find water. The owner shook his hand.

Juan ran into the sage and took the crook from the tender, and he gave the old signal to the dog with a lift of his hand and he was off and on his own. He did not permit himself to look back for some moments. When he did so, it was as if the truck, the men, the other bands of sheep had never existed, so quickly had the land taken them. And it was unlike any land he had ever seen, and vaster than any he had ever imagined.

The sage and the green buckbrush stretched as endlessly as eternity, broken only by a few small yellow sunflowers and a very occasional pine. No friendly villages. No small white houses with cheerful red-tiled roofs. Nothing but mountains which did not stand up proudly as mountains should, but lay rolling beneath his old high shoes.

He could scarcely bear to look at the sheep, so great was his disappointment. How ugly they were with their strange snub-nosed faces. The factory-made crook was awkward to his hand, and so long that he was sure he would never be able to trip a ewe neatly by her hind leg. Even the motley-colored Australian shepherd was unlike any dog he had known.

But the burro was the same. It trudged along with the sheep, carrying his supplies, topped by his big square bedroll. And the sheep baaed like sheep. The lambs frolicked like the lambs at home. And the dog let the sheep scatter only so far, rounding in the strays, circling watchfully.

He counted the black sheep—the markers—carefully. There were twenty-one. He counted the bellwethers. At the nooning-up he would unpack the burro, check his supplies and repack in his own precise way. He would make a fire and set a pot of beans to simmer, and cook himself a meal of ham and eggs. And this night when the coyotes yapped and the dog answered them, prowling the bed grounds, thoughts of home would creep to his little tent and he would begin the long battle against loneliness. And he swore now, by all the lady saints and the gentleman saints in the entire heaven, that he would fight it each night until he won.

It took him six weeks. He had no calendar and no watch, and he needed neither. Each day followed the familiar pattern. He was up before daylight, building his fire beneath the heavy U-shaped iron, brewing his coffee. When the burro was packed, the daily trek began, the sheep scattering over a mile, the boy following, his beat-up .30-30 in a sling on his back, the dog circling, alert to every sound of his voice, every movement of his hands.

Each nooning-up Juan cooked his meal while the sheep lay in the sage, chewing their cud. And every other day the sheep tender came bumping through the buckbrush in his four-wheel-drive truck, bringing fresh meat and food, even water if necessary, and an eight-pound round loaf of white Basque bread which he had baked in a long pit. The sheep tender was a Basque also, but he had been too long alone. He had lost his dream. He could not talk easily to anyone, and when he spoke, it was always of some café called Estrellita or Española in some valley town where he could fill himself up on red wine, poured from a goatskin, and eat prodigiously.

Sometimes on the rainy nights when the coyotes cried like women, the boy was so homesick for his land and his people that it was an agony within him, and he rose shaken and white. He dreamed one night of his *abuelita*, smiling and showing her toothless gums, and when he awoke, his cheeks were wet, and though never for an instant did he admit it was from anything but rain leaking in the tent, after that he felt better.

Gradually the sheep did not seem quite so snub-nosed and ugly. They became the familiar sheep. He knew them, and a few too well—especially the cantankerous ewe with the twin lambs which he called *La Bruja*, the witch. He grew fond of his burro, and he loved the dog as deeply as a man can love a friend.

Then the six weeks were over, and with his band he took the old trail toward the higher mountains, the little burro leading the way because it knew it well. They reached the river, followed and forded it into the great national forest, traveling twenty miles in three days into the juniper range.

They were in the juniper forest a week, working their way up to the ponderosa and the sugar pine, and here the boy's loneliness left him. Often he saw deer browsing at dawn and dusk; a doe keeping herself carefully between him and her fawn. Once, in the early evening when the sheep had settled for the night, he came on a mother bear, scolding, slapping and cuffing her two cubs to hurry them out of his way. Even the birds were a delight, the mountain bluebirds and jays, the sapsuckers and the black-and-yellow orioles. Here he was no longer a boy far from home. He was a Basque herder at his best, responsible and resourceful, like a soldier at some lonely outpost.

The tender's truck could not follow them now. The *Americano* who owned the sheep had established two cabins at seventy-five hundred feet from which several tenders took supplies to the various sheep bands by pack mule. And when Juan saw Ancelito riding through the trees leading a mule he laughed aloud, startled by the sound of his own voice.

The mule was a walking grocery, its pack bags heavy with flour sacks, each fat with supplies.

Then for the first time Juan Varra was afraid. He was so afraid he wanted to bolt like *La Bruja*, the witch ewe. On the mule bringing up the rear was a girl.

Ancelito dismounted. . . . Had it gone well? . . . Yes . . . Had he been lonely? . . . No—perhaps a very little at first. And as he spoke not once did the boy glance at the girl.

It was only Susana, said Ancelito; and she was his daughter, come to the cabins for a few days, as he had promised her. She was quite harmless. As women go, she was no trouble. She would get the noon meal while they unpacked the supplies.

And she did. While the boy and Ancelito unpacked the supplies and discussed the best sites for the bed grounds and the danger of bears, Juan could hear the girl moving at the fire.

When the meal was ready and they sat down for slabs of jack cheese, ham and eggs, fresh bread and coffee, he was forced to look at her. Her feet were as big as a boy's. Her legs were encased in thick blue cotton pants like a boy's. Her top half was submerged in a shirt like a boy's. Her hair was drawn tight to the back of her head, and hung in a thick brush, suitable only for a horse's tail. Furthermore, she did not look up at him from under her lashes and touch him with the briefest of cool, sweet glances to tell him she saw every single thing about him and found it good. She looked straight at him, and boldly, as one boy takes the measure of another.

He did not direct to her one word. When the meal was over and Ancelito and his daughter were mounted and leaving, he cast an *"adios"* into the air, which she could take to include her, if she wished.

"Is he alive?" Susana asked her father, when the mules had started.

"Yes."

"Is he stupid?"

"No. He is silent. He is a Basque. I am a Basque."

"When you came to this country you were not like that."

"I was exactly like that. He is afraid of you. But do not worry. I have told him you are harmless."

"Father, you didn't."

"But certainly. It would do you no good to make eyes at this one. He has a dream. He will save his money. He will go back to his village a *millonario* and marry the most beautiful girl in all Navarra. Now, if you were as wise as your mother—"

"*Papacito*," said Susana slowly, "are the girls so pretty in Navarra?"

And Ancelito smiled at her and said, "Beyond description."

The voices carried back to the boy in the high clear air, and though they were in English, he did not miss the scorn in the girl's voice. That night among the supplies he found that Ancelito had left him a beginner's Spanish-English reader.

Love may need no words, but resentment can use several. The next day Juan Varra opened the first crack in the dark tomb in which he was determined to bury himself for six years. He began to learn to read English.

Two days later, when the grocery mule came through the trees, the boy put on his most proud and silent Basque face, lest the girl think he was glad to see her. But it was not Ancelito and Susana who followed the mule. It was the dull camp tender who had lost his dream.

Juan did not admit to disappointment. He had no time to think of girls. The bears were troublesome. One old killer bear followed the sheep band, killing a ewe each night, and the boy tracked him and shot him. In all, he killed four bears.

In July the rams were brought in, and in August all the sheep bands were driven to a mountain valley, where the ewes were culled, the lambs separated into the fats and the feeders. On the way back to the high range with his reassembled band, Juan passed his first campers, and they were friendly. A little boy chased the lambs and couldn't catch them. The father gave him cigarettes, and the wife smiled at him and made him a present of a kitten.

After that, the cat followed along with the sheep, and though Juan told himself he kept her only to keep the chipmunks from his food, he carried her under his jacket in the thunderstorms, and let her sleep at the foot of his bedroll.

Then, in October, the long drive was done. The sheep were carried by two-and three-decker trucks down from the mountains to the low delta to browse on the corn stubble; the burro was left behind, a cook wagon carrying supplies. Just before Christmas the bands were driven to the home ranch to wait for the lambing, and it was here, in a neat white house, that Ancelito, the foreman, lived with Susana. The boy did not ask for her.

"Am I rich yet?" he asked Ancelito anxiously.

"In this country you are poor as a thin mouse," said Ancelito. "But at home already you can buy the finest house in the village."

It was Ancelito who helped him send money to his *abuelita* for the store teeth and presents for the family. It was Ancelito who brought from town the clothes he needed. After that, he spent nothing, and each month the *Americano* who owned the sheep deposited his wages in a savings account in his name. When, at Christmas, the other herders left the trailer houses and drove to town for a fine binge, he did not go. And when he was working with the sheep near the white house and saw something soft and obviously feminine fluttering on the clothesline in the rear, he looked the other way, so tight was the dream still within him.

Right after Christmas the drop band was collected in a big open field and lambing began. Four hundred lambs were born each night, the boy working out in the cold, helping the young ewes that were having trouble with their first-born, turning the lambs. One early morning the *Americano* was helping put each ewe and her new lamb into a portable *chiquero*, or pen, so she would claim her lamb, and he watched the boy work.

"He is wonderful," he said. "He will save twenty-five percent more lambs. . . . Andy, we must keep this one."

"I have thought of it," said Ancelito.

The last night of the lambing, through no fault of his own, the boy lost two little lambs, and this, to a Basque herder, is not cause for sadness, but for heartbreak. Ancelito took him to the white house for food and comfort, and there in the warm kitchen waited Susana.

Gone were the boy's shoes, the pants and the horse's tail. She was as shy as a forest creature and as sweet as any young girl in Navarra on her saint's day. She was the daughter of a Basque and she, too, could be silent. She placed the coffeepot before them without a word, and plates of ham and eggs. Then she left them, turning at the door.

"I am so sorry, Juan," and for an instant her glance touched his cheek and was gone.

He did not see her again, because this was the busy time. Lamb tails to be docked. New sheep bands to be formed. The ewes to be sheared and branded, and the winter was gone, and May here again, and the sheep driven to the campsite to go by train to Nevada. And the first year was over, and the cycle began again.

Now repetition had replaced newness, making the second year even lonelier than the first. In the buckbrush, loneliness became an entity, pressing constantly upon him. The boy talked aloud sometimes to the cat and the burro. The dog, of course, was his abiding friend.

Rarely the camp tender brought him letters from home. Those from his *abuelita* and his little brother were the same. They loved him; they missed him. But the letter from his eldest brother, who was head of the family, held a new tone. How fortunate Juan was to be in that land where everyone was rich and all was easy. How hard it was to be the one who was left behind. Oh, he must not stay away too long. If he worked harder and was given a raise—if he saved all beyond the barest necessities, perhaps five years would be enough, or even four.

* * *

In the juniper forest one June day he heard a strange little whimpering, crying sound, and came on a lone fawn. He longed to make a pet of it, to keep it with him, as the herders did sometimes. But he could not bear to take it from its mother, to teach it to be unafraid of man, to notch its ear so that when some hunter shot it he would know that once it had had too good a friend in man. It reminded him of the girl.

Then again he had driven the sheep band into the ponderosa and sugar pines of the high range, and he was home in the mountains.

When the grocery mule came through the trees, Ancelito was with it, but not Susana. This time the boy asked for her.

"And how is your daughter?" he asked formally, and Ancelito said she was well. She was going to school this summer. She was educating her head.

"It is that she does not wish a husband?" the boy asked slowly, and Ancelito said that, like all girls, she hoped to find one. But in this country it was the custom for many girls to help their husbands get started. Suppose Susana should marry a man who wished to own a sheep band of his very own. What a fine thing if she could help him. Did Juan know that the sheepman chosen as the year's best in all California was the son of a Basque whose father had come first as a herder? No doubt his wife had helped him, as his mother had helped his father. It was one of the strange American ways.

Several times this year the forest ranger came by at nooning-up and shared his meal. And once a party of mountaineers coming out from a climb passed by and hailed him. He had picked up enough English to say a few words now, but he was alone so much that the sound of a voice always startled him and filled him with uneasiness, because it broke the quiet monotony in which he lived.

Then at last it was fall and he and the sheep were back on the delta, working their way toward the home ranch.

"How rich am I now?" he asked Ancelito, who took out his pencil for a bit of figuring and replied gravely, "In this country you have a modest savings, but in Navarra you are a man of some means. All your relatives are trying to borrow money."

When the sheep band neared the home ranch, the boy watched eagerly for Susana to come home for the holidays from the school she attended, forty miles distant. And one afternoon just before Christmas, while he was working in the big field where the drop band was to be collected for the lambing, he saw her arrive, and the sight filled him with horror.

There was a loud and sudden roar, and into the ranch road from the highway bounced a small, open, ancient and rattletrap car, Susana at the wheel, her legs in jeans, her hair streaming behind her in a horsetail.

"She goes back and forth to school this way," said Ancelito calmly. "Scares the sheep. It is amazing what an *Americana* will do to educate her head and get ready to help her husband."

It was cold during this year's lambing, and again Juan worked each night in the big open field with the ewes, and late one night twin lambs lost their mother, arriving in this world so weak that in the morning he and Ancelito carried them to the house and bedded them in the warmth of the kitchen stove.

When the boy had finished working with the lambs and stood up, ready to return to the field, he saw that Susana was watching him quietly, sweet and feminine as she had been when she had prepared breakfast the year before.

"You had a good year, Juan?" she asked in Spanish.

"*Si.*"

"You were lonely?"

"A Basque is never lonely."

"See, *papacito*, he is afraid of me."

"I am afraid of no one."

"He is afraid of me. He is like the others. He learns nothing. He gives nothing. All he sees in this country is money. All he wants is to grab. He is stupid, *papacito*. He is more stupid than the sheep."

The boy followed Ancelito back to the field.

"She likes you," said Ancelito complacently. "If she did not like you, she would not be so *furiosa*."

One day from the fields Juan saw the little rattletrap car take off down the road, and he knew Susana had gone back to school. He put her resolutely from his mind, and the months slipped by until the sheep bands were driven to the campsite and the second year was done.

The third year was as like the second as the second had been like the first. The loneliness and the constant movement of the sheep. The nooning-up and the bedding-down, and the watchful eye that never forgot to count the bellwethers and the black sheep. The coyotes yapping in the night, and the bears coming in the night, and the cat, the dog and the burro. Only the details differed, and the girl's scornful words, and the thought of the girl was constantly in his mind.

In October, two days before the sheep bands were to leave the mountains, an early blizzard caught them; the snow falling so fast and heavily that they could not be driven out in time. The boy built a fire of green wood so much smoke would rise to guide the camp tender, and Ancelito saw it and came with horses and men to trample and pack the snow so the sheep could move.

"Am I rich now?" Juan asked, sitting beside Ancelito in the truck on their way down to the delta.

"You are not quite a *millonario*," said Ancelito. "You have a little more than five thousand dollars. In your village it would be a very large sum," and he spoke sadly.

"My work has not been good?" asked the boy. "The *Americano* is not satisfied?"

"He is much pleased. This morning when the sheep were safe from the blizzard, I called Susana to tell him. She says there are many letters for you. When a Basque family takes thus to the pen, the news must be bad."

They rode in silence, not to the corn stubble this time, but to the white house, and when they went into the kitchen, Susana handed his letters to the boy, her eyes big and worried.

They left him to read them alone, and when they returned to the kitchen, he was sitting quietly, the letters spread on the table before him, his face stricken. He did not look up.

"My *abuelita* is dead," he said, and when Ancelito tried to comfort him, he made no response, and when Susana set hot coffee before him, he did not thank her. He was silent as only a Basque can be silent.

"Shall I tell you what is wrong?" asked Ancelito. "Shall I tell you how I know?"

The boy did not answer.

"When I came to this country," said Ancelito, "I spent ten years alone with the sheep. I had a dream also. I thought only of my people and of the day I would return to them. When I did so, I could not stand it. I had forgotten such poverty. Things were bad in my village. Everyone was poor and I was rich, and between us was a wall of jealousy I could not tear down or climb over."

The boy did not look up.

"Have you not seen the wall in these letters? Is not your elder brother already resentful? Does he not complain bitterly of your good fortune?"

The boy was silent.

"I bought my parents the finest house in the village! I paid sixty American dollars for it. I gave them money to care for them, and I came back here where I shall never be rich. It is a friendly country. This is what matters."

"*Papacito*, it is useless!" cried Susana. "He is so stupid! Can you believe it? He does not know we love him of truth. He does not know you feel to him as a man to his own son. Let him save and go back. Let him be rich and miserable. Let him marry the most beautiful girl in all of Navarra. What do I care?" And she sat down at the table and began to cry as only a Basque girl can cry—loud and furiously.

Then the boy looked up. "Is it possible to bring my little brother to this country?" he asked slowly.

"It would take time, but it is possible. He could live with us. He could go to school. Susana could teach him to speak English."

"Is it possible Susana could teach me also? Could she teach me to tell her in English that in the mountains when I am alone with the sheep I do not think of any girl in Navarra? I think of her."

"This she would do gladly."

"Then if I have lost my dream, I can replace it with another. And if I do not return, it is nothing. I am a Basque," said the boy proudly, "and a Basque cannot lose his homeland, because he takes it with him always."

—*July 14, 1956*

RETURN TO GLORY

Eben Foster lifted his right arm
to highball the engineer and start the Cougar on its twice-weekly
run into the logging country. Then he saw Two-bits Billy Williams
weaving up the platform, followed by Mrs. Cutter, and he sighed
and dropped his arm quickly.

Two-bits Billy, last chief of the Nooksacks, had come to town to
attend a potlatch at the reservation of a cousin tribe. He was
returning now to his little prove-up shack in the deep woods, the
worse for beer and revelry, and he was giving Mrs. Cutter a spot of
trouble and enjoying it.

She was a prim, plump body, wife of the super at Camp 6.
Holding her skirts and sniffing her nose, she tried thrice to scuttle
past Two-bits Billy, but each time he lurched in her way. On the
fourth try she managed it, arriving full of sputter, one hand
feeling her placket to be sure she was still hooked tight.

"Conductor, I'll complain to Mr. Cutter!" she said furiously.
"This train is a disgrace!"

Eben hoisted her to the first step of the old combination coach
and said, "Yes, ma'am," because, indeed, it was true.

The Cougar had nothing to do with comfort or modernity, and
precious little with the rules and regulations of railroading. Since
the flats with the big logs were hauled out on the days it went
nowhere, it never had to dispute the right of way with anything
bigger than a bear. It was a most obliging and independent little
train. It stopped at many a clearing to deliver medicine to some
worried homesteader, and in the woods loggers listened for its
whistle as for a friend. When a man was hurt, it rushed him to a
hospital so fast it almost melted the soft plug in its boiler. And
there was no summer the Cougar did not traverse at least one
forest fire, the wood-burning engine with its big, screened barrel
stack snorting through the smoke, the sides of the coach blistered,
and the passengers—once they had stopped coughing and dried
their eyes—sharing that wonderful bond peculiar to humans who

283

have survived an adventure big enough to talk about all the long, rainy winter.

Two-bits Billy wobbled up now and was reminded of his thirst.

"Two bits, Mr. Foster," he pleaded plaintively; "two bits for Billy."

And Eben said, "Not a copper," and hauled him aboard and stowed him in a seat.

He returned to the platform and gave the highball fast before anything else could happen. And just as the wheels began to roll, the stationmaster came racing alongside, tossed a suitcase onto the landing and handed up a package and a pink slip.

"Stop at Cedar Crossing!" he yelled. "Emergency!" and Eben nodded that he understood.

The package was marked for Swanson's Mill, and Eben knew well what was in it. The Swedes at Swanson's had run out of snuff again. They had announced, "No snoose, no work," and were perched on logs like melancholy crows, waiting for the Cougar to come along and for Eben to toss off Copenhagen's Best.

Likewise the pink slip posed no mystery. It read: J. TAGGART—DONKEY ENGINE FIREMAN—CAMP 6, and it meant that among the passengers was one broke woodsman who, if he wished to repossess his suitcase, had better arrive at Camp 6 and start working off the price of his ticket.

Eben reached for the suitcase—and stared. It was like no receptacle in which a logger might be expected to stow his gear, his hobnailed boots tied usually to the handle by their rawhide laces. It was old, the fine leather still pliant beneath its scars, the metal of its expensive mountings still shining, on its sides remnants of baggage labels, the words "Paris" and "London" still legible.

Once there would have been no question as to the owner. A remittance man, of course. Some second son of a proud English family, and so difficult the Canadians had kicked him over the line at Blaine to be a nuisance to the Yanks. But the remittance men were gone now.

Eben placed the suitcase in the baggage compartment and entered the passenger end of the coach to collect the tickets. Two-bits Billy was asleep, his ticket stuck in his hatband between a fishhook and a porcupine quill. Mrs. Cutter was not speaking. He worked his way slowly down the aisle until he came to the last passenger, who was the only stranger. He was a big man, huge of shoulder, long of arm, the body truly magnificent and still youthful. But the face belied it. With the scar tissue about the eyes and ears, the face was tough and almost old, and center back on the

thick dark thatch was one small gray spot the man had missed as
he had combed the black dye into his hair.

Eben accepted the pink slip, which corresponded to the one he
had—J. TAGGART—DONKEY ENGINE FIREMAN—CAMP 6, and he knew
now who and what the man was, and why he was here.

When he spoke, his voice showed neither interest nor surprise.
"I'll let you know when you get off."

The man said dryly, "Do that, bub," and turned back to the
window.

Now the Cougar passed the stump farms which fringed the
town, smoke drifting up from the smoldering fires of the slashings. It entered the woods, the salt air of the sound giving way to
the fragrance of fir. And because it was not yet warm enough in
June to close the spread between the rail joints, the little train
played a loud and rhythmic melody which to Eben was the finest
music in the world. Yet today it depressed him.

He walked slowly back to the baggage compartment and looked
again at the suitcase. Big Jim Taggart! One of the great heavyweights of his day. Big Jim Taggart, who had gone twelve rounds
with Tom Sharkey, who had fought Philadelphia Jack O'Brien and
Joe Jeannette. He had been an idol of Eben's youth. Long ago, at
the beginning of his career, he had come to the Puget Sound town
on a Fourth of July, lumber schooners at anchor in the bay then,
and the mills and logging camps closed down so the men could see
the fight.

Eben coult not bear to think of the long slow years of descent
which had brought him here, come to hide himself in the woods
as many a man before him. But with a difference. He had not
signed on as a bull cook to empty the garbage and sweep out the
bunkhouses. He had not signed on as a night watchman to make
his rounds in the dark with only a dog to share his loneliness. He
had dyed his hair to get a man's job, and did he know how hungry
a logging donk could be?"

When the Cougar neared Swanson's Mill, Eben gave the way
signal and tossed off the snuff, and sure enough, a big Swede—the
top of his old felt hat cut out to ventilate his hair—was waiting to
pick it up. And when the train approached Cedar Crossing, Eben
did not forget to yank the bell cord for a stop. He climbed off the
train to ascertain the emergency.

The emergency was Grandpa Grant, accompanied by two little
girls, each carrying a small suitcase.

"My granddaughter and her best friend are traveling alone, Mr.
Foster," said Grandpa Grant with dignity. "Will you put them off

at my son's siding? If nobody meets them, start them on the skid road. They know the way home." He lifted up the children. "Don't climb on the seats," he said; "and mind Mr. Foster."

He paid Eben their fare. "Orley drove them over yesterday to spend a week," he confided. "So homesick they couldn't stand it, and a good thing too. Grandma's tuckered. Think they planned to be sent home so they could ride on the train all by themselves," and his eyes twinkled.

"I'll keep my eye on 'em," Eben promised. "I'll see they get there," and he highballed the engineer and swung himself aboard.

When he entered the coach, the two little girls were seated side by side, immensely pleased with themselves and the universe. They didn't squirm, they didn't whisper, they didn't giggle. Having raised considerable rumpus to get here, they were now proving they could behave like little ladies. The little Grant child wore a pleated wool dress of the family clan plaid. Around her neck she wore a string of red Mexican jumping beans, evidently new, because every now and then she squinted down her nose to see if they were hopping around yet. The other child, whom Eben recognized as the daughter of the town's judge, wore a navy-blue Peter Thompson suit. Since the town's doctor took a dim view of half socks in this climate, she had left home in long black stockings. Quite unwilling to be outdone by the Scotch, she had found a pair of scissors and whacked them off any which way. She sat entranced by the sight of her little white knees.

Eben kept his eye on them. They had to travel twenty miles, which on the Cougar was a journey. In the first ten, each child had two drinks of water and went to the women's room three times. They did not intend to miss any of the amenities of travel.

Then Mrs. Cutter proceeded to stick her nose into something which was none of her business. She whacked loudly on the seat side with her handbag, summoning Eben.

"Conductor," she said, "you certainly do not intend to put those innocent little children off this train with that dangerous Indian."

There was no use telling Mrs. Cutter that Two-bits Billy, though beer-soaked, had always been harmless.

"No, ma'am," said Eben meekly, and strolled down the aisle to Big Jim Taggart.

"If you get off at the company town, you'll get a ride to Camp Six," he told him. "But they won't pick you up until after dinner. If you get off at the next stop, you can take a short cut. 'Bout a mile's walk through the woods."

The old heavyweight didn't have the price of a meal, and Eben knew it.

"Thanks, mister; I'll walk."

Then Eben gave the stop signal for Grant's siding. He woke Two-bits Billy and dumped him off first. He helped the children down, who were followed by the prizefighter.

"This man's going to the logging camp," he told the little Grant girl. "He's a stranger. He doesn't know the way. You two will have to take care of him some. Do you understand?" He swung himself aboard, and the Cougar went off about its business and left them there at the siding in the woods, two rows of cedarshingle bundles stacked by the tracks, each marked: Orley Grant's Dandy Clears.

All the sound in the world seemed to go with the train. Then a bird spoke, a chipmunk chattered, and Two-bits Billy ambled to the nearest fir, lay down and resumed his slumber.

The two little girls looked at the prizefighter. The town child, who had been taught caution, was shy. But the woods child had known loggers quite as tough and almost as big, and they had saved her the little stars from their plug tobacco.

"I'll take care of him first," she said, "because I'm oldest," and the town child, not willing to be outdone by a Scot, said, "I'm the guest, and guests go first. And anyway I was born in a hospital and you were only born in a house," and the prizefighter, who knew nothing of children, but everything of fights, took a hand of each firmly, and they started up the skid road and into the forest.

Pretty soon the girls grew tired matching their little steps to his big ones, and they let him carry the little suitcases, and made a game of stepping on every other log in the old skid road.

Then they heard the clop-clop of hoofs and the jangle of harness, and two horses drawing a lumber sled appeared through the trees. Grandpa Grant had managed to get on the party line long enough to alert his son that the children were on their way, and Orley Grant and his wife, Janet, returning to the mill from delivering the shingle bolts to the siding, had turned around and come back.

The children ran ahead to meet them. "We rode on the train all by ourselves! We were homesick and we didn't like it there!"

The young couple greeted the children as if they had been gone a year, and, because he had accompanied them, welcomed Big Jim as a friend. Orley Grant hitched the team on the other end of the sled. He and Big Jim sat on shingle bundles in the front, the children between them.

"I'm oldest. I'll put the grease on the skids first," Ellen said, and from the shingle bundles on the end of the sled the mother said, "Judy is your guest, Ellen. She'll go first." And Big Jim hung tightly to the squirming child, doing her best to fall on her head beneath the hoofs as she dipped the ragged stick into the oilcan and daubed at the skids.

When they reached the shingle mill, the children asked if they might show him Bonnie Prince Charlie, and the mother said yes, leading the way to the little shingle house which was their home. And there he hung, done in oil and framed in gilt, kilted Charles Edward Louis Philip Casimir Stuart, the tragic prince.

"And a brave laddie he was, too," said Mrs. Grant, a bit of the heather in her voice.

She thanked Big Jim for being so good to the children.

"And drop in for dinner anytime," said her husband. "Our Letty is the best cook in the woods," and he walked with him to the point where the trail led to Camp 6, the children tagging along.

Then they told him good-by, and he was walking alone, the friendliness gone, the woods very still.

He walked slowly. Though he was not an imaginative man, it seemed to him he had been coming here forever, so long, so slow was the way of bitter descent. He remembered now the exact moment the long descent had begun. He couldn't get any more fights under his own name. He had fought anybody under any name, and the last had been a black boy, arrogant in his strong young prime. And when they had left the dressing rooms to go to the ring, the black boy had seen him. Relief had crossed his face, and he had laughed and said, "That ain't nobody but old Jim Taggart."

He had known it, but he had not admitted it. He had told it humorously many times to people who were still his friends, which is a man's way to prove he is bigger than a hurt. Now, when the trail broke clear of the woods at last, leading into the ugly, devastated logging camp, he told it again, and seriously. *That ain't nobody*, he said to himself. *That ain't nobody.*

He reported for work at the unpainted shack marked OFFICE— SAM CUTTER, SUPERINTENDENT, and though Mr. Cutter looked at him thoughtfully, his voice, like Eben's, showed no undue interest. He asked no personal questions.

"I'll take you over to the bunkhouse, Taggart," he said. "It's a bit crowded right now. Some of our older men have built one-room shake cabins for themselves. One of them's leaving next week. If you'd like to bunk alone, I can arrange it."

The bunkhouse was on skids and built like a freight car, a potbellied stove in the middle, six bunks on each side. Big Jim was looking it over when the first logger came off work—a man young and cocky because he was the high-rigger, which is an athlete's job.

The young man looked him over. When he spoke, his tone was patronizing. "You ever do any fighting, Pop?" And Big Jim Taggart recognized the tone and knew what he was in for.

"No, kid. I never did." His last battle had begun.

Every day he fought it out with the donkey engine.

"Isn't she a honey?" asked the engineer who handled the levers and the cables. "Now watch her haul in this log."

Even the little Indian boy who was the whistle punk considered the donkey engine a thing of beauty, deserving of respect.

But Big Jim Taggart hated her from the start. She dominated his life. She pestered and she nagged him, and she took his guts. He could never take his eyes from her water gauge. He could never rest his legs, rustling wood for her hungry mouth.

Except for the young high-rigger, the loggers did not question him, watching him quietly. When the men finished building a logging road across a ravine and topped the piles, they left the leavings, cut to the right length, where he could reach them. And when Sam Cutter came by on inspection, some young logger always passed the word. "Rustle 'em up, Pop. Here comes the super with his nose to the ground," and Big Jim would check the water gauge and toss in the wood.

At night he was too tired to do anything but comb a little dye into his hair and fall into his bunk. The young high-rigger baited him sometimes. "Who didcha fight, Pop? Were you any good, Pop? Tell us about it, Pop," and Big Jim would pretend he was asleep, and hadn't heard.

At the end of three weeks he moved into a shake cabin by himself, and the battle eased a little.

At noon the other men rode back to camp for a hot meal at the cookhouse, but Big Jim always carried his lunch with him. He would find himself a log in woods not yet cut, and rest there, sharing his food with the chipmunks. And always the past pressed close about him, of which he never spoke and could not forget.

One noon Two-bits Billy passed him. In a deserted camp up the river Two-bits Billy had found a drum of coffee beans. Since it was too heavy to roll home, he had removed his pants, tied up the ends of the legs and filled them. He came through the woods stark naked except for a tattered shirt, dragging his pants by the suspenders. Big Jim reported the incident in the cookhouse that night. It was the first time anybody had heard him laugh.

He did not go to the shingle mill. He mistrusted friendship. But he did not forget the children and Bonnie Prince Charlie. And one

Saturday afternoon he walked far from the camp and saw the children and Mrs. Grant on a sandbar by the river.

They were wading in the shallow, safe rivulets. The white glacier water was so cold that the children were squealing with shock and delight, the mother holding her skirt high and telling them they were quite purple enough and it was time to come out.

When she looked up and saw Big Jim, she dropped her skirt in the water and cried, "Look who's here! It's our friend!" and they came toward him with that outgoing and spontaneous joy of discovery with which people in the isolated corners find each other again.

Nevertheless when he took the trail to the shingle mill for the first visit, he did so in desperation. It was the week of the Fourth, and the camp closed down so the men could go to town and see the fight.

"You want to come, Jim?" they asked him casually, and he answered, "No, thanks."

But when they had gone, he could not stand the loneliness and took the trail to the shingle mill.

The children were in need of a friend. Convinced that it was time the baby ducks learned to swim, they had plucked them from the nest and dumped them in the slough. Orley Grant was on his hands and knees, rescuing the ducklings from an icy end, and Big Jim helped carry them to the mill and dry them out on the boiler.

He was asked to dinner, of course. A big circular saw with a crack in the middle hung by a chain in front of the cookhouse, and when big, blond and middle-aged Letty came out to wham it with a piece of crowbar steel, the children begged to take her place.

To strike the saw, except at mealtimes, was forbidden, since this was a call for help in trouble, but Orley Grant let the children do it now, one on each side.

"We don't have to hurry to table today because most of the men are gone," he told Big Jim. "Our Letty is such a good cook that when she strikes the saw, the men come arunning. If a man falls down, he doesn't bother to get up. Wouldn't do him any good. The food would be gone by the time he got there," and Letty hid her face in her apron to hide her blushing.

After dinner the bolt puncher and the cut-off man tossed a baseball back and forth. The children played house under a fir, and Big Jim and Orley Grant sat on the steps of the little shingle house, while Mrs. Grant sewed. And presently Two-bits Billy came by, leading his prize possession, his pony.

"Two bits, Mr. Grant," he pleaded plaintively. "Two bits for Billy."

"I'm not buying your horse, Billy. Now go along," and Two-bits Billy went along as far as the cookhouse, stopping to stare at the saw.

"Billy, leave that alone. . . . Honestly, he's worse than the children. He's the pest of the woods."

When Big Jim walked back up the trail to the logging camp that night, his bitterness was eased, and in the long twilight three days later he went again to the shingle mill. Orley Grant was not in sight, but the front door of the little shingle house was open, and he could see Bonnie Prince Charlie in his gilt frame, and the mother and the children. The children were dancing with the mother. They were barefoot and in their flannel nightgowns, and the mother had dressed up for them in a fine silk gown, remnant of the past. He went back up the trail, and for the first time he realized that this young wife was as exiled as himself.

When the loggers returned from their holiday, there was a change in the young high-rigger. The derision was gone from his voice. He walked over to Jim's cabin after work, a newspaper in his hand.

"Your name's in the sport page, Jim."

"That's not funny, kid."

"I mean it. See, here it is. Right here in the pink section of the Seattle P.I. I saved it for you," and he gave Jim the paper and went away fast.

WHERE ARE THE FINE FIGHTERS OF YESTERDAY? WHERE ARE THE GREAT OLD HEAVYWEIGHTS LIKE JEFFRIES AND CORBETT AND BIG JIM TAGGART?

Big Jim cut it out with his razor and kept it in the back of his watch. And sometimes when he was having lunch in the woods, observed only by the birds and the chipmunks, he would take it out and read it, and for an instant he was somebody again.

Every Sunday he went to the shingle mill, sure of his welcome. Once he and Orley Grant inveigled big, pink-cheeked Letty into trying to walk across the slough on the shingle bolts as the men did. The slough was solid with bolts, and it looked safe enough. But when Letty was twenty feet from dry land, the bolts slipped from under and away from her, depositing her waist-deep in the icy water.

"Why, Letty, I can't have this!" cried Orley Grant. "Look, you've left a hole in the water!" and they hauled her out, not one bit mad, and laughing as hard as anyone.

And sometimes in the long twilight after the children had been put to bed, the Grants told him of themselves. Of the quarter section they'd lost in Saskatchewan, of the wagon wheel on the roof of the sod house, of standing in the doorway watching the hail level the wheat three years running, and of Janet's uncle, of whom she was so proud because he had been knighted by the queen for helping build the railroad across Canada. But the little shingle mill was doing well. With luck, in another year they'd have a house in town, so Ellen could start to school with Judy, and not have to grow up wild as a woods rabbit.

Then the summer rounded to its end. In late October the logging camp would close. Big Jim knew what it meant. He would hole up in some shabby town hotel, its management setting trays of free crackers and cheese on the bar each noon, so that, with the price of a beer, its tenants could eke out the winter on two meals a day, until the fish traps of Alaska and the logging camps opened again and they could drift back to the job.

The thought of it filled him with a kind of sadness, and one night after supper his feet lagged on the trail to the shingle mill, because soon this, too, would belong to the past.

Suddenly the stillness was broken by the sound of a shot and the clamor of the circular saw that hung by the cookhouse. There was another shot, and another, until the woods rang with the shriek of the saw. Someone was using it for a target, and who could it be but Two-bits Billy?

Big Jim stood motionless and listening, expecting any instant that the noise would stop as abruptly as it had begun, which would mean that the men had run from the bunkhouse and Orley Grant from the shingle house, and boxed Two-bits Billy's ears, and put him on his pony and headed him into the woods to his prove-up shack.

But the clamor continued, and he remembered then it was a Saturday and that Orley Grant and the men had gone into the company town, probably to buy tobacco and supplies, and the women were alone with the children. He began to run.

In his mind he could see the kerosene lamp that hung in the cookhouse, that Letty always kept so polished and shining. If Two-bits Billy had a bullet left when he grew tired of playing Sitting Bull and massacring the palefaces—

Two-bits Billy had. There was one final shot, and, as he ran, Big Jim saw the first tendril of smoke rise in the trees. When he pounded off the trail into the clearing, Two-bits Billy had departed on his pony, quite unaware of the havoc he left behind him.

The cookhouse was a mass of flame. Letty, Janet Grant and the children had come out from under the beds and were dragging a ladder to the side of the mill, their eyes big with fear and fury.

"Oh, Yim," Letty cried, "he drank my vanilla extract! He shot out the light in my cookhouse! Oh, Yim, if the mill goes, these poor peoples—"

"Mrs. Grant, you and the children fill all the pails you can find with water from the mill pond and set them here by the ladder! . . . Letty, bring me an ax!" and Big Jim climbed to the roof comb and the water-filled barrels waiting there for emergency.

If he could hold the mill for fifteen minutes, help would come from the logging camp. He tipped the first barrel to wet the roof against the burning and falling tinder. Then Letty was there to help, to give him the ax, to watch where the sparks caught.

Once he looked down and saw Janet Grant filling pails in the pond, the children working as hard as she, filling the little toy pails they always carried when they went wading at the sandspit.

When the water was gone, and the roof burning in two places, and the smoke so thick it was hard to breathe, he made Letty go down to take Mrs. Grant and the children to the river, out of danger. He fought the fire with the ax. He beat it out with his jacket.

When aid arrived from the logging camp, Big Jim refused to leave the roof until the mill was safe, and he helped fight the brush fires until they, too, were extinguished. When it was over and one of the men led him to the shingle house for coffee, he could not hold the cup. He did not know that the shirt was torn from his back or that his face was black. Until Janet Grant brought the ointment and the bandages, he did not realize that he had burned his hands.

While they healed, he stayed at the shingle mill. Orley Grant put up a big tent as a temporary cookhouse, and the millmen made a long trestle table and benches for it. It was like being part of the fun and hustle of a big family. He did not let himself think of the long winter that lay ahead.

One evening when his hands were almost well, Sam Cutter and Orley Grant approached the fir where he was sitting on a log in the long twilight, and they stood there looking at him, almost shyly.

"The logging camp is closing week after next, Jim," Sam Cutter said.

"I'll be up for my gear," Jim told him. "It's O.K., Mr. Cutter. I've saved my wages. I'll find a room in town to hole up."

"No, Jim," Orley Grant said quickly. "We're not going to let you go. I want you to help me build the new cookhouse. When that's done, we'll build you a tight cabin of your own. You can help me at the mill."

Big Jim said nothing.

"If you don't want to work at the mill, Jim," said Sam Cutter desperately, "I think I can get you the contract to deliver the mails. You might like that, Jim, and in the spring the logging camp will open again. We'd be mighty proud if you'd stay with us."

Then he spoke. "I'll be glad to stay," he said. "I like it here."

Then the tension was gone. Orley Grant said he must go to the mill and check the boiler. Sam Cutter said he must be getting back to the camp.

"Someday, Jim, I wish you'd tell the high-rigger and me about the time you licked Root at Kalamazoo."

"Sure, I will, Mr. Cutter. Be glad to."

Then he was alone, and little Ellen Grant walked slowly through the trees and climbed up on the log beside him.

Judy, the town child, had gone home now, and Ellen was lonely.

From the shingle house, her mother called, "Jim, is Ellen with you? She has to come to bed in fifteen minutes, and no dilly-dallying about it."

"Yes, Mrs. Grant. I'll send her."

Then Letty stuck her head from the flap of the cookhouse tent. "Yim," she called, "it's getting cold! You put on a yacket! You hear me, Yim!" and he heard her, and it sounded good.

"Yes, Letty."

Ellen moved closer on the log.

"You want me to tell you about the little brown bear who was handy with his paws?" he asked her, and she said she did.

But first there was something he had to do. He took out his watch and let her hold it in her little hands while with one unbandaged finger he pried open the back.

He took out the little slip of newsprint, worn from so many readings. This time he did not bother to read it. He crumpled it into a little ball and he threw it away.

—*February 2, 1957*

FORBIDDEN YEARNING

When the hand of the adjutant touched her shoulder, the girl awoke instantly and to expectancy. This was the day the work schedule changed; she was to be a bread girl again, and of all the chores, this was her favorite.

In the first gray of day, the earnest new adjutant moved softly between the long rows of cots here on the porch where the big girls slept in summer, bending now and again to awaken the others who were to work on the bread also. Then she was gone, and the girl was up and out the door, slipping down the hall to the washrooms.

Her hand found the pigeonhole which was her very own, third row right, ninth from the end. She scrubbed her teeth with the salt and the soda. She splashed cold water on her face. She soaped and washed her hands vigorously. Alone in the little room she shared with two others, she dressed quickly in the dimness, and tying her work apron around her cotton frock, she hurried to the stairs to be the first one down.

In the eleven years she had lived here, sharing Mother and Dad Dorn with two hundred and sixty brothers and sisters, Gracie Hitt had seldom known the luxury of being alone. It was only at such rare times and lately that she had come to realize that she, too, was an individual, different from all others and therefore important.

Only the night lights were burning. On the second floor there was no whisper of blanket, no rustle of sheet. The aloneness was so big she was big also, and very bold, and flinging one slim leg over the balustrade, she swooped down the last flight, landing on her soft sneakers as deft as a cat. And there in her little white nightgown, head tousled, eyes big, waited Tina Dorn.

Tina was a courtesy Dorn, having been left on the stoop, aged three days, and wrapped in a blanket. She was six now, recently moved from the nursery cottage to the main house.

"Gracie," she whispered, "is it time yet? I'm going to be a dustpan girl."

Oh, the pride of the first chore. To hold the dustpan in front of the bedroom door while the big girl who had cleaned the room swept in the litter. Gracie knew it well.

"Sh-h-h, Tina; it's hours yet. It's not 'til after breakfast." She took the hand of the little dustpan girl and they started across the entrance hall toward the front door.

To their right was the open office, and on the wall above the desk they could see poor, dear, little Gilford gazing soulfully from his dark-brown frame. Little Gilford had been the Dorns' first-born, and all the children tried hard to feel sad that he was now an angel in heaven. Today, being bold, Gracie gave him an honest gratitude. It was little Gilford's death that had caused his parents to enter the Lord's army and accept two hundred and sixty children in his name. They had two more of their own now, and if there was any one reason why this was a home and not merely an orphanage, it was because they treated them like all the others. They ate the same food, shared the same chores, enjoyed the same treats and suffered the same punishments. If a bona-fide Dorn smacked a brother in the eye, he was exiled to the same Coventry: He had to stand in front of the main house in a pair of overalls with one brown leg and one blue leg, and take the gibes of his peers.

They came to the front door, which stood open in summer. No door was ever locked here, except, of course, the one of the closet under the stairs where the sugar and the dried fruits were stored. There were no fences, no walls. They stepped through the door onto the porch, into a day so new, so fresh that it caught the heart.

All around them were the rolling hills, the growing light glinting on the tracks where the small ones wore out the fronts of their clothes sliding down the slick dry grass on the sleds which the big boys made for them in the workshops. In the meadow under an oak grazed Dan, the old white horse, whose back was strung each afternoon with the nursery kids, their little bare heels thumping his sides to make him go faster. Beyond the grass and the flower garden near the old vineyards the gray cat was carrying the first of her new litter for safekeeping in the blackberry thicket.

But something was wrong. The little dustpan girl didn't know it yet, and the bread girl did. Almost all the children had someone, and anyone was better than no one, and they had no one. On Sunday afternoon the porch was always lined with squirming bodies and scrubbed and shining faces. And when a car turned off the dusty road and came up the drive and stopped, and out climbed the mother who had been ill, the father who had been out of work, the cousin or the aunt, something strange happened. The waiting child forgot all else—even Mother Dorn—even to say good-by to his best friend. And he went forward eagerly, yet a little shyly, with a look which was like no other.

"Why doesn't your mother ever come to see you? Don't you have anybody?" Gracie had been asked through the years. And when Tina was older, she would hear worse: "You're a foundling. You don't even have a name."

Gracie held the little hand with fierce protectiveness.

"I must go now, Tina," she said. "I have to work on the bread. Now you go back to bed. I won't forget you. I'll tell you when it's time to hold the dustpan."

They returned to the entrance hall, and the little girl scooted up the stairs, and the big girl moved quickly down the corridor to the dining room and stopped.

With the tables set for breakfast, each chair in place, each tumbler turned down, the room seemed to be waiting, hushed and eerie in the dawn, redolent of feelings and old echoes. This was the very heart of the place. Here, at Christmas, the little ones strung the paper garlands for the great tree which stood always at the far end, and the big boys carried in the piano box packed tight with dolls. Here, when she was sixteen, Gracie would receive her silver thimble, symbol of maturity.

Surely a little bit of God hovered perpetually above the ceiling, so many words had been addressed to Him here. At mealtimes the children lined up in the hall and entered, singing grace, and before leaving they stood for the hymn and knelt for the prayer.

Gracie entered slowly. It seemed to her that she could still hear her little girl's voice singing fervently her favorite hymn, "Pull for the Shore, Sailor, Pull for the Shore." And when at last the sailor was "safe in the lifeboat to sin no more," she had always been positive she had helped get him there. And she was sure now that all her life she would hear Dad Dorn giving the morning prayer, and see Mother Dorn as she stood after supper above the bowed heads of her huge family and asked that He hold every single one in the palm of His hand—and especially the bad ones.

Then why was she afraid of what she had determined to do? Was it because she was old enough to know that there are some who think faith possible only to the very young or the credulous?

She walked to the center of the huge room. She remembered having been told that when her mother brought her here, her little clothes had been clean and carefully made and hemstitched, and this gave her confidence.

She lifted her head and she spoke boldly to the Lord. "If my mother hasn't come for me, there must be a reason," she said. "And I want her to find me; and if she cannot, I want You to help me find her, and I ask it."

She dropped the words like pebbles in a sea, and almost running, slipped among the tables into the pantry, through it and into the big kitchen and the smell of the yeast.

Cookie was standing by the stove, stirring the immense kettle of oatmeal, her cotton robe wrapped firmly around her ample middle, her face framed in kid curlers.

"Bless you, Gracie. I'm glad it's you. Now I can get these bobbins out of my hair. Have a cup of hot chocolate, child," and Cookie whacked the spoon against the side of the kettle and put it down.

"And, Gracie, don't be lifting the flour sacks by yourself. The boy will be along with the milk cart directly. And when the others come, make them wash their hands, and watch they rinse them well. I will not have my good bread tainted of soap."

Then Gracie was alone, and when she had finished her chocolate, she heard the rattle of the milk cart coming from the barn, the boy singing as he pushed it, and she knew then he was Carl.

He came up the back steps and through the door, eager as the new day, a fine-looking lad in his worn blue overalls, sleeves rolled high on big strong arms. He saw her and stopped.

"Good morning, Gracie," he said shyly.

"Good morning, Carl."

He took the knife from his pocket and opened it, and he cut the chain stitch on the first flour sack carefully because it must be washed and bleached and used. He lifted the sack, Gracie ready at the bread table, and as he began to pour, she raised the board which dammed the yeast mixture into the three-foot trough and let it trickle through the softly falling flour.

There was a difference between them. Carl had a family. Carl belonged to people, and they to him. When his mother had died, his father had refused to separate the six children and brought them to the home, and he had found work nearby so he could see them frequently, and each month he had contributed toward their care.

When Carl had finished pouring the flour into the trough, Gracie dipped in her hands to begin the mixing.

"My father is coming this Sunday, Gracie," he said. "We are going to take my brothers and sisters on a picnic. If you will come with us, I will ask Mother Dorn's permission. My father says he will be pleased to have you."

Something big and bold within her answered. "Thank you, Carl, but I'm expecting to see my mother," and for an instant his face was empty of expression, so tightly did he contain his doubt.

"Some other time, Gracie," he said, and he put away his knife and left the kitchen quickly, whistling.

When the three other bread girls straggled in, Gracie made them wash their hands and rinse them. Now there were eight hands working the yeast into the flour, until it was smooth and spongy and ready for the raising.

After breakfast, Gracie remembered to tell Tina when the moment arrived to hold the dustpan proudly and without a wiggle. Yet already she was waiting for her answer. In midmorning, when she returned to the kitchen to help knead and shape the loaves, the dough seemed almost alive, and she pushed it hard with the heels of her palms, lifted and turned it deftly until it pushed back at her. And in the afternoon, when the big and middle girls gathered under the trees to mend socks, to shell peas into the huge dishpans, and they sang the old songs—"Juanita" and "Swing Low, Sweet Chariot"—Gracie forgot her turn to pick up the refrain, so big was the dream within her.

She held tight the dream, though she knew it was childish. It had been her companion on many a night through the years. To it she had given infinite variation. Now she added another. She added Tina; she and Tina would be waiting on the porch with the scrubbed and eager ones of a Sunday afternoon. Into the drive would turn a long and shining car, its back seat bulging with treats for all the kids, and when it stopped, out would step such a mother as the children's home had never seen—so blonde, so lovely—

"Gracie, you're woolgathering," said the adjutant. "You're a thousand miles away. Come back here," and Gracie shut off the dream and picked up the refrain, and wove another thread into the heel of some small boy's sock.

Gracie felt an instant's fear. Oh, she must be careful of this new green adjutant with the pretty face. But the fear did not come again. That evening when the adjutant was in charge of putting the smallest ones to bed in the nursery cottage, Gracie helping her, it was obvious no dumber help had ever been sent by the Lord to the children's home.

Even the two-year-olds knew it. When they knelt in the nursery for the "Lay-me-down" and the "God-blessing," it looked for a time as if the hated moment of climbing into the cribs was going to be postponed for hours, if not indefinitely.

They God-blessed all the brothers and the sisters and the help, and were working their way optimistically toward the pussycats, the puppy dogs, the woolly worms and the garter snakes, when the adjutant sent a frantic appeal for help above their heads.

"That'll be enough of that," said Gracie loudly and cheerfully. "Just God-bless everything and everybody in all the world and that will do it. . . . Now does anybody want a drink? . . . Does anybody have to go to—" And the small ones knew they were licked, and permitted themselves to be tucked in, and the adjutant sent Gracie a look of respect and thank-you.

While she waited, Gracie found it harder and harder to keep her mind on the chores, even the pleasant ones at playtime.

On doughnut night, when the big girls took turns dropping the sweet rings into the hot deep fat, Gracie was so busy with her dream that she let her batch grow too brown on the edges, and even Cookie looked at her strangely.

And one afternoon when Dad Dorn took some of the middle ones down the dusty road to the river to teach them to swim, Gracie sat so absent-mindedly on the bank, and held the rope so carelessly that the child dog-paddling at its end floundered just a little, and Dad Dorn had to yell at her loudly, "Gracie, pull him in!"

She avoided Mother Dorn's wise and gentle eyes. Each Thursday night after bedtime, Mother Dorn came upstairs to discuss with her daughters those facts of life suitable to each age group. Sometimes she brought her guitar, and when all the questions had been asked and answered, she sang to them. Gracie asked no questions. When Mother Dorn sang "Kiss Me Again, Little Darling," which was her favorite, she kept her face turned away, afraid she might meet those eyes and lose her dream by telling it. And once when Mother Dorn said, "Good night, Gracie," in her gentle voice, Gracie even pretended to be asleep.

Yet each Sunday Gracie avoided the porch where the children awaited their visitors. She kept Tina close to her, and they would sit under the trees, apart from the others, and watch the porch until even Tina looked at her a little anxiously.

On bread days, when Gracie hurried to be the first one down, and entered the eerie dining room, she did not remind Him of her request, determined to prove she could wait patiently.

Carl did not question her. One morning, lifting the heavy sack to pour the flour into the trough, he said, "I'm going to be a doctor,

Gracie. I'm going to start working toward it right now. I'm going to ask Dad Dorn to help me. What are you going to be?"

"I don't know. I haven't decided. I haven't even thought of it," and she let the yeast mixture trickle so fast into the flour that it splashed.

"You could be a nurse," Carl said. "Mother Dorn would help you. We might work together. We might come back here to the home and work. Some kids do."

"I don't know," she said quickly and almost resentfully. "I don't want to talk about it," and this was strange, since she liked Carl.

One day the green new adjutant sought out Mother Dorn, her pretty face worried.

"It's about Gracie Hitt," she said. "I'm worried about her. She's such a bright girl."

"Yes-s-s."

"It's as if she's waiting for something. On Sundays when the visitors come, she hangs around the front porch where the children are gathered. She never goes up on the porch to wait with them. She stays under the trees in the yard with Tina. There's a special bond between those two—something lasting. They're closer than sisters."

"They are the two who have no one of their own," said Mother Dorn slowly.

"I know that, but it's strange nevertheless. On bread mornings Gracie is always the first one down. You know where I think she goes? Into the dining room. It's so quiet then and sort of scary. It's not good for her. Why?"

"If your mother had brought you here when you were very small and left you and never came back, wouldn't you wonder why? And when you grew older, wouldn't you hope and pray she'd come? And if she did not, wouldn't you try and find her?"

"You mean she'll run away?"

"I mean she'll remember everything she can of the home she once had, and seek a chance to return and search for it. Since it was in a town only sixty miles distant, it should be fairly easy for her to begin her search."

"But you don't mean you'll let her? Suppose she should find her mother. There's no telling what kind of a woman she may be."

"Have you so little faith?" asked Mother Dorn.

Meanwhile Gracie waited and had no answer. Oh, it was obvious what was wrong. Dad Dorn was right when he said at prayer that the Lord loves those who help themselves. On the sleeping porch in the quiet night, she tried hard now to remember her life before her mother had brought her here. The memories were few and vague. Only a few stood out.

She could remember the time her mother had come into the kitchen with an apronful of baby chicks, and she had squealed with delight and reached for them, and her mother had said, "Be careful. You'll hurt them." There was a toy monkey on a stick. There were open shelves at one end of the kitchen where the cooky crock stood. The wooden house had stood on a hill—an old gingerbread house with an ornate porch. If the house still stood, she was sure she could find it in the hot valley town whose name she remembered.

Each afternoon, in the sewing room, older girls worked on the boys' shirts, and for this they were paid. Gracie asked Mother Dorn if she might work also, and Mother Dorn asked no questions and agreed.

No one worked so carefully to keep the seams straight, to make such fine buttonholes. When Mother Dorn inspected Gracie's first shirt and told her she had done well, Gracie could not meet her eyes. It was a rule in the home that if you had a problem, you took it straight to Mother or Dad Dorn, and she had not done so.

In two weeks she had saved enough money to buy a bus ticket to the valley town of her childhood, and the very next Saturday she had a chance to get away. It happened so naturally that Gracie could only consider it providential, and it seemed to her appropriate that providence had used for its instrument the green new adjutant.

Each Saturday morning the adjutant went to town to shop, and sometimes she asked a middle or an older girl to accompany her and help with the errands and the packages. This time she asked Gracie.

Gracie sat beside her in the ancient pickup in which they would carry home the supplies. In her pocket, wrapped in a handkerchief, was the money she had earned. She clutched it tightly, trying to hide her eagerness and to be natural. But the adjutant was so dumb that she noticed nothing, and the supermarket was so full of shoppers that escape was easy.

While the adjutant plucked cans from the shelves, Gracie slipped into the crowded aisle, around a corner into another and out. She knew where the bus station was, and she ran all the way, holding tightly to the handkerchief with the money, so breathless that when she arrived, she could scarcely ask for a ticket.

Only eight minutes to wait, and the bus already loading, and so crowded it was easy to make herself inconspicuous in a rear seat, hidden by the latecomers who had to stand.

When the bus started, Gracie pretended to be tying her shoe. She was afraid to look up. The adjutant must have missed her by now, and might be scuttling on the street like a frightened chicken. But when the bus reached the outskirts of the small town, she straightened and felt safe, freedom and daring like a wind in her face.

The bus stopped at every crossroads. People climbed off and people climbed on, and the driver had to help stow their luggage. When it reached the town of her early childhood it was almost noon, and she spent a precious dime for a glass of milk, swallowing it quickly because she was eager to begin her search.

It was little more than a village, dusty and hot in the summer sun, a cluster of old stores, and three roads leading out. In each store she sought the oldest employee and asked each if he had heard the name Hitt. No one had.

Each of the three roads led upward toward hills terraced with grapevines. She chose one, trudging along sturdily. But the houses were all new, set far back among trees, and this could not be right, so she returned and tried the second road. It was no better. Nothing was familiar. Not a bend. Not a tree; so, after following the road for a mile or so, she retraced her steps.

When she started on the third road, she was almost without hope. She was tired and she was hungry, and her feet dragged. There were new houses set back among trees, and they were wrong, and then there was a half mile or so with no houses at all. And then a small old white house, and the road began to climb. And suddenly it seemed to Gracie that her feet knew the way, knew the bend was there before her eyes saw it, knew the clump of trees would be waiting to the right.

Her steps quickened and suddenly she forgot her weariness. And then she saw it. She saw the house at the top of the hill. It had been long neglected, the fence unmended, the gate hanging on one hinge. It was a wooden house, a gingerbread house, with an ornate porch, and somebody lived in it, because washing hung on a line at the rear.

This is the house, something told her. *This is the house.* And she was afraid to go on, and determined to go on, and she walked through the gate and up the path, and she climbed the shabby steps to the door.

She knocked and waited. From somewhere in the rear of the house came the faint sound of voices, querulous, dulled by old quarrels. Gracie knocked again, more insistently, and the voices stopped, and a woman said, "I'll see who it is," and steps came to the door. It opened.

"What do you want, kid?" asked the woman, and Gracie searched the dull, worn face for some faint sign of recognition, and her eyes swept past the woman, down the hall to the kitchen, and found the open shelves where the cooky crock had stood. She was sure of the house then, and this gave her courage.

"I lived here once when I was very small," she said. "I lived here with my mother. She took me to the children's home and she never came back for me, and I'm trying to find her."

The woman stared. For an instant something flickered in her eyes and went out.

"You must know something. The name's Hitt—Gracie Hitt."

The woman said almost indolently, "Never heard it. We ain't lived here too long. Our name's Lombrosi. You can see it on the mailbox by the tree. Lombrosi's our name."

From the rear of the house a man's voice asked, "Who is it?"

The woman went quickly down the hall. "Just some kid. I'll get rid of her," and shut the door. Then she came back.

"Sorry I can't help you," she said. "You been living at the orphanage, you say? They good to you there?"

"Oh, yes!"

"They feed you good?"

"Yes, they do."

"Well, if I hear anything about the Hitts, I'll let you know. Not likely." Then there was a silence, and as Gracie turned to go, the woman took a step forward.

"Your mother'd be mighty proud to have a nice girl like you," she said. "She'd be mighty proud. You remember that, kid," and she started to close the door.

Gracie walked down the steps and the path. At the gate she looked back. The door was open just a crack and the woman was watching her. Then it shut with a click.

Gracie walked slowly back to the village, possessed by a huge and aching doubt. She waited on the battered bench at the bus stop, unable either to accept or to discard. On the bus trip back, she scarcely thought at all, only felt.

But when at last the ride was over and she was walking the last quarter mile on the road to the children's home, for the first time she realized she had run away. She had left without permission. No girl had ever been sent to Coventry, made to stand in front of the main house in a pair of overalls with one blue leg and one brown leg. She would be the first. She would suffer it gladly just to get home. She would accept it cheerfully, and more, too—even the words Mother Dorn would surely speak, and which she deserved.

She could hardly wait to reach the place in the road from which she could see the tracks on the hills where the small ones coasted their sleds down the dry grass, and when she reached it, she saw also Dad Dorn waiting in the road with a bunch of kids, and one of them cried, "Here she comes!"

They came to meet her.

"Gracie child," Dad Dorn said, "we're so glad you're home. We've been watching for you," and he put his hand on her shoulder, the kids tagging along, playing games as they went.

He did not question her. He did not ask where she had been. When they came to the main house, he said, "Cookie's saved your dinner, Gracie. Now run along. You must be starved."

It was so late now that the nursery kids were in their cots, the small ones going up to bed. The kitchen was empty and the dishes done, and Gracie's dinner was warm on the back of the big stove.

She ate slowly because she knew what she must do, and she both wanted and dreaded it. Then she walked through the dining room and down the long corridor to the office and knocked.

Poor dear little Gilford was gazing from his frame, and at the desk sat Mother Dorn.

"I'm glad you've come, Gracie," she said gently. "I knew you would. I've been waiting for you."

And Gracie sat down in the chair by the desk and told her everything. She spilled it out, holding back nothing, and Mother Dorn did not interrupt or question her. When she had finished, there was silence.

"I was so sure He would answer me," said Gracie.

"But didn't He?"

"Yes, I suppose—yes, I—"

"You are sorry you went?"

"No. Only"—and now she came to the part that hurt most— "only now I'll never know. I'll never be sure if she is my mother or is not."

"But you're sure of the thing that counts. If this woman is your mother, she brought you because she felt you would find here a better chance in life than she could give you. And if this is true, surely there are times when the love of giving up is greater than the love of keeping."

For a moment, Mother Dorn was busy with some papers on her desk.

"Carl's father is taking his family to the circus next Saturday," she said. "Carl has asked permission to take you and Tina. Tina's never been to a circus. Tina has no one, Gracie. I have hoped you would be her sister."

"But I am—I mean I feel I am. I'll take her. I'd love to take her. If she gets too tired, I'll see she rests. I'll be careful of her."

"I'll let you tell Carl, Gracie. A huge box of clothes came in today, and I've picked a new dress for you to wear, and one for Tina. Tomorrow we'll talk further. We've had enough excitement for one day. Off to bed with you, child."

She went with Gracie to the door, and opened it on a surprising sight. Tina was going up the stairs, the adjutant after her. Tina was holding up her little white nightgown, and under it she had on her bloomers, both legs bulging. Cookie had forgotten to lock the storage closet, and Tina was taking a treat for the kids in the small girls' ward.

"Tina," said Mother Dorn, and Tina turned quickly, and the bloomer elastics broke, and she stood there raining old dried prunes all over the stairs. And the adjutant burst into laughter, and Mother Dorn also.

"Oh, what a family I have," said Mother Dorn.

When the prunes were picked up, Gracie undressed in her little room, and slipped into her cot on the sleeping porch. She lay still in the dark, and she put down her old dream of the car coming up the drive. She put it down tenderly, as one puts away a doll, a monkey on a stick, a toy much loved in childhood.

Tomorrow was bread day. She could hardly wait for it to come. She would be the first one down. She would tell Carl she would go to the circus and she would thank him.

"When I grow up, I think maybe I'll be a nurse," she would say.

And when he had poured all the flour into the trough and put away his knife and gone, she would mix the yeast into the flour. She would mix it until it was spongy, and knead it until the dough pushed back at her.

In her mind the bread dough was life, and Gracie Hitt held her life now in her own two hands.

—January 11, 1958

ONE TO GO

The bishop arose early, as was his custom. He went quietly down the stairs and into the garden. The rain clouds had scattered in the night. The sky showed blue, and the sun was glinting on the waters of the bay.

Upstairs in the guest rooms the three young men were still asleep, come from the college in Montreal to report for their first work. Two jobs awaited them offering excellent, if usual, opportunities. The third job was so strange, so remote from the tempo of the day that the bishop had decided to assign it to none of the three. The one who went to the little, forgotten Indian settlement in the Queen Charlotte Islands must choose it for himself and with his heart or he'd be bushed in three months, to be plucked from the dock like an oil drum, drained and empty.

Deeply concerned, he went into the kitchen and brewed himself a pot of tea. He carried it into his study and had just poured the first cup when there was a knock at the door and in came Laird, his daughter.

She was a lithe and lovely girl, graduated from the University of British Columbia at twenty-one, home for her first holiday from eighteen months as a nurse in the Anglican hospital at Aklavik near the Artic Ocean. She was smiling, but in her eyes he saw that fierce honesty which he found so refreshing—and so disarming.

"Dad," she said, "you know those three know-nothings asleep in our spare beds?"

The bishop started to point out that the three know-nothings had spent seven years having their heads crammed with the very best; then he realized she was teasing him, a pleasant shock, since no one else dared.

"Yes."

"Have you noticed that one of them would make you a splendid son-in-law?"

"Frankly, no," said the bishop. "I'll have another look. Which one is it?"

"It isn't important. He's scared to death of me. Doesn't know I

307

exist. Anyway, you'll know after breakfast." The smile was gone now, the eyes serious. "You've mentioned the three jobs only briefly, I think. After breakfast you'll discuss them in detail. You'll save the one you like best for the last. Right?"

"Right."

"You'll knock every illusion out of their nice young heads. You'll bring them down to earth with a thump. But it won't matter, because one of them is going to say, 'Send me,' and he's the one I like."

"How do you know? What makes you so sure?"

"Last night at the big dinner he couldn't keep his eyes from the couple who are back from the north. They've been up there so long they look like Indians, they dress like Indians. Only a few people went out of their way to speak to them. Did you notice that?"

"I noticed it," said the bishop dryly.

"So did he, and it upset him. He said it was positively un-Christian. I told him that wasn't quite true. That it was just that most of us take all the everyday comforts for granted. It's a shock to see a couple who look as if they'd been dropped from another planet. Makes us almost ashamed that when we want a drink we turn a faucet, and when we want a light we flip a switch."

She walked to the door, then turned. "Dad, if one of them asks if it's a place a man can take a wife, what'll you say?"

"I'll say most girls would take one look and run for their lives," said the bishop cheerfully.

"I knew it. It's that horrible honesty. I'll spend the winter sitting on the Arctic Circle stewing about this lad. You could ask Captain McKenzie to keep a salty eye on him."

"I could and I shall."

"Tell him if he can't manage it, I'll have to alert Mrs. Clifton."

She was teasing him again, and the bishop knew it. Nevertheless he could not restrain a small shudder.

At breakfast the bishop looked at his visitors with a new interest.

The first was a city product, object of much love and expense. He was a handsome young man, an exceptional student, possessed of poise and a considerable charm.

The second was the eldest. He had served with the Royal Canadian Air Force and been twice decorated. He was practical, an excellent student, character already earned and molded on the face.

The third was twenty-three, the youngest, and of him the bishop knew only what the college had written. He came from Kerrobert in Saskatchewan and had asked to be sent west. He was a fair student only, having spent too much time helping earn his way to do better. He was resourceful, a bit original. He liked people.

After breakfast the bishop took his guests into his study. He discussed the first two jobs in detail, one as third assistant in a large Anglican cathedral, the second as a replacement in a small, well-established parish in a mill town.

"There is also an opening in the mission field," he said slowly, and all three tensed with interest, which was the old call of adventure.

"Now take those sparks out of your eyes. The man who chooses this job will be no Archdeacon Stuck of the Yukon, who traveled thousands of miles by dog sled and was the first to climb McKinley. He'll be no Bishop Fleming, who signed himself 'Archibald the Arctic.' Wasn't it Lord Tweedsmuir who called that the most romantic signature in all the world? This is not romantic. No living in igloos with the Eskimo. No flying over the tundra with the bush pilots. No breaking ice on the old *Nascopie*. She sank long ago. If this is an adventure, it is one of discipline. If it's a frontier, it is the frontier a man finds within himself."

Two of the three had relaxed a little.

"A branch of the Haida Indians has returned to a former settlement in the Queen Charlotte Islands. There is a small church they built long ago, and they have asked that a man be sent to it. It is a most isolated spot. No roads. No electricity. No running water. The only white people are the oil agent and his wife. No one goes there."

There was a silence.

"If none of you is interested, I shall understand, and I shall not be disappointed. There are two things I want to point out. Any man who takes this job will be considered stupid by the Indians. They can live off the land. He can't. Secondly he will never have the satisfaction of knowing if he does well, because as long as he's there the Indians will never speak of him. Years later some small word might drift back."

"If a man married, could he take his wife?" asked the ex-flier.

"Most girls would run. There are exceptions," and the bishop smiled. "I know. I married one."

Again there was silence. The third one broke it. "I'll go, sir," he said. "I'll be glad to go."

"You are sure? You have considered this carefully?"

"Yes, I have. Last night I was interested in the couple who are down from the north. I guess every man would like to think he can start right out as a prancing horse in his profession. Well, sir, after I saw them I knew I had to start as the mule."

When he smiled his face held that rare quality that makes a very little boy winsome and is so attractive in maturity because its owner never knows he has it and is, therefore, never tempted to use it consciously, one of the dangers of charm.

"And did you notice something else about them?" the bishop asked. "They've been up there thirty years. This is the first time they have been out in seven. Yet already their minds are homing back with eagerness. What is it that has stayed so green, so rewarding in the heart?"

He went to the door and called Laird.

"Mr. Neal has chosen to go to the Queen Charlotte settlement," he told her. "I want you to help him make a list of all he has and all he'll need. Bring it in and I'll check it with you. You can use my car to help him shop for what he must buy. There's a boat going in two days and I want him on it. Can you do this, Laird?"

She thought she just might manage it. "I'll scramble him some eggs first," she said. "I noticed he didn't each much breakfast."

Two hours later the bishop put in a call for Captain McKenzie, and when it came through he was succinct.

"Jock," he said, "when you stop at the old Haida settlement on your next trip you're going to unload one of my brand-new vicars. He's a good lad and I don't want him bushed. Laird hopes you can keep an eye on him. She says if you can't manage it, she'll alert Mrs. Clifton."

Over the wire came a strange sound which belonged surely in a bagpipe to be loosed only in moments of strong fervor. When the bishop hung up, he was smiling.

Two days later when the ship under Captain McKenzie pulled away from the Vancouver dock, the youth was aboard.

Nobody noticed him. He wore no clerical collar. He was just a sturdy young man with thoughtful eyes and a face that smiled readily, obviously on his first trip to the coast and interested in all he saw. No harbor so beautiful. No ship so fine. No passengers so fascinating.

There were Indians aboard, come to buy fishing gear, returning in new clothes bought in the secondhand stores. There were several minor officials on their way to Prince Rupert and three hard-rock miners sent by the government to blow ladders in the rock so the fish could get up to spawn. And there were loggers, all spruced up in their sunshine clothes, who, when the boat picked them up months later from some spongy dock, would come on board with their hair down to their collars and their calked boots tied around their necks by the laces.

He was surprised at dinner to find himself at the captain's table. Captain McKenzie asked him no questions, not even where he was going. Instead he told him something of the Indians.

"When I was a child, my parents had a summer place on one of the lower islands," he said. "Each year the Haidas used to come in their canoes and stop overnight at our beach on their way to the tribal potlatch. They brought with them the very old and the sick and the young. I remember once my mother and I took them medicine for a baby. After that every summer the chief gave mother a piece of fine beadwork."

"I suppose that's all changed now," the young man said regretfully.

"They use their seiners instead of canoes," the captain told him, "but they still do it."

The next morning when the ship started across Queen Charlotte Sound, the captain asked the boy if he'd like to spend the morning on the bridge.

It was rough, of course, the ship rolling, the man at the wheel friendly.

"Going to be a good trip," he told the youth. "Not like the last one with the female dragon of the line aboard," and the young man asked who was the female dragon of the line, and the seaman said it was Mrs. Clifton, widow of the founder and owner of fifty-one percent of the stock.

"Worst snoop in the Western Hemisphere. Raised her brood on the poop deck of a lumber schooner. Knows almost as much about navigation as the captain, and when she comes on board, he comes down with a cold in his nose and shuts himself in his cabin."

Mrs. Clifton, it seemed, considered it her pious duty to ride each boat of the line at least once a season.

"The chief engineer has it easier," the man at the wheel told the young man. "Turns off the ventilators, so if she dares come in the engine room, she'll roast. Even so he has to watch the combustion. One speck of oil soot and she'll find it and tell him about it too. She's a good woman, son. They're always the most pestiferous."

When the ship reached the islands, the youth felt like Cook himself at the moment of discovery. He drank the land in eager draughts—the thick spruce that grew to the water's edge, the lonely docks of the logging stops, the hidden coves and inlets and pebbled beaches. Once he saw three deer swimming from one side of a narrow strait to the other and, ambling along a beach, a black bear.

At one stop there was a government hospital. A seaplane put down on the water right off the beach, and two attendants waded out and carried in a stretcher with an injured logger or a sick Indian.

"What is the Indian's main problem?" the boy asked the captain, and the captain answered, "What's any man's problem? To be free. To stay free and yet adjust to a changing world."

On the third day, when he was to land, the young man felt as if he were waiting for the curtains to slide open on his own life—his real life, for which all else had been a preparation.

He had told the captain where he was going and why. Captain McKenzie made no comment, but when the youth was waiting to get off he came down to say good-by.

"The ship will be back on the twenty-third," he said. "I'll be looking for you. Just might be you'll need some tobacco for your pipe. Good luck," and the young man said he'd be there and thanked him.

Then he stood by the rail watching eagerly. He saw the lonely dock, the green-shored beach. The oil agent was waiting to catch the line. On the beach two dugout canoes were pulled up and turned over against the rain. Among the trees stood an ancient, weathered totem pole.

Then the line was thrown and caught. The oil drums and supplies were unloaded quickly. The young man was on the dock with his gear, and the ship was pulling away, the captain's hand raised.

The oil agent spoke first. "Name's Whitty. Guess you're the new vicar," and his eyes added plainly that any bishop should know better than to send so young a man to so Godforsaken a hole.

Now the obvious answer for a vicar—even a new one—was that no hole is Godforsaken, but the youth didn't make it. Instead the smile took his face. "I know, Mr. Whitty. But if I don't know anything, I have no mistakes to unlearn, have I?"

For an instant something flickered in the older man's eyes. The Indians were out fishing, he said. That's why no boats were moored in the little harbor. They'd be gone six days. Almost up to the Aleutians. The women were busy drying fish. There was a trail to the church, but if the vicar wanted to take his gear in one trip, he'd lend him a rowboat. Wasn't far. Just around the point to the right.

The young man borrowed the rowboat, and when it scraped the

pebbles of the little beach around the point, he carried his belongings through the trees to the cabin which was to be his.

There were two small rooms, simply furnished. He hardly saw
them. It had grown cloudy, the air moist with the coming rain, and
he must hurry. There was something he must do first. He piled his
gear inside the door, and he left the cabin, following the trail
through the woods.

The first growth had never been cut here. It was a brooding land
and it belonged to itself. "What can you do against me?" it seemed
to say to him. "I am big and you are puny. I am old and you are
young. For generations my rain forests kept the Indians on the
beaches. What can you do?"

And then he saw it—the little log church weathered by rain.
There was something ineffably poignant about it alone there in
the spruce, as if it were asleep, as if it had been waiting for him to
come and awaken it to life again.

He approached slowly. He stumbled and saw that he was walking through a small graveyard overgrown with ferns and bracken.
He unlocked the door and went in.

Inside it was dim, damp and chilly—and it was filthy. There was
one room, large enough to hold perhaps a hundred. There was a
row of handmade, backless benches. In one corner stood a potbellied stove, pipes from it running the length of the room. Under
each joint was a drip can.

He walked slowly toward the altar. The frontal piece had been
donated evidently by some church that had acquired a new and
better one. When he drew closer he saw it was supported on
packing crates.

But the cross was there with its hope and its promise, and to it
he put his question. *Where shall I begin?*

He listened, and heard nothing but the faint rustle of the wind
in the firs and the patter of the rain—the long, slow, patient
drizzle of the north. But he knew. Here, of course. His ministry
was to begin here—with a broom, a mop and a scrubbing brush.

"You're the first vicar I ever saw with washerwoman's knuckles," Mr. Whitty told him three days later when the young man
walked down the trail to Mr. Whitty's little store for his third can
of scouring powder. "Better come in and let Mrs. Whitty make you
a cup of tea."

Mrs. Whitty proved to be a small fussbudget, possessed of one
jewel. She owned the only parrot in the Queen Charlotte
Islands.

The parrot took an instant dislike to the young vicar. It hopped
onto his foot, walked up his leg and perched on his knee, staring

at him with malevolent eyes, while its owner extolled its virtues and its cleverness.

When the church and the cabin were as clean as he could make them, the young vicar was almost pleased. He had come to give, and he had not begun by asking help from any man. At the table in his cabin, the lamp lighted, the drizzle still falling, he went carefully over the church records.

There was a list of the Indians who had helped here in former years, their names written in a spidery hand—Mike, the warden; Joe, the caretaker. The women seemed to have no names of their own, known only as Mike's wife, Pete's mother.

He planned two services each Sunday, one at eight and one at ten. And every morning he would go into the little church and read the Morning Prayer—all of it, even if nobody came, even if nobody ever came—and he would do this for himself and for discipline.

Also he wrote Laird a thank-you note, and since there was much distance between them and he was, therefore, not quite so afraid of her, the note seemed to turn into a letter.

"The college taught me much of Greek," he wrote her, "but it failed to teach me how to wash wool socks without shrinking them. And how does a man learn to bake in a stove that burns everything on the top side and leaves the underside raw? And how does he make his own bread? I am practicing on biscuits. The squirrels like them."

On the fifth day the Indians returned from their fishing.

He had not been near the Indian settlement. At Mr. Whitty's store he had seen some of the women and children watching him from their bright dark eyes. He had made no effort to meet them. He must present himself first to the chief.

On the morning after the Indians' return he followed the trail to the harbor. The fishing boats were properly moored, diesel-driven and well kept. But when he came to the houses of the Indians, fringing the beach beyond Mr. Whitty's little store, he had a rude shock. They were little more than hovels. So much pride in the seiners; none in their homes.

The chief's house was a bit better than the others, and he also was a surprise. He was a large old man with an intelligent face and great dignity. He listened carefully when the vicar told him of the services he had planned. He promised to send the old wardens to help. And as he spoke the young man felt his wise old eyes watching and waiting.

During the first month he felt constantly the suspended judgment of the Indians. They were polite. They were respectful. They were willing to help. On a Sunday more of them came to the church than he had expected. But something was wrong; something was missing.

It was Constable Parkins who told him what it was. Each month the police patrol came by plane or by boat, and on his next trip Constable Parkins walked up the trail to meet the new vicar.

"You'll have little trouble," he told him. "The chief's a wise one and will handle most problems himself. He's a strong man too. In the powwows he can talk five hours without resting."

"I have the feeling he's watching me," the young man said. "They all are. But why and for what? They come to church."

"And they sing a bit off key," said the constable with a grin. "And they sing the same hymns over and over, and it's queer too. They're good with a brass band. Did you know the band at Kitkatla is famous?"

"I've worked hard on my sermons, but I don't seem to reach them."

"It's the ritual they like. What you say won't matter much yet. It's what you are and what you do that will count."

So now the young vicar knew. What he didn't know was what he was going to do, or what he was.

When Captain McKenzie stopped on his next trip, the youth was waiting on the dock. The captain had brought him tobacco and books, and he listened carefully while the young man told him how it was going.

"Ask the chief to take you fishing," the captain suggested. "You'll find out something, son. It won't be the ones for whom you do the most who will be most grateful. It will be the ones you permit to do something for you."

The fishing trip was the first of many. All the vicar did was watch and hope fervently he wouldn't fall in, to be hauled from the sound like a piece of limp kelp. When the seiner tied up at its moorings, he had acquired a healthy admiration for the skill of its crew of five. They were no longer Indians. They were individuals.

Then one day the youth had his first real breakthrough. When the first of the two fish runs was over, most of the Indians went to the mainland to work in the cannery, and Mike's wife ran wild and came home in disfavor.

At the Sunday service the vicar told them the story of the prodigal son, and after it was over he saw them lingering beneath the spruce, discussing it.

"This is true," they said. "This is the way it is. He speaks wisely."

And the next morning when he went into the church to read the Morning Prayer, for the first time he was not alone. Mike's wife sat watching him. When he had finished, she was gone, but that evening a huge sixty-pound salmon was left on his doorstep.

He kept on working to make the Indians *his* people. He fished with them. He called on each family and always on the sick. The ship's whistle was the voice of a friend. Each letter was a window into the great world so far away—and especially the letters of the girl.

She wrote of her life in Aklavik. She sent him a splendid recipe for skillet bread. She sent him an ivory rabbit, a seal and a bear cub carved by the Eskimo. In the Arctic, she wrote, the Christmas offering, given personally to the vicar, was in muskrat skins. Would it be in fish there? If so, fish were a splendid brain food, and surely by now his brains were prodigious.

. The young vicar wrote back that fish had failed to improve his brain power. "I borrowed Mr. Whitty's rowboat the other day," he wrote, "and found myself caught in a rip tide. Mike had to rescue me. It humiliated me, but it delighted him. Checks in every day to be sure I haven't managed to drown myself."

The Indians were working more in the church now. The women kept flowers on the altar and planned to grow tulips in a spring garden. And sometimes when the young vicar entered the church in the morning, he saw the old chief seated in the rear. Then summer slid into fall. The fall fish run was over, and something strange happened which nullified it all.

The men disappeared. They went without a word, though their boats were moored in the little harbor. When he asked one of the women where they had gone, she told him the medicine men and the chief had called a powwow. They were in the woods and would be gone a week.

It appalled him somehow. But if he wished them to respect his belief, he must respect theirs. When they returned, he asked nothing. He was told nothing. Shortly thereafter all the Indians, women and children, too, left in the seiners for the tribal pot-latch.

"It's their turn to take gifts," the constable told him. "You'll be lucky if they have enough blankets to cover themselves in the winter."

Now loneliness was a living thing. At night he turned up the radio for any sound from outside, as if he were the only man alive on the earth, as if all others were the strangers living on some far planet.

When the Indians returned, they brought a little boy who had been sick at the hospital. He had come home to die, not of the usual tuberculosis, but of cancer of the blood stream. For the first time the vicar realized that one Indian's sorrow was shared by all, and it humbled him.

Every day he went to see Johnny. He took him the ivory rabbit and the bear cub. He used up all his pipe cleaners to make him animals, and a really splendid lion with a dried fig turned inside out for the mane. When Johnny died, the men of the tribe made the box to hold him, and the vicar conducted the funeral. Everybody came, and when at the end he had asked that Johnny be given a safe lodging and the blessing, they seemed comforted, and he felt perhaps he had done a little something for these people who were teaching him so much.

One day he noticed the undergrowth had been cleared from the little graveyard and the low spots in the path had been filled. The lamps in the church had been cleaned. When he entered on a cold morning, there was a fire to warm him. And in the fall when the salmon run was over and the Indians went hunting, they left venison on his doorstep.

Then the long winter began. To keep fed. To keep clean. To keep the smile on the face, the hope in the heart. To keep his feet dry.

Always there was Captain McKenzie to encourage him and a letter from the girl and sometimes a package of books. He carried the package under his Mackinaw so it wouldn't get wet. He rationed his reading to fifteen pages a day to make the books last longer. The letters he read over and over.

He had come to know Aklavik, the hospital, the church, the Eskimo—and especially the girl. After Christmas he wrote her a long letter. The church had been filled—for once everybody had managed to sing on tune, and the offering had not been in fish or muskrat skins, but in money.

In the late winter he made his first trip out. He went to Prince Rupert with the Indians in a seiner. For days he awaited the trip eagerly, and when he clambered from the boat onto the mainland, the town seemed a city, the walks queer to his feet. He had a haircut, and it was hard not to run his hands over the back of his neck, so naked and light it felt. Yet when they returned the next day, laden with purchases, how blessed was the quiet, how lovely the woods. He could hardly wait to reach his cabin. And when he did so, a loaf of fresh bread was waiting on the table, the wood box was filled and the fire going.

That same month Mrs. Whitty's parrot died, and he went over to sit with her in sorrow. Mrs. Whitty was inconsolable. She wept and wept, and when she was done at last and mopping up, he made her a cup of tea.

"You know something?" said Mrs. Whitty. "He wasn't really a very nice parrot. He bit people. He even bit Mr. Whitty, and once when he was cranky he walked deliberately through my pies. It's just that—"

"That you loved him. To be able to love in a place like this, so far from everything most women prize, is an accomplishment, Mrs. Whitty. That's what counts."

"It is, isn't it? I've done fairly well after all, haven't I? That makes me feel much better, Mr. Neal."

"Mrs. Whitty," said the young vicar earnestly. "I'm not as nice as a parrot, but do you think you could take pity on me and help darn my socks. No matter how hard I try, I seem to end up with a little ball that makes a blister."

Each week Mrs. Whitty darned his socks, and each week she told Mr. Whitty that the vicar was so helpless, the poor dear, that if she didn't, he'd probably die of blood poisoning.

It was the thought of the girl that led him into his most ambitious project. He was falling in love with her, and he dared not. He knew now the problems that await the vicar whose work takes him to the forgotten corner. To be separated from his loved ones, or to watch his own children grow up like the Indians and no money to send them out to school.

Here only a few children were sent to the boarding school in the south. He noticed that if a boy who had been sent to school married a girl who had not, they lived in the old way. If both had been sent to school, they took pride in their home, they crossed the gulf from the old to the new.

So he began to hold classes in the church for the bright ones who wanted to learn. He built a long trestle table. Mrs. Whitty made him some curtains to pull over the altar. He used some of his Christmas-offering money to buy the books he needed, and he asked Captain McKenzie to bring two pairs of gloves so he could teach the older boys to box.

Now time moved swiftly. Winter slipped into spring. New sounds had come to the log church—the voices of the little ones reading their first words and the shouts of the older and the thud of the gloves.

He worried sometimes about the bishop's visit, and he watched anxiously for announcement of his pending arrival.

The statistics were not impressive. So few baptisms, marriages, funerals. The Sunday school and attendance at church had grown.

But the truth was not in these. It was the feeling that had changed. The Indians no longer watched and waited. He had become their friend and they his. But how to say it? That the children took pride in their spelling? That the loggers from the camp walked a mile of a Sunday and stayed after the service to chat? That even Mr. Whitty, a strict nonbeliever, had taken it upon himself to help with the singing?

Then early one Saturday afternoon the bishop arrived by rented boat and without warning. With him were two others, a pea-green archdeacon, who had been violently seasick all the way, and the head of the Women's Missionary Auxiliary, who was the formidable Mrs. Clifton.

The little church was filled with robust laughter. All the boys of the tribe were there, and the chief watching a boxing match, the vicar acting as referee. When the door opened suddenly, the shouting stopped. The old chief arose slowly. The small boys slipped out the door like wraiths.

The archdeacon spoke first and sadly. "Oh, Mr. Neal," he said, "in this consecrated place?"

Now the young vicar's own faith had deepened, strengthened and also simplified considerably. He was so surprised he showed it. "But, sir," he faltered, "we have no social hall. All we can do is pull the curtains in front of the altar."

"I think it's splendid," said Mrs. Clifton, coming forward like an ancient schooner in full sail. "I always insisted my own sons be able to defend themselves."

She walked over to the two boys who had been fighting. "That's a good left," she said to one. And to the other, "You're remarkably light on your feet." Next she shook hands with the chief.

"It's a good thing for the Sitkas they no longer raid down the Hecate Strait and steal your women," she said to him cheerfully. "You'd certainly be ready for them now."

Then she saw it—the article hanging on the hook on the church wall. She walked to it. She plucked it with two fingers. "What," asked Mrs. Clifton, "is this?"

"It's my surplice," said the vicar meekly. "I've been washing it on the rubbing board. I'm afraid those spots are candle grease. You see, the altar frontal was supported by old crates that wobbled. Oh, we've fixed it—the Indians and I built a new one—it's quite firm—"

"Disgraceful," said Mrs. Clifton. "Hereafter, young man, you'll send your surplices to the mainland to be washed. I'll speak to Captain McKenzie myself."

While the bishop and the archdeacon talked to the chief, the vicar showed Mrs. Clifton his cabin, so she could check those items which needed replacement.

She went straight to the dishcloth, which was sour. She snooped in his coffeepot, did not like what she found and told him so. When they returned to the church, Mrs. Clifton was still in full vigor. The young vicar was limp. "Have you checked what he needs?" asked the bishop.

"What he needs," said Mrs. Clifton firmly, "is a wife. Young man, do you have a girl?"

The young vicar said meekly, yes, but she didn't know it. That is, he didn't—he wasn't sure this was the kind of a place that any girl would—could—

"How do you know if you don't ask her?" asked Mrs. Clifton. "Ask her to come and see for herself, and I'll bring her over."

Then the chief took the archdeacon and Mrs. Clifton to see the Indian settlement, and the youth was alone with the bishop. They went over the records. The young vicar told the bishop all about it, and the bishop listened and made suggestions, and he watched the young man. The smile was the same. But on the face was a look a man earns only with self discipline in some far place, and he would wear it all the rest of his life.

"About this girl," said the bishop at the end. "Would she be anybody I know? If she is, let Mrs. Clifton bring her. Don't be afraid. It is possible now for a man to have his wife with him even in the Arctic."

Then, so soon, it was time for them to go. The young vicar and the chief went with them to the dock. Mrs. Clifton asked if there was anything else the vicar needed, and the boy said there was one thing. If he sent her the money, do you suppose she could ask Captain McKenzie to bring him a parrot, a live one, of course? "Mrs. Whitty needs a parrot," he said simply. "To love."

Mrs. Clifton said she could. "Captain McKenzie will sputter a little, but don't worry, he'll bring it," she promised.

Then they were gone. The chief and the vicar were alone on the dock.

"My friend," said the chief slowly, "what are you thinking?"

The funny little smile took the vicar's face as he answered. "I'm thinking that the Lord uses some very strange people to do some of His work for Him. Don't you agree?"

The chief smiled, and they stood there nodding in complete agreement—but with a difference. The vicar was thinking, of course, of the formidable Mrs. Clifton, who in a gruesome sort of way had turned out to be quite wonderful.

But the chief was thinking of the young vicar, and he did it thus: *Long after I am gone my people will remember this one. In the fall twilights of the powwows they will speak of him, and they will smile. He couldn't hunt. He couldn't fish. He shared our joys, and his heart ached with our sorrows. How good he was, and how stupid. Can you believe this? He was so stupid he never knew he showed us clearly the love of the great One who sent him.*

—*June 4, 1960*

THE TALE OF THE TOMMYKNOCKERS

When the price of gold remained
pegged and the most famous mine in the Northern Lode was
forced at last to shut down, the newspaper in Grass Valley asked
help for its Tommyknockers, a dispossessed and refugee people
without a home.

The Sixteen-to-One and the Best Mines said they'd take a few,
and men who had worked at the Golden Fleece in its prime sent
back word from the Yellow Jacket, the Ely Witch and even from as
far away as Flin Flon that the old mine could rest in peace, because
they'd find room somewhere in their winzes and their stopes for
every last one.

The Tommyknockers came to California with the Cornishmen
in the latter days of the Gold Rush, and there were those who
swore they'd seen them then—wizened little men scarcely a foot
high who knocked on tiny anvils with hammers the size of darn-
ing needles to warn the miners of impending disaster. "Knackers"
they were called in Cornwall, kin of the elves and the sprites. It is
said their origin goes back in a folk memory to some ancient,
forgotten race forced by the first Celt invasions to hide in the
moorlands and the cliffs; but when John Wesley rode his horse
from one Cornish village to another there were still many who
believed they were those who crucified our Lord, destined to work
out their doom forever deep in the dark earth.

When the knackers crossed the Atlantic and became Tommyknockers they were regarded with deep affection. There wasn't a
Cousin Jack who didn't heed his wife and leave them a bit of his
crust or his pasty—and they still do it. When the mules hauled out
the ore and a "super" berated a miner for a bad tally, he needed
speak only the simple truth: All night long the Tommyknockers
had raised 'ell in the barns, pulling the mules' tails and blowing in
their ears. His poor beast hadn't had a wink.

And even now up Grass Valley way if you ask a mining man if
he believes in the Tommyknockers—and this is true wherever a
Cornishman has worked in the dark and narrow stope—a strange

little look will take his face, and he won't answer you directly. Like as not he'll tell you about the time he was working a mile down in the old Empire when he heard a tap-tap on the air lines and a persistent knock-knock on the sills, and he put down his tools and he said, "This hole's deep enough," and scarcely had he reached the surface before the rock fell in the stope he'd just left. Now, he could say that when a man spends his life underground he develops an uncanny sense that warns him of trouble coming, and he could say that the sounds he'd heard were only the old timbers complaining of their terrible burden. But he won't.

"The Tommyknockers were talking," he'll say quietly. "And when they talk, lad, I listen."

So the Golden Fleece was closed. The yellow leaves of fall mellowed it. The green of spring softened it. And all its Little People went away forever. At least everybody thought so until summer came and the car turned up the lonely road.

It looked like something to deliver orphans to an asylum, a light truck aping a station wagon. In it were the young Prescotts, their twins, their cat, their most choice possessions.

The gentle little ghost towns of the Mother Lode had been a delight. John's knee had stopped its aching. Susan's face had lost its fine drawn look of worry. The twins, aged five, had been noisy, naughty and fun. And atop the highest mound of luggage, Pansy had purred loudly because her family was together again and hope was riding with it.

Just once Robby had remembered the dreary city apartment near the hospital where the doctors were trying to fix Daddy's knee. "Are we going home now?" he'd asked anxiously, echoed at once by Patty. "Is that where we're going now? Are we going home?" And John had said yes, in a way.

He'd explained that Grandfather Prescott had been born in this country they were seeing for the first time, and at the mine where his father had worked was a house he'd loved as a little boy. So when he was grown, he'd bought it, furniture and all. He'd permitted the original owner to live there until he should need it, and all his life he'd planned to return when he was old.

"And did he?" Robby had asked. John had said no, Grandfather Prescott didn't need a house where he was now, so he'd left it to them, and wasn't that nice?

It was only when they left Auburn in the Northern Lode—the sun hot now, Pansy and the twins napping—that hope slipped into "suppose." Suppose the house wasn't habitable? Suppose they had to find some other place to hole up while John's knee strengthened? Suppose it didn't—

"The only thing the lawyer knew was that the mine had been closed," John said. "He saw an item in the newspaper asking help for its Tommyknockers."

From the rear came a sleepy voice, "What's a Tommyknocker?" Susan said that it was a Cornish elf and she'd tell him later, and go back to sleep.

Then they came to the turnoff, and Susan drove as slowly as the car could go, afraid to hope, afraid to arrive. They rounded the last bend and saw the Golden Fleece sleeping in the sun, its blacksmith shop, its timber shed, and slightly below it and not fifty feet from its portal, the house, waiting like a friend.

It was a two-story white frame house surrounded by a wide veranda. Birth, death, sorrow and joy had marked it as definitely as character marks the face of one who has taken all life can hand out and still aged gracefully.

They stopped beneath the pines and climbed out and stood staring. The tinroofed mining cabins fell away, and the hard luck and the dreary city apartment. They saw the grass where the twins could run and the stream where they could wade and sail their boats. They saw the screened porch where they could eat outdoors, and where John could putter at a workbench—and more room than they could use.

They started forward exactly as the twins entered on Christmas morning, eager and shy and full of wonder—and then they stopped.

On the steps watching them intently sat a fine, fierce-looking old man. He knocked out his pipe slowly and stood up and came forward, something closed and guarded in his face, and the pressure of John's hand on Susan's said, "Now let me do the talking. I'll handle this." They stood ready to fight for what was theirs, for what they needed so desperately.

"I'm Ben Hutton, the caretaker," he said. "I'll be glad to have you picnic in the portal. Mighty refreshing place on a day like this." The voice held such dignity it made them feel like interlopers.

"Thank you—no, sir, we didn't come to picnic."

"You wouldn't be looking for a house to turn into an inn?" the old man asked. "With a bartender with a waxed mustache and a piano that plays tinny?"

They were truly shocked. "Oh, no—no, indeed." And for the first time they realized he was backing them slowly to the road's edge. Then he saw the car.

He looked at it long and carefully. When he spoke, it was as if to himself. "Forth-and-to'y transportation," he said. "It's been used to go to and from a mine. Yep, no doubt about it. Mining man's car, and a mining man's gear—a little more beat-up with each move."

Pansy descended from her perch and emerged majestically, and Patty awoke and stuck up her tousled head, the native embroidery on her dress plainly visible.

"All you need is a monkey on top," said the old man. "You been in the jungles, son? You get that knee in a plane crash in the bush?"

"It was an iron mine in South America," John said, "and it wasn't a plane crash. It was a shaft-sinking accident. Got myself clobbered by a sinking bucket." When he laughed his voice was still a bit shaky. "Clobbered good, sir—clobbered plenty."

"And the Indians had never seen a white baby," Susan said eagerly, "and they came smiling in a constant stream and stuck little bits of dirty wet paper on the twins' faces to ward off the spirits so of course—"

"You struggled to your feet and took 'em to the makeshift you'd made home," said the old man. "Typical mining man's wife." They all laughed, and the time had come to tell him who they were.

The guarded look was gone now. The character in the face, which was so much like the character of the house, was resigned, as if ready for a blow which would be important because it was the last. And they couldn't speak. They couldn't tell him, and so he did it for them.

"I think you must be kin of William Prescott," he said slowly. "Haven't heard a word since he died five years ago. Been kind of expecting somebody would come. I'm glad to welcome you. I'll show you the house, and then I'll leave."

The house was perfect for them. The twins scampered through the cool, high-ceilinged rooms and up and down the stairs, and Pansy held her tail high and nosed out the mouse holes. But the house was spoiled for John and Susan Prescott, and they didn't know why, and they had to find out.

While they were removing the first luggage from the car, they could hear the old man upstairs packing his personals getting ready to go. They carried in only two bags, and they whispered stealthily.

"Do you think it's safe to leave the twins with him?" Susan asked. John said of course it was safe, and not to be an idiot—anybody could see he was a fine old guy, and he'd go ask him.

He knocked on the bedroom door. "Mr. Hutton," he said casually, "would you mind keeping an eye on the kids while we drive into town for some supplies?" The old man said he wouldn't mind; he liked kids and cats. They might bring home some pasties from the inn of the Cornish widow, and he told John how to find it.

For the first time since the accident the young Prescotts had something to think about besides themselves. They drove fast. They could hardly wait to arrive and start snooping around asking questions. When they reached the town's edge, they saw a motor-cycle cop watching for speeders, and they stopped alongside; the man came over.

"We're interested in an old man we met at the Golden Fleece," John said. "Name of Ben Hutton. Do you know him?"

The officer grinned. "Sure I know him," he said. "Takes the combined force to keep him out of the pokey. The motor-vehicle department thinks he's too old to drive, but Ben doesn't agree."

He laughed. "Had a new spit-and-polish boy who insisted on picking him up, but we've worked out a compromise. Ben parks his old black sedan on the outskirts and walks into town. If he doesn't drive in traffic, we don't bother him. Why are you interested?" John explained that they had come to live in the house which he had inherited from his father.

"Mighty sorry to hear it," the officer said abruptly. "They don't come any better than Ben Hutton." And he turned away.

They had begun to feel like criminals, and for a moment they even harbored the thought that Grandfather Prescott must have cheated the old man, an idea too gruesome to ponder. John said there was only one thing to do—find the Cornish widow and put it straight to her.

When they found the place and entered, they saw a teen-age girl behind the counter, lips a little too red, blouse a little too low, the kind of a girl you see in any small town, certain that she is cooped and caught and determined to reach the big city where she can start to live.

She looked at them curiously, as if she were expecting them. "I'll call my aunt," she said. And when the gray-haired Cornish widow entered, a package in her hands, they knew instantly there was no use to ask a question. The closed look was on her face.

"You must be the Prescotts," she said. "Ben called you were coming. I have the pasties ready, and there'll be no charge—and no questions, please. Ben says a contract is a contract. He says you're a mighty fine young couple and you've had a mighty hard time, and you need the house more than he does." She handed them the package and went back into the kitchen.

When they reached the car, the young girl was waiting for them. "I'll tell you," she said. "It's the silliest thing you ever heard. Ben Hutton's as stubborn as the rest of this town. He's a refugee from a rest home. That's all."

"You mean—"

"That's right. And do you know something? The town's on his side. Every time Esmeralda, his daughter, comes to persuade him, somebody warns him and he hides out until she's gone."

"He does, does he?" said John with respect in his voice.

"They're jealous. That's all. Esmeralda got away from this burg. She has a big car and a mink coat, and they're jealous. But now that you've come, he'll have to go; and it'll be a lot better for him, and if nobody speaks to you, I will."

When they had bought their groceries and started back, they knew what they must do. They were mining people, and so was Ben Hutton. Susan said she couldn't bear to think of his sitting in the parlor of some dreary city rest home waiting for callers who never came. John said he was like the last of the buffalo caught in a blizzard with the wolves circling, and for his money Esmeralda was the lead wolf, the baby Quisling at her heels. And as for John's father—neither had any doubt as to what he'd want, and if they didn't manage it, blasts would pop off all over heaven itself.

"The old guy's proud," John said, "and that's the danger. We'll have to feel our way. I'll start it and you finish it."

When they reached the house and entered the kitchen, Ben Hutton had his bags packed and was ready to leave.

"Susan," John said brusquely, "you call the children while I carry out our stuff. Thank goodness we didn't unpack much of it. And don't forget Pansy. We can't leave without her."

"Wait a minute," the old man said. "What is this? What are you two doing?"

"There isn't any use disputing it," John told him. "We're leaving. We can't stay. Not possibly. Why do you think my dad bought this house? So he'd have a home waiting for him when he was old. That's why. So he could be his own man to the end in a mining man's country talking a mining man's talk."

He started for the door. As he opened it he turned. "And besides," he said, "if we stayed, nobody would speak to us. Not the Cornish widow. Not even the traffic cop. Nobody—except maybe the widow's niece, who wants to go to the city like Esmeralda and wear mink." And out he went.

Now it was Susan's turn. She sat down at the kitchen table beside the old man and she began to cry. "It's such a lovely old house, and it was going to be such a fine summer, and now it's spoiled. Oh, Mr. Hutton, couldn't we all stay? I don't think you'd mind us. Really I don't. We're nice people. At least I think so."

The old man was watching her carefully.

"Every child needs a grandfather, and the twins have none. And for a year John's had nothing but shattered kneecaps and sickness. We need you."

The old man's struggle showed on his face. Then John came in with the children, Pansy clutched in his arm. "Ready, Susan?" he asked.

She stood up slowly, but the old man remained seated, and she sensed the battle was over and pride had won.

"I appreciate what you're trying to do," he said slowly. "And a better try I never saw, and I thank you for it. I don't say it's easy to leave. I was born in this house, and there's scarcely a job in the old mine I haven't worked one time or another. It isn't that I wouldn't like to stay. It isn't that I wouldn't enjoy it. It's been mighty lonesome sometimes with the mine closed down and even the Tommyknockers gone."

A little look of complete understanding passed between Robby and Patty. They walked over and planted themselves at Ben's knees.

"Where did the little elves go?" Robby asked.

"To work in other mines, son. This one's closed. They're spriggins, you know, related to the piskies. They hide in the winzes and look after the miners. If a man leaves them a bit of his lunch, they're good to him. And if he forgets, they put out his light. They knock the tools out of his hands. And if he denies them, they'll plague his days with bad luck."

Another little look passed between the twins, and they pressed closer.

"But they'll be back, won't they?" Robby insisted, and Patty echoed him. "They'll come back, won't they?"

"They might. The Tommyknockers follow the good mines, and this is a good mine. Always was and still is. Yes—I guess if those noodleheads in Washington unpeg the gold and the Golden Fleece is worked again, they'll be back."

"But Patty and I can work it. We have hard hats. We have shovels. And Pansy's a good digger. And you could help us."

The old man lifted the little boy to one knee, and the little girl to the other.

"Ye-es," he said slowly. "I guess you and Patty and Pansy and I could have a small operation going. I guess maybe I could stay long enough for that."

This was the beginning of the lovely summer which was like no other. Ben was always the first one up. Upstairs in the big high-ceilinged bedroom John and Susan would hear him moving quietly in the kitchen, putting on the coffee, and presently they would hear a rustle on the stairs and know that Patty and Robby were going down in their sleepers, Patty clutching her favorite doll— the one who couldn't keep her clothes on and was missing an arm.

It was Ben who gave them their breakfast. It was to Ben Patty carried the garments with the tiny buttons she couldn't manage.

Susan insisted to John she was just a little jealous of Ben Hutton, bless his heart. With him the twins were such angels and with her sometimes such tartars. Even the hour before dinner which had a habit of slipping into howls and tantrums was relatively calm with Ben around. The twins considered him their personal possession.

Each midmorning there occurred an event which amounted almost to ritual. Robby and Patty put on their little hard hats, and Ben his big one with its carbide light and, armed with shovels and attended by Pansy, off they marched to work the Golden Fleece. They always carried a bit of food to place on some rocky ledge for the Tommyknockers.

When Susan was outdoors, she would watch them enter the portal, and Ben's voice would carry back to her, "Rattle 'em up, boys. Make the dirt fly. Here comes the super with his nose to the ground." Then there would be silence, and she would know they were walking a hundred feet into the old adit, and she would wait.

Their exit never lost its freshness. Out they came at fifteen miles an hour through the portal in the little ore car, Robby and Patty hanging on for dear life, Pansy tucked between them with her little white paws over the edge, and Ben standing on the back. It was so wonderful that Susan had to limit the event to once every weekday and twice on Sunday, or the twins would have worn Ben to a frazzle.

And when they came straggling into lunch on the screened porch almost always one of the children asked anxiously, "Do you think the Tommyknockers will be back soon, Ben?"

And he would answer, "I'm expecting them any day now, chickadee. Takes patience. Takes time for the news to spread that the Golden Fleece is a going concern again."

It was never lonely. John and Ben built a workbench. They made a dollhouse for Patty and a tree fort for Robby. They built a wheel to lift enough water from the Stream for Susan to have a vegetable garden.

When they all drove to town, they were greeted with broad grins, and there wasn't a week that two or three mining men didn't drop by—usually at lunchtime—for a chat with Ben and John. And the talk was always of mining, its efforts, its failures and its hopes. Then one day the Tommyknockers came back.

The little ore car seemed to emerge from the portal a bit faster than usual, and the twins came running to report the news. For the first time the food they had left the day before was gone.

Ben confirmed it. "Yep. They're back. No doubt about it. Hungry too. Gobbled up every smidgen." Neither he nor the parents mentioned the possibility of a night-prowling rat, no doubt grateful for so unexpected a cache.

The twins spoke much of the Tommyknockers when they first returned. Then not at all. Each afternoon after their naps they played together under the big old trees in a world which was their very own and excluded all others—even Ben.

One afternoon Ben took them a tray of milk and cookies, and from his chair on the veranda he saw them passing the cookies to playmates who were not there and talking to them earnestly.

"You know something, Susan?" he said to her. "I think the twins think they can see and hear the Tommyknockers." Susan said oh, yes she'd known it for the past week.

"It's because they haven't enough real children to play with, Ben. It's perfectly normal. When I was a little girl my best friend was a little boy called Charley Peters who didn't exist."

One afternoon Ben was sitting on the bank, watching the children wade in the stream, and Patty grew tired and came over to him and held out her hands for him to lift her out.

"Please, Ben," she said. "Lower me up."

This was a Cornish phrase, and he asked where had she heard it. "Patty, who told you that?" She grew very demure and said it was a secret.

"Couldn't you just whisper it?"

She put her little face close to his ear and whispered it. " 'Arry and 'Arvie told me," and off she scampered.

Then Robby came over. "I know what Patty said. She said 'Arry and 'Arvie told her."

"And did they?"

The same demure little look took Robby's face. "A'is," he said.

"Gave me the queerest feeling," Ben told Susan. "I haven't heard that word 'a'is' for years and years. 'Aye' is the closest you hear these days. And where did they get 'Arry and 'Arvie? It seems to me that when I was a youngster the miners had names for two of the Tommyknockers."

"Well, of course, that's it, Ben. They've heard it somewhere. Whoever said little pitchers have big ears simply didn't know children, Ben. They're better than that. They have a radar system all their own. It's normal. Just be thankful they picked up something nice instead of something naughty."

Then the lovely summer came to an end. The doctors said John could go back to work.

Ben and John started job-hunting at once. They visited the mines of the Alleghany. They drove north to see an iron pit where the mud swallows built their nests in the ledges, the rattlesnakes hid in the rocks and the miners ran for their lives when the lightning showed in the sky. Then one day through the chief engineer who had known Ben all his life, John found work as a project engineer to build a diversion tunnel on a new dam, near enough so the family could return to the old house for holidays and weekends.

When the Prescotts left, Pansy climbed a tree and refused to come down. She chose to remain with Ben, and though at first both missed the family, the old house was not lonely. It was filled with hope and plans. The kitchen to be painted as a surprise for Susan. Windows to be weatherstripped so the house would be warm for the twins. Bulbs to plant for the spring garden, leaves to rake and trees to prune.

Thus, the early fall passed quickly. The leaves fell, the nights turned cold and the Prescotts telephoned that they would arrive late Friday afternoon for a long weekend.

All Thursday morning and into the afternoon Ben worked to stack the last of the winter wood before the rains came. He was dusty with bits of wood duff caught on his sleeves and in his hair. He was thinking that at Christmas he and John and the twins must drive high enough to find a little fir, and cut it down and carry it home. And he must take Susan to the church to hear the Cornish choir sing carols so old they had never been written down, but passed from father to son over the generations.

Then he heard a car come up the road and stop, and he thought John must have managed to get off a day early. He put down the last piece of wood, shook the duff from his hands and straightened. In the car was Esmeralda, his daughter. He went forward to greet her as she climbed out, and they looked long at each other.

Ben saw a strong, capable and thoroughly good woman whom he didn't like very well, but loved dearly.

She saw a stubborn, willful old man, obviously unfit to live alone, to whom she was devoted. Why, he wasn't even bathing properly. And on the stove would be a pot of beans with a huge piece of fat pork—so bad for his heart. How hard to reach the day when a daughter must take charge. How thoughtful of the niece of the Cornish widow to have written her the truth. And this time she would not leave without him.

Esmeralda did not begin her campaign with direct action. Not a word. Not a reference. She inquired for friends. She discussed the weather. She discoursed on the joys of city living.

"Now I'll get supper, Father," said Esmeralda in the late afternoon. "I've drawn the water for your bath. Now run along, dear, and have a good soak."

Ben went upstairs slowly. The tub was filled and the towels laid out. He'd have to be watchful or she'd lock him in and vamoose with his pants. And sure enough—he was scarcely inside with the door shut when he heard a faint scurry in the hall. Esmeralda had come up to ascertain if her strategy was working.

He planned his own, and quickly. He performed some splendid splashing without wetting more than his hands. He emitted the proper puffs and snorts. He spilled water on the floor and sopped two bath towels. He removed one shoe and sock and left a large, wet footprint on the bath mat. Then he washed his hands and face, combed his hair and went down to dinner.

Dinner was deplorable. The pot of beans was gone, and Ben too wise to mention it. No spice. No pickles. Not a taste of onion. In place of his strong, dark brew was a cup of something so remotely related to his favorite bean as to have neither taste nor fragrance.

Breakfast the next morning was even worse. More weak coffee and not one slice of thick bacon. It was obvious that Esmeralda was softening him for the attack, and for the first time Ben felt afraid.

It began as soon as the dishes were done, and it was direct. It was kindly, or meant to be, and it went on and on with that patient, persistent hammering of the woman who is sure—absolutely sure—she is right.

"Now, Father, you know you must go back with me. You're too old to drive. You're too old to cook for yourself. It's too far from a doctor. You're my responsibility, not the Prescotts'."

And Ben said the Prescotts had come into his life like a benediction. That they had given him every reason to believe they needed and wanted him. What more did a man want? Suppose living here as he wished did shorten his life? What did it matter, if he lived it and put it down at the end like a man?

Esmeralda wept, and promptly repenting such weakness, strung her bow with her sharpest arrow. "I know how you feel, Father. I do understand. But the Prescotts are young. They don't want to be burdened with an old man. They can't say so. They can't come right out and say they'd rather have their own house to them-selves. Can you accept kindness given out of pity?" And when she saw the flinch of pain on his face, she was so sure of success she gave him a respite.

Ben walked into the kitchen. He plucked his hard hat from its hook on the back porch and followed the path to the Golden Fleece. He lighted his carbide lamp and entered the portal. This time he went farther than he and the twins had ever gone, deep into the adit. In one place a small slide had fallen, and when he saw it, he knew the mine was weakening—and so was he.

He turned back. There in the portal was the little spot of day-light a miner can see for hundreds of yards, that waits all his life to guide him home to a safe lodging after his work is done. For Ben it led to the old house, to John and Susan and the children, and he felt the will to fight on still within him, and he walked toward it steadily.

When he was within fifty feet of the portal, the light blurred an instant. Esmeralda had come after him. He stopped, and he spoke first and firmly. "Esmeralda, you ought to know better than to come into a mine. It's bad luck. Now get out of here."

"Oh, Father, that's superstitious nonsense. Come on, dear, I'll help you pack. We'll stop on our way and have a nice dinner."

For an instant there was silence, and then he heard it, the tap-tap on the air lines, the knock-knock on the sills.

"The Tommyknockers are talking."

"Father, if anybody heard you say that, he'd think you were childish."

"He would, would he? Well, let him try and certify me. He'd have to do it in Grass Valley. The judge would throw it out of court. He'd have to, or he wouldn't dare run for reelection."

He walked toward her, and on his cheek he felt a slowly increas-ing flow of air coming from the workings deep in the mine and moving toward the portal. But the fan wasn't going—it was dis-connected—and he yelled to Esmeralda to run, and because he was too old to run, he jumped into an old powder-storage crosscut.

There was a deafening howl, and Ben's light went out. Some-where in the old adit the rock had fallen, pushing out the air as if from a balloon down a straw. His poor determined Esmeralda had become airborne, and when the current that had picked her up reached the unrestricted atmosphere outside the portal, it would drop her with a rude thump.

Then it was over. He could hear the faint rumble of the stopes that had caved and compressed the air.

He hurried to the portal and, illuminated in the sunlight, he saw Esmeralda sitting between the tracks, covered with dust and surrounded by old powder boxes, wedges and leaves. She was unbroken.

"Esmeralda," said Ben gently. "You've made a mess. What you need is a good, long soak."

Esmeralda didn't want a soak. She found her voice. "Those horrible little Tommyknockers—they did it on purpose."

"I thought you didn't believe in the Tommyknockers."

"I don't; of course I don't—the nasty little things. I'm going home. I've had enough. I've had all I can take. I did the best I could. Nobody can say I didn't try. Heaven knows I tried!" Ben agreed, and he soothed her and he calmed her, and at last he saw her on her way.

What sweet release. He made himself a pot of strong, fine coffee. He laid the fires. He placed the doll Patty had left behind to await her return on the pillow of her little bed. He put the model of a gold dredge which he had made for Robby on a card table. He cleaned the bathroom and remade the bed in which Esmeralda had slept. Then he put on his jacket and went outdoors to wait.

Far down the road he heard the car coming up the grade. He heard it with that eager lift of the young heart, as a child hears a sleigh bell or a youth the long whistle of a freight train in the night.

Then the car came around the bend and stopped, Patty running toward him with her arms out, Robby just behind her, content to be second because he was a boy and girls go first.

It was Susan who spoke first. "Oh, Ben—we were so afraid. The traffic cop told us your daughter had passed him. If you weren't here, we were going to start right out after you."

So, of course, he told them all about it, and it was solemnly agreed that the Tommyknockers must have pried loose the rocks that started the slide that compressed the air that blew Esmeralda through the portal. And John said this was no night for cooking. They must celebrate. They would dine at the inn of the Cornish widow, and if the suet and the onion in her meat pasties gave Ben a bit of heartburn, it was worth the risk.

When they were ready to start, Ben said he had a bit of business he must tend to first. He picked up Pansy and, with Patty on one side and Robby on the other, walked again to the Golden Fleece and through the portal just far enough for the dark to find them. There was not a sound.

"Are you listening, lads?" He felt Pansy stiffen, alert as to the flicker of a mouse tail no human eye could see, and from deep in the old mine he heard a faint, benign tap and a sound that resembled a small—a very small—chuckle.

Ben raised his right arm in greeting as one mining man to others. "'Arry and 'Arvie," said the old man. "We're obliged to you gentlemen."

—*February 1, 1961*

Two Against Terror

From the big old ranch house John Ferrer saw his Basque foreman coming from the corrals. Ancelito had worked twelve years for him and twenty-two for his dad. Ancelito had known his grandfather when old Miguel could no longer trail the sheep through the ponderosa and the sugar pine, but spent his last summer on the rock beneath the oak because he still found a house too confining and a chair too soft for comfort.

He came steadily, direct as a sheep dog bringing the ewes to his master. He wore his best jacket and a hat, and when Ancelito came thus on the evening of a workday it was for one reason only—to plead clemency for one of his young herders. John knew which one and hardened, waiting for the knock.

"Come in, Andy," he said. "Please sit down."

Ancelito came in, but he did not sit. It is difficult for a Basque to beg, even for another. In his country of Eskualherria, which is no country at all but parts of southern France and northern Spain, the house of every man is a noble house, and his *fueros*, his rights, were protected before the Magna Charta was an idea in the mind of any man.

"The boy is back," he said simply.

"You found him asleep in a ditch, I suppose, or under a bush?"

"I found him in the back room of the tavern at the crossroads. My friend Pietro had been kind enough to cover him with a quilt."

"He's no good."

"He is twenty and far from home. He came from the Spanish Pyrenees just after the *Natividad*, and we put him to work that very night. He worked well in the cold and the rain in the long nights of the lambing. Is this not true?"

"He worked well for four months, and if he spoke a word, I never heard him. And then what did he do? He deserted it. He

336

lifted the *bota* so high and so often he ended up drunk in a tavern."

"*Ez—ez—ez,*" protested Ancelito. "He did better than that. When he realized that a herder from another ranch had filled the *bota* with a strange hard liquor, saying it was a wine of the *Norteamericanos,* he stayed on his feet long enough to knock out four teeth."

"This Baskie's no good."

Ancelito despised the word "Baskie." He never even used the word Basque. He was an Eskualduna. He sat down slowly, and he looked at John steadily.

John knew the look well. He had seen it often enough in the eyes of his little old lady. She was twelve now and still working, though she stiffened a bit on the long drives. When a ewe stomped in her face, she fixed the ewe with the look Ancelito was giving him now. Then she walked up slowly, lifted her right paw, gave the ewe a sound smack on the nose and penned her. He must be careful or Ancelito would pen him also and shut the gate.

"I won't have drunkenness and brawling among my men."

"But *Juanito,*" said Ancelito gently, using the diminutive he had used when John was very young, "it was so small a fight. No bones broken. No sheriff. No lawsuit. Not like the other one here on your own ranch."

"Another? One of my own men? Why didn't you tell me?"

"One of your very own. He told me himself. He was sitting on the rock under the old oak, and even then in his last summer it pained him to remember the loneliness of that first year. He said the fight was his *adios* to the boy in him who had to grow up too fast and too soon. You have forgotten."

He stood up. "You will see the boy?" he asked slowly.

"Yes, Andy. Send him over."

He had not forgotten. He simply had never known about the fight. There was too much he had never known. As a small boy he had loved his grandfather, and secretly he had been a little ashamed because he was so different from the grandfathers of the other boys in school. He had been ashamed of the language old Miguel spoke when he came down from the hills, and he'd been glad when his father had Americanized the family name into one his friends could pronounce and spell. It was only when he was older that he had come to realize his was a double heritage, twice precious, and it was then he had put to his grandfather his question.

"*Abuelito,* how was it when you came here as a boy?"

Through the window he saw the boy, Esteban, coming and heard again the answer. Fundamentally it had not changed much. It had been for the young Miguel as it was for this one. It had been so hard he had screened it with the same *altivez,* that wonderful and dreadful Basque quality which we can only approximate with our word "pride."

When the boy knocked and entered, the man was standing. The boy waited as if he expected to be made into little pieces and was determined to take it without apology or explanation. And when the man spoke, his words lashed not the boy but himself.

"It was my fault," he said. "I am to blame. I put you to work too soon. I forgot that the other herders have been here for many years. I forgot what it means to leave one's homeland and one's people. Sit down, Esteban."

They both sat.

"Ancelito tells me that when my grandfather came, he was in a brawl much worse than yours. I did not know it. But I remember he told me once he let his beard grow that first summer in the mountains, and when he drove the sheep down in the fall, he looked so fierce the children were afraid of him and hid under the beds. He said he felt like a *Cagot.* You have heard of them?"

For the first time some emotion flickered in the boy's face. "They could not appear in public places," he said slowly, "or marry or mingle at the church. They could not kiss the cross, and nobody knew why."

"Lepers maybe, or descendants of the Saracens. For hundreds of years, until they were absorbed by the race, they were the outcasts of the homeland. My grandfather felt like a *Cagot,* and I had forgotten."

He took out his pipe and filled it. "I am sending you on the long summer drive with a sheep band. I have a little old lady who will go with you, but you will need a second dog also, and this is a problem. We're short of dogs."

He stood up and walked to the door, the boy beside him. "Tomorrow you and Ancelito will take the rams to the big yearly sale in Sacramento. Then we will go to the ranch of a friend who trains dogs. He may have one we can use. If he does, you will have to learn the commands in English until you can teach the dog your own words. Can you do this?"

"I can do it," the boy said eagerly.

"Then until tomorrow, Esteban."

Ancelito was waiting in the early dusk. "You have seen almost a miracle," he said. "You have seen a rich *Norteamericano* as proud as you put down his pride and bend to you. Is this not true?"

And it was true. The boy walked beyond the corrals into the soft May night. Homesickness had been an agony within him, and he had run from it. He could admit it now. Now he could think of home.

How many times he had walked with his own grandfather beside the oxcart and sat with him under the big umbrella that stood at its rear, sharing the lunch of sausage and cold omelet. And the green valleys, the cows with their long, curving horns, the creaking of the wooden wheels that made so fine a *chirrio* it could be heard far away. Now he could think even of his mother.

When he was very small and frightened in the night by some loud noise, his mother had always come to him, and she had said, "Go back to sleep. It is only the Laminak."

The Laminak were the little stubby-fingered ghost people of his homeland. By day they spied on the grownups, and by night they tried to duplicate their actions, breaking the crockery and dropping the furniture, and wailing horribly with frustration.

Now he knew that in his homesickness the small boy in him had wailed louder than any Laminak, and he could bend to the boy who already was stepping back into the past.

The next day he and Ancelito loaded the rams into a truck and accompanied John Ferrer to the ram sale. Esteban helped unload the rams and drive them into a pen to await auction. When their turn came, he tapped their ends gently with a short sheep hook, sending them into the ring like a *corps de ballet*, wheeling and turning together so the bidders could see how fine and strong they were.

Then he was free. He stood alone by a barricade, watching and listening to the chant of the auctioneer, and he heard the soft tones of his own tongue, which is like a chant also. Old friends were greeting one another on the other side of the fence. Their rams were not selling quite so well, they said. Their lambs were smaller this year. Their taxes were higher.

"And how is your grandson?" one voice asked, and Esteban turned to see the man who answered. He wore a suit like those of the rich *Norteamericanos* and on his white head a blue beret, which meant he was a French Basque. And in his voice was the old pride, but with a difference. "He is doing well, Fermin. He is in the last year at the university. He wants to be a doctor."

One son for the church, and one for the sheep. This was the saying in Esteban's village. Not for his own sheep on his own land, of course. To migrate to one of the Americas and herd another man's sheep. But these Eskualdunak were speaking of their own rams and their own lambs and their own taxes—and of a grandson who could choose to be a doctor. And this was also almost a miracle.

Then Ancelito beckoned. They returned to the truck and followed John Ferrer through the city and deep into the flat valley to see the friend who might have a dog. When at last they turned into a driveway, the friend came to meet them, two Scotch border collies at his heels.

They were black with white markings and a faint touch of brown, smaller and shorter-haired than the usual collie. They had the leanness and alertness of sheep dogs. They had the ears attuned to every intonation of the master's voice. They had the eyes so highly trained that when the wind was wrong and the voice could not reach them, they could see a step to the right, a lifted hand at half a mile and take their order.

John Ferrer and his friend spoke in English, and when they began to discuss the dogs, Ancelito translated the words so the boy could follow.

"You might be able to use this one, John," the friend said, motioning to the older of the two dogs. "He knows his job, and he'll do it. But he's predatory. He's a sly one."

"He pulls wool?"

"Worse than that. When he knows he's out of sight, he'll lure a ewe over the hill and break the windpipe."

"He's a killer. That's almost unforgivable."

"Almost. Last year we had to use him. Couldn't get along without him. I gave orders the herder must never let him out of his sight. Worked well."

"And the other?"

"I'll give him away. He's no good."

"What's the matter with him?"

"He's just no good. Never saw a smarter puppy. Began training him at three months with a piece of rubber attached to a cord at the end of a stick. Ten minutes a day, and he'd have the lesson second time around. Then I trained him on a band of range sheep."

"And he's no good?"

"He's mechanical. Doesn't like livestock."

"What does he like?"

"Other dogs. Nothing but other dogs."

They both looked at the dog as if he were indeed beyond hope.

"Of course, he's still young. He's only eighteen months old, and you know how it is. Sometimes a dog will be worthless for two years and then find himself."

"You think he might?"

"Well-l-l—it's possible. If he grew fond of a herder and knew that when he did well, it pleased him. He's sensitive. Can't punish him much. You want to see him work?"

They did, and the friend took Tonto, which is Spanish for "fool," into a field and whistled him out to bring in some old ewes and bummer lambs.

The dog went out fast and well to the left. He came in behind the sheep, not too far, not close enough to spook them. He hunkered down, one old ewe watching him warily, and he brought them in straight and gently. When one ewe started to break and the friend called out, "Take care," the dog headed her back with a clean, quick turn; and when he had delivered the sheep to his master, he waited, as a child waits to be praised.

"He has an eye," John said.

"Oh, he shows off well. I'll say that for him. But when it's a hundred and ten, he doesn't want to work."

"Neither do I," and they both laughed. Then the friend said soberly, "You know the danger, John. He'll do well until he's bored, and he'll hear a dog call somewhere back in the pines, and he'll desert."

Nobody spoke.

"Well, Esteban," John Ferrer said finally in Spanish. "It's your choice, and it's a tough one. Which one do you want?"

The boy spoke quickly and surely, "Este," and he chose Tonto, the one, like himself, who found it hard to grow up.

Ancelito had worked dogs with English commands. He went over them carefully with the sheepman who had trained Tonto so that he could teach them to Esteban. Then they started back to the home ranch, the dog at Esteban's feet.

In the evenings that followed, John Ferrer could hear Ancelito drilling the boy. His friend had learned his first lessons in the training of sheep dogs from a Scotchman and retained some of the old orders. These Ancelito gave to Esteban with the smell of the heather still on them.

"Come up a'hint," Esteban would say over and over, which meant come up behind. "Come in," come closer to the sheep. And a splendid, loud "hist" to stop the dog.

"Steady" . . . "take care" . . . "get over" . . . "keep back" . . . "stop there"—the boy practiced until he was sure of each one. Later in the high range he would replace them gradually with Basque commands, and since the most modern Basque words go back to the time when Latin was a spoken tongue and the oldest words are sheep terms and go further into antiquity than any man knows, even if Tonto never made a sheep dog, he was bound to be a very erudite failure.

The boy did not let Tonto roam. He fed him, kept him beside his cot at night, played with him and made friends with him. Just once he worked him with a group of sheep, John and Ancelito watching, the boy sure of his orders, the dog obeying.

"He is putting himself into the dog," John said. "And if he fails, it will break his heart."

"If he fails," said Ancelito philosophically, "he will make a man of himself trying."

Now the wild grass had dried. An ancient engine hauled thirty freight cars onto the siding to take the bands to the mountains, the air filled with the baaing and the bleating of the sheep, the barking of the dogs, the calls of the herders.

The bands were kept separate, and when it came time to load Esteban's, Tonto nosed the sheep toward the chute, but it was the little old lady who loaded them into the cars. When they stopped in the chute, refusing to enter the ramp, and tried to turn back, she needed no orders. Into the chute she went, working her way under the sheep, turning them as she wished them to go, and when some old ewe refused to budge, she gave her a sound smack on the rump or showed teeth in her face.

When the sheep were loaded and the herders resting in the caboose and the wheels clacking on the track, it was Ancelito who paid the little old lady the highest compliment a man can pay a female.

"She thinks like a man," he said. "And what is more natural. So did her father."

One summer when the sheep were still driven home from the mountains over the old trails, a mountain lion frightened a hundred ewes deep into the hills. The herders and the dogs could not find them and had to go on without them. But the father of the little old lady stayed behind. He found the sheep, and he kept them together. He let them rest at the nooning-up, and guarded them at the bedding-down, and he brought them fifty miles safely home without a herder. It took him five days.

"What a pity he is gone, Esteban," said Ancelito. "If he were still alive, he could teach Tonto for you."

"When we see you again, Esteban," said another of the herders, "you will be a foot shorter. You will have chased so many sheep over so many mountains your feet will be worn to the knee."

They were teasing him to make him fight better in the test that was coming, and Esteban, looking very proud, did not answer them.

At dawn the sheep bands were unloaded from the cars, and when Esteban had packed his supplies on his burro, he waited his turn, the two dogs at his side.

The little old lady stood close and quietly. Once she touched his hand with her soft nose as if she were saying, "Now don't worry. You have me. I will be like a wife who has been married so long and so happily she needs never ask, 'Do you love me?' because she knows it well."

But Tonto waited impatiently, and when Esteban cautioned him to be still, his eyes were questioning. "To command me you must command youself, and can you?" No anger must show. The voice must be always encouraging and hopeful. When he thought of it, Esteban turned his head so that Tonto could not see his doubt.

Then it was their turn. Ancelito gave the directions and promised that the camptender would bring supplies by truck every other day. The band was spilled into the sage. The burro led the way, Tonto and the old lady driving the sheep away from the train.

When Esteban saw the great, rolling country with its green buckbrush and occasional pine, he felt hope. So few places for sheep to hide and a chance to build the bond between him and his dog—a bond invisible to any eye and yet so strong the lives of the sheep would rest upon it, and his honor also, and his pride.

It was fun at first. The nights were cool. The days were sunny. Tonto found the smells delicious. Surely this was a dog's life, and he went into it with his nose sniffing and his tail wagging.

Nothing to do but trot along beside the old lady circling the sheep, scattered over a square mile, and keep them from straying. And each day the man played with him. There was the game of the stick, the man holding it out as he came forward, Tonto grabbing it with his teeth and learning to walk backward. There was the exciting running game in which he learned to take an order on the run instead of stopping and looking back. And there was the game in which Tonto must jump on a sheepskin nailed on a wobbly log and balance there. When he did well, the praise was always effusive, and the bits of sheep liver which rewarded him were delectable. So the man became the master, and the master became a kind of god.

Esteban had no time to be lonely. He was up before dawn, swallowing his first coffee, well sopped in bread. He was on the move until his second, his real, breakfast. And all day he must watch the dog lest he crowd the sheep, quick to stop any false move before it could develop into a habit.

Sometimes at the nooning-up, the sheep chewing their cud, the day's lesson over and Tonto asleep, Esteban would sit musing and talking to the old lady.

"Tell me, wise one, how do you think he's doing?" he would ask, and the old lady's eyes would answer, "Surely you know, Esteban, a parent cannot buy loyalty from a child with bits of sheep liver."

At night Esteban kept Tonto in his little tent beside his bedroll because he dared not let him stray.

For six weeks they worked their way through the rolling sage and the buckbrush, and the bond grew and strengthened.

Then the weather changed. The rain fell in a slow, persistent drizzle. The sheep woke early, restive to be off. The old lady's rheumatism bothered her, and for the first time Esteban sent Tonto out alone.

After a week of rain they came to a river which must be forded. The water was cold, and the sheep refused to enter it. Again and again Tonto and the old lady drove them to the edge, the ornery old ewes breaking and darting off to be rounded up again. It was a day of utter frustration, and when at last the river was crossed and the band bedded down for its first night in the juniper forest, Tonto pouted, the first rebellion in his eyes.

In the juniper forest the weather cleared. The lambs were frisky and the ewes so delighted to be warm and dry again that they took pleasure in thinking up tricks. On the second afternoon thirty ewes hid themselves in a small ravine, and Esteban, knowing they were there, sent Tonto after them. He came back with twelve.

"Can't you count?" asked Esteban, and sent him back again— and again, until he had brought every one.

At the next nooning-up Esteban and the old lady discussed matters.

"He works well when it's easy," said her eyes, "but surely, Esteban, you know you are coming to the first time of testing, and how will he do then?"

They worked their way higher and higher into the ponderosa and the sugar pine. Once lightning struck a near tree and frightened the sheep, and again the rocks were so sharp they cut the feet. And in the distance Esteban could hear sometimes the sounds of campers, and he was always listening for what he dreaded, for what he knew would come.

He heard it at night in his little tent with that part of him that was watchful even in sleep. He dragged himself up and awake and heard it again—faint and clear in the night, a dog was calling. When he spoke Tonto's name sharply, there was no answer.

Tonto was gone all the next day. Esteban and the old lady held the sheep in the same grazing grounds and waited, and that night, the sheep bedded down, Tonto returned.

He did not come tail down, afraid to hold up his head. He came proudly, with a splendid indifference, and he sat down by the fire and looked at the boy.

Esteban stood up slowly and motioned Tonto to come to him, and the dog obeyed. In some strange way Tonto was himself back there in the office of the ranch house and the boy was the sheep-man. He held out his left arm. When he struck, the blow was so sharp it made the face wince. But he struck not the dog but his own arm. Then he reached down and pinched the dog's ear once, and sharply.

"You have done wrong," he said, "and I have hurt you. But first I hurt myself."

He put out Tonto's food. He did not touch or speak to him again. When the dog had eaten, Esteban motioned him to the tent.

Once in the night Esteban felt a cold nose touch his hand. The wind blew gently, and from far away in the pines it brought the call of the bitch. Tonto whimpered and lay still, and when the boy awakened, the dog was still there.

The next week a bear made a shambles of their camp, and each day he followed the sheep band, keeping hidden among the pines. And each night he came to the bedgrounds for the joy of killing some fat ewe.

Now the old lady took a hand in Tonto's training. When he smelled the bear coming and whined for her to wake up and help with the night prowling, she refused, feeling her years.

Instinct taught him now to bark and awaken Esteban to the danger. For the first time he knew he was responsible for the sheep, and when he and Esteban had failed to find the bear in the dark, he learned to paw the man awake so the bear would not be warned off by his barking.

When the bear had killed three ewes in four nights, Esteban did something Ancelito had told him he must not tell the forest ranger. He made a bait of bacon, setting and triggering his gun so that with the first bite the bear would shoot himself. And when he and Tonto rushed out at dawn to find the bear dead, they were as pleased as conspirators who share a deep secret.

In July the rams were brought in, and in August the sheep

bands were gathered in a mountain valley, the ewes culled and the lambs separated into the fats and the feeders. Then Esteban headed back for the high range.

His way led through country which had been logged two years before, desolate and ugly, and when the camptender came with his pack mules, his voice was serious.

When some of the loggers had gone, they had left their dogs behind to forage for themselves. The dogs had formed a pack with others deserted by hunters, and the pack preyed on the sheep bands. Esteban must be careful.

"You can trust your dogs?" the camptender asked him.

"I can trust both dogs," answered Esteban staunchly.

Nevertheless he felt a growing fear. He drove the sheep as hard as he dared. Once in the night he heard dogs barking far away, and he heard Tonto whimper softly.

"Even against your own kind could you be faithful?" he asked him, and found no answer.

The next day it thundered and rained. The sheep were as troublesome as sheep can be. When they were bedded down and night fell, Esteban was sure he could feel danger waiting in the dark.

No owl hooted. No small animal scurried in his quest for food. The night was too still and the old lady knew it and for the first time in many nights she accompanied Tonto in prowling the bedgrounds.

Esteban did not sleep. He had oiled and cleaned his gun. He took it from its sling, and he sent the old lady to circle the bedgrounds from the left, while he and Tonto circled from the right.

Slowly—around and around—they went, but the beam of the searchlight revealed nothing hidden in the fallen timber. Only Tonto's nose and ears told Esteban he had been right and danger waited. He stayed close by Esteban's side and whimpered a little, as if he knew exactly what danger waited and what Esteban expected of him, as if he hesitated at so hard a choice.

Thus they prowled without a bark or a command, and when the night held all its darkness just before the first faint light began its daily tug of war, the pack struck.

Esteban heard nothing, but Tonto did and shot forward. At the same instant the old lady barked. Then the night turned hideous with the baaing and bleating of the sheep, the snarling of the dogs and the report of Esteban's gun.

When Esteban reached the other side of the bedgrounds, the pack was gone as fast as it had come. Three ewes lay dead with their windpipes broken. Already the old lady was rounding up the sheep that had scattered in fright. And Tonto was lying very still with a deep gash in his side.

Esteban kneeled beside him, and though he did not know it, his words were those spoken by el Cid, the bravest knight in all Christendom, when he lay dying and said good-by to the horse that had carried him in battle. *"Caro amigo—dear friend."*

He carried Tonto back to the camp. He cleaned and bound the wound as best he could, and in the morning when the sheep were on the move he carried Tonto until the tender found them, and helped rig a sling to take the dog out.

Each time the camptender came thereafter Esteban waited for news of the dog of whom he could not speak because he cared so much.

"The *Norteamericano* took Tonto to the hospital at the university at Davis," the camptender told him. "He has had four blood transfusions. He is as important as a person."

And again, "He misses you, Esteban. When the *Norteamericano* took him home, he had to find an old jacket of yours on which the dog could lay his head."

The little old lady did the best she could. She even tried to be young again and playful, as Tonto had. And sometimes at the nooning-up they spoke of him.

"Little grandmother, will he work again? Will he forget everything he knows? Will he be afraid? Will he be good for anything better than chasing butterflies and his own tail?" And the old lady would look up from her soft, wise eyes as if she were saying, "Who knows, Esteban? You know how it is with the young. When they're little, they step on your paws. When they're bigger, they step on your heart."

It was as if Esteban waited to rejoin part of himself. If he were not whole again, how could he hope that he would be strong enough to take his own rams to the big yearly sale and speak proudly of a grandson at the university? Would he, too, be like so many who never succeeded, who were afraid to return to the homeland, who said, "Next year I will go home," over and over all the rest of their lives?

Fall came. The nights grew colder. The first snow fell. The sheep bands were driven from the high range to the road where double-decker trucks waited to carry them back to the valley.

There was a difference now in the way the other herders treated Esteban. He was one of them, and they seemed to know it by something they saw in his face.

"We will take you to the Basque barbecue," they told him. "You will hear the old songs and see the old dances. And we will introduce you to the prettiest girls of them all."

But on the long drive down from the mountains Esteban was silent. His truck was the last to arrive, and when he climbed down, John Ferrer and Ancelito were waiting and with them Tonto, the dog barking and wriggling with joy as Esteban hugged him.

"I want you to drive your band through this field to the one beyond," John Ferrer told him, and in the field to be crossed was already a sheep band. Esteban sent the old lady to drive this band into a corner of the field and hold it there. Then he ordered Tonto to drive through his own band without mixing the two.

There was nothing mechanical about the dog now. He drove the band through gently with no barking, no false move. He hunkered down and nosed the sheep forward, watchful for any sudden break, not once looking back for an order.

From the fence John Ferrer watched, and he felt that quickening of the heart every sheepman feels when he sees a dog and a herder so attuned that none of the work shows, only the smooth and flowing skill.

Just at the last Tonto had a bit of trouble. When most of the sheep had passed into the field beyond, several old ewes stood crosswise in the gate and refused to budge, the last hundred sheep mobbed behind them.

Tonto knew exactly what to do, and he did it expertly. He ran up along the side of the sheep, cutting in just behind the leaders. Then he turned and came back through the middle of the sheep so that to get out of his way they were forced to flow around him and through the gate.

When the sheep were all through, Esteban closed the gate, while Tonto waited. Not for flattery. Not for a bit of sheep liver, but as one partner waits for another. And Esteban stooped and put his hand on his head, and he said, "Well done."

Then they started back where John Ferrer stood, Esteban first, Tonto trotting at his side, head turned, eyes watching, ears listening.

Thus they came proudly—the man and the sheep dog. Behind them, like a grandmother at a graduation, walked the little old lady.

—June 3, 1961

CHANGE OF HEART HILL

The time of the tadpole was
drawing slowly to an end in the small town, as it does periodically
in towns big or little everywhere.

All the youngsters had grown up together with little disparity.
They'd paddled in the same pools, played hopscotch on the same
streets, gone to the same schools and coasted their sleds down the
same hills. Then one summer came the change.

As if by a signal the parents began to look ahead and worry a
little, suddenly aware that there weren't going to be enough good
jobs for all the boys and enough good husbands for all the girls
and if they didn't do the very best they could for their children,
who would? Who indeed?

Pat Jacoby, who worked at the mill, mentioned to the boss
mechanic that he'd like to apprentice his boy Sam. Mr. Hutton, the
lawyer, and Doctor Blake, the surgeon, began to put aside money
each month to send Peter to Harvard and Jim to Johns Hopkins.
Mrs. Turner, mother of three girls, sent an unexpected check to
her old sorority at the state university to help the sisters reshingle
the roof.

And Mrs. Kenilworth, undisputed social matriarch, decided to
give a luncheon—to be followed later by a dance at the country-
club—for her granddaughter Lucy, thereby initiating a new
young set and setting it firmly on the first rung. She wrote the
invitations at once, deftly separating wheat from tare. When she
came to Judy Drew, she hesitated. Judy belonged on the list, of
course, but Mrs. Kenilworth was not at all sure it would be a
kindness to put her there. Poor child—no matter how gallant her
dear mother might be, Judy would never be able to keep up now
with the others. Nevertheless Mrs. Kenilworth did not wish to be
the one to leave her out. She wrote the invitation and mailed it
with the rest.

Thus the jockeying for position in the serious race to come
began in the town and, although the tadpoles did not know it,

their common and happy childhood branched here—and for some it stopped.

One afternoon Ellen Drew, a widow, lifted a troubled head from her work and looked into the rear garden, where Judy was washing her red bicycle for its last ride. This morning at breakfast Judy had asked if she might sell it, and when Ellen had said yes, if she wished, but didn't Judy want to ride it anymore, she had heard those words all parents know are coming—and dread. They came from across the chasm that separates any two generations. "Oh, mother—girls my age don't ride bicycles."

Since when, Judy? Since Friday? Since you went to the luncheon for Lucy Kenilworth?

Ellen had not asked it. She had not even asked what Judy wanted to buy with the money the bicycle would bring. The bicycle itself had been a symbol, and four years ago any little tad-girl who didn't have one was absolutely sure she might as well be dead.

For a moment Ellen Drew felt a helpless yearning, because she knew what the daughter did not. The symbols were growing more frequent and more expensive. She could not replace the old with the new and, even if Judy sold the bicycle, neither could Judy. Then she remembered suddenly how Judy had behaved the day they bought the bicycle, and she felt an unexpected courage and her first hope.

They had walked to the little shop in Old Town on the last of the wooden streets, built on piles above the tide flats and spongy to the feet. And if prayer is man's deepest desire, they had prayed every foot of the way that Mr. Tully would have a bicycle for fifteen dollars, which was all that Ellen, newly widowed, could afford. When they had reached the shop and entered, there it stood—the beautiful red bicycle—all by itself and beside it on a white placard the gruesome black figures—$60.

Judy had taken one long awed look and turned her back and kept it there. Yes, Mr. Tully had a girl's bike for fourteen dollars, and he had brought it out. It was so old its handle bars were wooden, freshly painted that bilious gray peculiar to back porches and attained by dumping all paint remnants into one pot. Judy had sought desperately for something nice to say about it—and found it. "It won't show the dirt." And Mr. Tully had said dryly that it certainly wouldn't. Good thing, too, because it didn't have a skirt guard and was bound to spatter mud on its rider. "I'm sure it will go fast."

And Mr. Tully had said, "Oh, yes, it will go fast enough all right. It will go too fast. Matter of fact, it doesn't have a coaster brake."

Ellen had opened her purse to take out the money, when Mr. Tully had said earnestly, "Mrs. Drew, I knew your husband, the young doc, and I liked him. Mrs. Drew, a little girl doesn't need much in this town. One good doll and, if she's a tomboy, one good bike."

So they had bought the fine red bicycle and, to pay for it, Ellen had become the first lady in the town to work. She had let it be known among her friends that she was not averse to plying a fine needle for hire.

Now in the rear garden Judy was polishing the last few spokes, almost ready to deliver three packages for her mother on her way to sell the bicycle back to Mr. Tully.

Ellen took the last stitch and snipped her thread. Three pink crepe combinations, hand hemstitched and sprinkled with French knots for Sue Gordon, who was going east to finishing school. A blue silk robe for the hope chest of Agnes Drury, who taught fifth grade and evidently was not yet reconciled to her fate. And a beautifully mended rosepoint wedding veil, heirloom of the Britton family, richest in the town, which could only mean that Emily Britton had succeeded at last in snaring the only young man with any hope at all of maintaining marriage at a level attained by Emily's parents after a thirty-year pull.

Ellen placed the garments in tissue in their boxes, then carried the boxes to the door. Judy was unrolling the sleeves of her middy blouse, her eyes bright and anxious.

"Mother, how does it look?"

"Splendid, dear. You've taken fine care of it."

"Do you think Mr. Tully will give me thirty dollars?"

"I wouldn't be surprised. He's an honest man."

They placed the packages in the basket over the rear wheel and tied them firmly.

"Judy, I haven't asked what you plan to buy with the money, and I'm not going to ask. But remember. The bicycle is your one resource. I'd look before I bought."

"Oh, I will. It's so terribly important."

"Now, be careful, dear, and don't squash the packages." Judy slipped onto the bike, gliding off before she was in the seat. Momentarily the door held her mother as if in a frame, the expression on her face one of deep concern. She rode as if the bike were part of herself. Nothing had ever given her so much joy. Yet so great was her desire to conform that she could not pedal fast enough to deliver the packages and sell the bicycle to Mr. Tully. Already in her mind she was spending the money on those things which, since the luncheon for Lucy Kenilworth, had become the newest symbols.

First, the sweater. Soft blue and a cardigan it must be and buttoned by the second button from the bottom. The blouse must be white and the collar pointed. The sleeves must be long, and around the collar and the cuffs must be a fluting—not a ruffle. The skirt must be beige and box-pleated, and under the skirt must be that mysterious article of which the new young set spoke little, content to squirm under an unaccustomed restraint.

There were other things too. The slippers must be thus and so, the hose this and that, and in the pocket of the sweater must be a small round cardboard box with a French label—HIGGINS's DRUG-STORE, 75 CENTS—and in the box a tiny feathered puff without which not a nose of the young set could be properly daubed. And all these things were almost as important as life itself.

Judy had come to the driveway of the Britton's gray-stone mansion and, because it was hard to pedal on the soft gravel, she slid off, stopped and wheeled the bicycle to the portico. There she untied the box with the rosepoint veil and walked up the steps and rang the bell.

Now footsteps were coming. The door opened, and there stood Norah, the cook.

"Bless my soul, if it isn't Judy. Mrs. Britton and Miss Emily are gone for the day. Come in. How's your dear mom? Come in, child. I just took a loaf of bread from the oven. We'll have a slice with strawberry jam."

"I can only stay a minute, Norah. I have a terribly important errand." But Judy had two helpings of bread and jam before she prepared to leave.

"Thanks, Norah. It was awfully nice of you," Judy said before Norah let her out. Judy wheeled her bike back to the street.

Now the street began to climb. She had to work harder—standing up, leaning forward. One block, two blocks, three blocks—and she turned up a side street where Agnes Drury had a little apartment in an old house. She leaned the bicycle against a fir and untied the second package.

Agnes Drury was the prettiest teacher in the town and one of the most popular. The kids loved her and were sorry for her too. They knew that each fall the town's mothers turned over their obstreperous offspring to the teachers' care with loud hallelujahs, but they never asked them to parties. The teachers were spinsters all. They had to be. Most of them cared for aged parents, or helped educate younger brothers and sisters. If one should marry, she was promptly dismissed.

Judy rang the bell of the little apartment. The door opened at once, as if Miss Drury had been waiting for her.

"Oh, Judy," she said with relief. "It's you. Your mother promised me the robe this afternoon. Come in. I'll write the check."

On the couch Miss Drury's suitcases were packed and ready to be closed. When she sat down to write the check, she was so nervous that she dropped ink on one and had to tear it out and do another. She handed it to Judy, and then she opened the box and took out the robe. Scarcely looking at it, she placed it in the top of the larger suitcase.

"You're going on a vacation?" Judy asked.

"I'm going to Canada tonight to be married. Judy, don't leave me. Stay with me a minute—I think I'm a little scared."

She laughed shakily.

"Isn't it silly? He's a nice man, Judy. He'll be good to me. He's generous. He's going to look after my sister, the one that's sick. He offered—all by himself. He'll be good to me, but now—at the last minute—I don't know. I guess I——"

The doorbell rang. She went slowly to the door and opened it, and something very strange happened. Miss Drury was nervous no longer. She was all charm and animation—and even coy. She introduced Judy gaily.

"John, this is one of my old pupils. I'm all ready. Only have to close the bags. . . . And thank your mother for me, Judy, and good-by, dear. Everything's going to be lovely," and Judy remembered to wish her happiness and to congratulate the man, and she slipped down the steps and away from there.

She returned to the main street. It was too steep to ride farther. She wheeled the bicycle slowly up the long hill. She stopped to rest once by a door that had always fascinated her. It was in the face of a rocky cliff and was said to lead through a small tunnel to a house in the back.

She now could see over the green firs to the bay, where the freighters rode at anchor. She could see the thread of smoke from the sawdust burner at the mills. Then at last she reached the top and the Gordon house, where she was to deliver the last package.

She untied it and ran up the steps with relief. Sue Gordon was her friend, and the house as familiar as her own. She even knew the attic and the plumed hats in the old trunks.

She rang the bell. She heard Mrs. Gordon coming on her high heels, and the door opened. "Oh, Judy, dear, how nice. Come in.

Come in. Mrs. Schubbie's here shortening hems. Do you know the summer's slipping by, and it won't be any time until Sue leaves?"

They went up the stairs—Mrs. Gordon chatting every instant—and there in the sewing room on a footstool stood Judy's friend, Sue. On her knees was Mrs. Schubbie, her mouth full of pins.

"Sue—stop wiggling. You can talk to Judy later. Put your arms down. How can Mrs. Schubbie get the hem straight with your arms up? All right, I'll just take Judy in the other room until this skirt's hung."

She led Judy into the guest room and shut the door. The bed was covered with luggage, and the door strung with garments on hangers.

"I want you to see her things. Look, Judy, isn't this a darling? And look at this. And this too—of course, she won't wear it much, but she'll need it for weekends. I do think it's important for a girl to learn to wear her clothes well, especially one who isn't a raving beauty, don't you?"

Judy heard herself saying, "Oh, I do. Oh, I love it. It's just perfect."

They were all there. The soft sweaters that must be buttoned by the second button from the bottom. The fluted blouses. Not just one of each, but several. And other things not yet even imagined. The evening slippers with the heels that looked high, but weren't, and the party dress with the neck that looked too low, but wasn't. And when the new young set saw them all, out would go the old symbols Judy didn't even have yet, and in would come a whole new set—and beyond it another and still another.

"We're going east a little early. I want to show Vassar to Sue. That's where I went, you know. Had you heard that Lucy Kenilworth has put her name in for Stanford, and Peter Hutton for Harvard? Of course, it's some years yet, but you have to plan ahead. Don't you think so?"

And suddenly Judy could hear the words that hadn't been spoken yet, the words that were coming. "I'm going to State." "I'm going to Stanford." "I'm going to Smith." "Judy, where are you going?" "I'm going nowhere." And as if she heard them also, Mrs. Gordon answered.

"Of course, we're very fortunate to have the Normal School here for those who—who won't go away, and especially for those who want to teach."

At last it was over. Judy had explained that she must go. She had an important errand to do. No, don't bother, she'd let herself out.

As she wheeled the bicycle away from the house to the street, she heard Sue's voice come through the open upstairs window. "Oh, Mother, how could you?"

She did not think. She only felt. For the first time in her life she felt an emotion bigger than a desire to conform, to be like the others. She felt a terrible rebellion against the smug small town which for some was an open door and for others a trap. And because she didn't care, because the feeling within her clamored so fiercely for action, she slipped onto the bike and over the brim and down the hill—the dreadful hill—the one that in winter the common boys called "the belly buster."

For an instant she saw the scene as she had seen her mother—hours, oh, years ago—framed, like a picture. The blue of the bay was far below. At the bottom of the hill Mike, the delivery man for the town's leading grocery store, had left his horse and wagon. He had walked up the hill with a box of groceries on his shoulder, stopping to ring the bell at the door in the cliff. He was standing there waiting, and she saw the door open and a man come out. Then it was gone. The bicycle was gathering speed. She saw nothing but the street going down at a perilous angle. She felt exhilaration, the wind in her face and her hair blowing.

Faster, still faster. She was a third of the way down. She was halfway down. Vaguely she was aware that Mike and the man who had come from the door in the cliff were yelling loudly and waving.

Then exhilaration was gone, and in its place was fear. She was afraid to put on the brake, and she was afraid not to. She pressed against the pedal—gently, then stronger—and the bicycle veered, lurched, skidded sickeningly toward the curb and hit it. She felt herself fly over the handlebars and land on the grass of the parking strip, and she heard the air knocked out of her.

Then the two men were on their knees beside her, and she heard Mike say, "It's Judy Drew. It's the widow's girl. Oh, she's hurt bad."

"Nonsense," the other man answered. "Stunned—that's all. Skinned a knee. Hasn't even broken an arm or a leg. Deserved to kill herself, but she didn't. Darn fool kid. Why, not even the tough boys come down this hill except on their sleds. Now easy, Mike. You take her feet—up we go—slowly, slowly. Here's the door."

They carried her through the door in the cliff, through a little tunnel into a garden and onto a porch, and they laid her on a couch.

"Agatha," the man yelled loudly. "Come a-running, come instanter. . . . Now don't talk—don't try to get up."

Then the man's wife came and bandaged her knee, propped some pillows under her head and brought her a cup of tea. Mike said good-by and went away. The husband carried the bicycle in from the street and surveyed it critically.

"The chain's off, but I can fix it. Lost a little paint too. Otherwise it's in pretty good shape. Agatha, where's my pipe?"

"In your pocket, dear, and your tobacco's on the magazine stand in the corner."

The wife was a nice-looking woman, no longer young. She sat by the couch, knitting quietly. The husband stood tamping his pipe slowly, a wiry, slender, gray-haired man, his eyes behind the glasses direct and questioning.

"How did you happen to come down our hill on your bike?" he asked. "No sensible girl would do a thing like that, and you look like a sensible girl."

Judy didn't answer, and the wife said to him, "Stand still a minute, dear. I want to see if I have the shoulder wide enough," and she held her knitting against his back.

"I'll write an editorial about kids with bikes. That's what I'll do, Agatha. I'll call it HEEDLESS YOUTH."

"I just don't think this is a case of heedless youth, dear. I think Judy had a reason and a good one. I know Judy's mother. She's a splendid woman."

"I was on my way to sell my bicycle," Judy said. "I had delivered some packages for my mother, and I was going to sell the bicycle back to Mr. Tully because there were some things I wanted to buy."

"I suppose it would be impolite to ask what you wanted so much that you risked your neck?"

"Of course it would," his wife said quickly, "and anybody but a man could guess. I can remember exactly what I wanted at Judy's age. I wanted a hat with bird wings on it."

"Revolting."

"It was a divine hat. I remember my grandmother bought it for me. She bought it because when she was young she wanted a shoo-fly."

"A what?"

"A shoo-fly, dear. It's a kind of a bustle that sticks out behind. Her older sister had a splendid shoo-fly, but hers was skimpy and made of remnants. And you know something, even at ninety my grandmother had never forgiven it. When you were Judy's age, what did you want?"

"Well—let me see. My first long trousers? No, I had those. A twenty-two? No, I had that. Oh—I know. A double-breasted suit.

All the boys in my crowd had new double-breasted suits, and all I had was my old blue serge. I remember my mother sponged and pressed it every week, but it was still single-breasted, and it shone."

He walked up and down the porch vigorously.

"Agatha, remind me to write an editorial on the pains of youth. This whole country's in love with youth, but most of us wouldn't go through it again for anything in the world. Agatha, where is my toolbox? I must fix the bike."

And now Judy had to speak. Even if she didn't understand it, she had to explain somehow, and she heard the words coming out of her.

"I wanted a sweater. A certain kind of sweater. And a blouse with fluting on it. And other things too. And I wanted a little cardboard powder box with a French label on it and a feather puff that you get at Higgins's Drugstore. But it doesn't matter now."

"Why of course it matters."

"No, it doesn't. It doesn't matter because, when I delivered the last package at the Gordon House at the top of the hill, I knew I couldn't keep up with the others. It's the strangest thing. Last week all the kids were alike, and all of a sudden everything's different. Already the others know what they're going to do— even years from now. They're going to Stanford, and Vassar and State. I'm going to be the one who's supposed to go to the Normal School and teach—and I won't do it, I simply won't do it."

"Good for you," he said. "In this town it's a life sentence. So you came down the hill because you didn't care. *Ring out, wild bells, to the wild sky!* That's what you felt. The first rebellion. How well Shakespeare put it."

"It's not Shakespeare, dear. I don't know who it is, but it's not Shakespeare."

"Nonsense, Agatha," and he ducked into the house and came out with a book. "Here, Judy, look it up in *Bartlett*," and she did, and it was Tennyson.

"Remind me to remind you to write an editorial on WIVES ARE SMARTER THAN HUSBANDS," said Agatha gently. "And now, if you'll excuse me, I have some errands to do. Dear, why don't you ask Judy to read to you while you tinker with the bike? By the time I return you'll have it fixed and all the materials for your editorials gathered," and the husband said it was a good idea, and he'd do it.

It was so natural, Judy was not even apprehensive. The man tinkered with the chain of the red bike, his long sensitive fingers sure and deft. The wife brought her a pile of newspapers that had come in the day's mail—*The New York Times*, the Manchester *Guardian* and others. She read the headlines, and the articles he chose. Sometimes he would say, "Skip it—just give me the gist" and, since in the Northwest, where there are so many rainy days, most youngsters could read well, this was easy. She was an old expert at skipping the dull descriptions and landing on the juicy bits. He'd had an accident long ago, he said. Mistook a celluloid eyeshade for his pipe. Got along fine. Couldn't read easily. That's all.

"And don't get that horrible poorpussy look on your face. I don't permit it. It's the one thing that can make me swear. I'm not totally blind by a long shot."

When the papers were all scanned, Agatha was back from her errands, the bicycle fixed, and from his pocket the man took a dollar and handed it to Judy solemnly. "I always pay my readers, and you've earned it. The last girl I had up and married, and Agatha's been pinchhitting for her. Hard on her too. Takes two hours every afternoon, and she has enough to do without that."

Judy sat very still, struck by an enormous, a fabulous idea. The nicest thing that can happen to youth was happening now. From no other motive than pure goodness of heart someone was opening a door in her life and so gently that she would feel no strings of obligation and think she had opened it herself.

"Do you suppose—" she said slowly,"—do you think I'm old enough to apply for the job of reader?"

"Why, yes—yes, I do. Of course, I'm a hard man to work for. I'll correct your pronunciation. I'll make you learn to spell. . . . What do you think, Agatha?"

"I think Judy's a bright girl to think of it. If she saves her money she'll have almost enough for the first year of college. It's the first year that's the hardest, but there are more scholarships now than ever before. Yes, I believe it might work out. And if she learns to type, you can dictate your editorials to her directly on the machine, and then she'll earn more."

"I can type forty words a minute," Judy said. "That's not fast enough. I'll have to practice."

"You talk it over with your mother," the man said. "Tell her I'll call her in the morning and, if she agrees, you can come to work tomorrow at three."

He stood up, and Judy also.

"Now wheel the bicycle to the foot of the hill," he said. "I don't want you to arrive tomorrow in splints."

"Oh, yes, I will," and she shook hands with both very formally, and they walked with her through the little tunnel to the street.

Only when the door in the cliff was shut did she remember that she did not know their name.

She went down the hill carefully, but as fast as she dared. At the foot she slipped onto the bike, pedaling swiftly down the street. When she reached the cross street that led to Old Town, she went right by. She had forgotten Mr. Tully and the musty bicycle shop. Head up, she sped homeward.

Her mother would be waiting and watching for her, careful not to pull against the fine lace curtains that would not stand another washing or drying on the wooden frames. She remembered the look of concern on her mother's face framed in the door, and she knew that all the time her mother had understood everything. It was the words unspoken she heard now. "I would sacrifice anything to give you the advantages the others will have."

She would answer in kind. She would not go leaping up the front steps three at a time, like some silly kid. She would go quietly as befit a wage earner. She would say with dignity, "I have a job. I have a wonderful job, and I got it all by myself. I'm going to work hard and save my money. I'm going to college. I didn't sell the bicycle because I'll need it. And I've brought you a present." And she would put in her mother's hand—the first, the big, the most beautiful silver dollar.

Faster and faster. Down the last street. Up the home walk, and off the bicycle and into the woodshed. Then she saw in the basket at the rear a small package that hadn't been there before, that Agatha, the wife, must have placed there after she returned from her errands. She picked it up and opened it.

It was the little cardboard box with the French label and, when she broke the seal and removed the cover, there was the little feather puff without which no member of the new young set could daub a nose. She held it as if it were a pearl. But something had changed. It was a sweet and precious thing. That's all it was. Not a symbol. Only a thing.

Then she walked along the path to the front door. The sun was low in the sky, the shadows lengthening on the grass. And the small town and all the world, even the shabby white paint on the front door, were touched by the tantalizing challenge and the promise that are known only to those who are both young and brave.

—*March 10, 1962*